FATAL INSTINCT

ROBERT W. WALKER

JOVE BOOKS, NEW YORK

FATAL INSTINCT

A Jove Book / published by arrangement with
the author

PRINTING HISTORY
Diamond edition / October 1993
Jove edition / August 1995

ISBN: 0-515-11913-X

A JOVE BOOK®
Jove Books are published by The Berkley Publishing Group,
200 Madison Avenue, New York, New York 10016.
JOVE and the "J" design
are trademarks belonging to Jove Publications, Inc.

PRINTED IN THE UNITED STATES OF AMERICA

10 9 8 7 6 5 4

Good instincts are to be treasured and I have terrific instincts about my son, Stephen, to whom this book is affectionately dedicated . . .

This book has been helped tremendously by the editorial instincts and tireless efforts of others who have worked on my behalf, especially John Schline, who has kept the torch burning. Thanks also to Leslie Gelbman, the guru who has kept the faith.

Also to the faithful who've been with me in spirit and perspiration throughout many long years in a topsy-turvy, checkered career kept alive BY INSTINCT ALONE on my part, and by love and understanding on the part of all around me.

"He was such a doggone good Jaycee."

e

"I didn't ask for this thing to come live inside of me, but now it's here and it killed all those girls, not me. Those teeth marks aren't my teeth marks, they belong to Stainlype."

One

𝒆

Each day that Gerald Ray Sims awoke in the Federal Penitentiary for the Criminally Insane, he was amazed at having survived another night locked up with Stainlype. Nor could he believe that the authorities, with such total control over him, could do nothing about Stainlype's comings and goings. Would they never understand the nature of the beast? That it was Stainlype and not he who brutally attacked and killed all those defenseless women?

Each day Gerald spent in captivity gave Stainlype more reason to hate him, just as Matisak had said via prison communiqué. All of Stainlype's venom, once directed outward, was now cut off with no measure of release, so the anger twisted back on Gerald himself.

Stainlype was feminine by nature, and when she spoke to Gerald, she called *him* Stainlype, a clever attempt to throw off the doctors, but the doctors couldn't be that dumb. Arnold and the lady doctor who visited from Washington, D.C., couldn't possibly believe that she—Stainlype—and he—Sims—were the same. No way . . .

Gerald was convinced that Dr. Coran had to know the truth. She must understand that Stainlype remained so murderous and malevolent a force that Stainlype simply could not be denied her needs; that when she wanted human flesh to feed on, she would take whatever she craved, whatever was at hand, and currently this meant *his* flesh. The bite marks all over his body proved it, bites in places not even a contortionist could reach. This Dr. Arnold could not explain away with psychobabble and mumbo jumbo.

The bites were steadily enlarging whole fleshy chunks

1

ripped from him. The doctors couldn't possibly believe that he'd inflict such pain and torture upon himself, could they?

"But you did that with your own teeth, Gerald," Dr. Arnold had countered.

"They're not my goddamned teeth anymore; they're her teeth, and she's using them on me! She hates it here and—"

"We provide for all your wants here, Gerald."

"Inside me!" he'd shouted. "She hates being trapped inside me, inside this place, unable to feed."

How completely at her mercy he was when Stainlype claimed possession of his hands, his body, his mind and heart. When she used him, he had no power to stop her from cannibalizing those girls. Stainlype had an insatiable appetite for the young ones.

Now he was locked away with her in cell number H1-32, deep inside the federal facility in Philadelphia. He shared the same cell block with an assortment of infamous serial killers, many of whom were being studied, watched, filmed and tested like so many rats in a laboratory.

Alongside him was Dominick Jeffries, "the Collector," and down from him was Mad Matthew Matisak, "Teach" to some, who had terrorized the Midwest with his wide-ranging, blood-draining kill spree in which his victims gave up every ounce to literally quench his thirst for blood. They called Matisak a vampire, a true-life Dracula. Gerald didn't belong here with such monsters; Stainlype did, but not him.

The last time Dr. Coran had come around she had been nice to him, and she was so pretty, with fresh, smooth skin and soft eyes, a glistening moisture in them, and those lips that she frequently wet with her tongue, all very beautiful, framed as it was in her long, auburn hair, her hazel eyes like a final floral touch. Stainlype, who refused to talk to Dr. Coran or Dr. Arnold anymore, whispered to him that Jessica Coran looked tasty. Stainlype made his eyes bulge as *she* tried to get a good look at Dr. Coran through the 3-inch-thick glass casing.

Dr. Coran told him that she liked seeing the recent progress Dr. Arnold and he had made. "Although it's far from a break-through," she'd said, "it does appear that you are finally accepting responsibility for your own actions and that Stainlype has stopped or slowed in her efforts to harm you."

That had been a month before. He'd agreed with her, as Stainlype told him to. She was recording their conversation on camera, the lens just outside his glass cage, staring in at him like some ever-present evil eye. He'd forget that the camera was there, running twenty-four hours a day, until she came. Then it bothered him, made him nervous, fidgety.

Now that Stainlype had been in hiding for a long time, Dr. Arnold had seen this as a sign of progress. Apparently so did Dr. Coran. But Stainlype was very much with him, biding her time, through with doctors and talk. What did the doctors really know? They couldn't feel Stainlype's slug trail inside his head, the leaden feeling when Stainlype invaded the pit of his stomach, twisting and turning through the coiled passageways of his intestines, squeezing at his heart and flitting shadow-like over the irises of his colorless eyes. No, Stainlype was not any weaker, just patiently waiting.

Dr. Coran made Gerald review in detail what she had done to those women, what she'd done to their flesh, making his body mount them after they were dead, making him perform carnal acts on their corpses. Dr. Coran had a word for it: *necrophilia*. Knowing that there was a word for it helped just a little, the way a salve helps a sore. Dr. Coran made him tell her about how Stainlype had lured the women to their deaths, how she had struck them, the weapons used and what happened after, about the cannibalism, everything. Dr. Coran told him it was good for him to relive the events and that what she learned from him would help the FBI and law enforcement across the nation, and that his case would be written up in journals. He had wanted to forget, but she had made him remember, and it was only after she came that he learned that the demon within him was a woman.

Dr. Arnold called that progress.

Gerald had made it clear to them both that during the horrid attacks, he could see and hear what was going on around him, but that Stainlype had made off with his feelings of touch and taste, his motor capabilities, his powerful arms and legs, the hands used in killing, the mouth and teeth used in eating.

Stainlype was now filled with frustration and rage, her anger directed more and more at him, as attested to by the new bites. He'd remained too afraid to tell Dr. Arnold that his worst fears seemed on the verge of coming true, because Arnold would have his guards strap him down again, further restricting Stainlype and adding to her now burning hatred of the body she'd possessed for all these years. Dr. Arnold would take away the few privileges he now enjoyed, a stack of comic books, the occasional newspaper, a deck of cards.

Stainlype kept up a constant complaint over the fact Gerald had allowed himself to be locked away inside a mountain of mortar, but he felt like a free man by comparison to the Gerald Ray Sims who'd spent almost a year in a rubber-walled cell where he was constantly strapped down.

"Free man," Stainlype scoffed. "What a joke."

Dr. Coran worked for the FBI and was at first talking only to Matisak down the way, but then she started coming to see Gerald. She'd told Gerald that she liked him. So where was she now? Quantico, Virginia, Arnold had said, and Arnold was no help, either. He just kept saying, "You get what you give, Gerald. You've got to cooperate with her if you want her to keep coming all the way back here to see you."

"I told you," he'd replied, "I can't tell her any more about where the bodies are buried. Stainlype warned me that if I told any more, she'll kill me!"

"But what can Stainlype do to you? And besides, why should she care, Gerald, what you tell us?"

"She cares . . . she cares plenty."

"Why?"

"I don't know why! She just does."

Dr. Arnold had gotten up, saying he had more important matters to attend to.

"Stainlype will kill me!"

"Dr. Coran is not going to return here unless you are willing to talk seriously, Gerald."

"Stainlype still hates her victims, still wants them to suffer, even in death, and wants the families to suffer. I know Dr. Coran wants to help people, but Stainlype could give a fuck."

That had been the reason he'd given Dr. Arnold, but there

was another. Stainlype had told Gerald that she knew what the FBI woman really wanted, that Coran wanted Stainlype's power for herself; wanted to trade places with Gerald Ray Sims; wanted to accept Stainlype into her life and body, to become one with Stainlype.

Dr. Coran was going about gathering up as much power as she possibly could, Stainlype had told him. This was why Jessica Coran was interested in such men as Matisak. The good doctor's reasons were far from pure. She, like Stainlype, wanted to take power from men . . . and maybe Stainlype was right.

"How else could she have overpowered Matisak?" Stainlype had asked, hammering home the point. "It was she who put Matisak away."

"She says that we—me and her—could do some good," he had tried to explain to Stainlype. "That together, we could help stop killings in the future. That's power, Dr. Coran says, to alter what's going to happen."

Stainlype caused a milky white froth to bubble up from his stomach and over his lips, and she was shouting at the same time, "That mind-whore is looking for a mental fuck, Gerald. She is fucking your head, you stupid bastard."

Down the hall from Gerald's cell, a guard was on the phone with Dr. Gabriel Arnold, excitedly saying, "It's Sims, sir! . . . Yes, yes, he's getting agitated again."

At the other end, Dr. Arnold leaned back into the folds of his high-backed, cushioned chair, sighed heavily and looked around the book-tiered room with its polished, modern milieu beating out a rhythm that spoke of comfort and longevity. He'd survived as head of psychiatric disciplines at the federal facility since it opened its doors in 1979, and now with a staff numbering seven and two part-time internists, not to mention his teaching duties at nearby Philadelphia University, he was dug in and in control.

"Talking to himself again, or rather to Stainlype, is he?" asked Dr. Arnold.

"More like cursing and shouting, sir."

"Well, we've all seen that before."

"Spitting up, too, sir."

"Spitting up?"

"White stuff, sir, all over the glass."

"Christ," moaned Arnold. "Look, take two men and get in there. Restrain the bastard before he hurts himself."

"Full restraints, sir?"

"Yes. Now go! I'll be right down."

"Yes, sir, Dr. Arnold."

Arnold took a moment to clean his glasses with a handkerchief and then wiped excess grease from his forehead. He buzzed his secretary, telling her where he would be, and after a moment's hesitation over a file he'd been looking through before Lewis had called, he got up and went for the elevator that would carry him to lockup. When he got to level H, the doors opened and he stepped out, calling to a guard with keys to follow him. He had to pass through three security checks and locked doors. Disregarding any paperwork, as it was in the nature of an emergency, he was passed through without the usual sign-ins, which even he had to adhere to, under normal circumstances.

Over the comlink, he could hear the commotion up ahead. Lewis was calling for backup and, thinking himself off the comlink, he added, "Shit, we got to jump through hoops every time one of these freaks goes off his bean."

Arnold had just reached one of the TV monitors when his attention was riveted by a strange sound like that of a huge kettledrum. Arnold stared in horror, seeing Sims repeatedly throw himself viciously against the glass, totally out of control, sending up a chorus of gong sounds.

"Lewis! Lewis!" Arnold began screaming through the comlink, and the entire cell block went into bedlam. Over the chorus of catcalls, Arnold clearly heard Matt Matisak's voice, shouting, "Do it, Gerald! Do it right! Do it, babe!"

Sim's face was already a mask of red, his nose broken and blood covering his scalp, when Dr. Arnold stormed to the guards who stood transfixed and staring in at the sight of a man killing himself against the blood-streaked, smeared glass.

The *poooooooong, poooooooong, poooooooong* beat was punctuated by a bone-crushing counterpoint—Sims' skull cracking. Any normal man would by now be sprawled out and unconscious, but some demonic force within kept hurtling the man's body—as if independent of him—into the killing wall of glass. With each crashing gong sound, the other inmates cheered. Matisak roared out, "Stainlype one, Gerald zip." Hideous laughter filled the cell block.

Then the pongs stopped abruptly and Gerald Ray Sims' bloodied form slid Jell-O-like down the face of the filthy glass and into a formless heap on the floor.

"Get the hell in there!" cried Arnold.

Lewis had been fighting with the key in an uncontrollable hand, but now the cell door came open.

"Careful, Lewis!" shouted Matisak from two cells away. "Sims may be dead but Stainlype isn't!"

"Shut up, Matisak!" Arnold replied.

"You touch Sims and Stainlype's going to get you!" Matisak shouted, and laughed, causing a chain reaction of barking and laughter from the row of inmates.

Arnold ordered the other two guards inside with Lewis. They must get Sims to the infirmary immediately. Lewis, without touching the body, replied, "He's dead, sir."

"Check for a pulse!" shouted Arnold, pushing his way past the guards and doing it himself, getting Sims' blood all over his hands and white lab coat.

"Watch you don't get his blood on you, boys!" shouted Matisak, whose voice was ominously muffled here in Sims' cell. "One drop of it and you could be Stainlype. It's like AIDS, you know, what he has ... contracted through the blood. If you want, Dr. Arnold, I'll drink it all up for you, so you don't have to worry."

Arnold was trying desperately to ignore Matisak. "He's dead, all right ... Bloody fool killed himself."

"Stainlype killed him!" Matisak shouted.

"Well, don't just stand about, you men!" said Arnold. "Get this ... cleaned up."

The guards hesitated, not wanting to touch Sims. Hardened, seasoned men, they shied from any thought of touching him. They had all come to feel superstitious about this thing that had hold of Sims. Could it possibly be catching? Sims had said it, and now Matisak said it, and what they had seen also said it could be.

"Lewis?"

Lewis, the senior man, crouched over the body and told Dr. Arnold it would be taken care of.

"There'll be papers to fill out, reports, no doubt an investigation into the man's death."

Lewis said to another of the guards, "Haines, get a stretcher from the infirmary. Malone, get what you need and clean this place up."

Both junior men looked relieved and neither man hesitated leaving. Dr. Arnold quietly and slowly left behind them, leaving Lewis alone with the devil at his feet. A creeping, eerie feeling began to invade Lewis's insides, moving outward from his abdomen, climbing up his spine one vertebra at a time as his skin began to prickle, sweat and cool. He felt an odd sensation verging on fear, an emotion he had never allowed a moment's sway with him in his life. He recalled Sims' left eye, just before he died, looking out at him as if he were the only man in the room. Lewis thought he had seen something there, a ghostly sliver of curling smoke wisping up and away from the raw, red cranium, like a lingering ring of smoke . . . something escaping.

When they carried Sims' body out on the stretcher, his disfigured face was covered with a white sheet. A brownish purple stain rose and grew where the sheet clung to the sticky face. Carrying Sims out past the other madmen brought on a new wave of cheers, hoots, laughter and remarks.

"Did he shit his pants?"

"What're you going to do with him?"

"Dissect him, dummy. We're all going to have our heads cut open and studied at close range someday."

"Is that true, Lewis? Lewis?"

Matisak had the last word as they passed from the cell block. "You know Stainlype's got you now, don't you, Lewis?"

Two

The heavyset man in the seat beside her kept staring, and his eyes played over Dr. Jessica Coran's inconvenient, pearl-handled cane. It was a gift from those who knew that her long recovery had been filled with anguish and that, at least physically, she meant to overcome the most awful mistake and setback of her life.

She wrestled the cane back from below the seat where it rested no better than in her lap, now finding a place alongside her. The Boeing 707 was a lumbering pachyderm here on the taxi strip, and she still hadn't gotten her seat belt fastened. A wary flight attendant prompted her now to do so, and she tried to return the plastic smile.

It would be a long short flight from D.C. to New York City. The big man beside her initiated a prolonged smoker's cough and afterward began pontificating on the "unconsitutionality of nonsmoking rules aboard aircraft."

She hated flying commercial and especially coach, even more so when she was working, preferring instead a military transport with seats as hard as a '57 Chevy's. Despite the so-called bennies of a modern jet—plush seats, films, Bach at fifty thousand feet and a cuisine slightly less appetizing than a Big Mac and fries—she'd take the gutted F-14 on the runway at Quantico any day. Any day it was available, that is.

She did her level best not to meet the eyes of the stranger beside her or to encourage his smoking speech, tearing open her briefcase as a clear sign that she was occupied.

The evening before, Chief Theresa O'Rourke had handed her everything the FBI had on the maniac who was now terrorizing New York, a horrid case of serial murder and cannibalism. The unknown predator stalking the city was, like

9

Gerald Ray Sims, a flesh-eater, the kind of killer whose mind-set and M.O. were startlingly similar to Sims'. She ought to know. She had logged hour upon hour with Sims at his cell in Philadelphia, taping his various confessions, and in a rare instance or two, catching Stainlype's voice on the tape as well.

She had become something of an expert on madness. It had become her métier, along with her expertise as a medical examiner for the FBI.

"How'd it happen?" asked the man in the seat beside her.

She pretended that she was engrossed in the file into which she had buried her face.

"How'd you bum out your leg?" he persisted, a Rolex on his wrist above an ancient burn scar. "Pretty thing like you? Skiing accident, right? Must've been some sorta sport, huh?"

She kept her eyes down. "Yeah, skiing accident," she lied, wondering if she shouldn't have bummed him out with the truth—*maimed by a madman who was trying to drink blood from my throat at the time.* Whether he believed it or not, it would put him off the air-travel cordiality he was going for. But suppose he then wanted to hear all the details? Risky, she thought.

"Don't ski myself. Don't get a chance to do much of anything that calls for muscle these days. Make my living in computers," he said with a gingery laugh. "Work out of D.C. with H and P, you know, the *Pack*?"

"I'm sorry, but—"

"Hewlett-Packard! I do—"

"Please, Mr. ahhh . . ."

"Dorrington. Jack, my friends call me."

"Mr. Dorrington, I've got tons of work to do, so if you don't mind?"

There was a moment's pause and the jet went airborne, and this was followed by an enormous sigh out of Jack Dorrington of the *Pack*, who, without any more talk, began to fan through the in-flight magazine, leaving Jessica to herself.

Jessica knew that she drew attention wherever she went. A strikingly tall woman with the good looks of her parents, and now the damned limp and cane. Mad Matisak had changed her appearance, altered the way others saw her, dealt with her, judged her, and ultimately how she judged herself.

The plane ascended through the rain, rising on the air above the clouds and into sunlight denied the Virginia and D.C. area for several days now. The brilliance of the sun was a balm to her soul.

Beside her, Dorrington said, "Do you mind closing the window shield? The sun's glare ... making it hard to read."

She gave a few more moments to the sun before quietly closing the shield and delving back into the dark business at hand. Moments before leaving her Quantico pathology lab, she had gotten word that Gerald Ray Sims had literally crushed his own skull in an attempt to rid his mind of Stainlype at last. Perhaps in death he'd find peace but she rather doubted it.

Now the information on the New York City killer, dubbed "the Claw" by press media, was staring her in the face. Closing her eyes, she began to lightly doze with the hum of the plane.

When she'd first gone to the prison in the City of Brotherly Love to seek additional information from Matisak, who was "ready to cooperate with federal authorities," it was for the express purpose of learning as much as she could about both him and his victims, many of whom remained unaccounted for. It was also important to learn what she might of his motivations, the methods employed to lure his victims, the reasons he selected the women and men he chose to kill.

Matisak was one of the hundreds of serial killers now being interviewed by the FBI, the information correlated and fed into computers in an attempt to better understand how such social monsters came into being and how best to safeguard against them in the future.

Matisak was bored. All of his nutritional and medical needs were being taken care of by the U.S. Government. But his mind, he told them, was not being nourished. He started to barter and he wanted files and information on Gerald Ray Sims, a.k.a. Stainlype, saying that he wanted to help in understanding a man who enjoyed flesh over Matisak's own preference, blood. Jessica had not wanted to indulge Matisak in what was obviously an aberrant game. She saw his interest in a fellow madman as sick curiosity, while Matisak called it training for more important and ongoing cases! He said he wanted recognition as a consultant for the FBI.

Jessica's superiors wanted her to go along with Matisak, who refused to deal with anyone but her, the agent who had placed him behind bars. They had seen this as a chance to glean more information out of Matisak, particularly to learn the whereabouts of a large number of bodies still unaccounted for, moldering in shallow graves all across the Midwest.

Feeding Matisak's prurient interest in Sims meant she must play to the crazed killer's ego trip, but on her last visit, Teach Matisak refused any more "trash" on Sims; he now wanted information on the lurid Claw case, the very case she had been assigned to, somehow knowing that it would fall into her hands even before she did.

"You can go straight to hell, Matisak," she'd told him.

"Don't be a fool, Jessica." His iron blue eyes held her prisoner for a moment. She knew what he was picturing in his mind, the moment when she was completely under his control. His hideous grin revealed his jaundiced gums.

She'd gotten up, prepared to leave.

"I can give you Tracy Torres ... Ana Pelligrino ... a list of others," he'd teased.

"I won't be returning."

"Check an area called the Old Downs Glen section southwest of Lexington, Kentucky, a broad field surrounded by trees, a winding, unpaved road with a ranch house on one side and a lake on the other. Dredge the lake." He spoke coldly, smugly, in that tone he used when he had whispered in her ear that he was going to drain her of all her blood, the night he'd killed Otto Boutine, her mentor and lover.

Sometimes his information unearthed a body. Sometimes not. She had shut down her recorder, but someone watching on the TV monitors might have heard the "latest Matisak revelation." She'd wanted to push through the door and not look back, but she couldn't. When Matisak had stood trial the previous year, the number of blood-drained bodies attributed to him stood at twenty-four, but it had now risen to twice that and counting.

The FBI liked closing cases, liked being able to write up a tidy ending to a missing person's case. It was great P.R. and great press when a victim's family could finally recover remains and put them in a sacred place. It all made good sense to deal with the devil for such results, but it turned her stomach even to look at Matisak.

In the end, she had called his bluff and stepped through the door without another word, infuriating him. She failed to report his request for information on the case of the Claw. So far as she was concerned, and from what Dr. Arnold had told her of his behavior and remarks upon Sims' suicide, Matisak was having too damned much fun yanking everyone's chain when by rights he ought to have been gassed or electrocuted for his crimes, but the sovereign State of Illinois hadn't been a death-sentence state.

Sims was a pitiable creature by comparison to Matisak, though his crimes had been even more ghastly and hideous in the public mind than those of the vampire. Cannibals killed quickly, vampires with slow deliberation. Matisak drained his victim's blood slowly, in torturous fashion, with the use of a tracheotomy tube. His bloodletting was called in FBI terms the ninth level of torture. Sims was a meat-eater, a cannibal, and his crime in FBI parlance fell at the sixth level of torture, or Tort 6. After having incapacitated his victims, he subjected their bodies to indignities unimaginable to the average citizen, but their suffering was ended relatively quickly. On the FBI torture scale, the scale was tipped by the number of hours a victim actually suffered.

There weren't a lot of blood-drinkers or cannibals in captivity, and so each one, from the sometime cannibal to the full-blown, such as Jeffrey Dahmer, was seen as an important source of information regarding the darkest and most depraved of human desires. From a psychiatric point of view these rare species were priceless. And so people like Arnold and O'Rourke treated them like celebrities.

But what had they learned from Sims, whose own character was so weak as to be dominated by a shadowy second

self, a delusionary double that he claimed to be a woman
named Stainlype who was the meat-eater, not him? Jessica
wondered which one, Sims or Stainlype, would pay for his
sins in the hereafter. As with Sims, her Matisak talks had
located a number of otherwise lost bodies, and this was
the only reason she'd agreed to return to the asylum penitentiary.

Nodding off in the peace and serenity brought on by air
flight, Jessica felt for a time safe and untouchable when
she heard Matisak's grating voice, saying, "The Claw . . .
the Claw . . . the Claw . . ."

Jessica jerked awake and found Dorrington shouting at the
flight attendant, who'd handed him chicken instead of the club
sandwich. He was repeatedly saying, "The club . . . the club."

"And anything for you, miss?" asked the attendant.

"Just coffee, please, black," she said over the noise in the
plane. Once she'd gotten her coffee stabilized, she went back
to the case file in her lap.

The New York City police were baffled by a vicious, sadistic woman-hater brutalizing, maiming and cannibalizing victims across a wide area. The handiwork of the so-called Claw
was so awful that it went beyond anything Jessica had seen
in or out of an autopsy room.

An NYPD captain of detectives named Alan Rychman had
placed multiple information checks through VICAP—the Violent Criminal Apprehension Program at the National Crime
Information Center, Washington, D.C. Rychman was asking
for cooperation on a nationwide scale by utilizing the FBI
computer where all information on violent crimes was pooled
and screened for pattern crimes and similarities. NYPD had
been unable to obtain anything in the way of evidence on the
killer's identity, or identities. Enough damage had been done
on the victims to warrant the possibility that the Claw was
more than one assailant. Along with Rychman, the renowned
New York City chief medical examiner, Dr. Luther Darius,
was asking for limited assistance through his contacts in the
FBI medical community.

Jessica knew of Darius' reputation, and if he was asking

for help, then things had gone badly in New York. As it was, five known victims of the maniac were spread across several boroughs, further complicating matters, as this involved various police jurisdictions and pathology labs. The killings had recently ceased, but fear ran high that the ugly mutilation murders and cannibalized corpses would return.

She found it of great interest that the killer had chosen to play games early on with the police, intentionally placing the bodies in high-visibility locations. The killer wanted the bodies found either because he felt some remorse and wanted his victims to be given a decent burial or—and much more likely given the severity of the attacks—he took great delight in showing off his carving talents and enjoyed frightening and disgusting the public, the authorities or both.

The fifth victim was found after a phone caller to an all-night radio talk show told authorities where to look; the caller had timidly identified himself as Ovid. A trace on the call turned up an empty phone booth in Manhattan, but Ovid's voiceprint was on record.

A search of the area where Ovid told police to look revealed a woman gutted, her entrails gone, presumably eaten, since the cannibalistic nature of the monster had already been established forensically, making the Claw the most notorious serial killer in the city since the Son of Sam.

The bastard hasn't been very selective, Jessica thought. His victims ranged from age seventeen to seventy-one, from blondes to gray-haired grandmas, leaving the NYPD without an apparent victim type, further limiting knowledge of the kind of killer they were dealing with. The only common denominator was that the victims were female, leading to speculation that this ripper killed out of a deep-seated hatred of women, which was no big deduction at this point.

NYPD hadn't any fingerprints, hair samples, or fibers of any significance, and with no one in custody whose teeth impressions matched the bites left in the flesh of the victims, and no other leads, neither Forensics nor Captain Rychman was holding out for any miracles. The killer was meticulous about not leaving any trace of himself behind, giving Jessica to believe that he was what the Bureau called a highly *organized* killer.

Dr. Luther Darius had recently requested and received useful crime-fighting software from the FBI which might pinpoint the size, style and type of the weapon being used on the Claw's victims. Jessica Coran had had a hand in developing and refining the software, a dream that had begun with the now retired Dr. Holecraft. He'd been one of Jessica's instructors in the crime lab. Darius could get no better computer-assisted aid than the FBI Evidence TACH Program. This evidence technician software would save Darius weeks, perhaps months, of painstaking evidence-gathering and measurements.

With this thought, Jessica closed her eyes once again, drifting off toward sleep. All information regarding the NYPD troubles seemed now to be floating like the debris of a sunken ship atop mounting waves, flotsam in her mind, unrelated, disjointed and disorganized. Her mind fought to put it away, to find rest, and she did so for a brief time until the floating debris coalesced into one disturbing, familiar form— the face of Gerald Ray Sims. Was the Claw cut of the same cloth? She might warily assume so on the basis of their mutual taste for human flesh, that they were both Tort 6 killers.

Then she watched as Sims' face darkened and shape-changed into a bestial monster, Stainlype; then Stainlype was Matthew Matisak, his eyes glaring out at her from the window of his glass-encased cell.

Matisak's form suddenly rises up in her dream, moving toward her at a threatening pace, stepping to and through the glass that separates them, a supernatural being unhampered and unimpaired by the glass. His hands extend ten feet before him, poised to grab her. She quickly reaches down to the gun she has smuggled into the jail, raises it and fires, blowing half of Matisak's face away. But he keeps coming, one eye dangling, the other eerily focused on her.

She gasps when he grabs her and wakes with a start to find the plane descending toward La Guardia.

Three

e

"What do you think, Ovid?"

The Claw insisted on calling him Ovid. He didn't know what it signified, but the Claw told him that he renamed all of his followers.

"She'll do . . ."

"You sure, now? Don't wanna rush you into anything."

"Let's do it, Claw."

"You got the hammer?"

"Got it."

"You worked out the place?"

"Quit worrying."

"Time to feast?"

"Time to feast."

Sometimes Ovid thought it was like talking to himself, and sometimes it was like talking to an entirely different person.

But when the Claw was stalking a victim, they were of the same mind.

She was about thirty yards away. She had come out of a grocery store, her arm wrapped around a bag. She looked troubled, preoccupied. She didn't notice his approach. She took exactly the right course, toward the area he had planned to drag her after hitting her with the hammer. Once she was unconscious, he would have his way with her, and so would the Claw.

He knew the Claw liked to rip women open. He knew the Claw liked to bite and tear with his teeth, too, and eat some of the parts. The Claw was a real animal.

He, too, liked some of it. He liked using his teeth on her.

17

At first, though, when he tried tasting what the Claw tasted, it made him vomit. He had become more accustomed to it now, and he no longer threw up, but he still didn't much like it.

He lessened the distance between himself and his victim, feeling the hefty hammer in his hand beneath the coat. He had slit the pocket to accommodate both hand and hammer. All the other tools he required were in the safe place.

She looked over her shoulder, saw him and quickened her pace. He sensed her fear. He liked the feeling it made in the pit of his stomach. He took longer strides toward her. She would reach the alleyway entrance in a moment. He must be quick.

She looked around again, half stumbled on seeing him so near, and she let out a scream just as the hammer came down. Her groceries spilled and he dragged her limp form down the darkened alley, out of the streetlights that cast his shadow in the horrible shape of a hunchback. But the hunchback's shadow was due to the cumbersome woman he had slung over his shoulder.

He passed a house where some lights had come on, pressed himself and his victim against the fence and held his breath. The people inside had heard the scream that had been curtailed by the blow to her head. She was bleeding. He could smell it. He reached up to her scalp to touch the warm spot, getting his fingers sticky with it. The Claw would be pleased.

He made his way toward his destination with his burden, wishing the Claw would be of more assistance during this stage of preparation, but the Claw said it was a way to show faith in him, and that it would be wrong of the Claw to assist in this part of the ritual.

He and the Claw swore never to be weak ever again, never to go hungry or without power. They took power when they took life, the Claw said. They took sustenance when they took life. They had every right to what they could take.

He dragged her into the blackness of a city basement at sublevel. Earlier he had snapped the lock and placed his tool-box inside. He expected the Claw to enter behind him, knowing the Claw was nearby, watching out there in the night.

The woman moaned. Heat rose off her as if she had a fever. He guessed her to be in her late twenties. She was rather thick with a pleasant, plump face, her hair left to fall straight to each side. She hadn't taken very good care of herself, he thought. She reminded him of his mother.

He wondered what was keeping the Claw; he feared she would regain consciousness too soon and wake up screaming, before the Claw arrived. Where was he?

He laid her now on the grimy floor. She rolled to one side. She was waking. He didn't want to hit her again for fear another blow might kill her. The Claw wanted her to be alive when he ripped into her.

Then the Claw was in the room with them. Ovid hadn't even seen him come in. It was amazing, as if he had materialized out of the black emptiness all around them.

"We need light," said the Claw, and it was as if the words were whispered into his brain through some kind of weird telephone. He heard the words as if from far away.

"Light could draw somebody."

"Light," ordered the other.

"All right, light."

Ovid set up a small flashlight fished from his tool chest. "How's that?"

"Better."

He saw the Claw extend his shiny, metallic, scissorslike right hand. It was a devastating weapon, sparkling in the weak light, the ice-pick ends seemingly hungry for flesh. The Claw extended the razor-sharp, three-pronged piece of metal over the woman's body, and with a mere swipe, cut open the fabric of her cotton print dress. Then her bra and panties were cut. Next came the skin, the blood bubbling up. But this was just the Claw at foreplay.

Ovid swallowed hard, watching the claw pendulum back and forth slowly over the helpless victim.

"You want to take a bite out of her?" the Claw asked him.

"Yeah, can hardly wait," lied Ovid, who knew he could wait.

"Do it . . . Do it now!"

He clamped down on her throat, and with his teeth he drew

back blood and tissue. At almost the same instant, the Claw dug deep into her chest and jaggedly pulled down and down and down. The woman's scream was lost with her vocal cords, which Ovid ripped out with his teeth.

The Claw now bit at her lower parts, tearing away chunks of her flesh, rolling it around in his mouth, spitting some out, swallowing other pieces.

The Claw went into a frenzy over the still-kicking, nerve-rippling corpse, digging again into her and ripping away. He then did it a third time. When he finished, he asked for the eyes. These were cut away, handed to him, and he fed on them.

Spent, lying against the dead woman, the Claw dug out her insides, carefully placing the intestines alongside the body before looping them in a winding, circular pattern about the limbs. He then went back inside her for the heart and kidneys. They both became perturbed at finding only one kidney.

"Take what we have," said the Claw.

He found the plastic bags in the tool chest. The heart was severed and put away first. Then the left kidney was bagged.

"We'll finish the liver here," the Claw told him.

"All right, all right."

"I want the head," said the Claw.

"What? Whataya mean?"

"The head."

"You want to take her head with us?"

"Yes, dammit."

"What for?"

"For later."

"All right, all right." With a carpenter's knife used for cutting linoleum, he began an effective slice all around the throat. He could feel the head coming, held now only by the cervical vertebra. The linoleum cutter soon severed this last connection. The head tumbled from the body as if scurrying off. He grabbed it and instantly the Claw snatched it from him. It dangled at the end of the claw.   •

The eyeless face was further disfigured by the Claw while Ovid went for the raw liver, but there was a noise outside.

"The light!"

Ovid shut it down.

Someone was coming down the stone steps, was just outside the door. Whoever it was saw the broken lock and had seen the strange glow inside; whoever it was dropped what he or she was carrying and rushed away.

"Tools, collect up everything, everything!" cried the Claw.

Ovid did so as quickly and as carefully as he could, and when Ovid turned around, he found himself alone with the decapitated, mutilated corpse. The Claw had left empty-handed. He'd have to leave the head, and hope that he could get away with his tools and the two organs in his toolbox.

He rushed out into the dark. No sign of the Claw.

The rookie cop that Tyler Davis was training told him they'd gotten a call over the radio while Davis was inside getting coffee. "What kind of call?"

"Routine 10-22, Sergeant Davis."

Tyler had been a training sergeant for eleven years, and rookies never ceased to amaze him. "Nothing routine about a 10-22. You go answering a 10-22 thinking the way you're thinking, *Officer* Chase, just go right ahead and get your friggin' brains blown out for ringing on a doorbell. Seen it happen."

"Well, I figure it's maybe a prowler," said Bryan Chase to his training sergeant, shrugging it off.

"Call like that's the trickiest kind. Let's roll, you got the address?"

Chase hit the siren and peeled out the moment Davis' hefty behind was on the seat, spilling the man's coffee in the bargain, further aggravating him. After the cursing stopped, Tyler Davis cleaned himself off with a handkerchief. He then slowly spoke to Chase in calm, even tones. "You get a 10-30, you know what's going down. You get a 10-11, you pretty much know what's waiting at the end of the ride. *This* shit . . . could be a burglary in progress, sure. Could be a break-in for any number of reasons. Jealous boyfriend or husband hitting on his wife. Could be a man with a gun."

The radio car stopped in front of an old brownstone where three people—a crowd for this time of night in this area—had gathered. The strobe beacon on the radio car drew more onlookers and curious kids. The superintendent of the building told them that he called when one of his tenants had run to his door with a report of something awful going on in the basement laundry room. The super led the way.

The rear basement door stood open, the black interior staring back like a gaping dungeon. Davis had brought along his flashlight, and now he cut the darkness with a thin line of light, shouting, "Come on out of there, all of you! This is the police. Step out with your hands up in front of you!"

There was no response.

"There a light switch inside there?" he asked the super.

"Sure, center of the room on a chain."

The flash reflected back off the dull finish of an ill-matched washer and dryer. "Calcutta in there," muttered Davis. "And something smells wrong."

"I don't smell anything," replied Bryan Chase.

Davis had been a medic in Vietnam. "Smells like blood, man. Anybody in there? Anybody hurt? I don't think nobody's here."

"I'll get the light switch," said Bryan, going for the center of the room, his gun pulled and poised. Suddenly the rookie tripped, his firearm discharging, Davis cursing, asking what happened.

"Fell over something ... something big."

Tyler Davis was trying to help Chase to his feet when his beam picked up the unmistakable form of a corpse—the something Bryan had tripped over. A decapitated head was still skittering around like a spinning bottle where the kid had kicked it with his boot. Davis' light watched it until it slowed, revealing the destroyed features of the dead woman.

Chase scrambled to his feet, his clothes wet and clinging. Cursing, he slipped a second time on the pool of blood and juices he found himself in, saying, "Jesus Christ! God, oh, my God, Sergeant!"

"Get on your feet and back out to the radio, kid," shouted Davis. "Call it in! Get everybody down here—*everybody*!"

A yapping dog on the scent raced into the dungeon, going for the body, rooting around in the spilled fluids. People had pushed forward and were staring like so many ghouls. Davis kicked out at the dog to get it from the body. The crime scene had already been contaminated enough by him and Chase. "Christ, get this mutt out of here or I swear I'm gonna blow him away!"

His boot now caught the dog in the ribs, sending it flying toward the door. It yelped and ran out, but the motion required on Davis' part had sent him onto his butt, his elbow landing in the grisly open torso.

Just outside he heard some woman moaning about the mistreatment of her dog. The moment Bryan Chase returned, Tyler Davis ordered him to clear people from the area and get it cordoned off. Davis had seen mutilated bodies by the truckload in Cambodia and Vietnam, yet he wasn't hardened to the corpse at his feet tonight. Still he knew from training how to conduct himself calmly and what must be done. This had to be the work of the creep the papers had been calling the Claw. It wouldn't be long before every brass ass on the force was down on him. He had to do everything by the book.

He returned to the door, seeing that young Chase wasn't getting the job done outside. He knew how to clear out a crime scene fast.

"People! Folks, now listen." Once he'd gotten their attention, he continued. "Now, folks, in a matter of minutes every cop in New York's gonna be here, and the first things they'll want to know is how much you saw, or heard, or thought you heard and where you were standing when you saw or heard it. Now, it's true, there's a dead lady inside there. What the police detectives is going to want to know is this: where were you when the woman was getting herself murdered?"

This had the immediate and desired effect Davis was going for. The gawkers began to disappear.

Chase, some vomit residue on his lips, looked at his duty sergeant with newfound respect. "You sure are cool about all this, Sergeant."

Tyler Davis nodded and stood silent sentinel at the door, awaiting superiors who'd have to turn that light on inside; people who would have to flash an intense light on the ugliness Chase and he had merely to glance over.

"You don't tell anyone you were all over the corpse, Bryan," he said, and when the kid hesitated, "You got that?"

"Yes, sir, if you say so, sir."

"I say so."

He knew the routine.

"What a goddamned mess. Why'n hell can't we get those lights up? This going to take all bloody night? Like I don't have anything better to do?" Dr. Kevin Perkins was young, disgruntled, loud, rude and obnoxious. He disliked the profession he found himself in, and he had an abiding dislike for cops, which was never more apparent than tonight.

Capt. Alan Rychman watched the younger, educated man verbally assault those around him. A field generator was droning on, but the juice was intermittent, the equipment faulty. The guy who had brought it was taking a lot of flak from Dr. Perkins, whose white lab coat was smeared with an obscene array of dark, viscous fluids.

Alan Rychman had driven at top speed to get here, having been routed from a party where the mayor and the commissioner of police had just told everyone that the Claw was a matter of history, that he was now believed to be locked up in an asylum somewhere.

It appeared such talk was over.

"You're right, Perkins," he said to the younger man, "the light in here really sucks."

"Damned inconvenient. Been waiting for your photographers to get in and finish, waiting for your guy with the generator over there! It's crazy, like a Mack Sennett film. You got any idea what this is like on my homelife? Maybe you don't have a homelife, but I do."

Rychman nodded at the young doctor, who had obviously been roused from his bed and now had a gut-wrenching, tedious task ahead of him. "Still," Rychman said, "you're pulling down good money on the rotation." As an associate M.E. with the city, he was on call, making many times over Rychman's salary.

"Good money, hell. In private practice, I could make six, seven times as much."

"Then maybe you'd better go into private practice, Doctor—after tonight, that is."

Perkins' eyes fixed Rychman's but they did not lock for long. Rychman valued forensic information, but he didn't care to work with the disenchanted Perkins and he'd told Darius that, but Darius had become ill, and so it had fallen to Perkins to investigate an important killing, to gather evidence and arrange for an autopsy, to do the necessary paperwork declaring the victim dead and to give "reason" of death.

"Cause of death is fairly obvious, wouldn't you say, Doctor?" Rychman said, his eyes staring in sad disbelief at what one human being was capable of doing to another.

"It would appear so," Perkins managed as he worked to scrape a few fine, blond hairs off the body, putting them neatly into a plastic envelope. Perkins had seen only one other victim of the Claw, but that had been at the morgue on a gleaming steel table, by then the wounds cleaned, the body made as presentable as possible for burial. His hands now shook as he worked, a bad sign for an M.E., Rychman thought.

"The beheading's something new."

"Yeah, a new twist, you might say," muttered Perkins in a rare bit of gallows humor.

Rychman moved with measured step about the body and crime scene. Cops in plain clothes and uniform had been coming in and out all night, most simply to have a look.

"Something else not quite to pattern here, either, Doc," added Rychman in a conspiratorial whisper.

"Oh? And what's that, Captain?"

"Not like this guy to hide his handiwork away like this. This guy likes to leave his victims out in the open, Times Square if he could manage it."

"Maybe he'll provide you with an exhibition later."

"Meaning?"

"Meaning he either ate or took with him some of her parts."

"What parts?"

"You name it: heart, kidneys . . ."

Rychman ground his teeth together. "Anything else?"

Perkins pointed with a pen to a few brown, lumpy portions of what appeared to be dog droppings amid blood splatters. "Most of her liver was eaten here on the spot."

"What about the brain?"

"Intact."

"Can't figure the decapitation."

"The killer was surprised in the act. I think he meant to take the head away with him."

Rychman nodded. "Yeah, quite possibly, but it may also be that some joker's trying his hand at *playing* the Claw."

"A copycat to throw the police off? So far, Captain, everything marks this corpse as just another hapless victim of the same brutal predator."

"Has your office come up with anything on the kind of cutting weapon he's using, Doctor?"

"No, no, we haven't. Sorry, but there you have it."

"Sorry?" Rychman sensed that Perkins had for some time now been coming unglued. He had noticed it on an earlier case which dealt with a younger, attractive woman named Laura Schindler. "We need to know what kind of murder weapon he's using. If we knew that—"

"Sorry, we've come up with a big zero!" shouted Perkins, his eyes shading over in a zestful anger.

"So far your people've got no semen, no bodily fluids, no prints. What have you got? A few fibers, hairs and teeth marks, all useless without a match."

"The goddamned teeth marks have been placed in a computer and sent to every major police information system in the country and abroad."

"Yeah, I know, because I pressed you guys into doing just that."

Rychman started away but suddenly felt Perkins grip his arm. He spun on his heels to face the other man, who was now shouting in his face. "Why haven't your people found this animal?"

"What do you think we're—"

"The bastard's got to stick out!" Perkins continued. "He must be covered in blood after he does a thing like this. He must be a madman, a raving lunatic, one of your bloody

MDSOs! Don't come down on our office when you guys haven't done a fucking thing to stop this kind of bloodletting!" He finished by pointing to the mutilated woman.

Rychman grabbed Perkins by the shirt and shoved him against the washer-dryer unit, causing a metal boom that alerted everyone to stand clear.

"First of all, sonny, we're investigating every one of the 6,092 mentally disturbed sex offenders in our computer, and secondly, we've logged 110,000 man-hours on this sonofabitch, so don't hand me any more shit, okay? Okay!"

Rychman was a tall and intimidating man, and under his grip, Perkins felt totally powerless. For a moment, he read in Rychman's eyes the instinctive animal drive to kill. Perkins had covered his face with his bony arms, expecting the blow to come, but Rychman was pulled away by several other cops. Having cooled, the big captain left with a final word for Perkins. "See that my office gets a full report first thing in the morning, Perkins. You got that?"

Shaken, Perkins was actually glad to be feeling something. Earlier, his senses had completely shut down. His mind had been assailed by the sight, smell and feel of the cannibalized victim. He allowed Rychman a chance to get past the door before he shouted a response. "You'll get the damned report as soon as it's available."

As Rychman stormed away, Perkins thought him a force not unlike the Claw, a man interested in power and control and humiliating others. Only in Rychman's case, he carried a badge.

Four

Capt. Alan Rychman arrived at Police Plaza One the following morning with raw nerves only to find an army of reporters camped on his doorstep. The battery of questions was like a rapid-fire automatic. He waved his hands for the assembled members of the press to quiet down and he pushed more than one microphone out of his face. "We're doing everything humanly possible—"

A gang groan rose from the press people and several shouted questions that amounted to *What've you done for me lately?* One reporter that Rychman knew as Jim Drake, an up-and-coming with the *New York Times*, pointedly asked, "How do you expect people to believe you're doing all you can? Vacations, black-tie parties, and it's become obvious you're running for C.P."

"Nobody's declared on that score, but if I do, Drake, you'll be the first to know."

"Do you think as commissioner of police you could more effectively handle cases such as the Claw?"

"I'm not about to be sucked into that ... issue," he told Drake, his steely eyes fixed on the reporter for the first time. "Now, I assure you, ladies, gentlemen, we're moving on this case."

Rychman's aide, a large, round uniformed sergeant named Lou Pierce, tried to run interference for his boss, but he may as well have been trying to hold back jackals from a carcass.

"What about the C.P.'s office? What about the mayor's office?" shouted Drake as Rychman pushed his way forward.

"Everybody's moving, Jim, Andy, Martha." His attempt to reassure the press fell flat. His polite police P.R. tone wasn't enough to cut it anymore with these guys and he knew it.

"Speculation has it that the Claw is a medical man of some sort. Any foundation in that, Captain Rychman?" pursued Drake.

"No foundation in fact, but it hasn't been ruled out."

"Has there been a sixth and a seventh victim, Captain?"

Rychman had heard about the so-called seventh victim, a housewife who'd been mutilated early that morning by her husband, who was in custody. The husband thought he could get away with the killing if he made it look like the work of the Claw, but his work couldn't stand the close scrutiny of the chief assistant M.E., Luther Darius' right-hand man, Dr. Simon Archer, who had called Rychman, telling him what they had over on the Lower East Side.

"We have a sixth victim," replied Rychman. "The seventh was a copycat killing. You'll have full details in the press kit being put together at this moment. Now, please."

"What about the homeless couple?" pressed a female reporter.

"There was nothing to connect those deaths with the Claw, so far as can be determined."

"Busy night last night, huh, Captain?" asked another reporter.

"Typical Saturday night in the Apple."

Drake returned to his earlier question. "Is it true, Captain Rychman, that you want to be our next police commissioner?"

"I said no further comment." Rychman's glare held Drake hostage for a moment before he disappeared through the door held open by Lou Pierce, who now stepped in for his boss and fielded questions of the disappointed reporters.

Rychman knew that Drake, along with a lot of other people, was fishing for a commitment, one that he couldn't at this time make. He had given the idea of becoming C.P. a lot of thought, but should he lose such a race, he'd have to forfeit a great deal, and besides, he wasn't sure he wanted the headaches that went with the office. Still, he had a lot of support in the rank and file, although that could simply be because everyone hated Commissioner Carl Eldritch, a man whose tenure was synonymous with bland and uneventful.

Until now. Thanks to the Claw. The NYPD was being par-
boiled and burned raw daily in the press, not only in the city
but across the nation, being made to look ridiculous and incompetent. Allegations of gross ineptitude were nothing new,
but now the cry of reform was in the air, reform at all
levels, and since Rychman was a man decorated several times
for bravery in his career, and since he had come up through
the ranks ... But even he hadn't escaped the sometimes
cruel barbs of the cartoonists and columnists, the so-called
wrath of the public via publishers who weren't above manu-
facturing almost as much news as they might legitimately
find. *All that's fit to print* had long before become *Print all
that fits.*

"And if it doesn't fit," he muttered to himself, "make it
fit."

Rychman had to work hard to hold his anger at the press
in check. Good relations could make or break a campaign,
and he did indeed have aspirations to become the new C.P.
He had ideas, plans for reform that would shake up the entire
system, his top priority to effect the exchange of information
across all boundaries and boroughs.

He had personal reasons to dislike and suspect the press as
well, since his recent divorce had been given the *National
Enquirer* treatment, the sensationalism verging on slander and
libel. They took words uttered in passion and anger, twisted
them just so, words out of Nancy's mouth as well as his own.
Any chance of a reconciliation was demolished by the beating each of them had taken in the arena of the press. He'd
lost his calm exterior over that one and lost friends among the
fifth estate. Soon any utterance from either of Nancy's lawyers was confirmed as truth by the power of the printed word.
He'd read where she had suffered emotional torment, mental
torment, sexual torment and sixteen other forms of torment in
their marriage, and to keep from going down to Lowenstein
and Rutledge to find the vipers and crack their heads together, he'd have to rush down to the firing range to pull off
as many rounds as it took to relieve the venom and the sense
of injury and the confusion of not knowing what had hap-

pened to bring Nancy and him to such a place in their relationship.

After twenty-odd years in the department, he ought to know how to kiss ass and when to shut up. But lately, his nerves sheared raw by this case and the infuriating way in which it had so far been botched, he knew he could lose it at any time, on or off camera. He'd lost it with Perkins the night before. The mechanism by which he maneuvered on tiptoe with both the press and his superiors was grinding gears, threatening to halt altogether, if he didn't get control first.

He rode the elevator up and got off at his floor. He stared down the busy, teeming hallway that led to the hastily got-up evidence room where a meeting with the mayor's deputy for public safety, Commissioner Eldritch and others with a vested interest in the case of the Claw were supposedly waiting. People spilling in and out of the offices lining his way offered practiced and solicitous greetings, none genuine. Rychman's well-perfected cold stare greeted them each in turn. P. P. One was not yet his precinct, but his image was recognized throughout the city, thanks to the divorce. He strode quickly past cops who jokingly asked for favors in his new regime, his chiseled, granite features like those of a bronze statue. Bronze due to his recent trip to Bermuda, which had turned him more contemplative and brown. He'd gotten to like Bermuda's sun and rum, and he'd enjoyed a world without ties—ties of any kind. He seldom wore a tie himself, but today he'd made an exception. The tie lay across his broad chest, unable to reach to his waistline. People stared.

He knew he could be intimidating, and that it wasn't an endearing quality—not for most. He knew he intimidated the younger cops, due to his record of service, which could be a positive kind of intimidation, he thought. Being persuasive without having to say a word was a useful tool in the right hands, at the right time, especially for a commander. It certainly hadn't hurt him any in the war.

Most other cops understood him. He was fierce, ferocious if need be, unforgiving if circumstances warranted. Still, the fact that no one felt comfortable around him bothered him at times.

A career cop, he'd come up the hard way. Not once had he been appointed to or promoted to any rank on the basis of anything other than ability. Even the press couldn't find fault here. But he hadn't carved out a political place for himself and remained without political ties; truth be known, he was not a political animal, not in the sense that Eldritch was. Rychman hadn't the guile or the stomach for what Eldritch termed "political astuteness." The lack of this "quality" was his chief weakness should he move against Eldritch. Despite the fact he had turned precinct after precinct into well-organized, result-getting organizations, he still didn't dance effortlessly along the tightrope of the police superstructure, which was much harder than doing the minuet with the press corps. Maybe he wasn't a dancer, and maybe he wasn't C.P. material.

Before looking in on the evidence room, a room filled with the compiled information on the Claw killings, he remembered that Eldritch wanted to see him. The cop grapevine was quicker than a potato creeper. Word about Eldritch's having got up a special task force to oversee the investigation into the Claw killings was being spoken of in every sector. No one knew the particulars. Today everyone would know.

He was told by Eldritch's secretary, "They're waiting for you, Captain Rychman. Go right in."

Eldritch had ordered him out of his office only two weeks before, and in a fit of rage told him there was no need of such a task force and finished by ordering him to take a week's vacation. It had been the first days he'd spent away from the job and the city in several years and he knew he was feeling burned out, so he raced off to Bermuda, where, for a time, he put thoughts of the Claw out of his mind. In the meantime news of another victim and news of his lounging in Bermuda at the time—conveniently leaked to the press—made him look bad.

Eldritch, ever the astute politician.

Now inside Eldritch's office he found two other men, Ken Stallings, deputy mayor of the city, and Lt. Capt. Lowell Morris, a capable man whom Rychman both liked and respected. Eldritch introduced Stallings to Rychman, the men sizing one another up.

"I called you here, Alan, because we need a man of your caliber to head the Claw task force and head up—"

"Whoa, wait a minute." Rychman was searching the room for answers, his head twisting and turning. "I don't get it, Carl."

"You're the best man for the job."

"Am I?"

"We're all agreed. That is, the mayor and this office."

Stallings jumped in. "His Honor reviewed a lot of men and you came out on top, Captain Rychman. It's a high-profile case; certainly can't but help you if you ever aspire to any political office—not necessarily this office!"

Eldritch and Stallings laughed but Morris remained silent.

"What about Morris here?" Rychman asked, not sure he wanted to head such a task force. Task forces were grueling, the hours murder, and he didn't fully understand what was motivating Eldritch.

"Morris'll be taking charge of your precinct duties while you're on the task force," explained Carl Eldritch.

"I see."

"I thought it natural that you take over, Alan. After all, you were the one who initially came to me with the idea, remember?"

"I remember, all right."

"Look, it was you who contacted the FBI, and they're sending a man. You've had your hand in since the first of these murders. It seemed only natural that you should carry on," Eldritch continued.

Stallings jumped in again. "And you were the mayor's first choice, Alan."

Rychman looked at Lowell Morris, who just stared back, saying nothing.

"I suppose accepting is the politically correct thing to do, then. And from the congestion in the hall, I take it you expect to hold a press conference."

"Does that mean you'll accept?" asked Stallings.

Feeling trapped, a part of him wanting to run and a part of

him wanting to take on the greatest challenge of his official life, Rychman quietly said, "I should have my head examined. Only one thing, Carl: I don't want anyone—anyone—second-guessing me or undermining me. Understood?"

"Perfectly, and you won't regret it, Alan."

"Somehow," Rychman said, "I'm not so sure."

Eldritch told him that the evidence room and offices for the special task force were being set up in the building. Rychman told him that he knew that much, down to the room number.

"Can't keep a secret in a police precinct."

"I don't know. Naming me to this task force came as quite a shock."

Everyone shook hands and Ken Stallings said, "The mayor wants immediate action on this, Alan. You understand?"

"Sure, he wants the Claw behind bars yesterday."

Stallings smiled, his grin like the lip of a large pitcher. The three cops watched the Brooks Brothers suit as it hurried off.

"I thought he might stay for the pep talk to the task force," said Rychman.

"Thank God no," replied Eldritch.

Morris stood, poked a cigarette in his mouth, which he didn't light, and said, "I'll take care of your guys, Alan."

"I know you will, Lowell, and good luck."

Morris disappeared.

"You'll have the best men available, Alan," said Eldritch the moment they were alone. "Best from each sector, and most have been working on one or more of the cases. Hand-picked, all good men."

"When did all this come about? Last night there wasn't a word of this. Now—"

"We'd recruited everyone earlier, while you were away. Then when the killings appeared to have stopped . . . well, then last night. Ahh, what the hell difference does it make now?"

"I might've liked to choose my own team."

"Hey, Alan, we're all on the same team, remember? Besides, you know most of the men that will be working under you."

Rychman's eyes bore into Eldritch. "Most but not all isn't

good enough, Carl." Rychman knew that working within the team would be at least one and possibly two moles who'd be reporting back to the C.P.

At least Eldritch was transparent, he thought.

Rychman stepped into the homicide incident room, which would in all likelihood be his home for some time. Photographs of the victims shot from every angle immediately assailed the senses. Several blow-ups revealed the gargantuan injustices played out on the dead women. In this room, what few clues the police from various boroughs had gathered now belonged to the task force—the shredded clothing of the victims; their shoes; a pathetic display of purses, the contents of which had once surrounded their corpses; a few scraps of paper; a footprint set in concrete which had been lifted from a muddy alleyway; police reports; dossiers on the victims, their friends and relatives; detailed, tedious forensics reports on precisely how each woman had died—all lying across a line of cheap folding tables. Rychman thought that each item desperately cried out its meaning, but no one could hear. Lipstick tubes, keys and petite, childlike key rings, wallets with photos, scattered nail files and makeup kits. All the so-called evidence amounted to victim paraphernalia, nothing noteworthy and all pointing toward the victims, not the perpetrator. Frustration had crawled in before the task force was under way.

Eldritch had left him amid the collection of officers assembled from each of the city's five boroughs. Carl had a press conference to attend where he would present the details of how Alan Rychman would be heading up the newly formed task force. As soon as Eldritch disappeared, Rychman went to the front of the room, picked up a gavel and called for order. Some of the faces looking back at him he knew from previous cases, some he did not know and others were still milling in.

Among the late-comers were people Rychman didn't know, and he feared the press might infiltrate. He called for an ID check at the door, one of his detectives doing the honors. Then Rychman's attention, along with everyone else's, became glued on a tall, leggy and rather stunning woman in a

gray suit. Her hazel eyes were clear, wide, intelligent and curious, Rychman thought. She carried a cane and walked with
a limp. She could be press. He certainly didn't recognize her,
but then he didn't know every detective or cop in the city.
She might also be a police shrink, someone to help with the
killer profile they'd have to work up. His man at the door, be-
latedly checking the woman's ID, nodded that all was well.
The lovely stranger limped only a few feet when a detective
rose and offered her a front-row seat.

Rychman grunted at the noise level, and asked for people
to settle in.

"Gentlemen ... ladies ... detectives ... people!" Over
Rychman's head, to the rear, the large photographic images of
the victims of the phantom killer stared down over the assem-
blage. The dead faces, many with missing eyes, looked to
Jessica Coran as though they belonged in a dark gallery in a
wax museum of horrors. The skulls were crushed like soft
melons by a ball peen hammer, axe or hatchet, depending on
the mood of the sadistic monster, she supposed. The torsos
presented an even more horrible array of destroyed flesh
where the Claw had used some unknown tool to tear open the
area usually reserved for the autopsiest. The contents of
the victims' chests and abdomens had been turned out to feed
the flies and rats.

The killer apparently relished the brutalization of female
flesh.

The savagery was not altogether new to Jessica or the other
police officials in the room. Violent crimes against women
were on the rise, so much so that three out of four American
women, at some point or other, would be the victims of at
least one violent crime. The Justice Department statistic was
more than just a number to Jessica, who had become
Matisak's final target before he was captured and incarcerated. She knew that each year women were the victims of ap-
proximately 2.5 million violent crimes, from assault to rape.
It was a low estimate, since the statistics didn't take into account the 3 million to 4 million women who were battered in
episodes of domestic violence.

But it wasn't just the statistics that frightened Jessica; it

was the *randomness* of so much of this crime, the brutality
for the sake of brutality alone. She remembered a time when
it was rare to see physical injury to a woman who'd submitted to rape when threatened, but now, when a woman
submitted, she was often hurt, anyway.

Certainly the Claw hated women, and his crimes were hate
crimes. Most crime could be traced back to the witch's brew
of social ills: street gangs, the availability of guns and drugs,
the overall breakdown of family and community values. But
what did such *explainable* crime have to do with the inexpli-
cable doctor of death known as the Claw, who, like a
modern-day Jack the Ripper, targeted women for mutilation
and cannibalism? Very little, she guessed. It was more likely
that they were dealing with a criminal with a very high IQ,
above-average education, a white male who had a great deal
more going for him than the street gang member; a fellow
who, if he did drugs, did only light drugs; a fellow who very
likely had a hate relationship with his mother, a hate that had
boiled over, sending him after surrogate mothers to kill again
and again. Had this to do with the overall breakdown of
"family values"? No, it had to do with a single, insidious and
hideous perversion that had poisoned the mind of the killer
against women.

Neither she nor the other police officials could confuse the
case of the Claw with the rise in street crime and violence
against women, no matter how alluring the concept. No, it
was apparent they had a dyed-in-the-wool misogynist, a creep
who hated one thing to his core: *women*. Still, this meat-eater
would be wise enough to hide his hatred by day, in the well-
lit room, bringing his hatred out in the dark to look at it and
massage it, to allow it full vent, like a vampire thirsting for
blood; except that this bastard thirsted for flesh and quenched
his hatred only when he battered and ripped women to death,
and then desecrated the body. This was the true purpose of
his mutilation and cannibalism, she believed: to denigrate the
body and perhaps the sanctity of the human female form.

As the room around her settled, she thought of the lyrics of
a song by the Geto Boys. Before there were cop-killer raps,
there were woman-killer raps.

Jessica got the message loud and clear, and she recalled that after Matisak's attack on her, she had been unable to shower alone. It was sheer animal fear and a great, growing hatred of her own at the person who did this to her. Fear changed the way she went to bed each night, the way she woke in the morning; it changed the way she did everything . . .

Rychman's voice cut through her thoughts. "I've been *told* to be here, people, just like you, but I received one additional order—"

"And?" asked O'Toole, a burly detective Rychman had worked with before.

"*And* that I'm to inform you folks that we—*you and I*—are to be the nucleus of a special task force—"

"So you're heading up this task force," replied O'Toole, his brows knitted in thought.

"That's the gist of it, yeah. Any problems with that?"

O'Toole only laughed before saying, "Better you than me."

"Good choice. Congratulations, Captain!" others piped in.

"Not so sure congratulations are quite appropriate here, people," he said, looking around the room.

"So what's your first call, Alan?" asked O'Toole.

"I say we use every detective we can collar."

"What about regular caseloads?" someone asked.

"To hell with regular . . . back-shelve the bastards. Send some of your casework over to Missing Persons and the DMV, I don't care."

One of the other detectives wailed, "That's easier said than done. Do we have topflight clearance on this, Captain Rychman?"

"It comes from the top."

"Why the sudden change in policy?" asked another.

Rychman's face turned stony; he was obviously not used to being questioned.

"We are not here to question policy, people. We are here to carry out policy, understood?"

The quasi-military organization was having its military straps pulled tight, he was saying.

Rychman took the measure of his newly formed task force

again. "People, the press and others are saying we're sitting with our fingers up our asses on this case. They're drawing little cartoons of the mayor and the C.P., and if it keeps up, you and me. Some people are comparing this to the Yorkshire Ripper case in England, 1980. And that's not good. Police had questioned the killer nine times without realizing who they had. Not even Scotland Yard could catch this guy because none of the police agencies were cooperating with the others. And that's what the press is saying about us, that we can't play well together in the New York City sandbox, and maybe that's so, and maybe there'll always be a certain amount of that; maybe it's inevitable, given the fact we're all cops and cops are very territorial. But I tell you what: this killer we have on our hands, he's not so territorial. In fact, he doesn't know Queens from Bronx from Manhattan, as we've seen. *He's grazing.*"

"So we're supposed to be a super-squad?" asked Louis Emmons, a detective from Queens.

"That's right. We're it, so if you've got family, if you've got girlfriends or boyfriends, you'll have to put them at arm's length."

The men began to complain and moan.

Rychman held on to his calm. Watching him from where she sat, Dr. Jessica Coran thought him handsome in a rugged way. He was slim for so large a man and those eyes commanded such attention and respect.

"Now, we have no lack of red tape, computers or not," said Rychman. "And we've got no lack of quacks, crackpots and idiots giving information, and enough confessions to fill St. Pat's, but what we don't seem to have is a central clearing-house on this. The FBI has been called in and they're sending a crack man to help us coordinate efforts. I'd expected him to be here by now, but—any of you guys see anyone wearing a three-piece suit over steel-plated B.V.D.s?"

The remark drew laughter from every cop in the place, except the pretty auburn-haired lady in front. Most city cops refused to wear vests and most feds refused not to. She kept still, biding her time.

"Anyway, the feds'll be helping us with a profile of the

killer and with forensic backup any way they can, now that the mayor's finally given us the go-ahead."

"Good move," said Jessica Coran, drawing a few stares. "And first thing you might wish to do—"

"And what's that?" asked Rychman a bit disdainfully.

"Put a gag order on every police agency and officer; nothing is released to the press except what goes out from here."

"Good thinking," said O'Toole, with others agreeing.

Rychman nodded. "I was getting to that. Thank you for saving us time. Now, on to the next problem. Time to swallow our pride, and time to work together at all levels. That's what this team is all about. No showboating, no hot dogs or supersleuths, just hard-hitting, teeth-grinding police investigation. All of you've been handpicked by your captains because you're dogged, determined, hardworking cops ... like me."

"Right on!"

"We're being asked to do the miraculous, to find a needle in a haystack ... a rather large haystack of over eight million people, to trace this mystery down to one man. We're to set up a Ripper-type special squad to combat the sick creep the press is calling the Claw. So far the actual weapon the bastard uses across his victims' bodies hasn't been determined. Forensics hasn't an answer. So we're working blind as to weapon, and as far as motive, we haven't a clue. Maybe there is none ... maybe it's just plain old-fashioned evil, the same that's been spawning these monsters since time began."

Rychman allowed the notion to settle in.

"While we wait for that FBI guy to get here," he continued, "I want each captain present to tell us in capsule form what his division has, and then I want assurances that this information will get to this computer." He stopped to point to the machine. "This is the incident room and the only incident room on this case, gentlemen. Does everyone understand this?"

Everyone nodded and the various captains got up one at a time, each offering a few crumbs. The killer was very adept at leaving nothing whatever of himself behind. He appeared to be as swift and relentless as a gale-force wind.

Jessica could not fathom such callous disregard for life.

One of the captains said, "You've got to remember the kind of area we're talking here. Nobody wants to get involved. They see a man hit a woman with a hammer, they think it's between the man and his wife, and that's that."

"The hammerblow is just the beginning," said Rychman, "to render the victim defenseless. The actual murder occurs later. This guy drags his victim to a secluded area, usually a basement he has broken into, or below some stairwell, behind some cans, whatever, and there he takes out this incredible rage on the body."

"This guy is really sick . . . sicker than . . . than . . ." Louis Emmons began.

". . . sicker than O'Toole at last year's annual?"

This brought some mixed laughter.

"Sicker than that vampire creep the FBI stopped in Chicago last year," finished the good-looking female detective.

Jessica felt it was time to come forward when Rychman regained the attention of the assembled men and women. "I'm Agent Coran, Dr. Jessica Coran, of the FBI crime lab," she said.

Rychman's deep-set dark eyes narrowed, showing his displeasure at her having sat through the meeting to this point without identifying herself. She could also see that he was mentally flipping back through the files of his memory for any and all remarks he had made regarding the feds.

"Bad assumption that the fed would be a man," she replied. "Who did you think I was, the cleaning lady?"

"Christ, I don't know everybody in the entire department. I thought . . . Well, never mind what I thought. Would you like ahh . . . to add to anything that has been said here?"

She turned to the assembled detectives, holding onto her cane. "We recently put away Gerald Ray Sims, and you may have read that he killed himself in his prison cell. I . . . I had seen him in the prison only days before. Sims and your Claw have much in common." Her eyes scanned the room of silenced detectives.

"His doctor—and I concur—believes that his other self, the murderous side of his personality, talked him into killing himself."

"We can only pray the Claw does the same," said O'Toole. "Not likely so long as he's at large."

She allowed this to sink in for a few moments before she calmly said, "My team was also responsible for the capture of Matthew Matisak."

This brought about a great deal of murmuring as many in the room now realized exactly who Dr. Jessica Coran was. They had all read about the spectacular break in the vampire case and how she had been maimed in the process of catching Matisak.

"So you can rest assured that my team and I are not exactly amateurs at this. At any rate, I'm glad to have been selected to help you here. We have the best forensics lab on the planet. If there's an iota of information that has been overlooked, our lab will find it. In the meantime, I have to concur with everything—almost everything—that Captain Rychman has had to say to you. It's vital that all areas of the city work in close harmony against this . . . creature."

Five

After the meeting broke up, Alan Rychman asked Jessica Coran into the adjacent office, which Eldritch had designated as his. Once they were alone, he said, "I didn't appreciate your little masquerade in there, Dr. Coran."

"I was informed that you were told of my—"

"I'd say it's fairly apparent that I was unaware that you'd arrived. How long have you been in the city?"

"I arrived late yesterday, took the evening to familiarize myself with the case—as much as possible, given the lack of information. I had a meeting with Commissioner Eldritch and was asked to be here this morning. No one notified me about last night's homicide."

Rychman followed her speech with a series of "I sees."

"In the future, I'd like to be on the call list," she added.

"Whatever you say, Doctor."

"I'm anxious to help in whatever way possible."

"I guess you've seen this kind of thing before."

"A killer whose teeth imprints were lifted from the intestines of one of his victims? Not quite, but you might say I've seen enough ghouls so that I won't swoon."

She had a tough line, he thought, appraising her. She was a stunning woman, even with the distraction of the cane. "Matisak's victims surely suffered longer, and Gerald Ray Sims may've been sicker than this freak we've got on our hands, Doctor, but the way this bastard operates, the way he leaves their bodies . . . it may even shock *you*."

"What's that supposed to mean, Captain? That my reputation has preceded me? That I'm unshakable? That you'd like to see me shake?"

She'd read a complete file on Rychman, who was born in

43

1948 to working-class parents, the third of five children. He attended New York City schools, spent two years at John Jay College, dropped out for a stint in Vietnam and entered the Police Academy in 1973 on his return. He'd quickly risen through the ranks from patrolman to detective after a series of dazzling arrests. He moved from Vice to Homicide in '79 and had remained a homicide detective since. In 1989 he was named captain of the 31st Precinct, a precinct considered the worst in the city until he turned it around, making it immune to corruption and internal problems. Now the 31st had one of the highest arrest rates in the city. He'd done so well with the 31st that he had since been moved to two other "dirty" precincts to clean them up, and he had succeeded admirably. She understood that his successes were due to his unrelenting nature and a hands-on style of management. He was called "the Boot" by men who served under him because he had given so many burned-out cops a kick in the ass.

He'd also been decorated for bravery under fire in two wars, Nam and New York. In some ways he reminded her of Otto Boutine; the two would have been either extremely close friends or archenemies, butting heads like a pair of rams, she decided.

"Where're you staying?" he asked.

"Marriott."

"Downtown? Nice if you can get it. Close, should a call come in."

"I hope that's not an indication of how vigorously you intend to pursue this case, Captain."

He looked askance at her, confused. "What?"

"By waiting for a call." She picked up her cane and her bag, making for the door.

He thought of pursuing her, setting her straight, but tossed a disdainful wave in her direction instead, letting her go. But then she stuck her head back inside.

"Yes?"

"I'll want a copy of the forensics report on the sixth victim. Can you direct me?"

"I'll see you get a copy. It'll be on my desk sometime today."

"Is Archer or Darius the M.E. on the case?"

"Fellow name of Perkins."

"Hmmmm, I see. New?"

"Not exactly, but first time he's done a Claw crime scene. Seems Archer was occupied elsewhere and Darius ... well, he's been under the weather lately."

"There's been no continuity."

"You might say that, yes."

"The only constant at all the scenes has been the killer. The M.E.'s office has been playing musical chairs."

He frowned, pursed his lips and apologetically said, "We do the best we can with what we got, Dr. Coran."

"Unfortunately, that's not always good enough."

"We've got the best man in the country here and the men under him are equally good, Doctor. You go second-guessing a man of Dr. Darius' reputation and you might get burned."

"I don't want this to be an adversarial relationship, Captain."

"You could've fooled me."

She managed a smile, something he hadn't seen until now. It warmed the room, he thought. "If we're going to stop this madman, we've got to do as you preach—cooperate with one another. That means your crime lab has to cooperate with mine."

"And I have to cooperate with you."

"Couldn't hurt."

Despite her rough-and-tumble verbal display and the rigid exterior, the cane and limp, something about her eyes marked her as soft, caring and warm. But this was gone in a second, retracted in what might be an unconscious and automatic response to his stare. He was smiling but hers had faded. She had stood up to him; it had been a long time since last he met a woman capable of that.

Jessica Coran was learning the labyrinth of Police Plaza One and adjacent buildings by trying to follow directions given her by Sgt. Lou Pierce as to how to get to the crime lab. She'd been told that Dr. Luther Darius, world-renowned for his advancements in the field—his two textbooks were required reading at the FBI Academy—was not available. From the way Lou Pierce had mumbled it, she assumed the seventy-year-old forensics genius was bedridden. With most of the work going on at his lab now being performed by younger men and women, Darius spent his working hours grooming interns as they came through the co-op program associated with New York University, John Jay and other colleges in the vicinity. However, inside information or careless hearsay had it that the old man was at least partially responsible for careless oversights made in the past year or so, resulting in lawsuits and settlements against the city. If Darius had lost his edge, perhaps he ought not to be handling what precious little medicolegal evidence there was on the Claw. But how do you unseat a Milton Helpern or a Luther Darius?

One step at a time, she thought. First she wanted to see the remains of the Claw's latest victim. She could do so, Pierce informed her, by locating Dr. Simon Archer, Darius' second-in-command.

She now found the lab and adjacent autopsy rooms and freezer compartments. A helpful young technician pointed out Dr. Archer, a tall, good-looking and muscular man with a firm bearing and large brown eyes so intense they seemed to see through her as she introduced herself.

"Ahh, yes, the task force and you're Dr. Coran. I got a call from the C.P. Welcome aboard and let me be the first to congratulate you on surviving the Matisak affair."

"Yes, well, if I could have a surgical gown, I'd really like to see the Claw's latest victim."

"Of course. You'll find what you need through here and the body'll be waiting on the other side."

He held the door, stared at her cane, making her feel uncomfortable about her limp. Inside she suited up in surgeon's gown, mask and gloves while Dr. Archer put his people in motion to retrieve the body from a freezer compartment and have it waiting in the inner room. She found Dr. Archer also waiting, standing alongside the body like a mortician fishing for praise over his handiwork.

"Did the autopsy myself," he muttered. "Understandably

SUPER CROWN #736

YOUR SAVINGS AT CROWN... $ 0.70

	PRICE	CROWN
SAVINGS		
CROWN		
PRICE		
PUBLISHER		

THAT INSTINCT .... YOU
FATAL

PRICE PUBLISHER   12.95
PRICE CROWN   9.95
SALES TAX @ 8.25%   0.82
TOTAL   10.77
TENDERED CASH   11.00
CHANGE   0.23

REFUNDS WITHIN 30 MIN SALES ENHANCE
RETURNS WITHIN 30 DAYS WITH RECEIPT AND
12/11/94   10:03   1   10   3300

```
SUPER CROWN #736

12/14/'97   10:53   I        18      5300
REFUNDS WITHIN 30 DAYS WITH RECEIPT ONLY
            MAGAZINE SALES FINAL
    PUBLISHER              CROWN    CROWN
      PRICE                SAVINGS  PRICE
FATAL INSTINCT
 1@  6.99 051511913X        10%  $   6.29
SUBTOTAL                         $   6.29
SALES TAX @ 8.25%                $   0.52
TOTAL                            $   6.81
TENDERED Cash                    $   7.00
CHANGE                           $   0.19

    YOUR SAVINGS AT CROWN... $ 0.70
```

nervous, having you look Mrs. Hamner over, what with your reputation. What is it the papers call you?"

"There's no need for nervousness, Doctor."

"*Scavenger*, isn't it?"

"I'm called that, but only affectionately." She smiled below the mask, trying to get him to loosen up.

"Do you mind my hovering?"

"Truthfully, you're making me nervous, Doctor."

"Oh, I don't mean to. It's just that since I did the autopsy ... Well, if I've missed anything, I'd like to be the first to know. I took the case out of Dr. Perkins' hands for ... well, personal reasons."

"Personal reasons? Did you know the victim?"

"No, no, no! You misunderstand. Dr. Perkins ... well, he hasn't really been on the beam, so to speak. In fact, he walked out during the autopsy. So I ... I took over, and given the kind of night we had ... well, I did my best."

She seemed to be hearing that phrase a lot around here.

"I've been up all night, spent nine hours with Mrs. Hamner."

She liked the fact he used the woman's name instead of calling her a body, corpse, cadaver, victim, subject or stiff. He seemed a sensitive man. "Nine hours is a lot of time." He knew that she understood how grueling the hours spent over a murder victim, especially one so disfigured and dismembered, could be. Her eyes, the only visible feature left unmasked, met his again.

"There was nothing easy about it, I can tell you," he replied.

"Let me have a look," she said, snatching away the sheet that covered Mrs. Hamner's remains.

The sheet flew and curled away, sliding to the floor and beneath the table. She found that Mrs. Hamner had been reassembled with sutures across chest and abdomen and encircling the neck. The sutures and the cleaning could not hide the hideous original slashes to the woman's torso, three parallel but jagged rupture lines from breastbone to navel. The murder weapon was as crude as garden shears and as delicate as a surgeon's scalpel all at once, she instantly thought. This meant that it had more than one edge. She imagined a weapon that was double-edged, perhaps serrated, but how, then, the three perfectly formed zigzags at what appeared the same depth? Had the killer performed a kind of ritual pattern drawing across the skin, a New Age swastika?

"The decapitation?" she asked.

"After death."

She nodded, saying, "Small comfort."

Her eyes had at first avoided the ghastly, nauseating sight of the destroyed facial features. She examined them now, the wounds cleaned with an alcohol-based solution, the skin and puckering scars arid, barren of moist suppleness.

There were no eyes, only empty sockets, like all the other victims. It was surmised the cannibal thought the eyes a delicacy.

"Initial blow to the head was not sufficient to kill?"

" 'Fraid not; that would've been merciful. Just a skull fracture, caused by a blunt instrument, the shape confirming our suspicion of a hammer."

"Round-headed?"

"Ball peen, yes. But she was alive when he tore into her torso."

"Splayed her open like she was a marlin," she muttered, feeling sick at heart.

"Are you all right, Doctor?"

She sighed heavily, pushing back the threatening nausea. "Yes, I'm all right."

Archer loosened his collar below the gown. "My first Claw victim put me under one hell of a strain, let me tell you. I've seen all six, either as autopsiest or assisting. After that first one, I thought of running out of here, the way Perkins did, but now—"

"Do you mean Perkins quit?"

"It appears so, yes."

"Then you'll be handling the evidence he gathered at the scene?"

He shrugged. "Me, the tech team here, yes, unless Dr. Darius returns and wants to handle it himself, which is fine with me, but . . ." His voice trailed off. "Sorry, I'm boring you, I'm sure . . . talking too much."

She sensed that loyalty to Darius had made him stop short of another word. "It must've been wonderful to train under a man like Luther Darius."

"None like him, and yes, it has been."

She turned back to the work at hand, her own hands going gently to the wounds and the patchwork of stitches that made Mrs. Hamner look like a Frankenstein monster. In the empty eye sockets lived a deep, disturbing mystery.

"I would've liked to see her before you put her back together and stitched her up," she said.

"I . . . I had no idea you were going to be here. If I had—"

"Show me," she said, "at what areas you found teeth marks."

"Several areas, actually, but the best were lifted from the throat, at the voice box. Here." He pointed with a penlight.

She stared at the animal markings.

"Where else?"

He pointed to marks on the thighs, rolled the body and pointed to tears in the buttocks. "Only partials lifted here; didn't photograph under the electron microscope too well. Computer enhancement helped little."

She nodded. The bite marks were discolored abrasions, looking like bruises, easily seen while the blood remained in the body, but not quite so easily seen now, since samples had been carved away for use under the electron scope.

"The bites," she began. "Do they come before or after death?"

"Both. Some showed vital color reaction, others no."

"Anything else I should know?"

"He may've eaten the liver during the attack; chewed fragments were left behind, and he carried the heart and kidney off with him. Police believe he was surprised, left hurriedly."

"But still left nothing of himself behind?"

"Nothing but the teeth imprints. He's cunning."

"Anything else?"

"He may've been shocked to learn she had only one kidney, one of the items he made off with, we theorize."

"Only one kidney?"

"Old suture wounds and her medical history reveal she'd donated her other one to a better cause, donor for her sister."

"Did Perkins diagram the crime scene? Where were the disemboweled organs and the head in relation to the body?"

"Perkins didn't do much of anything, I'm afraid."

"That's a crime."

"Ought to be punishable, but—"

"What did his report say about it?"

"Intestines yanked out, coiled alongside the corpse rather neatly. No, no, that was an earlier victim. Perkins said the intestines were looped about the body and limbs."

"Looped."

"You know, like rope."

"Around the waist, legs, neck?"

"Head was severed, remember?" A note of annoyance had filtered into his voice. He looked dead tired, up all night.

"Bites taken out of the intestines again?"

"Several."

"So what have you on the murder weapon?"

"The twenty-four-thousand-dollar question?"

"Come on, you've got to have made some conclusions."

He nodded, stepped away from the body, and she pursued. "I believe it is some sort of serrated scissors or tool. Hand-held, honed razor-sharp, to be sure."

"A common pair of scissors?"

"Or something damned close, maybe garden-sized?"

She glanced back at the silent body of evidence which wasn't giving up its secrets. "I've seen enough," she told Archer, and with her cane she returned to the adjacent room, where she discarded her mask, gloves and gown.

She was feeling a little faint. The emotional response brought on by the sight of Mrs. Hamner's devastated body, like a timed fuse, began to burn down. She rushed into an adjacent washroom, aware that Dr. Archer had entered the area to discard his own surgical garb, and that he was watching her until she closed the door behind her. How much weakness had he seen? she wondered from inside the claustrophobic washroom.

She went to the basin and washed cold water over her face, fighting the rising tide of fear and loathing, desperately seeking the control over herself that her shrink had told her she was capable of maintaining.

It was all Matisak's fault, his doing. He had crippled her not only physically but mentally as well, robbing her of something more precious than the easy use of her legs.

And now she was in the city where the Claw lived and preyed on women not unlike her, women who lived with fear every day of their lives. He was not behind an unbreakable wall. He was at large. He had risen from bed this morning and had likely scanned the papers for an account of himself and what he'd done to Mrs. Hamner. He was *nearby*.

He was the same kind of maniac as Gerald Ray Sims and Matt Matisak, perhaps both of them rolled into one. She stammered to her reflection in the mirror, "Bastard . . . bastard thing."

Six

ℰ

The night had passed without incident related to the Claw, the poised city like a bride relieved to have been stood up. Getting in early to his new office, Rychman felt, would give him time to get organized, to prepare for the day, gird up for the inevitable surprises. He'd gotten Dr. Archer's less than helpful forensics report on the Hamner woman, had sat up with it, searching for something—*anything*—that might lead to a breakthrough or at least a direction they might take. But there was nothing new, beyond the beheading. Why'd the creep add that?

He'd avoided reporters by driving straight into the underground garage, where he now had a parking slot. He had purposefully avoided reading the morning news, knowing it would be filled with a lot of trash about the case and the department, none of which helped. Why didn't they print the facts? Literally thousands of suspects had been hauled into custody, questioned and released; more man-hours had gone to the case prior to the formation of a task force than any in the history of the department. The cops were doing their job. Maybe the formation of the special task force to which he was assigned would get the press off their backs, at least for a time, but he doubted it.

He'd successfully led task forces before and was responsible for the white-collar crimes of Charles Dean Ilandfeldt coming to light. He had routed the Lords of Satan biker gang before that, infiltrating as a fence for automatic weapons. They had so come to trust him that they'd allowed him to film a bit of "biker justice" from inside the walls of the L.S. hideout. He'd never witnessed such cruelty before, but the work of the Claw made the L.S. guys look like a Girl Scout troop.

As for his new duties, Rychman didn't mind an interesting change, but Police Plaza One—and his new, upscale office—were going to take some getting used to.

He tried to get comfortable in his new, temporary office, switching on the soft-rock channel, playing now a Gordon Lightfoot medley which ended with his favorite, "If You Could Read My Mind." It made him wish that he could read the Claw's mind, and the mind of Dr. Jessica Coran, for that matter. Did she really think she could see into the killer's mind? Perhaps she'd just gotten lucky in the Mad Matisak case in Chicago; coincidence and luck often played a large part in detection and police work, after all. "Son of Sam" Berkowitz was caught because some beat cop wrote him a ticket for illegally parking, a stroke of dumb luck. Then again, Rychman believed that when coincidence struck, most people failed to recognize it for what it was, because most were not *tuned in*, were not observant, especially of the commonplace and everyday. Perhaps this female M.E. Coran was tuned in. She certainly seemed observant.

He thought for a moment about how pretty she was, the radio now blaring out the traffic report, promising the news soon. He'd begun to take a cursory look at his correspondence and several files that cluttered his desk when Lou Pierce came in, an odd look on his face. Rychman and Lou had been together now for nearly seven years, and he knew when Lou had to shake off to the can and when he had a toothache, and when he had bad news.

"Something in the *Times* you ought to see, Captain."

"Not so sure I want to see anything in the *Times*, Lou. Not yet, anyway."

"This won't wait, Captain. C.P.'s on his way, and the mayor's been up all night."

"That bad, huh?"

Lou slumped down in the chair across from him and dropped the paper in front of his captain all in one languid movement. He seemed to be melting into his chair, shutting his eyes, feigning sleep. "Been reading up on self-hypnosis techniques, Captain," Lou said. "Everywhere you look, everybody's saying how important relaxing is—to the health, the body, the soul, I mean . . ."

Lou kept his eyes closed tight as he spoke and as Rychman scanned the story on page one. The byline was that of a now familiar reporter, Jim Drake III.

The headline was scorching: "6th Claw Mutilation Murder—Police Without a Suspect, Leads or Clues."

"Just heard it on a talk show the other day, 'Donahue.' Had a lot of doctors on and they all stressed the same thing, about learning how to relax," Lou prattled on. "Say if you can't relax, you'll wind up with bleeding ulcers, a heart condition or in a mental ward, or all three."

Rychman wasn't relaxing as he read down the column, his anger rising with each printed word. He was now at the center of the story where he was, named as a questionable selection to head the special task force put together by the city to end the terror.

And the bastard actually brought up a bar fight that was sixteen years old, along with Rychman's controversial and nasty divorce.

"Christ," he muttered, "Jesus Christ." He imagined Dr. Jessica Coran in her hotel room reading the story over her coffee.

"Consider the source," said Lou cautiously.

Rychman stood up, knocking over his coffee, cursing and slapping the paper down so hard that papers flew in all directions. "Lou, I'd like to consider the source. I'd like to hang the goddamned source. I want a fucking gag order on this whole damn building, you got that, Lou?" And as he spoke, the door burst open and in walked the mayor, his Commissioner, Eldritch, and Dr. Jessica Coran.

So she's an early riser, too, he thought as he stared across the disheveled desk at them, Lou trying desperately to pick up the loose papers and dry up the still-dripping coffee.

Rychman made no attempt to hide his anger. Everyone must know that the press seemed to be stalking Alan Rychman. But he calmed long enough to say, "I guess you've seen the papers."

"Making us look like idiots, this bastard," said Commissioner Eldritch.

His Honor the mayor, Dan Halle, came right to the point, his style, which Rychman liked. Halle was concerned about the image of his office and the police department, but he seemed also genuinely concerned about the realities of the situation. Alan Rychman had learned on earlier occasions that His Honor had studied the facts and details of the Claw slayings. He knew what they were up against. "Alan, I'm very concerned that we make some kind of break in this bloody case. We've got to show some progress. That's why we called in the FBI, and that's why they sent Dr. Coran, here."

The commissioner was not so straightforward, and while Coran was nodding, saying they'd met, Carl Eldritch said, "That's why you were selected to head the task force, Alan."

Rychman knew a lie when he heard one. The C.P. wanted to remain the C.P., and Alan presented a real threat to him, and they both knew it. Eldritch knew that it was a make-or-break case, and he also knew that the department was coming up empty at every turn. He was gambling that Rychman and company would be as inept as the press painted them. He continued, his tongue greased, Rychman believed, so that he wouldn't choke on his own lies. "I'm sorry I couldn't have been in two places at once yesterday when Dr. Coran arrived. The mayor had hoped to be here, too, but circumstances—"

"Circumstances being as they are, I fully understand," Rychman said with an edge to his voice. "Not to worry, everything's in hand. The ball's rolling, right, Lou?"

Pierce had remained silent and had slipped toward the door. He was about to disappear when Rychman asked the question.

He inched back through the door, saying, "Absolutely . . . everything is under way. And might I add, sir, that everyone associated with the task force is enthusiastic and hopeful."

"Good, good," said the mayor, "we need all the enthusiasm we can muster for this heinous work."

Lou finished his disappearing act.

Rychman exchanged a look with Jessica Coran. Lou had

turned off the radio, tidied the mess Rychman had made, and had done so like a doting servant or faithful wife.

"It must be good to have such a loyal aide," she said.

"I insist on loyalty."

"So," interrupted the C.P., "what're your plans at this point, Captain Rychman?"

"Plans?"

"For the apprehension of this . . . this Claw character."

"We are proceeding as quickly as we can, but the task force was just begun yesterday; if you remember, sir, I suggested such a special team two weeks ago, but—"

"Two weeks ago there were only a few deaths, one victim a prostitute," countered the C.P. "Allocating a fortune in city funds to this madman—at that time—"

"—would have reflected badly in the papers, I know," Rychman finished. "Now we've arrived at the same destination. So tell me honestly what sends you gentlemen here, besides this?" He punched his large forefinger at the copy of the *Times.*

"It's not just the press, Captain Rychman," said the mayor. "It's everyone, the clergy, the PTA, the Rotarians, for Christ's sake, the whole city, the community."

Alan put up his hands. "You think I don't know that everyone is on us?"

"We need to make an arrest." The C.P. finally got around to what the visit was actually about.

"Arrest, huh?" he said, muttering under his breath, "Jesus." Rychman began to pace like a large, caged bear, then stopped before Jessica and coolly stared her in the eye, asking, "That'd look good? Calm the community brain? Do you agree with this . . . *thinking*, Dr. Coran? That we ought to make a wholesale arrest?"

"No one said wholesale arrest, Alan," interrupted Eldritch.

But neither Jessica nor Alan Rychman heard him, so intent remained their attention to each other. She said calmly, "No . . . no, I don't believe an arrest for the sake of an arrest will, in the long run, serve any purpose."

Rychman's face brightened, but he quickly squelched his

smile when he saw the confusion in Eldritch's eyes. Eldritch had apparently believed Dr. Coran was sold on the idea.

She stood up and paced, her cane tapping out a soft requiem. "Gentlemen, detaining and questioning your thousands of MSDOs has already cost more time, energy and paperwork than you can afford, creating several thousand paper trails that will likely lead nowhere."

"We can't stand idly by a moment longer!" shouted Eldritch.

She met his eyes. "This killer is not your usual sex offender; he's not a rapist; he's in no way a typical killer."

Mayor Halle asked her what she was driving at.

"This maniac is the rarest of murderers. A man who has acquired a taste for female flesh and female suffering. He kills women because he hates women; he is a predator, and people of my sex are his prey."

"Is that how you see it, Captain?" Halle asked.

Rychman nodded vigorously. "That's about how I see it, yes."

Dr. Coran continued. "His taste for flesh is an integral part of his gaming."

"Gaming?"

"Fantasizing, fantasy fulfillment, sport, if you like."

Mayor Halle swallowed. "Well . . . yes . . ."

"He hunts for flesh, for the excitement of it all, to quench a perceived need," she said, pacing nervously before the three men. "A flesh-eater, like a blood-drinker, is an aberration far beyond your normal sex deviant. He's gone so far beyond what we know as our *normal lunatic* that . . . well, this man has returned to a state of cannibalism; in his head and in his genes he is a cannibal doing only what comes naturally, like the flesh-eating ape from which mankind evolved."

"A bloody animal," said Eldritch, trying to imagine the man.

"But don't be fooled. He's no simple animal," she countered.

"Go on," said the mayor.

"He displays a very complex personality . . . perhaps too complex."

"Can you be more specific?"

"I don't believe he will be a simpleton, a crazed drug addict, a street person or one of the names in your MSDO files."

"We've already looked at all our deviants and've cut them loose," added Rychman.

"Whoever this guy is, he shows careful ritualistic patterns; he's working out a deep-seated fantasy which, as horrible as it is, requires a high level of cognitive thought and planning."

"Well, yes, the crimes have shown significant repetition," said Eldritch. "Pattern crimes . . ."

Halle took in a great breath of air. "What you're saying is that this guy could elude us for a long time, if we ever catch him at all."

"I'm afraid so. And if you're going to force your people to make arrests at this point, it could backfire."

"We're not talking about arrests," said Eldritch. "We're talking about *one* goddamned arrest."

Rychman said sharply, "I stand with Dr. Coran. Any arrest at this point is bound to come back to haunt us as the lie it is."

"If it takes a lie—" began the C.P., but the mayor put up a hand, silencing him.

"May I suggest, Captain Rychman, that you do as Carl says and make *one* arrest. Get a man you've wanted off the street, anyway . . . a good stand-in for this, this Claw. Bring him up on charges, hold him as long as possible, while you continue to investigate. Who knows, could turn out to be the Claw."

Rychman stared out his new office window at the teeming life of the city below. He turned and said, "If that's what you want, Your Honor."

"Have one of your detectives bring this other fellow in, and have others go through the motions. And when you get the real monster, then all will be settled. I should think it would make for a calmer working environment," said the mayor.

Rychman nodded. "Sure, yes . . . yes, you're right . . . if we could get some of the heat off."

The mayor stood, took Rychman's hand and shook it firmly. "Good, I'm glad we came to some consensus on this matter." He turned, faced Dr. Coran and said, "Well, Dr. Coran, I'll be anxious to hear that progress toward apprehending this fiend is going forward with your help. Do maintain a low profile."

"Yes, of course." She shook his hand.

The C.P. followed the mayor out, but stopped at the door and said, "Alan, I have complete confidence in you. Good luck."

Rychman allowed his frown to surface only when the C.P. was gone, and then he turned his attention on Dr. Coran. "Thanks for being straight."

"They've got political reasons for what they do. I don't."

"When you came in here together, I thought you were all of one mind."

"So did they, apparently."

He laughed a full laugh, something he'd not done in a long time.

"I told them," she continued, "that any bits of information on the investigation they could feed the public might help calm the situation, but I didn't know they were advocating false arrest."

"They're getting desperate, but who do they have to blame but themselves? Or me, now that I'm in charge. As to false arrest, if anyone should bring up due process, well, they've still got me as their patsy."

"They can deny every word of it," she agreed, "except that I have it on tape." She revealed the miniature recorder to his startled eyes. "I use it for autopsy notes. I don't know how I could have left it on."

Rychman smiled approvingly, laughing again. She liked the sound of his warm, magnetic laughter.

"You're something else, Dr. Coran," he said when he regained his composure. Lou ducked in for a quick glance inside to see what the commotion was all about before disappearing again. "I hear you paid a call on Archer yesterday."

"That's my job."

"Heard you hang tough."

She nodded, her chin up.

"Come on," he said, guiding her to the adjacent crime incident room where they had first met. "At nine we're reassembling for an old-fashioned rap and think-tank session. You're cordially invited."

"Would love to, but I've got appointments most all day."

"Oh? You're wasting no time."

"At nine I begin meetings with each division head in the crime lab," she said. "I'll listen to each for ideas, suggestions, information and maybe a few tips."

"Learn what each is working on; I get it."

"And you," she countered, "you have to find a suitable Claw to arrest."

"For the likes of Jim Drake III and the public."

"And the mayor."

"And Carl."

"I'm sure you've got men on your list begging to be arrested for these crimes."

"We have *that*!"

"Who knows, you might get lucky like the mayor says."

"But you and I know better."

"We do."

She started out of the incident room, where the eyeless faces of the photographed victims stared down at them. Alan Rychman, watching her go, almost pursued, thinking he'd ask her for lunch, but he stopped short, afraid of her answer.

Seven

ෙ

Rychman learned that every detective in the city had a "favorite" killer who was, in his or her mind, the Claw.

He'd simply told his detectives in strict confidence that "in order for us to work with the press off our backs, we gotta put somebody in the lockup, then we dummy up on this guy, make 'em think we've got someone hot. So I want our *hottest* guy, and only you people can tell me who that is."

It had started a bidding war of sorts, each detective fighting for his choice, his favored Claw. They all sounded like good, likely candidates.

"Cameron Reeves, a real mixed-up wacko," said one detective. "I've been after his ass for years. He fits the profile and has a long list of prior sex offenses."

"That'd make good copy for the press," Rychman said, as if now enjoying the idea of screwing the press.

"I got a better guy," suggested another detective, a gruff, big-shouldered, wide fellow called Marty. "A guy named Lamb, Earl T. Lamb."

"What's his story?"

"Climbs trees."

"Climbs trees?"

"But he don't just stay in the tree. He jumps down on women who happen by."

"Christ." A mutter went around the room.

"Does he have a rap sheet?"

"Does a shark shit in the ocean?"

"Does he use a weapon?"

"A lead pipe."

"Sounds like we ought to pay Earl the Claw a visit."

"We have."

"And?"

"Loony tunes."

"So he's out on the street?"

"Lives with Momma, aged forty-three. She says he's harmless, so long as he takes his psychoactive drugs."

"And so long as he's kept out of trees?" asked Rychman.

"I got to admit, Lamb would serve up well to the papers. 'The Claw is a Lamb,' all that," said a female detective, flipping open a pocket-sized notebook. "But I got a creep that makes Lamb sound like a Boy Scout."

"You're Emmons, right?" asked Rychman.

"Yes, sir."

"Whataya got?"

She took a moment to review her notes. "We got a call at the 54th desk one night about this guy. Seems he lurks around back alleys, breaks into basement windows, rapes women after he knocks them out."

"How? How does he overpower his victims?"

"Renders them unconscious with a hammerblow."

"He's done time?"

"Fourteen years, Rockaway."

"Released?"

"Six months ago."

"About the time the Claw came on the scene," said Emmons' partner, Dave Turner. "We think—"

Rychman put up a hand and said, "How old is this man?"

Louise Emmons checked her notes. "Thirty ... thirty ... thirty something ... thirty-four."

"Been incarcerated most of his adult life," said Rychman, looking to see everyone's reaction. "Got to be a lot of anger and hostility toward society in this guy. Is he white, black, Hispanic, what?"

"Caucasian," said Emmons.

"Lives with a common-law wife," added Turner. "They live very close to the bone."

Some of the others began to heckle, calling on Rychman to reconsider their choices. Rychman banged his fist on the podium. "Call this bastard's parole officer. See how many of his terms he's already violated ... see if any of those terms prohibit him from work using anything like a hammer. Let's see just how lucky we can get here. Also see what came of the call that had him lurking in that alleyway. Did he talk his way free, or did he go before a judge?"

Emmons had taken to jotting down his requests, but she stopped now to say, "He was just rousted. Cops found him roosting between some trash cans, like he was just waiting for a victim to come along."

"What's his name?"

"Conrad Shaw."

"Shaw . . . claw," said one of the other detectives. "Least it rhymes."

"Press'll like that."

"Let's drag his ass in, put the screws to him," suggested another.

"Check it out, like I said, and if we learn any more, we'll go for it. But so far, my vote goes with Shaw." Rychman settled in.

He glanced over his shoulder at Lou, whose nod seemed to place a final stamp of approval on the discussion.

"Now, as for you other stiffs who have favorites. Don't abandon them. In fact, pursue them like before, even more relentlessly. If you think you can do something to strike this guy or that off your list, if you can make him show his true colors, do so. We've got to work fast and carefully at the same time."

He turned to the map of the city behind him and told them the red pins represented the areas in the city where the maniac had struck. Thus far, they had no witnesses and every victim was dead. No one escaped this guy.

"Geographically we have no pattern. The only pattern we have," said Rychman, "is the M.O., how this pervert operates. So we'll be examining this from every angle very closely, and we will be examining the forensics evidence thoroughly. I've already got some ideas along those lines. As for now, we have a cannibal on our streets, a human predator, and he will . . . *eat again*." He came from behind the podium.

"That's all for this morning," Rychman said. "Remember,

every day, here nine and six, no matter your shift or other duties. The task force is cleared as your number-one priority."

People began to file out. It was ten-twenty A.M.

It was late in the day, nearly five, and dark clouds had con-
verged over the city, turning the sky and the area all around
Police Plaza One into a grim, dismal, charcoal painting. Rain
threatened and in the distance the rumble of thunder gave everyone a catlike sixth sense of impending danger while radio
and TV announcers called for a besotted and blackened city.
Everyone paused over their work, some staring out at the
coming storm.

Rychman was going between offices when he saw Jessica
Coran coming down the hall. He went to greet her.

"All finished for the day?" he asked.

"Pretty much, yeah. I was about to call a cab, try to beat
the storm."

"Don't. I'll have Lou send a radio car around for you. You
know your way to the garage?"

"I passed a sign for it, yeah."

"So what do you think of Luther Darius' operation?"

"Excellent lab, terrified people."

"Terrified?"

"Nervous, let's say. Course I haven't met Darius himself
yet."

"Yeah, I understand he's under doctor's care."

"A euphemism for what?" she asked pointedly.

Rychman shrugged, his eyes alert. "Just talk . . . Some say
he has Parkinson's, others say it's cancer. Some say he has
both."

"Poor man. I didn't know." She thought momentarily of
the debilitating disease that had claimed her father, made him
a prisoner within his own body. "Think I'd rather go quickly
and cleanly."

"Agreed. Luther's lab people are extremely loyal to him,"
he confided. "They weren't likely to discuss his condition,
I'm sure, but his problems have had an ill effect on the lab.
Reports aren't as timely or complete as they once were, mis-
takes have been made with the handling of evidence. You

know how that looks. I don't suppose his people would have revealed a thing about that, either, so . . . Oh, and here's the report on the Hamner woman."

"So my dealings will almost certainly be with Dr. Archer," she replied, taking the report and watching for his reaction.

"You could do worse," he said. "Perkins, for instance."

"Yeah, I heard about Perkins quitting."

"Quitting? He actually quit?"

"I thought you were about to tell me!"

"I was just going to tell you he was an asshole."

"From what I've heard of him, I'd have to agree. Lou tells me you slammed him into a wall at the crime scene? Sounds like clever crime scene tactics, a boys' fight over the corpse? Really . . . I'm sure the integrity of the evidence-gathering wasn't compromised."

"You certainly have a way with sarcasm, Doctor."

"I was reared on it, sorry. Well, I'd best run. I didn't bring an umbrella."

"Lou," he shouted suddenly, spying Pierce. "See to it someone gets Dr. Coran back to where she's staying."

Pierce shouted back, "You got it, Captain."

"Just wander down to the garage. Someone'll be along in a moment."

People with papers in their hands were streaming by them in the hallway, some trying to get his attention. He continued to stare at her until he said, "Your examination of the Hamner woman? Did it tell you anything I should know?"

"Nothing new, no . . . sorry."

"Well . . . keep me informed."

"What about an arrest? Has your task force come up with any suggestions?"

"Several, but we took the mayor's advice and arrested only one. *Shaw the Claw,* they're calling him. Detaining him on charges other than murder at this point, but letting it be known that he is suspected of the killings. Press is doing as expected, eating it up."

"That should cool the brew a bit. Later, then, Captain."

"Right, later."

He turned and hurried fullback fashion to the confines of

his new office, Jessica staring after, watching him go and wondering what had changed their relationship so drastically. Had it to do with her being on his side against the C.P. and the mayor? Adversity made for strange bedfellows. As for her, when she had read about his troubled divorce, she'd come to realize why he posed as such a hard-ass. She sensed that deep below the surface he was repressing a great deal of pain and grief.

Her ankles throbbed and twitched, a nervous reaction that she'd come to know as a sign that she'd been standing too damned long. She found the police garage where a young, aggressive reporter had somehow penetrated the barricades, and now rushed up to her and said, "You're with the FBI, aren't you?"

"And who are you?"

"I'm with the *Times*, and I'm just interested in you. I understand you're the agent who ended the career of that crazy guy in Chicago who thought he was a vampire?"

"I was one of a team, Mr. ahh . . ."

"Drake, Jim Drake."

She recognized his name from the byline accompanying the twisted-knife story on Rychman. "I'd like you to stand away from me," she said firmly.

"You're a hero—heroine—what you did in Chicago." He glanced at the cane, his eyes glued there long enough to embarrass her. "You're big news, and now you're here to help the NYPD find the Claw, aren't you? Aren't you?"

A uniformed police guard rushed over to them just as her car pulled up. The driver was Lou Pierce, who got out and joined the other uniformed man to help usher the reporter out of the restricted area, shouts filling the basement garage.

She got into the car, kicked off her shoes and massaged her ankles.

Lou returned and settled into the driver's seat, a broad smile, sandy-brown hair and blue eyes forming a pleasant demeanor. "We drew straws who'd get you, and I won," he said triumphantly as he put the car in gear and started from the garage, the car tilting almost straight up on the exit ramp.

It was overcast out and there was a picket line in front of

the precinct. The picketers carried signs, denouncing the police as fools, and they chanted, "The Claw controls the city . . . the Claw controls the city . . ." They had no idea just how true the slogan was.

Just as the car was turning out, a camera was all but slammed against the back window and Jessica saw a flash, realizing that Jim Drake had gotten his photographer to capture her before she could get away.

"Damn, damn," she muttered.

Lou was cursing under his breath, too. "Bloody reporters can be like camel shit on your shoe, Dr. Coran."

"How's that, Lou?"

"Ever try to kick camel shit off your shoe, ma'am?"

She laughed for the first time that day.

"You sure got one beautiful smile, Dr. Coran," he said.

She smiled wider. "Thanks, I'm glad you won the draw."

"Oh, there was no question of it, ma'am."

"No?"

"I cheated, ma'am. Had to pull this duty. You know, a lot of us guys see a pretty woman, and we just can't help ourselves."

"You're very flattering, Lou . . . Thanks." Something had told her there'd been no drawing.

"Some of us think a lot of what you did in Chicago, ma'am . . . really. That took some guts."

She dropped her head, her eyes pinned on her sore ankles, her mind returning to that awful room where Matisak had begun to drain her of her blood, where Otto Boutine had come crashing through a window to her rescue, getting himself killed for her. "I lost my partner in Chicago," she said.

"Yes, ma'am . . . I know, ma'am."

The rain started, slowly at first, like fairies appearing from nowhere on the windshield and the windows, and then suddenly the fairies were deluged by a thick, heavy, angry downpour as if the powers of heaven meant to destroy their own. Sometimes nature was as much at war with itself, she felt, as was the human psyche, filled with rage, chaos, violence, deposited there by some unseen and unknowable force. The human propensity for murder seemed to her quite closely akin to the universe's propensity to create black holes and violent, explosive stars. The dark New York landscape, sheathed in a slick downpour, made her cold inside, despite how warm and dry it was in the radio car. There was a steady, unending stream of human outbursts, turmoil and entanglements being reported over the police band. Not even nature's storm could quell the human fury of the large metropolis.

"Have you home in a second, Dr. Coran."

She missed her apartment home in Quantico, a refuge.

"Honestly, Doctor," Lou continued as he weaved expertly through traffic. "There wasn't any drawing to see who gets to drive you home, but that's only because I didn't give the others a chance."

She smiled again. "I like honesty, Lou."

"Then you'll like New York and New Yorkers. They're . . . painfully honest, ma'am."

She wanted to ask him twenty questions about Alan Rychman after his assurance of honesty. She wondered if she dared.

"You and Captain Rychman seem close—for subordinate and superior, I mean."

"Hell, ma'am, I owe the captain my life."

"How's that?"

"He saved my life, Doctor."

"Really?"

"All in the line of duty, he'd say, but he put himself between me and danger, and I can never forget a thing like that, Doctor."

"Nor should you." Her thoughts returned to the night Otto Boutine had done as much for her, except that Otto had not lived to reap the benefit of her undying gratitude.

"Hell, I didn't even hardly know Rychman at the time, ma'am. He'd just taken over the 31st and was cleaning house good, and even me—a clean cop—was worried about 'the Boot.' That's what we called him back then—'bout nine, maybe ten years now. Been with him as his aide for seven. Anyway, back then, I was a real gung-ho fool and I charged into this crack house ahead of the others. The captain, he could've just parked it outside, but not Rychman. He wanted in on the action from the start, same as I did that night.

"Anyway, if he hadn't come storming through the back when he did, I'd be in a box in Greenlawn instead of telling you all this."

They were at the hotel and she hurried from the car, wind rippling and beating at her clothes. Inside the lobby, Lou caught up with her and asked if she needed anything else.

"You didn't have to leave your unit, Sergeant," she told him.

"Rychman told me to see you safely inside, ma'am."

"Well, you've done that."

"You've got *carte blanche* in this town, Dr. Coran, just remember, no cabs for you. You just call the squad room."

"Thank you, Sergeant."

"Oh, it isn't my doing, Doctor." On that note he rushed back out into the stormy night.

Ovid was worried.

He had become progressively more brutal with each murder, as if he were working up to some sort of bizarre final brutality.

So had the Claw.

The Claw taught him everything.

But he didn't know that much, really. He didn't know where the Claw lived, for instance. Once, he started to follow him, and the Claw turned as if he felt him near. He had stared so long at the place where Ovid hid in the brush in Central Park that Ovid had almost begun to believe the Claw had cat's eyes, and could see him there. It so unnerved Ovid that he never dared to follow the Claw again.

He always feared that one day the Claw would turn on him, make a meal of him.

He knew he walked a thin, dangerous line. But it was the most thrilling thing that had happened in an otherwise dull and empty existence.

He even had a new name to proclaim his rebirth: Ovid. He'd wondered why "Ovid," wondered if it held some special significance to the Claw, and so he had gone to the library and found a book on names. Opening it to the *O*'s and trailing his finger along the column, he found Ovid there. It was strange and obscure and filled with ancient meaning, his new name. "Ovid" was Latin for "divine protector." And in a sense, he did help and protect the Claw, who came to him in the night, needing him, needing his assistance. It was the first time anyone had ever needed him.

He located the history of the ancient poet Ovid, and began to feel some connection with him. He took out translations of Ovid's work along with the Latin subtext, and slowly he began to teach himself some Latin words and phrases.

The Claw had opened up a whole new world to him, and he began to wonder if he could, like his namesake, write poetry.

That was what he was doing now, writing a poem, a poem he intended to send to the *New York Times*, knowing somehow that they'd print it, if it was good enough and graphic enough.

But he worried about sending his poem to the newspaper. What would the Claw do to him? How would he react? Still, the poem proclaimed the inevitable power of the Claw over everyone in this life; it also spoke of disease and aging and death. It told the world that the Claw was good, not evil; that he ended suffering. He didn't create it. He ended it.

Still, Ovid hesitated sending his words without talking it over with the Claw first. Perhaps if he read it to the Claw, he'd have to see the importance of it, that it was preordained, and that Ovid was important to the cause, too. *Maybe* he'd see it that way . . .

The Claw had contacted him in the usual eerie manner last night, leaving a note under his pillow like a goddamned visiting ghost, a night creature, a bloody, dark tooth fairy. How he came and went, how he got in, leaving everything intact, Ovid hadn't a clue. He seemed capable of walking through walls, walking on air . . . and maybe water. Maybe he was the Antichrist, a god in his own right, a dark angel.

You don't cross a dark angel, he kept telling himself all through breakfast and the writing of the poem, and the rest of the day as he studied and refined and rewrote the poem. It was his day off, so he didn't have to work at the factory, and so he had too much time on his hands to think. The poem, while about the Claw, ironically kept his mind off things he didn't want to think about; kept him busy so time wouldn't weigh heavy, and so he wouldn't be so nervous when the Claw next stepped from a shadow to speak to him and direct him.

It was good to have someone to tell him what to do, when and where and how. He'd missed that since his mother's death. Before he had the Claw in his life, he had Mother. And while Mother wasn't a cannibal, she shared a lot of other characteristics with the Claw.

They would've liked one another, he thought.

Once when Ovid had telephoned a radio talk show, careful to use a pay phone, the Claw was so upset with him that he'd struck him hard across the face several times, and he'd slashed Ovid with his claw for good measure, just to show him that Ovid could easily be another victim. The Claw had torn his arm badly, but Ovid knew it was all his own fault. He shouldn't've done anything to anger the Claw.

He reviewed the poem once more, made a few more refinements, trying desperately to make it succinct and rhythmic at the same time. He thought it was good, and he toyed with the idea of sending it straight out and telling the Claw about it afterward, but no, he knew better.

He thought of the first time he had met the Claw, and how strange it had been. It was when his mother died. Everyone had gone and he was left alone with his mother's corpse at the funeral home, tearful and resentful that she had left him. He had been afraid to go home alone. He was talking to her as she lay in her coffin, asking her what he was going to do without her.

And then *he* appeared from nowhere, and it was as if he knew the depth of Ovid's pain and grief. He placed a gentle hand on him. He promised to befriend Ovid and said he'd go home with him for the night, if he was afraid to go into the empty house alone.

Up until that moment, Leon was the name Ovid went by in the neighborhood and at the factory. Leon Helfer. The firm

hand of the stranger he later came to know only as the Claw
had materialized out of the weave of a heavy, burgundy-red
curtain; the spirit had literally pulled its way from the
haunted cloth. In a soft whisper he said, "You are Ovid. I
know you from the ages. You are not alone; your mother sent
me. You're not a factory worker, you're a speaker of divine
truth."

At the time, Ovid had not understood the allusion to his
being a speaker of divine truth, but he did understand the
remarks about his mother, and the fact that the Claw had
been sent by her, that he was there to guide and direct
him.

That was enough for Leon Helfer. He liked being Ovid,
once he got over his horror and disdain for the blood and the
evisceration, and the feeding on flesh.

According to the Claw, in the distant past his family had
always eaten flesh, and in time his genetic makeup and in-
born need for human flesh would make itself felt. And it did
. . . it did. The Claw, for all his ill temper and tantrums, had
never told Ovid a lie. He had that in common with his
mother, too.

"Together, we can work miracles. Will you follow me?
Will you do my bidding? Will you accept me as your master?" He could hear the Claw's voice in his head as if it were
lodged there, as if it had been implanted that first moment he
had been asked these same questions.

He looked down at his poetry and read aloud what he had
written:

> Eyes no longer see
> The power vested in me . . .
> I am the Claw
> who makes the law . . .
> Those who come to me
> Are redeemed in a sea
> of blood and cleansed
> of their unholy sins . . .

It read too much like a catechism, far too Catholic for his needs. He set about the business of rethinking and rewriting.

After a few hours and innumerable drafts, his poem was complete. It read:

> My teeth will have your eyes
> And feed on your banal cries . . .
> Your sins will be eaten away
> That you might live another day . . .
> The Claw is no name for him
> Who gives you eternal life
> By eating away your sin . . .
> My rabid, hungry sin-feast
> Will out in the end
> To give you eternal peace.

"Not bad," he told himself. Not half-bad for someone who didn't understand the first thing about iambic pentameter, or whatever they called these things, someone who had never written poetry before. The Claw was right. It was in his genes, this desire to destroy and to create, all wrapped up together like two hands clasped.

Still, he dared not send the poem for publication.

He wondered again if the Claw would come to visit tonight.

Eight

ℰ

The following day Jessica was in the lab early. She had pinpointed the crux of the forensics problem with regard to the Claw. What Rychman needed to know was the type of weapon used, and so she had gone to work on this in earnest. Secondly, she wanted to review the information on the bite marks thoroughly, to be certain there was only one set of marks and not two. This determination, and the exact nature of the weapon, might be the most important information she could provide for Rychman at this time.

From her reading of the files, the way the victims were attacked, first by a blow to the back of the head and then the mutilations, the idea of a team at work rather than a single individual appealed to her instincts. It wouldn't be the first time that the so-called killer turned out to be two men, or a man and woman, lust-killing in tandem. But to prove this, she'd have to prove the NYPD crime lab wrong, as all the evidence thus far pointed to a single perpetrator.

It would take all of her resources and those of the Quantico labs and a lot of help from J.T. there to rule out the possibility of a team of killers.

She had already faxed notes of her thoughts on the matter to J.T. Even with so many miles separating them, she was using John Thorpe as her sounding board. Her list in part read: All victims were taken by surprise. Victims had been struck in one location and dragged to another, where the attack took place. Further, the bodies, in all but the Hamner case, were removed and placed elsewhere, suggesting either a very strong man or two men. Possibly one man acted as decoy, distracting victim, while second slipped from shadows to overpower her.

Only possibilities, she'd finished.

She had also air-expressed J.T. the one good set of teeth impressions lifted from the Hamner woman along with all those lifted from previous victims. If J.T. determined that the teeth marks all came from the same man, then she'd be satisfied, but as it was, with rumors abounding about the slipshod condition of the NY lab during Darius' bout with illness, she hadn't slept easily knowing a mistake of great proportion might have gone unnoticed. Worse things happened in a laboratory.

Jessica tried to consider all the possibilities, so she'd be open to clues when they arose. She was working in the lab when a technician called via the intercom and said that there was a Dr. Gabriel Arnold on the line for her.

"Just what I need," she muttered under her breath. "A sadistic shrink calling from the asylum in Philadelphia." The last time she'd been alone with Dr. Arnold, the slime had pulled out a bottle of brandy and tried to cajole her into having a drink with him. She sensed that he had somehow learned of her recent battle with drinking. Who among her colleagues would have told Arnold about her bout with alcoholism after Otto's death? Who but Chief O'Rourke, either intentionally or unintentionally?

When she got to the phone in the office that had been turned over to her, she asked, "What can I do for you, Dr. Arnold?"

"It's not what you can do for me. It's what I can do for you, Dr. Coran."

"What is it, Doctor?"

"I've been working steadily with Matisak since you last saw him."

"That's commendable, Doctor." She didn't intend to give him an inch.

"Anyway, I think we've had a breakthrough. He's told us where the Torres woman's remains can be found, and the authorities in Ohio—she wasn't in Kentucky, after all—have unearthed a body fitting the general description—"

"Dr. Arnold, I'm in the middle of an ongoing case here that needs my attention, so if you don't mind—"

"But that's just it. This relates to the Claw. I've gotten Matisak to cooperate with us on this, and he wishes to speak to you. He says he has vital information bearing on your case there."

"Forget it, Dr. Arnold. He's using you for a fool."

"This was not my idea."

"What're you saying?"

"I'm saying that a copy of the FBI files on the Claw was forwarded here for Matisak by your superiors, and—"

"O'Rourke, dammit!" She'd pleaded with O'Rourke to give her some time; that she didn't need or want any input from Mad Matisak; that the man was yanking everyone's chain.

"Look, Matisak refuses to talk to anyone but you at this point."

"There is nothing Matisak could possibly say of interest about—"

"He's sitting beside me and he tells me to tell you that the Claw is not one but *two.*"

This made her pause. How did the bastard know that? Was he simply taking a wild stab? Was he trying to throw her off guard? Was he trying to predict what her thinking would be? He was doing an eerily good job of both.

"Dr. Coran? Doctor? Are you there?"

"Put the bastard on the phone, Arnold."

She heard the noise of a phone being passed through to Matisak in his cell.

"You're so far away dear Doctor, my old acquaintance," mewed Matisak, whose voice was like a knife sliding over her nerves. She felt her blood pressure rise with her anger.

"What is it you want, Matisak?"

"Please, I've asked you a hundred times. Call me Teach or Matthew."

"Get on with it."

"I have had time—lots of time, thanks to you—to review the records and documents your superiors forwarded, despite your apparent reluctance to, shall we say, have me on your team . . ."

Jessica imagined how the small man's chest was expanding. He was so full of himself. She took in a great breath of air and bit her lip, trying to maintain her control, saying nothing.

"It's Stainlype. Stainlype went out-of-body, out of Gerald Ray Sims, just long enough to find another Sims, there in New York, where you are now. Stainlype came back here to destroy Sims, and then she returned to New York. It's a real force, Jessica: demonic, evil, powerful beyond your wildest imaginings, and if you get too close to it again, well . . . I fear for your future, dear Dr. Jessica."

"Arnold, you fool. You interrupted me with this trash?"

"Trash!" shouted Matisak. "Are you telling me you did not know it was *two* all along? That Stainlype escaped? That's why you're there, but if you get too close, then I fear for you, Doctor, I do . . . I really do. Stainlype is a monster and she will eat you alive."

She ridiculed him with her laughter and said, "I'm going to hang up now, *Teach*. I suggest you pray to the demons in your own mind."

"I had help, just like Sims did, when I took their blood, but you never knew that."

"That's a lie. You acted alone, just as Sims acted alone."

"Alone? Really? Alone with the devil, perhaps. Besides, if you will just look more closely, you will find there are two sets of teeth marks. Those of some dupe like Sims and those of Stainlype, or maybe the demon that once lived within *me*."

She could see the direction Matisak was moving in. He was trying to bolster the "guilty by reason of insanity" plea he had maintained throughout. If he could convince the authorities that his aberration was identical to Sims', the parole board might cut him some slack in twenty years—or even ten.

"Just the same, Matisak, your so-called information is worthless. I've already moved in that direction."

"Then you do feel Stainlype is there with you?"

"No, damn your soul, and if you have nothing further—"

"Stainlype's teeth marks were distinctly—*distinctly*—different from those of Gerald Ray Sims, remember?"

"That's what I'd expect a crazy person to believe, Matisak, so go right ahead."

"It was proven at his trial, remember?"

"That's more garbage. The difference was attributed to the degree of puncture, the rending. Any expert—"

"It was more than that and you know it! It was physical proof. The same phenomenon as in Joan of Arc and others throughout history who've been possessed, such as the appearance of stigmata, disease spots, burns on the body. Careful examination of the difference in the two bites *proved* Sims was possessed of an evil force, a demon. There were several dental experts who testified to the fact Sims left the marks of two different sets of teeth, and not of two men but a man and a *woman*! One set was daintier than the other." He allowed his hideous chuckle to creep into the conversation.

She could hear Arnold breathing heavily into the extension, monitoring every word even as it was being recorded. He was wondering, no doubt, if he should or should not cut Matisak off.

"There were just as many experts who didn't see it that way," she replied to Matisak.

She was mad at O'Rourke, at Arnold, at the asinine situation they had created, but she was also mad at herself for letting Matisak bait her this way; but what he'd said earlier gave her pause. Perhaps her theory of two killers was shaky; maybe the Claw *was* another Sims a.k.a. Stainlype case.

Matisak continued on about Sims. "You know the poor bastard died alone with the devil, and why, Doctor? Because he angered Stainlype, and why'd he do that when he knew the consequences? Why'd he anger Stainlype? Because he wanted to please *you*, Doctor. Sims did please you, didn't he, Doctor? But in doing so he pissed Stainlype off, because *you* kept dragging her secrets out of him. You're as responsible for Sims' death as you were for Otto's, Jessica."

She wanted to scream for him to shut up, but she wouldn't give him the satisfaction. "If you say so, Matisak, then it must be so."

"If you ask Dr. Arnold for a video of exactly how Sims was killed by Stainlype, I'm sure—"

"God damn you, Matisak," she coldly said.

"Dr. Arnold, you wouldn't mind, would you? Sure, sure he'd oblige. I understand Stainlype cracked open his skull in three places before she was through with him."

Arnold broke him off, shouting into the phone, "That's enough, Matisak, enough!" When they had gotten the phone away from Matisak, Arnold came back on line, saying, "I hope this hasn't been a waste of your time, Dr. Coran; truly, I had no idea Matisak was going to launch into . . . well, all that nonsense. I hope . . . Well, I'm sorry."

"Is Matisak off?"

"Yes, of course. You may speak freely."

"Is our conversation on tape?"

"As you might expect, yes."

"I don't want a single word about the possibility the Claw is two people leaking out. Do you understand?"

"You may depend on it."

"For how long?" she asked, not expecting an answer.

"Teach is full of surprises. I apologize for my part in this. But if we are to continue to glean information from him, then—"

She blew off his apology. "Whataya think his master plan is, Arnold?"

"Minimum security in ten years."

"And from there an easy escape."

"And if he is ever free again . . ." He let it hang.

"He'll feed again like the vampire he is, Doctor. He has an instinct for evil."

Lights began to go on everywhere in the lab as day became night. Jessica felt like throwing things, the way Alan Rychman had that day she, Eldritch and the mayor had entered his office. Maybe she'd feel better if she could let out the anger the way Rychman did. She tried it, pushing a pen set to the floor, but it had no effect on her. She went back to work instead, faxing some additional information to Quantico. She wanted J.T. to have everything as she got it. She had tried to get her mind off Matisak, Dr. Arnold and the asylum in Philadelphia, as well as Sims and Stainlype. But the more her mind played over Matisak's being allowed, if not encouraged, to telephone her here, the angrier she'd become.

She didn't hear the knock on her door because she was cursing too loudly, saying, "Why doesn't O'Rourke just get Matisak a fucking fax machine in his cell?"

"Sorry if I caught you at a bad time," Alan Rychman said. "Is everything all right? You want me to come back later?"

"No, no, come on in. Sorry about the tantrum."

"No reason you should be having tantrums, any more than I." He tried a laugh and this brought a small smile to her lips.

"That's pretty," he said.

"What's pretty?"

"That smile of yours. Does it get better with a little help?"

"Haven't had much to smile about in a long time."

"Then this is a good sign?" he asked, but she only looked back at the fax machine, finishing what she had to send, speaking with her back to him.

"It's a wonder I can find anything to smile about, if that's what you mean. We've got one hell of a problem on our hands, Rychman."

"So what's new? And what's got you so riled up?"

"Long story," she said, finishing with the fax and wheeling around in her chair to face him again. "It'd just bore you."

"It's going to be a long night. Why not tell me about it over dinner?"

"Dinner? Jesus, what time is it?" she asked, and glanced at her watch. "How'd it get so late? I missed the six o'clock meeting. I'm ... I'm sorry."

Rychman waved it off. "Forget it. You didn't miss much. Assignments, fresh leads that don't smell too fresh; nothing I can't fill you in on, Doctor. But I can tell you that *you* were missed by all."

This made her smile again. "Really? By everyone?"

"Heard you were up here working hard, so I came to haul you out."

"Haul me out? You do have a way with words, Captain."

"For dinner, I mean."

"I've had some training in cryptology; I figured you meant,

'Would you care to have dinner with me?' when you said, 'Haul you out,' but I'm just a little rusty, so it took me a moment."

He half frowned and squinted at her. "Is that a yes?"

"You haven't deciphered it yet?"

"Working . . . I'd say it was an affirmative reply."

Nine

ᛩ

Rychman suggested an Italian restaurant named Donatel-lo's Greatest Achievements, in the heart of Manhattan. Along the way, she filled him in on what the FBI had been trying to accomplish with Gerald Ray Sims before his suicide, and what they were trying to do with Matisak. Rychman agreed that her bosses were pandering to Matisak, to the point that any information gained from him was suspect. He was sympathetic and very understanding about her earlier outburst. He seemed genuinely concerned about her well-being, she felt. She sensed a gentleness that perhaps only a few were privy to.

"So what credence do you give to Matisak's theory, if it can be called that? I mean maybe it's not a demonic possession but what about a pair of madmen?"

"I'm sorry, it's just too early to tell," she replied, saying nothing of her own suspicions along these lines. "Have you any reason to believe it could be two men instead of one?"

"No, not really," he readily admitted.

After arriving at the restaurant and being seated, they ordered a carafe of Chablis and she was soon asking him about his home life. "Any children?"

"A pair of 'em. Sweet, gentle kids. Raised far from their father's profession, thanks to their mother."

"You get to see them on weekends?"

"When the job doesn't interfere, which isn't often, lately. My ex jokes that I'm a merchant marine and I come around when my ship's in."

She dipped her head and bit her lip. "It doesn't sound like the perfect amicable divorce, but it takes a special person to understand how important the job is to a dedicated cop, or agent, as in my case."

"It's been difficult, to say the least, not seeing the kids when I come home at night, and as for a woman's company . . . well, let's just say, I miss that, too."

"Guess we've got some things in common, Captain."

"I think it'd be okay if you called me Alan under the circumstances."

"Maybe not. Wouldn't want to slip around your men."

"We're not around my men. Go ahead. Try it. A-L-A-N, Alan."

"Alan," she said.

"You've got it, and you make it sound better than 'Captain.' "

"I'm starved," she replied. "Where's that waiter?" In a moment someone was there taking their orders. He opted for a small New York strip steak, she for the red snapper.

She caught him staring at her before he realized what he was doing. To cover, he said abruptly, "I'm given to understand that you're extremely good at reading people, at psychologically dissecting killers; that you have an instinct for it."

"I have some talent in that direction, yes."

"Then you've already made some judgments about our friend or friends, the Claw?" He seemed to be drawing inward again. Maybe he wanted their relationship to remain on a firm professional footing, too. Perhaps talking about the case would accomplish this.

Or was he slicker than she'd given him credit for? Was this Alan Rychman's way of maneuvering her into talking more openly about her initial impressions and findings than she had intended?

"I know that the Claw's appetite grows," she said.

"Grows? You mean the stepped-up calendar of his kills?"

"I mean that with each victim, apparently, he has either eaten more or walked off with more of the organs. He's working his way up to feeding jackal fashion on the brains of his future victims."

Rychman stared across at her. "You can tell that from what you've seen in the lab?" The same notion had crossed his mind at the Hamner murder scene.

"First victim was only lightly hit over the head. Now he's murderously battering the cranial matter, splitting open the skull. He'll take the brains of his next victim, because he has been working his way through the organs, tasting each in turn. He gorges himself on the entrails, disinterested in the intestines themselves, but fascinated with the organ tissues. He's fed on heart, lung, liver and kidney tissues, as well as the eyes of his victims. He's bored now with this and he'll go on to their brains next."

The waiter gulped back bile as he stood listening to her. She'd been unaware of his presence. Rychman looked up at the man and said, "We're testing dog food materials at the plant. Don't mind us."

The waiter quickly deposited their meals and backed off, hurriedly asking if they needed anything else, quite anxious to make his exit. Rychman waved the poor man off.

They dug in, both hungry, the aroma of the hot meals and juices swirling about them. Rychman poured them both more wine until she placed a hand up to him.

Jessica's cane slid softly away from the unoccupied chair she'd propped it on, slapping the floor. She reddened and began to reach for it, but Alan was faster, lifting it and laying it gingerly across the arms of the chair.

"That'll do better there." He stared at the Irish shillelagh. Its clublike pearl handle had a brass band around it, like the markings on the neck of a wild goose, the rest of the cane a simple black.

"Nice cane, a real beauty."

"A gift," she said.

"Oh? From a friend?" He was fishing.

"From several friends at headquarters."

"I'm sorry I'm so nosy."

She waved it off. "Not necessary, really. As for any more details on the predilections of the Claw, it's going to take a little more time. You'll have to remain patient."

"Tell that to everybody that's after my . . . neck."

She took a deep breath. "Is this why you asked me to dinner? To interrogate me? To draw at straws?"

"No, no," he replied. "I just don't know what else to talk to you about."

"Tell me about yourself."

"Me? I'd have thought you'd learned all you wanted to know from Lou by now."

"I did, but there are a few holes. What do you do to relax?"

"Firing range helps me, sometimes."

She nodded. "Me, too."

"You a good shot?"

Grinning, she replied, "The best."

"You're on, anytime."

"How about after dinner?"

"All right ... you're on!"

She could feel his tension easing.

"What do you do for fun?" he asked.

"Recently learned to scuba dive."

"Really? That's a kick, isn't it?"

"You dive?"

"Since I was seventeen, sure."

"I love the feeling of freedom it offers."

He nodded knowingly and their eyes met. "We do have something in common, after all."

"I'm not what you're used to, I know. Not your typical M.E."

He thought of Perkins and some others he'd worked cases with and this made him laugh. "No, you sure aren't."

"Lot of men have a hard time dealing with a woman who isn't easily intimidated," she said.

"A lot of women are easily intimidated," he countered.

"By you, I'm sure."

"But not you."

"No, not me."

"Good."

The food beckoned, and they drifted into other areas of discussion as they ate. She talked passionately about hunting deer and bear in Minnesota, Canada and Alaska. He had hunted deer in northern New York but hadn't gone after larger game. She talked about her father and how he had brought her up to be proud and independent and a capable gunwoman. The evening seemed to evaporate around them, and when she looked at her watch, it was nine forty-five.

"I guess the range is out, huh?" she asked.

"Closes at ten, but I've got a little pull. Come on."

He took her to his former precinct headquarters where they rode an elevator down to the sub-subbasement to find an enormous indoor shooting range unnaturally silent and unlit. He shouted an order to the cop on duty to bring up the lights.

"Captain!" came the quick reply. "Been a while. Hope you're not turning into a full-time desk jock. Just lock up when you go," said the sergeant as he tacked a pair of targets to the electronic runners and sent them on their way.

"How many yards?"

"Make it fifty," he said.

"Seventy-five," she countered.

"A hundred, Pete. Make it one hundred."

"Wanta make up your mind?" Pete, a wizened, leathery-faced man, lightweight and short enough to pass as a jockey, stared first at Rychman and then at Jessica, his eyes twinkling with mischief. "Havin' a little contest, huh?"

"Just put 'em up, Pete." Rychman whipped out his Police Special, a standard .38, and she pulled out hers, a near identical Smith & Wesson, but hers was a .44-caliber.

"Nice-looking weapon," he complimented her.

"Put up or shut up," she replied, turned and without hesitation drilled the target at a hundred yards with successive rounds until she had emptied the chamber.

He was impressed and she knew it. "Your turn," she said.

He took a casual stance and clicked off bullet after bullet as quickly as she had.

Pete had been about to drift out, but was held back by their display of shooting. "I want to see this," he said, punching the buttons that returned the targets to their owners. As they approached, the two targets looked almost identical in every detail, every bullet hole. It was impossible to tell which of them was the better shot; both had several shots going through the same hole.

Pete was bug-eyed, stammering.

"I knew you were good, Captain, but ... wow ... Young lady, you're quite a shot."

"Thanks, Pete."

"Come on, I'll drive you home," Alan said.

"That'd be some drive. Home's in Virginia."

"Your hotel, then. Pete," he said, turning at the elevator door, "log these for us, will you? I need the points."

When they got into the elevator and were going up, he said, "So, you relaxed a little now? Got some of that stress out?"

"It feels great, getting a few rounds off. Relieves a lot of tension."

He came across the elevator toward her and took her in his arms, kissing her passionately. She pushed him away.

"Stop it, Captain, stop," she said, and he backed off.

"Sorry, I shouldn't have done that. Too much wine lingering in the brain, I suppose, but ... well, dammit, you are—"

"Captain Rychman, we ... we are going to be working together, and I don't think it's wise to get involved in ... in any other fashion until our work together is ... is complete."

She was feeling the effects of the wine, too, and finding it hard to put into words what her exact feelings and thoughts were. It seemed odd to her that a little alcohol gave her a sharp edge as a shooter, but that it dulled her emotional senses. She wasn't sure how she felt at having him kiss her. She wasn't sure if she had invited or allowed it, whether she enjoyed or disliked it. It had been a long time since she'd been touched—either physically or emotionally—by a "sane" man.

And the big, strong Alan Rychman, although very different in appearance, so reminded her of Otto. In his mannerisms, in the fact he was trying so hard to hide the little boy curled up deep within him.

"I'd still like to take you to your hotel."

"Hotel, *yes*, hotel room, *no*."

• • •

It had been nice having Alan Rychman escort her to the hotel, and he had no idea how much she had honestly wanted him to stay. She dreaded nights alone, especially away from her Virginia home in Quantico, the only place she felt completely and wholly safe. But even home had been invaded by her night visions and the shadows.

Jessica got into bed and sat up reading a recent report put together by one of the best psychological profiling teams at the FBI. The report served a double purpose: to induce a sound sleep, along with the pills given her by her shrink, and to bring her up-to-date on the most recent advice in dealing with *killer couples*. She knew that reading had lately become a way to avoid thinking about her continuing insomnia and what amounted to fear.

She concentrated on the cold, explicit, factual report in her lap, desperately trying to stay on her train of thought. It was well known in violent crime cases that there was often a dominant-subservient partnership involved, in which two killers formed a symbiotic bond of need and lust that led to mutual gratification through torture and murder. Killer couples weren't always a man/man team; quite often it was two women, and much more often, a man and a woman. Often one was so infatuated with the other that he felt a "spell" had been cast over him.

It wasn't a new notion; in fact, there were many such case histories available at the FBI Academy. She had read many of them while researching killer couples for a paper that had won her high marks. There were instances throughout history in which one person was so dominated by another that he or she would act out any unlawful or immoral act put to him or her.

The brutal Jack the Ripper murders in London in the fall of 1888 might have been the work of more than one man. In the early part of the twentieth century there were Leopold and Loeb, and since then there had been multiple examples of killer couples, making them almost commonplace. There were Bywaters and Thompson, Snyder and Gray, Brady and Hindley, Bonnie and Clyde, Fernandez and Beck. Killer couples, as in the Aileen Wournos lesbian killer case, were not as common as the lone-wolf serial-killer type, however they were on the rise along with cult murders.

If her time in the FBI had taught her anything, it was that a man and a woman, teamed for the murder of a third person, were one of the deadliest combinations known. Between them they had a powerful arsenal to bring to bear against their intended prey: cunning, deceit, sex appeal, physical strength, boldness, resolve and amorality. Few victims of such teams survived such an unholy assault.

Usually, such teams were only caught as the result of a sure erosion of trust between the two murderers, the erosion beginning after the first murder, because each partner was by then the sole witness to the other's crime. The relationship steadily crumbled under the weight of such responsibility. They would begin to suspect each other, begin to doubt and question every move, and would soon be unable to live from moment to moment without fearing one another.

"You're afraid of your own shadow by now, aren't you? Aren't you?" she asked the empty room, trying to imagine the state of mind of the killer or killers at this time. Even if the Claw was an individual, she reasoned, he would eventually begin to fear *himself* as he might an accomplice, the way that Gerald Ray Sims feared his shadow self, Stainlype.

She had come to believe, since the death of Otto Boutine, with whom she'd shared so many intimacies, that everyone, herself included, had dark second selves within, doubles or doppelgängers, as the Germans called them. The trauma she had gone through had revealed to her the dangerous double held in check at all times by her more dominant personality. The dark double was a frightful being, a creature that truly disturbed its owner to her core, one that rattled sabers that turned into snakes that fed on the good and wishing-to-be-good self.

Jessica believed meeting the shadow within—not just glimpsing it from a distance—could cause a person either to become whole by facing down the murderous impulses that raged below the still volcano, or to become fragmented, as in the case of Gerald Ray Sims, and quite possibly Matthew Matisak. She had long been accustomed to the power of the dark side in killers, but had always denied it in herself, until she had been maimed by Matisak, until she had wanted vengeance against the maniac. She knew about her undesirable other self now, her less than pretty side, the shadow within. At times she now experienced something that felt like her two selves crossing, and it frightened her. The dark brute was, in its way, so much more powerful, as if negative energy drained off positive impulses at every turn.

It was what the shrinks called an intrapsychic "problem" that could evolve into a "conflict" if she didn't get control of it. It was one of the scars left her by Matisak, part of a legacy of fear and self-doubt created in her by the vampiristic madman. It was worse than any nightmare or replay of the events that brought her near death at his hands, because this creature was *like* Matisak, and yet it was *her*.

Her lady shrink, Dr. Lemonte, had told her it was dangerous, at this point, to ignore her "shadow" shelf.

"Or to fear one's own shadow?" she had replied. "What the hell am I supposed to do?"

"Face it . . . recognize it for what it is."

"And what is that?"

"Another and legitimate aspect of your *self*. The self that as a child you allowed vent to, that escaped when you picked up an object and hurled it across a room."

She thought of Rychman hurling objects about his office and wondered if he ever had any shadow fears. Perhaps her psychiatrist was right.

"How do I let it out safely?" she had asked.

"Play with it."

"Play with it? I don't want to play with it. I'm afraid of it."

"Play out harmless aspects of your rejected self—"

She was shaking. "Suppose it, this rejected self, takes hold. Hell, it already has begun to!"

"You're intelligent, levelheaded, and from what I've read of your record, Jessica, you're a very brave woman. All you need do is face this as you would one of your cases. Investigate intelligently."

"But this isn't a case; this is me . . . *me*."

Donna Lemonte had then leaned forward, uncharacteristically took Jessica's hands into her own and stared hard into her eyes. "You can beat this thing; you can shake it, Jess, but in order to heal the split between what you've come to know and accept as your true persona and your shadow persona, you must face the shadow, recognize it for what it is and put it back in its place."

Ten

e

After Alan Rychman had dropped Jessica at her hotel, he checked in at headquarters long enough to see that the order he had reluctantly given to arrest Shaw had been carried out. The interrogations had already begun and it looked like Conrad Shaw was going to be so cooperative that he'd confess to anything put to him. He stayed long enough to be certain that proper procedures were being followed. Since his detectives had the situation well in hand, he made the long drive to New Jersey, where his brother Sam lived.

He'd called ahead to his brother, a computer consultant for Pioneer, who owned a roomy home. The phone number was a secret to all but Lou Pierce. Surrounded by gates, bars, and a fail-safe, state-of-the-art security system, "Samhaven"—as Alan jokingly called the place—afforded him the ultimate hideout whenever pressures became unbearable in the big city. Sam didn't mind, because it was the only time he ever saw big brother Alan anymore.

Now Alan was propped up in bed in his perennial guest room. It was near midnight, and Sam and his family of four were fast asleep while he second-guessed the bogus direction the Claw case was taking with the indictment of Conrad Shaw, ideal as he was as a press scapegoat. Rychman's only comfort in the nasty affair was that Jessica Coran had felt as he had about Shaw's then impending arrest. Sharp lady, he told himself, with great instincts of her own, instincts that put her squarely on the plane of the killer. Not to mention her good instincts about men.

He'd hoped she might change her mind when they'd arrived at her hotel, invite him up to her room for a drink and talk. They'd been getting along well before he had clumsily pushed himself on her. He cursed himself as the vivid memory returned.

He pictured her again at the shooting range with him. She had been extremely good with her weapon. She held it as if it were an extension of herself, part of her flesh, and God save the man who tried to take it from her. Tough, dangerous, yes, she was ... but there was also something else, something he sensed when his lips had touched hers for that fleeting moment, a certain vulnerability born of pain perhaps? He could not be sure. Something deep within her beautiful eyes told of a well of sadness; yet, she was so alive.

He thought for a moment of the cane, her limp, the doing of that bastard Matisak.

He tried to imagine what she had gone through, the pain and suffering, the loss of her superior and friend, the well-respected Boutine. He could imagine the loss of a partner in the line of duty. He'd had this happen to himself more times than he cared to recall, but he couldn't imagine being at the mercy of a vicious killer like the blood-taker, Matisak.

The case had become required reading at the FBI Academy, not only for the *do's* but for the *don'ts.* Dr. Coran had messed up royally, by what he'd heard. She'd gone after this guy Matisak on her own. She was lucky to be alive. Some army personnel guy that'd gone along with her hadn't been so fortunate.

Rychman wondered which was worse, Matisak, the blood-drinking vampire killer, or the Claw, who took delight in rending the flesh and feeding off parts of the body. He knew which man's victims suffered longer.

It was late and he was tired when he turned out the light and rolled over, his mind swimming with the next day's agenda, all the hundreds of administrative jobs that needed to be done to pull his task force properly together. One thing was lacking for certain, he told himself, and that was a sense of teamwork and camaraderie, something he must instill in all of the divergent cops from across the city who were working on the case. But how? They seemed at such odds with each other, little wonder it was taking them so long to pull together.

• • •

Ovid's house was beginning to smell like a hospital ward, what with all the disinfectant and formaldehyde. Ovid had put up whole organs in jars all around the house. He sometimes wondered what his mother would have made of his and the Claw's collection.

She most certainly would not approve; she'd be disgusted by the sight—and odor—of his *things,* and the idea he would consume them. She would order him to stop what he was doing, and she would fight the Claw and likely be killed by the Claw, if it came to that.

Sometimes Ovid awoke in the night to find the Claw standing over him, staring, as if considering the possibility of opening Ovid up, turning him into just another of his victims. Ovid was terrified of the Claw at times. He did what the Claw told him to do out of fear as much as any sense of loyalty or purpose, although he had tried desperately to understand the purpose of the Claw.

The Claw came and went from Ovid's place in the night. He often wanted one of the treasures they'd taken from their victims. Ovid had eyes put up like pickles, a pair of kidneys, a human heart, and the Claw wanted to add to their collection.

The Claw was like a spirit, the way he moved in and out of the shadows, disappearing into the night mist. It was almost as if he came with his own thick fog, the kind you heard about in England, as thick as soup, floating about him. His features were always cloaked and indistinct. Sometimes he just came for one of the jars, taking it off with him. Other times, like tonight, he ordered Ovid up and dressed. While Ovid was dressing, he disappeared, only to reappear again, telling Ovid he had a prize for him. Ovid went downstairs to the living room and found a rolled carpet in the center of the floor with a bloodied body inside.

"What the hell's this? You can't bring one of your kills into my house. This is crazy!"

"You're going to help me get rid of it, Ovid, now. But first, I want you to take a good look at the face."

With that the Claw tore open the carpet, revealing the

bloody, eyeless corpse. The body was that of an elderly, white-haired woman, and the Claw turned up the face so Ovid could see it clearly in the dim light.

"Hold on, *ohhh*, no, *ohhh* no! You've gone too far this time, dammit, too far," cried Ovid. "It's Mrs. Phillips. You killed Mrs. Phillips!"

"A present for you, Ovid."

"What? A present?"

"It's clear enough, Ovid. Or do I have to spell it out? You can't be so thick. I can kill anyone, including you, with this!" He held up his powerful claw and it glinted in the moonlight filtering in from outside.

Ovid got the message loud and clear: the Claw had killed all on his own, without Ovid's help. It was a demonstration of the fact the Claw did not *need* him, and that the Claw could easily implicate him to the authorities by destroying his neighbors! Mrs. Phillips was one of his goddamned neighbors!

He had angered the Claw the night before when he had shown him the poem he had written in the Claw's honor. Ovid had pleaded that he be allowed to send it to the *Times*. The Claw had said nothing, but in the depth of his silence, Ovid felt his hopes decrease while his fears increased. Then in a rage, the Claw had cried out that he wanted every scrap of the poem destroyed, calling Ovid a moron and an idiot, and his poem stupid. "Destroy it all!" he had shouted as he ripped apart the papers in his hands. "I want every draft, every copy burned, do you understand? And do not go out of this house until I return."

Now he had returned but he was not alone. He had Mrs. Phillips with him. It was a clear indication that he could just as easily destroy Ovid as anyone, and that the Claw could carry on his work alone if need be.

The familiar leathery old face of Mrs. Phillips, who had been his mother's companion, and lately his own, made Ovid's stomach turn. She was eviscerated like the others, except there was more. Her skull was cracked open like a melon and her brain had been removed. Undoubtedly it had been consumed by the Claw's insatiable cannibalistic urges.

Mrs. Phillips' grimacing face indicated her tortured death had been prolonged. The Claw had not been kind to her. She had lived a block over. They used to sit together on the same park bench feeding the pigeons and talking about his mother. Mrs. Phillips remembered her fondly.

The memory made Ovid shudder, a quaking panic rippling through him until suddenly the Claw grabbed him and shook him, tearing the flesh of his arm as he did so.

"Put what's left of her in the car."

He did as he was told, taking Mrs. Phillips' remains out to the little sedan that Leon Helfer used to get to work. Leon, not feeling as strong as Ovid, lifted both rug and old woman into his arms and stumbled out the back way, presumably the way that the Claw had entered with the body in tow. In the darkened garage, he popped the trunk, part of his mind questioning why it was that the Claw always insisted on using Leon's car, Leon's house and now one of Leon's neighbors as a victim! It was like waving a flag to tell everyone that he, Leon Helfer, was Ovid, the accomplice to the awful and deadly Claw. He wondered privately if he dared cut a deal with the authorities to save himself before it was too late, but he instantly feared the thought, because he believed that the Claw, if not distracted, could read his mind.

He stuffed the rug and body deep into the trunk, knowing it would be the devil to get it all out again. Suddenly the Claw said in his ear, "Now, go get some of those Hefty bags, Ovid, and let's go."

Ovid saw that the Claw had already carried out two of the jars with organs of earlier victims swimming in the soup of the preservatives. "Where're we going?"

"I have a little surprise for you."

"Another one?"

"Even better. Hurry, do as I say . . . hurry."

Leon Helfer was no longer there; it was just Ovid and the Claw. Ovid returned to Leon's house, found the bags and returned, sliding into the car alongside the dark shadow of the Claw.

"Where're we going?"

"Hunting."

"But we've ... I mean, you've already got the old woman tonight."

"And now I want a young one! Just drive! Will you?"

"Which way?"

"We're going to Scarsdale."

"Scarsdale?"

"A lovely name when you think of it ... *scars* ... dale, Scarsdale. Where better to scar someone?" The Claw's laughter filled the dark car, and Mrs. Phillips' body thumped behind them with each bump in the alleyway as they ventured forth for Scarsdale.

"What're we going to do with the old woman's body?"

"We'll find a suitable use for it, dear Ovid."

And they did, later.

Ovid, home again, thought of the awful chance he had taken, the terrible fear welling up inside him, threatening to crush him. If the Claw should find out—and he would, he must. He found out everything. So why did Ovid do such a foolish thing?

They had driven to Scarsdale as the Claw had ordered. The Claw seemed to know exactly where he wanted to go. They pulled into a secreted backyard, where the Claw ordered Ovid to take Mrs. Phillips' body from the trunk, rug and all, and to follow him around to the front and up the steps to the door. The Claw rang the bell as if on a normal visit. A young, dark-haired woman answered, and while she was no great beauty, she excited Ovid's interest. She was the picture of surprise on seeing the Claw. The Claw, whom she seemed to know, grabbed the rug Mrs. Phillips was wrapped in and said, "Here is that Oriental rug I promised you, Catherine."

"But I wasn't expecting you—"

"You do want the rug!" he shouted, grunting as he pushed the rug through the door and into her, its contents falling out, sending blood rivulets over the woman. She quickly tried to make her way out the back of the house, but the Claw was far too fast for her. His deadly three-pronged weapon ripped down across her skull and sent her toppling over, moaning, still very much alive. Ovid had never seen the Claw act so quickly and surely on his own. He certainly didn't need Ovid any longer. Now Ovid feared for himself.

They had fed over the bodies but Ovid took no delight, while the Claw seemed to take greater delight than ever before. He also took his time over the head. Now Ovid understood why he had wanted the head from their last victim, because before Ovid's eyes, the Claw consumed the young woman's brain. Ovid was sure he had done the same with Mrs. Phillips.

In a state of confusion, Ovid had taken the final and only copy left of his poem, which he had folded tightly into a ball to keep it hidden from the Claw, and moments before they'd left Mrs. Phillips with the young woman in Scarsdale, he had plunged the note into a hiding place. At the time this had seemed his only course of action. He sensed that his days with the Claw were coming to a close and that he must protect himself in some manner. Perhaps this was the way. Then again, it might be a little like suicide, he told himself now.

When the phone rang, Alan Rychman didn't feel as if he'd gotten an hour's sleep, much less several. It was Lou Pierce, calling from Queens with bad news. Lou apologized but said that everyone was trying to get in touch with Rychman. Rychman's brother, awakened by the call, stood in the doorway, and Rychman grumbled something about its being an emergency. His brother waved as if to say he was going back to sleep, and Rychman rolled over and took the information from Lou.

"The Claw has put in another appearance, and Captain, this one's extremely bad because—"

"What's the location, Lou?"

"Twelve forty-nine Nantucket, Captain, in—"

"Where the hell's that?"

"Scarsdale, Captain."

"Jesus, since when's he going to Scarsdale?"

"It's not that far from his last one, Captain. Fifteen, maybe twenty minutes."

"He's on wheels, that's for sure . . . hell on wheels," Rychman sleepily mumbled, but his mind was on the question of jurisdictional lines. Scarsdale meant complications; it meant arguing with Scarsdale authorities as to exactly whose case it was and who got first dibs. He'd have to telephone Mayor Halle and have him call his counterpart in Scarsdale to make sure that the NYPD special task force would be in charge.

Hopefully, the cops in Scarsdale would see the wisdom of cooperating. It amazed Rychman, however, just how stubbornly territorial the various jurisdictions were. If and when he became C.P., the question of cooperation between boroughs, cities, counties and states would be uppermost on his agenda.

"This one's doubly bad, Captain," Lou said.

"Bastard did a real hatchet job on the vic, huh?"

"Christ, Captain, he took the brains this time, and—"

"Jesus," moaned Rychman, on the edge of the bed now, pulling on his pants. Coran had called it like some psychic. She was as good as her record indicated. "Locate Dr. Coran, Lou, and see to it she gets to the scene. I'll see you both there."

"I'll see to it personally, Captain, but there's one other thing you ought to know—"

But Lou heard the click of the receiver before he could get out the fact there were two bodies this time. Lou decided that the captain would find out soon enough. For now he had to roust out Dr. Coran. It was his understanding that someone had already notified the coroner's office and that Dr. Archer was already on his way to Scarsdale.

Rychman was yawning and driving rapidly toward his destination, his siren and flashing light parting the relatively sparse traffic at 3 A.M. He was only half hearing his radio, alive and crackling with news of the Claw's recent kill. So the place would be deluged with reporters and thrill-seekers, he thought. There'd be a thick crowd to part just to get to the body, so he called ahead to the scene, shouting for whoever had taken charge of the body. By protocol this was the first on-scene officer until a coroner or superior arrived to relieve him.

"This is Officer Calvin Boyle, Scarsdale Police Department, Captain Rychman."

"Boyle, are you in charge there?"

"For now, yes, sir."

"Have you secured the body?"

"Bodies, sir, and yes, they are secured."

"Bodies?"

"Weren't you told, sir? There's two vics."

"That's what Lou was trying to tell me, damn."

"Sir?"

"Never mind, Boyle, just do me some good, will you?"

"Anything, Captain."

"I want you and any other first-on-scene to be there when I get there. Want to talk to you."

"Not a problem."

"I want you to maintain control, Officer, you got that?"

"Control of the bodies, sir?"

"That's right."

"But our coroner's already arrived and ... well, it's his show now."

"You just tell him Dr. Darius is on his way, and so is an M.E. with the FBI. Tell him it's an NYPD task force matter." Rychman knew that the famous Dr. Darius wasn't likely to put in an appearance, but the lie would be effective.

"It might mean more coming from you, sir."

"Think you can get him on the horn?"

"I'll do my best."

Rychman didn't want the crime scene disturbed until Jessica Coran could have at it; given her accurate prediction, and what he had read about her, he believed that she might be instrumental in stopping this madness. Anything he could do to delay the Scarsdale coroner, he decided, was good at this point.

Rychman got a Dr. Stanley Permeter on the line and he began the tedious job of keeping Permeter wondering about whether he should or should not go ahead with his investigation there in Scarsdale; whether he should wait for the renowned Dr. Darius and the FBI's Dr. Coran. Rychman kept the doctor entangled with words until his car pulled up to the

crime scene area, where, as he expected, everyone with a
police-band radio was waiting and watching.

Dr. Permeter was arguing with the Scarsdale chief of police
when Rychman stepped up to them and introduced himself
with a large handshake. Once more he launched into the
many reasons for waiting on Darius and Coran.

The Scarsdale chief was Bill Flemming, a friendly enough
sort, but he was concerned about how his department was going to look if they simply stepped aside and allowed
Rychman in without contest. The killings were, after all,
within his jurisdiction. A radio call from Flemming's superior
took him away. Rychman prayed it was the right call, and it
seemed to be, for when Flemming came back he agreed to
wait.

Rychman gathered members of his task force about him
and gave each an assignment. One was to interrogate Boyle,
to find out how the bodies were discovered and who made
the call and what had alerted them. Another was to question
Boyle's partner, a rookie who was badly shaken. She hadn't
been prepared for what they had found inside the house on a
residential block of Nantucket Street.

The Claw, if it was the work of the Claw, had deviated
from his normal pattern: he had apparently killed two victims
at a single location, and he had chosen to kill indoors, gaining
access to the house without apparent difficulty. There were no
broken windows, no broken locks. But Rychman knew it was
the same bastard, or bastards. He knew it because Jessica had
warned him that soon the Claw would be graduating to cannibalizing his victim's brain. He had done so with a vengeance, and he was playing a game with the authorities,
seeing just how daring he could be, for the bright streetlamps
of Nantucket Street must have shone on him clearly as he
stepped up to the front door of the little home.

Eleven

The keening of the telephone beside her bed was a welcome shock to Jessica's system. She'd been in the throes of a nightmare; an endlessly long snake had been coiling about her, making her feel pinned to the bed. She'd been frustrated by the fact that she'd known it was a nightmare, but could not break free of it. She was prisoner until the phone, an object outside herself, had forced consciousness from unconsciousness. The snake's head had had Matthew Matisak's face.

She grabbed the phone, and for just an instant, she wanted it to be Otto at the other end, but of course, that was impossible.

"Dr. Coran? This is Sergeant Pierce."

"Something's happened?" She immediately feared for Alan Rychman.

"Captain Rychman asked that I fetch you, Doctor."

"The Claw?"

" 'Fraid so, ma'am."

"Can you send a car?"

"I'm in the lobby, ma'am. I'm to take you myself."

"Good, good . . . I'm dressing . . . Be right down."

She pulled herself together quickly, dressing in jeans and a pullover sweater, grabbing her cane and her medical valise. Inside a compartment in the valise was a medical smock she'd throw on at the scene.

Lou Pierce greeted her in the lobby, and it was good to see a friendly face. He instantly took her medical bag, showing her the way to the squad car. He deposited the bag on the backseat, but she asked to ride up front with him. Lou was pleased. He opened the door for her and watched her slide in gracefully, save for a brief fight with her cane.

Lou sped toward the scene, telling her that she had a long night ahead of her.

"Anything you want to tell me, Lou, that I should know?"

He'd been thinking about the double murder and the missing gray matter from the heads of each victim, and he felt a little unnerved that she could read him so easily. "Well, yes, ma'am, some information . . . by way of preparation."

She knew that words could do little to prepare a person for the kind of work she must do tonight. "Go ahead, Lou. What is it?"

"Well, there're two bodies, same location—"

"Two? My God."

"One's older, one younger; they're thinking it's a mother and daughter, but there's some question about that."

"How awful."

"And ma'am, well, this time the lunatic took their . . . took their . . . well, he took their brains, or ate them. Nobody's sure of that, but the brains are missing."

She felt chilled, recalling the prediction she had made to Rychman. She hadn't expected the maniac to advance to this stage quite so quickly, and certainly not so dramatically, killing two women in a single night.

"You okay, ma'am?"

"Yes, Lou. Just get me there quickly."

Lou felt uneasy and awkward, and he tried small talk, but it was a poor opponent for the silence that had settled in around them. "Your injury, ma'am?"

She looked up at him. "Yes?"

"Is it temporary, or will it never heal?"

"Doctors say it could be almost right someday."

"Then you can throw away your cane. That'd be nice."

"But only if I stay off my legs."

"If you don't mind my saying so, Doctor, maybe you're doing yourself a . . . a disservice."

"I don't put much store in what the doctors have told me. Besides, I'm stubborn, and I'm in a profession that doesn't allow you to be on your behind, so . . ." She paused. "As for the cane, it's kinda become a part of me; lends character, don't you think?" She smiled. "And it's a constant reminder to never again be naive or foolish."

"Tell you this much, Dr. Coran."

"What's that, Lou?"

"Sure hasn't slowed Captain Rychman down; I think he likes your *character*, if you get my drift."

"I think I do."

"The Captain, he knows good character."

Lou returned his attention to the road, and her thoughts drifted back to the Claw. The psycho seemed to be baiting them all, taunting an entire population, daring them to come nearer and nearer only to discover a phantom they could never actually put their hands on, much less cage. More and more, the Claw reminded her of Stainlype, but she wanted to cling to the belief that he was two separate physical beings, and not the single being that Stainlype/Sims had been.

She mentally began to psych herself up for what lay ahead, knowing she could not fully do so until she was in the midst of the carnage with her eyes and hands directly over the remains left her by the Claw.

The squad car pulled up to the police barricade, and when she got out she saw the reporters, among them Jim Drake, who gave a perfunctory wave from the sidelines. She hurried toward the door that would take her into the nice-looking little bungalow that had become a torture chamber for its inhabitants.

Rychman stepped out onto the front stoop and stopped her before she entered the house, saying, "Brace yourself, Jessica. It's the worst yet."

"I can handle it," she said flatly, about to move past him.

"I managed to secure the scene, and we were able to keep the bodies intact, where they were left. Dr. Darius is inside."

"Dr. Darius? I thought he was—"

"In good shape and saucy as ever. Between the two of you, get us something we can go on."

"No witnesses, I assume."

"No one useful, and little hope in that direction. We have determined that one of the victims doesn't live here."

"The younger woman?"

"No, the old lady. The younger one lived here alone, parents are Upstate, Albany area. No one knows who the old woman is, and there's no identifying her. Missing Persons is working on a match, but so far, zip. Jess, did anyone inform you of . . . of the fact that—"

"It's a little scary, about the brains, Alan, but it simply stood to reason. He treats a corpse like his personal smorgasbord. He was bound to get to the entrée soon, the only major organ he had left untouched so far. I'd better get inside now."

"Sure . . . Meantime, the task force detectives are fanned out, checking every possible lead, asking questions. Seems a neighbor became curious when she saw a strange car out her back window. Made a call to the Olin woman—the young one—but got no answer. She didn't see the car's occupant enter or exit. I've got O'Toole and Mannion trying to jog her memory regarding the vehicle."

She nodded and entered the death house, Rychman just behind her. He watched her go to where Darius was kneeling over the body of the older woman, whose head, like that of the Olin woman, was split completely open, the brains scooped clean from the cranium.

Jessica sensed that Alan was nearby, and part of her wanted him there. She had managed to keep her eye from wandering to the center of the brutality here, concentrating on the details of the crime scene first to maintain her professional bearing. She knew that Darius had already passed through this phase, because he was now on his knees with his gloved hands inside the open wounds, searching for clues to the double murder.

She registered the blood trails and strange trajectories in the foyer, on the walls and floorboards; on the surface, it looked as if Miss Olin had struggled to get away from her attacker at the open door. She might have been tripped or become disoriented. A large pool of blood showed the exact location where she'd been rendered unconscious by a blow to the head. The blow had sent her into a convulsive state, if the reading of the blood trail could be believed. There was much smeared blood, because each body had been dragged into the center of the living room. At least, these were her initial impressions. At the moment she could only speculate, but she guessed that Darius had to have seen the same tell-tale signs as she.

The air was stale, thick and rank with odors meant only for the embalming room. A police photographer was snapping shots of the two victims, and Darius was grumbling to himself and shaking his head sadly. Darius' form was thin and small and white-haired, making him look like one of Santa's elves as he knelt over the deceased. His snowy-white hair was in sharp contrast to the blood and bile on his hands when he turned to greet her. His handlebar mustache was also white and it tweaked from side to side as he tried to scratch an itch below it without the use of his soiled hands.

Jessica had suited up and she reached out her gloved right hand to take Dr. Darius' as she said, "I've so wanted to meet with you and work with you; I'm just sorry it has to be under such horrid conditions."

"Yes, well, I've been anxious to meet you, too, Dr. Coran. I knew your father for a time; excellent medical examiner."

"Thank you. He always spoke very highly of you, too, sir."

"I worked on a case with your father once; had to do with a bit of an epidemic here in the city back in the late fifties. After it was over, I offered him a job with my office, but he was stubborn; thought he could improve the military, so he stayed in. What a waste, I thought at the time, but he did make a difference in the way M.E.s in the service are perceived, wouldn't you agree?"

"Yes, he did, and he spoke of your work together often."

"I was so sorry to hear of his illness and his passing."

"Thank you, Dr. Darius."

"Well, we'd better earn our keep here. We'll have to talk later," he said. "As usual, the Claw has us up to our hips in gore for reasons unknown."

Darius offered her his jar of Vicks VapoRub to cut the stench, but she declined, pulling forth scented cotton balls, which she offered him.

"Oh, something new?"

"It beats Vicks for this."

"I'll try them next time."

"We've got to ensure that there will not be a next time."

"Right you are, but I fear otherwise, my dear."

The old coroner returned to his work, and for the first time Jessica allowed her eyes to take in the full extent of the damnable, godless crime against these women. They were filleted from throat to groin, their intestines removed and looped in the neat little coil that had become the trademark signature of the Claw, along with the crushed skulls where he had used his awful hammer. The two bodies had been robbed of their organs, she guessed, as in the past, and added to this horror was the missing gray matter from each skull. From the appearance of the heads, the brain tissue was removed after a surgical-like incision by a rough cutting instrument, most likely the same instrument used on the torsos. Once again the eyes had been removed, presumably eaten.

Jessica felt a wave of revulsion sweep over her, but she managed to maintain a firm hold on her emotions. She kneeled beside Dr. Darius, trying to keep her sanity and professional edge. Darius had found his amid this; she must do likewise.

Darius, as if to help her along, held up a kidney that he had fished from the soup of the younger woman's body.

"What do you make of this, Doctor?"

"She was suffering jaundice?"

"You might think so, but guess again."

The kidney was shriveled, tiny even, and the color was that of a several-days'-old pâté. "It's . . . it's not her kidney. It's the old woman's?"

"I think not," replied Darius.

"Whose is it, then?"

"That's the problem."

"Are you saying it doesn't belong to either victim?"

"That is what I believe, yes."

She stared into Darius' luminous eyes. She saw a little boy deep within him looking back at her, trapped there in his decrepit body. She liked him instantly, and she now understood his riddle. "The bastard brought it with him; it belongs to one of the earlier victims, maybe Mrs. Hamner?"

"Precisely. It will be tested for a match."

"Then he may have left other such items."

They began to look closely at the organs, finding that none were connected to the bodies. "This appears to be the young woman's," she told Darius when she lifted out the heart that had been posited inside the old woman.

"And this no doubt belongs to the young woman," Darius reciprocated.

Police standing about listening to the M.E.s instantly spread the word that the killer had switched the victims' organs like a child at play.

They found several other older, shriveled organs that matched neither victim. The Claw had made off with the fresher meat, as he had with the brain tissues.

Rychman told the others he didn't want a word of this to leak to the press, that it was the kind of information they could use at a later date, if and when they had the murdering psycho in custody.

"A three-way switch," said Darius, "and for what reason?"

"For the hell of it," suggested Rychman. "To shove it in our faces, that's why!"

Rychman informed them that the house belonged to the Olin woman and that the identity of the second woman remained unknown. He explained that the second body, along with the additional organs, had been transported to the house and dumped here.

"Such a fiend," said Darius, shaking his white head, strands of the thin hair falling forward. "And to think that he is one of us, one of our species."

"He seems drawn to the most defenseless, the gentlest of victims," Rychman added.

His words recalled something Jessica's father once told her when she had asked how a gentle person such as he could possibly want to work as a medical examiner, to investigate the crimes of the cruel and inhuman.

"My father used to say that the gentlest among us are fascinated with the cruelest among us. Maybe it works in reverse, too. That the cruelest among us are fascinated with the gentlest."

"That might well be our common denominator so far as the victims go. They were all shy, retiring, quiet types. Even the first victim, a streetwalker, was known for being a timid, reluctant streetwalker," replied Rychman.

The M.E.s returned to their work, and after a few hours an impatient Rychman came back, asking if they had found anything useful.

"Some fibers that don't appear to match the room, and we've been unable to find a match elsewhere here. They were clinging to the old woman, matted in the blood. We know she was killed elsewhere, and it appears she was wrapped in some sort of blanket or rug. We will analyze the fibers in detail back at the lab," Jessica explained.

"That doesn't tell us a whole lot," replied a frustrated Rychman.

"We're doing the best we can, Captain. Like your identifying the old woman, it will take time."

"Still searching."

"Dr. Darius has stated that he believes the killer could quite possibly be two men instead of one," she now added.

"Is that right, Dr. Darius?"

"That is what we have been speculating about, yes."

"I can't go on speculation. What makes you think so?"

"It's just a . . . a feeling," Jessica answered.

"A feeling?"

"At least until we can prove it otherwise through the microscopic evidence."

"Did you find two sets of bite marks? Two footprint sizes? Give," he ordered her.

"No, nothing concrete, but for a single man to pull this off—it just seems highly unlikely."

"Hell, I've thought of that myself, but if he's a big man, a strong man, my size, he could do it alone. I need more to go on than that."

Rychman's ire was getting the best of him. They were all tired and frustrated. "I can only tell you what my gut reaction is," she defended herself.

"From day one there's only been one set of fingerprints we've been able to match at the various scenes, one set of bite marks, according to your office, Darius, and as for hair and saliva samples, the story's the same. Now, in midstream, you're talking two instead of one? It makes no sense."

"It does if the second man takes extreme care, uses gloves, takes his portion away with him to cannibalize elsewhere," replied Darius, his eyes widening.

"But you've got nothing whatever to go on here, except your gut reaction."

"My gut reaction," Darius defended, "is the result of long meditation and maybe plenty of medication as well, Captain."

He didn't have an answer for this. "All right, how soon before the lab can come up with something to prove this theory? I don't want my people going down a wrong alley, searching for a killer couple, going through all kinds of gyrations on nothing other than a hunch I can't justify."

The Claw already had the NYPD looking like the Keystone Kops, and Rychman didn't want to add to that bleak picture.

Dr. Darius groaned and Rychman helped him to his feet. Jessica's legs were stiff from kneeling, and she was also exhausted. She followed the old coroner's lead, standing and stretching; she, too, had taken all the samples she wanted from the crime scene. Everything else must wait for the autopsy room.

"Well, Dr. Coran, you've got your samples and specimens, and I've got mine; between the two of us, we're going to give this sonofabitch a run for his money. Oh, by the way, should your specimens reveal any new hair samples, check what you've found here against the ones I have on file first. Saves time and keeps you from looking like a fool later. Which reminds me, young lady, you had best file samples of your hair with the lab, too, unless you want Rychman here or some other gung-ho cop arresting you as the Claw."

It was sound advice and standard procedure for M.E.s to have fingerprints, hair, and blood samples on file with the lab, so that stray prints and hair found at a crime scene could be ruled out right away as those of the examiner.

Dr. Simon Archer came through the door and went directly to Darius and scolded him. "Why didn't you tell them to contact me, Luther? I could have handled this; I can't believe you've been here since three this morning."

Archer's concern for his aged colleague was touching, Jessica thought as she made for the door, but Darius didn't quite find it so. He returned Archer's kindness with a bitter outburst, saying, "God damn you, Simon, I'm not a fucking cripple. I can do my job. You needn't have rushed down here. Who's minding the office?"

Rychman and Jessica left the two doctors to war it out. As he walked Jessica to the car, Rychman told her that he had to hang there a bit longer, something about a possible witness with a very shaky story that he doubted would pan out.

Darius came out of the house, joining Jessica at Lou Pierce's squad car, asking, "Is this carriage going downtown?"

"You got it, Doc," replied Lou.

"May I join you, Dr. Coran?"

"Absolutely."

"Sorry about that outburst. Archer doesn't mean to be such a pain in the ass, he just is. He thinks he's doing the decrepit old man right by disqualifying me from fieldwork. Meanwhile, we've gotten nowhere on this case. It's not that Simon isn't a good, thorough man, but he simply lacks that special something. Your father had it, and I suspect you do, too, Dr. Coran, that special . . . ahhh." He searched for the word.

"Imagination?" she asked.

"Precisely, yes. Imagination and instinct."

"Both very necessary in our business."

"Dull man, really, that Archer, but he means well, and I suppose he does his best. Perkins was a greater disappointment, actually, not finishing out his term with us. Ahh, well . . ."

They got into the backseat of the car after depositing their medical bags in the trunk. She asked him, "Will you be pursuing the case from here out, Doctor?"

"So long as my health allows, Doctor."

"It would be wonderful to work closely with you, sir."

"Butter the other side, my dear. That feels good."

"But I mean it in the most sincere way, Dr. Darius."

"Me, so out of step with the times I didn't even know about your scented cotton balls?" He laughed and she realized that he'd been joking the entire time. "Fact is, it would do me a world of good to work with you, Jessica Coran. I've read everything about your case of the vampire killer, what was his name? Madson, Manson?"

"Matisak."

"Oh, yes ... vile creature that one. Not wholly unlike our Claw."

Twelve

❧

Rychman was a frustrated man. The C.P. had him exactly where he wanted him, on the firing line. The Claw case made anyone connected with it look the fool; it could not have been better for Eldritch if he had planned it himself for this election year. By maneuvering Rychman into the catbird seat, he had both the perfect fall guy and a way to make his competition look bad. Maybe Eldritch was the better man for the job, after all; he was certainly the better politician. Where was he now? Miles from Scarsdale, that was for sure.

The half-baked notion of making an arrest was another fine stroke of genius on Eldritch's part. Arresting Conrad Shaw would make Rychman look as if he were leading a witch-hunt. He had to find some new *some*thing, some sort of lead, anything, if he planned to survive. But for now, feeling tired and weary, he slumped against his car and waited for the rest of his task force people to report back to him what they had, or more likely had not, learned from the surrounding neighborhood. He himself had learned that the Olin woman was quiet and retiring, a model neighbor, hardly spoke a word above a whisper. Those who knew her best didn't really seem to know her at all, but there was some hint of money problems, and her wealth seemed an issue. As for the old woman, still no word.

His mind raced back over every victim of the Claw, trying to take a new tack, to think about two killers. It was like sailing against the wind to pursue an idea that opposed what seemed concrete fact. It was always the hardest part of police work to keep options open, to keep the sea of information from solidifying too quickly into one idea. For so long now, everyone had assumed the brutal killer was a single individual . . . but what if Jessica and Darius were right?

113

And why couldn't they provide him with something un
equivocal and binding, some proof he could believe in com
pletely? Something other than hunches and suppositions
however informed?

Maybe these murders weren't even the work of the Claw
Rychman thought in disgust. The fact it was Scarsdale and
the fact the killer or killers had deviated by brutalizing two
victims in one night made Rychman suspicious that they were
copy cat killings. Someone reading the nonstop news cover
age on the Claw could have planned and executed the double
murder to make it appear the work of the Claw, thereby
throwing suspicion away from himself.

It had not helped matters that the newspaper reporter
across the city had been able to piece together almost all o
the various clues that pointed to the work of the Claw
Throughout the investigation, they lifted one detail from one
precinct, another from a second and so on, while the mayo
and the C.P. were gabbing about gag orders.

Meanwhile advantage the Claw.

So much wasted effort and time. Translating into eigh
wasted lives, he thought. When he was a kid he had seen the
movie *Psycho,* and it had left an indelible mark on him. I
changed the way movies dealt with bad guys and heroine
when Bates murdered Janet Leigh in the shower scene. There
was no boyfriend running in at the last moment to save her
no cops or cavalry to the rescue, and somehow, even as a
child Rychman understood the simple truth that *real life* sel
dom meant justice or fairness, or saved-in-the-nick-of-time
happy endings. Still, he had wanted to be a cop; he'd wanted
to be one of the good guys, and do whatever he could wher
ever he could to at least make reality bearable. And what had
it gotten him? A divorce, the estrangement of his kids and a
nasty fight ahead for Eldritch's job, *if* he had the stamina to
go through with it. There were a lot of people who were be
hind him, but most of these had their own agendas. "Hell,"
he moaned as he opened the car door and sprawled out on the
back seat, hoping to catch a few winks.

His detectives were still rattling doors, asking questions
They were all coming up empty-handed. The woman lived

alone, never had relatives or visitors over, was as quiet and unimposing as a church mouse. Neighbors used to see her waiting for the bus on the corner.

Then who in hell was the old woman? What was the connection? Was there a connection, or was the Claw having them all on once more? Some sense of humor, he thought. But there must be something that attracted this demonic killer to his victims in the first place; something the two of them had in common, some shred of a connection. But what could it be?

He played over the similarities and the differences again in his head. All the victims were women who were alone when they were attacked. In no instance had the killer dared attack a woman in the company of a man. The attacks appeared random, but he knew that random violence was unlikely, that what at first appeared random very often was far from it. No, the Claw had a plan, however bizarre the plan might be. There was nothing random about the killer's obvious decision to murder women only. The bastard either feared men or had no interest in feeding on male organs. Why? The bastard was a coward at heart, afraid to attack even two women together, it would appear, since the new victims had been attacked at separate locations.

"Captain, Captain!" Lou Pierce interrupted his thoughts. "We've got word on the old woman."

Rychman had no idea how long he had been lying in the car, but a glance at his clock told him it was almost 6 A.M. "A positive ID, Lou?"

"Amelia Phillips. The super in her building reported her missing. Her place was searched a few hours ago by some guys in the 23rd. The place was a mess and there was blood, but no body. Missing Persons put two and two together, had someone go down to the morgue to ID her, and *voilà*."

"Good to know somebody around here can still put two and two together. All right, hop in and let's have a look at her place."

"You want me to drive, Captain?"

"Good idea, Lou. Dr. Coran get back okay?"

"I dropped her and Dr. Darius off at the morgue."

"She'll wanta hear about this. See if you can get dispatch to put us through."

But dispatch was unable to reach her or Darius. The two had seemingly disappeared. Only Simon Archer was available to take the call. He took the address and said he would be right behind them, and that he was sorry but he didn't know where the other two M.E.s had gone.

On the way to the second crime scene, a Brooklyn apartment out of the 23rd Precinct's jurisdiction, but not out of the jurisdiction of the citywide task force, Rychman learned that Amelia Phillips was a live-alone with multiple health problems that'd turned her into a recluse. When she did venture out, she might visit the corner store, the free clinic or the neighborhood park where she fed popcorn and seeds to squirrels and pigeons.

Once at her apartment, Rychman could see at a glance just how close to the bone the woman lived. Her fridge was bare, and her cupboard was scantily stocked with a handful of tuna and soup cans, a box of Saltines and a bag of Fig Newtons gone stale according to O'Toole, whom Alan had found munching in the kitchen. The woman's furniture was early Salvation Army and had come with the apartment, but she kept the place neat and orderly, *a place for everything and everything in its place.* So the ugly red stain on the hardwood floor, indicating the likeliest place where Amelia Phillips had died, seemed that much more alien here in this place she called home.

No forced entry—nothing to indicate she had any reason to fear her attacker any more than the Olin woman seemed to have had—gave Rychman a glimmer of hope. If both women knew their attacker, then some thread of commonality existed between these two victims which had gone unnoticed among the previous victims. Somewhere in each woman's past she had crossed the path of the Claw before last night, and when he came to call, each in turn had allowed him inside. Perhaps he was a neighbor, someone to be trusted, someone clever and cunning who had targeted these women in anything other than a random way after all.

"This . . . this is dreadful," whispered the building superintendent who'd crept in behind the detectives. Rychman thought the super was understandably upset by a tenant's death until he heard the man telling Lou that it was going to be hell to get the bloodstains up if they were allowed to remain much longer, and this would make renting out the place even more difficult in these recessionary times. He also complained of a missing rug.

"What kind of a rug?" asked Rychman sharply.

"An expensive one, Oriental."

"Hers or yours?"

"Mine . . . at least, it was."

"Whataya mean, was? Either it belonged to you or it didn't."

"I didn't get it in writing. It was the only thing she had of worth, and she purchased her last month's rent with it. I figured it lent the place a touch of class, and if she moved out and it stayed, I figured . . . well, I figured . . ."

"I get the picture, Mr. ahhh . . ."

"Gwinn, Donald W.," he told Lou, who was jotting information down on a notepad.

"And the rug was here the last time you saw her here?" Rychman asked.

"It was."

"And when was that, sir?"

"Yesterday afternoon. Then I knocked on the door about nine, but I got no answer. I was supposed to look at some pipes; been puttin' it off. So I think it's odd she don't answer, on account she's always in after dark, you know, and so I tried again at ten, because the next day's my day off, and I didn't want her calling down and disturbing me. So when she didn't answer again, I used my passkey, and this is what I find."

"But you didn't call the police until ten-twenty?"

"I did some looking around. Thought she might've been trying to ditch out on me. Another month's rent was coming due, and the rug was gone. I figured the blood was just her way of, you know, throwing me off. She was smart, that old bag. She'd been a teacher at some college once down South, and she was putting me on all the time. Used to be we had a nice relationship when her checks came in on time."

"Welfare checks?"

"That and sometimes she got money from her daughter, or so she claimed. That's her on the bureau." He pointed to a picture of a rather plain young face. Beside this was a picture of the same young woman with a man, their arms entwined.

"That's the daughter. Never comes around."

Rychman stared at the black-and-white photos, realizing they were somewhat old. He slipped one from its holder and scanned the back for any notations. There were none, only the marks of the processor and the date, 1952.

"This isn't her daughter," Rychman concluded.

"What?"

"This is her, when she was young."

"Damn, then the old girl did have me fooled," said Gwinn. "According to her, that was her daughter and son-in-law, some big-shot lawyer in Florida where the kids lived with her newborn grandchild."

"A boy or a girl, Mr. Gwinn?" asked Rychman, shaking his head.

Rychman considered the fact the killer hadn't bothered to clean up after himself, but the amount of blood on the floor was not enough to account for the condition of Mrs. Phillips' remains. "She was obviously carried out of here rolled in *your* rug, Mr. Gwinn, which has not been located." He turned to Pierce. "Lou, I want our people to fan out and crisscross this neighborhood and speak to everyone within sight of this place about seeing a man carrying a rug out of here. You got that?"

"I'm on it, Captain."

Rychman recalled what Darius had said about finding several unusual fibers matted in the old woman's blood. It was like two puzzle pieces had just gone neatly into place, and it gave Alan Rychman a minor feeling of hope.

"And where the hell's Dr. Archer?" he bellowed as Lou started out.

Archer showed up in the doorway at the same moment. "Sorry, but that driver I got was timid about getting here."

Rychman nodded, knowing full-well that anytime a coroner was called out, he had to be escorted by an officer who also escorted the M.E. and his findings back to the morgue. No one was above suspicion when it came to evidence in a murder case, so there were formal rules of conduct for everyone on the crime scene, thanks mainly to Dr. Darius.

"You can get out of here for now," Rychman told the superintendent. "It's all yours, Dr. Archer."

"Sorry I couldn't locate Darius for you, but I think the all-nighter took a lot out of him. Heard he was recuperating with orders not to be disturbed. He'll likely be back at the lab later. Leastways, that's what I was told."

Archer's voice held a subtle edge. He probably felt he should have handled the scene at Scarsdale. Alan knew Archer was in line for Darius' job if and when Darius finally called it quits.

"Well, we're glad to have you here, Doc." Alan tried to reassure him. "Anybody but Perkins, I always say."

"High praise," joked Archer. He got down to business, opening his black bag and taking blood scrapings, searching for fibers, fingerprints, hairs, anything he could bag up for microscopic analysis back at his lab.

Rychman took this opportunity to investigate the room further, careful to steer clear of where Archer painstakingly worked. Rychman stared at Mrs. Phillips' card table and single chair, wondering what had happened between her and her long-ago husband; what had driven them apart and left her alone. Fights, money, drugs, lust, dishonesty, divorce or death? Life was brutal. He parted a curtain that acted as a divider and saw an alcove being used as a bedroom. A single bed with neatly tucked corners stared back at him, apparently untouched by the murderer.

Rychman searched the coverlet for any tell-tale signs, and when he saw what might be a stain, he got excited.

He called Archer in to look at the stain. Archer was skeptical, but he took a pair of scissors and cut around the stain, giving it wide berth, then placed the tiny patch of cloth into a specimen envelope to examine closely later. "Nothing's getting by me," muttered Archer, "but don't hold your breath on this one, Captain."

"Understood."

"Still, you've got a good eye for this kind of work."

"I've had enough experience, God help me."

Rychman continued his tour of the little apartment. Yellowed plaster on the walls was crisscrossed by occasional cracks, apparently painted over at some time only to return to haunt the occupant. The small icebox sat like a silent sentinel over the horror that had occurred here, atop it another photo of the woman's so-called daughter, herself at a young age. Wedged between the corner and the wall was a bag of bird feed, half-empty. Rychman saw a roach peeking from around the bag, and its antennae twitching nervously and avoiding any contact with the blood of the victim, as it made its determined way into the shadows.

Rychman knew from experience that a body—whether fit or frail—was heavy and cumbersome. The super's missing rug likely meant that Mrs. Phillips had been concealed within and carried down the back steps and into the darkness; in fact, a blood trail indicated as much. Did the killer have help in transporting the body? He speculated on the probables here. It seemed more tantalizing than ever to adopt Jessica Coran's idea that the ungodly work of the Claw could well be the work of a pair of killers, especially since the madman's handiwork had taken on this added dimension of two victims in a single night. The creeping notion of an innocent-looking decoy entered Rychman's thinking, a dupe who might do the Claw's bidding, someone he could control, and someone who presented no threat to others, someone Mrs. Phillips and Mrs. Olin might, without fear, open their doors to.

"Christ," he muttered to himself, "maybe Jessica's theory has merit." The hypothesis was tempting for another reason: if his detectives accepted the supposition, they could narrow the field, focusing on criminals known to have worked in tandem before. He'd give it more thought, talk to Jessica again, and perhaps at the next task-force meeting, which had now been postponed until tomorrow morning at 6 A.M., he'd pursue it.

While teams of detectives scoured the neighborhood, he and Lou Pierce found a nearby diner and ordered up breakfasts. Just as the steaming second cup of coffee, their bacon and eggs with toast and jelly arrived, so did the TV and radio reporters. It was already a long day.

Thirteen

e

Jessica Coran and Dr. Luther Darius had enjoyed a peaceful breakfast. Darius had shut off his beeper, as was his habit when he had had enough. He'd announced the fact with a mischievous grin. While they'd eaten, they'd been treated to a delightful sunrise in New York Harbor where the tugboats bellowed out their intentions and large freighters and cruise ships were assembled below the watching eyes of thousands of sea gulls.

As they walked back to the lab, their heads cleared of the spiderwebs that had accumulated from lack of sleep. Each was anxious to get deeply involved in the forensics information they had gathered, and Jessica was particularly interested in hearing from J.T. in Quantico.

They spoke of many things, but the conversation somehow worked its way back to Darius' physical condition and his present situation with the coroner's office.

"They're shopping around for a replacement, but haven't done one so well. Who wants the headaches? I gave it the best years of my life, and what happens? The moment I have a bit of a health problem, they want to discard me like yesterday's newspaper."

"I'd say a stroke is more than a little health problem, Doctor."

He frowned. "It was a small stroke."

"And now they've asked you to return?"

"Until they can find a suitable replacement."

"No one could replace you."

"We're all expendable, Dr. Coran, believe me."

She knew what he meant. She felt her relationship with her own superiors was shaky and she mentioned this.

"Then you have some idea how they can make an old man feel."

They spoke no more, simply enjoying the walk and the company.

When they arrived at the lab, they found the place buzzing and learned the search for them had been on. Apparently the police had located and entered the apartment of the elderly woman, and it was clear that she had been killed by the Claw in her Brooklyn apartment—miles from Scarsdale.

"I want to get out there," she told Dr. Darius.

"Archer is there; he will do a fine job. You should get to work here."

She took a deep breath, considering this. "Perhaps you're right."

He smiled. "I am right. I am always right."

A few hours later Jessica stopped work and went to the telephone in the office that was temporarily hers. She dialed FBI headquarters in Quantico. Her assistant, J.T., came on with a glum tone, and after the amenities, she asked him what was wrong.

"I got back this morning and found your first-priority case was back-shelved."

"What?"

"I had Glenn working on the materials you forwarded, thought all was going well, and then found out O'Rourke ordered him off it and onto something she called more pressing."

"God damn her. If I didn't know any better, I'd swear she was trying to drive me out. Undermining every damned thing I do, lately."

"Let's not get paranoid, huh, Jess?"

"It's paranoia that's got me as far as I am."

"Not this time, Jess. You must've heard about Senator Keillor's death?"

"Heart attack, right?"

"They're not so sure anymore. Seems he had some track marks."

"Drugs? Christ, wasn't he on the President's Drug-free USA Committee?"

"He was."

"And so Glenn Hale was yanked to study his tracks instead of my teeth marks?"

"That's right."

"Well, Hale's not the only guy at Quantico who knows flesh marks. Get Kinnon or—"

"Kinnon's in Africa."

"—or Springer. Springer's had some experience in—"

"Jess, I'm doing it myself—"

"You?"

"And I'll get your results to you this afternoon."

"All right, J.T."

"Got the specimens in the SEM right now."

"No second chances here." She knew that the SEM destroyed the evidence as it photographed, bombarding the tissue with a shower of electrons. If the photos were marred, there'd be no evidence and no way to tell if the teeth marks sent J.T. were identical or not.

"Not to worry, Jess. Now, how're you doing in New York?"

"Not so good. Two more victims last night."

"Jesus . . . two . . ."

"Yeah, our boy—or boys—is or *are* getting bolder."

"This guy's shaping up to be another Matisak."

She was silent a moment, thinking of Matisak's involvement in her case, wondering again how he had arrived at the same theory as she. Maybe it took a madman to understand a madman, and if that was the case, did it mean that she, too, was mad?

She hoped the syllogism held no water.

"You still there, Jess?"

"Yeah, J.T., and thanks. I'll be hearing from you soon, then?"

The moment she hung up the phone, she decided that as much as she loved J.T., she'd better start doing what she could on her own. She returned to the two corpses brought in from Scarsdale. Dr. Darius was overseeing the autopsy of the younger woman, with Jessica assisting.

The autopsy took less than the usual four to five hours because the body had already been eviscerated, usually the job of the coroner. The autopsy was, however, complicated by the fact that a number of the organs did not belong to the subject. It made for a most uneven examination of the victim.

Where appropriate, they had returned the correct organs to the second body, the process making Jessica feel like a reanimator, a Dr. Frankenstein attempting to force order onto death and chaos.

Dr. Darius, by comparison, seemed composed, at ease, in his element. All of her professional life Jessica had been looked upon by those outside of medicine—reporters, lawyers, even rugged cops—as something of a ghoul for being capable of doing her work amid the most horrific of conditions. But she now had to bow to Darius as far more detached and capable than she.

But suddenly her estimation was qualified. The body jerked in a spasm and Darius jumped in response, laughing nervously. "I . . . I'll never get used to that," he said before continuing on with his report. He was fastidious and sharp, she thought, as she watched him work.

"It appears the slash marks came from a right-handed man from across this way." He pointed to the body's right shoulder and drew an imaginary, jagged diagonal line toward her navel. "The killer did this three times. It seems his favorite number, as it corresponds with all earlier victims. As can be seen by the vital reaction around the rents, the bruised blue, the victim was very much alive when she was ripped open."

The overhead microphone taped the words automatically. It also taped Dr. Darius' cough and the sound of him clearing his throat. The typescript would eliminate all nonessential information, and copies of the autopsy reports on both victims would be on Alan Rychman's desk before 3 P.M., if the second autopsy went as smoothly as this one was going.

She noticed that Dr. Darius worked with a coverlet over the head of the victims. This was not unusual, especially for

nan of his generation. For many years it had been standard
practice, something about gentility and concern for the dead,
respect.

It also cut down on the unnerving problem of having
closed pupils popping open, giving the autopsiest the chilling
impression that the deceased was watching him or her while
t work. In this case, with the eyes removed, it was even
more disturbing.

Now that she was older, Jessica didn't think it was such a
bad idea. The older she got, the more superstitious, too, she
conceded, feeling the thick crystal gem that'd been given to
her by a dear friend who promised that it would bring her, if
not luck, comfort, and when she did hold it in her palm, feeling the heat from her hand rise and ebb like a tide, it gave her
pause, and calmed her nerves.

Still, regardless of Dr. Darius' obvious aversion for the
corpse's eyeless face, the head was part of a complete autopsy, and he would not only have to unveil the head, but
stare into the cavities with a brilliant light.

But he didn't do this. He asked Jessica if she would see to
the stitches, now that most of the woman's organs had been
returned to her, and he began to walk away.

"Doctor . . ."

"Yes, my dear?"

"What about the throat, the head, the eyes?"

"Hammerblow to the forehead, occipital lobe. It's on the
tape, Dr. Coran."

"But in a complete autopsy—"

"No need to disfigure this poor soul any more than she already has been. I am . . . we are . . . done here. Close her up
and let's get started on the other one." Darius went out.

She uncovered the face, finding the woman's eye cavities
disconcerting. Jessica ran her eyes along the throat and found
multiple bite wounds there, all mentioned in the autopsy, but
she wanted to take the bite marks for more intensive study,
and that meant cutting the sections out of the dead woman's
throat with a scalpel.

Maybe New York is unfortunate to have Dr. Darius back in

on the case, she thought. Maybe he's too old for this kind of
thing. Maybe . . . maybe . . .

"What're you doing there?" It was Darius and his face was
near white, his cold stare holding her. "We must get on," he
said, softening his tone.

"I want to take these bite marks, study them in more detail."

"You've *got* bite marks. More, in fact, than we can deal
with. Didn't you say you sent some off to Washington?"

"Yes, but we have to be sure these match the others, that
it's the work of the same man, or men."

"I suppose you're right. I just thought we could spare the
woman any further . . . indignity . . ."

"I understand and appreciate your concern—"

He was nodding as he interrupted her, "But she won't feel
a thing, I know . . . I know."

Darius had a cup of juice in his hands, bloodlike in color—
cranberry, she guessed from the aroma. He popped a capsule
and took a swallow.

She stared a moment too long.

"Nitro," he said, "for the ticker."

Nitroglycerin, she thought, averting her eyes. That meant
his attack had been far more serious than he had let on.

"My body has, as they say, turned against me."

Jessica took samples from the dead woman's throat as she
had from the thighs, the buttocks and arms earlier. Bite marks
in the entrails appeared rather useless as impressions, so she
stuck with the others.

"If we have two killers, the teeth marks ought to show it,"
she said.

"Not necessarily," he countered. "Not if only one of them
does the biting. I think we have to concentrate on hair, fiber
and particle samples, Jessica."

"And what about the weapon? What kind of a . . . an instrument could possibly cause the rents opening the body?"

"The answer to that eventually leads to the killer."

Jessica finished taking her samples, dropping each into
fixative formula in various small jars beside the autopsy ta

ble. Dr. Darius buzzed for a pair of attendants to replace the Olin cadaver with the elderly Mrs. Phillips now.

The Phillips autopsy was as painstaking as the previous one, for once again the missing organs, as noted at the crime scene, caused untold problems. Some of the organs removed from Miss Olin had been those of a much older person, and now some of Mrs. Phillips' parts were proving to be too young for her; even so, not all of Miss Olin's parts could be accounted for. Despite the monster's ugly idea of hide-and-seek, he'd obviously been tempted and had either eaten or carried off some of his carrion with him.

With his every word being recorded, Dr. Darius said, "Whoever our maniac is, he bloody well knows his anatomy. He's extracted every major organ. No small task in and of . . . What the hell?" He paused, his gloved fingers probing Mrs. Phillips' chest cavity. "There's something odd here."

Jessica was instantly curious. "What is it, Doctor?"

Something foreign materialized in Darius' hand and even the magician was startled at his trick. It appeared to be a small patch of cloth or square of cardboard covered in dark blood. "My God, what've we here?" he asked.

She reached out for it with a pair of forceps, gingerly taking it between the prongs. "We've got to rush this to your photo-document section, Doctor."

"My thinking, precisely. I'll alert Lathrope of your coming."

"It could prove very valuable."

Darius' eyes spoke of his disbelief. Finally he said, "You don't suppose . . ."

"What?"

"That there might've been something like this in other victims? Say, the Olin woman? The Hamner woman?"

"Recall them," she replied. "Thoroughly search any of the victims you haven't released for burial."

He nodded, obviously shaken. She asked, "Are you all right, Doctor?"

He nodded again, sweat beading his brow. "I've got a grip on it. Go now; go quickly."

But she hesitated. He looked pale. "Get some rest before you do anything else, Doctor, and wait for Archer, okay?"

"Perhaps you're right. Go now! I'm fine, really, I am."

As he began dialing the head of his photo-document section, Jessica grabbed her cane from where it was propped against a lab table and started through the door. She bumped into Dr. Archer, who stared at the odd item between the bloody forceps she was holding before her. A dark fluid dripped from the matted paper camouflaged by the soupy blood and bile it had been fished from.

"What the hell's this?" asked Archer, curious.

"No time to explain, Doctor." She rushed past him for the stairwell and the floor below.

Archer looked across the room at Darius, who beamed at him, saying, "I think we may have finally gotten a break in the case of the Claw, Simon. And now I will need your help. We have to reopen the Olin and the Hamner cadavers."

"What for? What's going on?" asked the confused Archer.

"Hurry, come with me, and I'll explain everything," said Darius, who went for the freezer compartments. He had composed himself and was anxious now to get on with the work at hand.

Fourteen

❧

Jessica couldn't help thinking that she held between the pincers of the forceps a clue that might break the case wide open. It had to be something left by the killer, intentionally. Her heart was beating so fast and her hands shaking so much that she feared she'd drop the paper before she got to the door marked "Documents." People in the hallway watched her as she rushed by, curious and wondering. At the end of the hall, she saw the reporter that had confronted her in the garage two days before, and for a moment their eyes met, telling him she had something important dangling at the end of the forceps and dripping a string of gruel.

She rushed through the door, her cane batting out her arrival. She didn't have to shout for help; everyone was surrounding her. The document guys were all aflutter, anxious to be involved in such a high-level case.

"Walter Lathrope," the head of the department said, cursorily introducing himself. "And you must be Dr. Coran."

After his initial, cursory inspection of the bloodied paper, Dr. Lathrope assured Jessica that his lab could free the message, but that it would take some time. And it did.

The paper was ordinary 8½″ by 11″ copy paper, 20-pound weight, grain long, color white. It had been tightly folded, and the document experts were opening it slowly so they wouldn't tear the wet, spoiled paper, trying desperately to keep it all in one piece. It was placed in an air-drying compartment with bubble gloves at each end. The experts had their hands in the gloves and were manipulating the paper with the pincherlike fingers on the ends. The gloves made her wonder about the Claw's awful, flesh-rending weapon or tool.

129

Under the force of the drying air in the compartment, the paper began slowly to regain its shape and bond, but it took another twenty minutes for it to be unfolded completely. There were words on one side, but blood and bile had been absorbed by the fiber, obstructing most of them.

"It's some kind of message, all right," said Lathrope.

Jessica had been pacing, drinking coffee, and she had telephoned for Rychman to join her here, just in case.

The handwriting was large, childish and done in green ink. She saw loops and swirls like a roller coaster, but much of the writing was covered by stains that ran the entire length of what looked like a child's poem. Her heart sank. Maybe it wasn't something from the killer, after all; maybe it was something picked up in Olin's house, a note from a niece of nephew, that the sadistic killer had simply crushed into her gaping body as some kind of final, sick prank.

"Can you clean it up?" she asked, staring.

"I believe we can," said Lathrope, who disappeared with his assistant into a darkened room, Jessica following. He placed the piece of paper below a Tensor lamp, on a table encircled by enormous magnifying glasses on robotic swivel arms, and the two men continued their painstaking work.

They began the slow, careful removal of the dried blood and other matter clinging to the paper, concentrating on the areas where they could see green ink.

"Green," she said aloud. "Why green?"

"The color of hope," said Lathrope with a twinkle in his eye. Lathrope was a head taller than she, with large glasses and an elongated face. He looked the quintessence of the scientist. His partner, by comparison, was a short, balding man with round shoulders that looked perpetually hunched over.

"Can you make out any of the words?" she asked just as Alan Rychman joined them.

"Understand you have something important here?"

"Maybe . . . maybe," she cautioned.

Lathrope studied a line of the green-lettered verse, the first to be completely cleared of the obstructing grunge. "It is some sort of poem . . ."

"Poem?" Rychman almost shouted.

Lathrope began reading aloud. "My . . . my teeth will have your eyes . . . And feed on your . . . banal cries."

"Doesn't sound like a child writing to his aunt," she said.

"What?" asked Rychman.

"Never mind. Dr. Lathrope, how long before you can extricate the entire message?"

"Give us another thirty minutes; we'll go to a dissolving solution."

"Good . . . good . . ." Jessica replied.

Rychman escorted her out, asking, "What's this all about?"

"We found what appears to be a message from the killer lodged into the Phillips body, Alan."

"A poem? Now our creep is writing poetry to us? Left inside the victim? Christ, I want to fry this bastard."

"I think it's a new ripple. I think he wants to talk, to communicate."

"Talk, communicate . . . sounds familiar. What is it makes these lunatics want to buddy up and talk, like maybe it'd be nice to have a beer with the sonofa—"

Rychman stopped in midsentence, seeing Jim Drake at the other end of the hall on a telephone. "That creep gets ahold of this, it'll be in the evening paper, you know that?"

"I haven't spoken to him."

"You don't have to speak to him. He's got rabbit ears."

"Come on. Let's get a bite at the machines downstairs."

"Where'd you and Darius disappear to this morning, if you don't mind my asking?"

"Not at all." She launched into a description of the best time she'd had in New York since her arrival.

"Hmmmm," replied Rychman as they entered the elevator, "better than the fun we had at the shooting range?"

"Let's just say I didn't feel any tension with the good doctor, no expectations, no games."

"And you do with me?"

"Some, yes, especially the last time I entered an elevator with you."

"Hey, I'm sorry 'bout that, really. I . . . It was the wine and . . . and you . . . being alone with you."

"I'll try to take that as a compliment."
"You should."

Dr. Lathrope's secretary, Marilyn Khoen, whispered into the telephone receiver. "That's all I know. No, don't push me on this, not unless you can guarantee . . . No, no way. I'm not going to do that."

At the other end of the line, James W. Drake III was making promises the reporter wasn't sure he could keep, but if he could show a break in the Claw case, he believed he could write his own ticket. Hell, he could practically guarantee Marilyn a job with the *Times*, maybe as *his* assistant . . . but it all depended on the nature of the contents of the piece of paper fished from the body of one of the victims. He needed details, facts only Marilyn could secure for him. He knew it was asking a lot, but it could also mean a great deal. Everything was riding on what the Claw did these days.

He realized that the deadly Claw had, in effect, the power to make or break any number of careers in the city, from lowly reporter to mayor to commissioner of police. He wondered how it would work out for Alan Rychman, whom he didn't particularly like, anyway.

"Marilyn, sweetheart, it's for me, for Jimmy, huh?"

He waited for her reply. When it didn't come, he urged her on. "Whataya say? Come on, you can trust me."

"You're making me feel like . . . like a damned whore, Jimmy, and I deserve better from you!"

"No, no, baby, I'd never do that. I love you, and I want to make things right between us, the way they used to be, remember? Remember when we took the boat out on the harbor? Remember how it was, doing it at sea? Remember the salt air and, and—"

"What're you saying? That we can get back together if—"

"I'm saying I'll be eternally grateful, babe, eternally."

"Is that like a marriage proposal?"

"I'll get you a good job at the paper."

"I . . . I don't know."

He was about to slam the phone down in frustration, but he held onto it and calmed himself instead. "You'd be doing the city a favor. When they hide all the facts about this maniac running around the city ... Marilyn, a killer that feeds on women like you, babe, slices and dices and actually eats their flesh ... I'm telling you, honey, the public's got a right to know, to protect themselves, to be on the lookout, and you ... you're in a unique position to help see that happens. You might even save a life."

"I ... I don't know."

But he could tell by the change in her tone that she did know. And he knew that he had her where he wanted her, hooked on the idea.

"Just start keeping notes. Anything you overhear, anything relating to what Dr. Coran is working on, okay?"

"I like Dr. Lathrope. It's just these all-nighters and you never know when you're on call."

"Baby, you think I don't know that? It's got to be grueling for you ... grueling. With me, it'd be strictly nine to five." What was one more lie? he told himself.

When Jessica and Alan Rychman returned to the documents division, they were hopeful that something useful might await them. Lathrope was staring at the supposed words of the killer, a scowl disfiguring his horse-sized face, his glasses perched at the end of his nose as he crinkled it in consternation.

"Makes no damned sense, Rychman. See for yourselves."

Rychman and Jessica read from the sheet of paper, now safely under a blue light that illuminated bloodstains, separating the messy stains from the ink lettering and the plethora of fingerprints that lay beneath. The words were bizarre. She began to read them aloud, trying to pick up on the meter.

> "My teeth will have your eyes
> And feed on your banal cries ...
> Your sins will be eaten away
> That you might live another day ...
> The Claw is no name for him
> Who gives you eternal life
> By eating away your sin ...

My rabid, hungry sin-feast
Will out in the end
To give you eternal peace."

It was signed "Ovid, Divine Protector."

"Christ, what're we supposed to surmise from this?" asked Rychman. "That it's the work of one guy, or a *collaborative* effort?"

He could not hide his disappointment.

"There's more here than meets the eye. We need to get a shrink's advice, but I'd be willing to bet there're some clues to this guy's head in all this," Jessica said.

"We got a guy named Ames, fresh from the Chicago Police Department," said Rychman. "Supposed to be a helluva head man. Let's get a few copies of this made," Rychman replied.

Lathrope called his secretary in and handed her the poem in its glass case, carefully holding it by its sides. "Careful with this, Marilyn. Make a few copies for Captain Rychman."

"This stays in-house, people," Rychman told Lathrope and his assistant. "Who else knows about this?" he asked Jessica.

"Only Dr. Darius and Archer. Archer saw me with it when I left the lab, and I assume Dr. Darius told him about it."

"Good, let's see it stays that way, everyone."

"You got it, Captain," said Lathrope.

Marilyn returned with several copies and Rychman quickly confiscated them.

"We'll get what we can from the original," said Lathrope. "See if these prints can be matched."

"Thanks for dropping everything for me, Dr. Lathrope," said Jessica, shaking his hand.

"Not to give it a second thought. A most interesting challenge, actually."

His assistant piped in from the other room where he had started back to work on another project, saying, "It's a wonder Darius fished it from the dead woman's insides at all, from what I saw down there in Scarsdale."

"Yes, it was quite a surprise for him; something of a shock," Jessica answered.

She and Rychman said their goodbyes and were soon making their way to see Dr. Richard Ames, the police psychiatrist. Not knowing anything about Ames, she faxed a copy to Quantico for O'Rourke to turn over to a psychological profiling team there.

Rychman had no objections. "We need all the help we can get with this Claw or *Claws*."

Dr. Richard Ames was a very tall, broad-shouldered, handsome black man with fine features and huge hands, which appeared both gentle and dexterous. Jessica judged him a basketball star in college, and a number of plaques and trophies behind his desk corroborated her guess. Ames got up from behind the desk and offered them comfortable, large leather chairs that fronted a window overlooking the Avenue of the Americas in lower Manhattan. He enjoyed a private practice here and charitably gave sixteen hours a week, at ninety dollars an hour, to the NYPD. His credentials were impressive and he had worked extensively with psychotics, sociopaths and serial killers.

Rychman had informed Jessica that Ames had been instrumental in the Handyman case some years before in Chicago. The maniacal killer in that case had only indirectly murdered his victims. They had died of shock after coming out of a hypnotic state induced by the charming murderer, who had left them intact, except for their hands. When the man was finally caught, he had a collection of human hands the likes of which could not be comprehended.

After introductions, Dr. Ames was anxious to get to work.

"I understand you have a written statement from this madman the papers are calling the Claw. I am anxious to examine it. How did it arrive? Did he contact a reporter, a TV personality?"

"None of the above," said Rychman.

"Oh?"

Jessica explained how they had come by the communiqué.

"It's not your usual method, to say the least," replied Ames, biting the inside of his cheek nervously, as if recalling something disturbing. "It's almost as if the sender were afraid of his own message. As if he largely wished it not to be found, and yet was compelled to . . . *forward* it."

"It's not your usual evil-killer communiqué, either," she said. "A bit literary for a killer, in fact."

"Literary? In the Jack the Ripper school of letters, you mean?"

"The Ripper was fond of rhyming."

"Rhymes? Really? I'm surprised you didn't send it to a cryptologist."

"Don't worry," she assured him, "we have. They're working on it in Virginia as we speak."

"I see. How daunting, then, that you should bring it to me. Well, let's have a look."

She handed a copy to him in a manila envelope. He took it to his desk and lay it out before him, scanning it quickly, almost instantly saying, "This fellow is very disturbed."

"We know that much, Doctor," said Rychman.

"Captain, I may need to keep this for a while."

"It can't go beyond this office. The papers don't have this, and we want to keep it that way, understood?"

"Yes, of course. I haven't a problem with that, but I would like to be free to take it back and forth with me."

"Of course," he said. "But time is important here. The fiend killed two women last night, and he's going to go right on killing until he's stopped."

"I heard," said Ames. He paced a moment before going to his intercom and speaking with his secretary. They were engaged in an argument when he shouted, "Priscilla, you'll just have to arrange it. I've got to take the afternoon. It's police business that won't wait. Now, please, no more argument." He clicked off a bit disdainfully and looked up at the two law enforcement officials. "I'll make it my only priority this afternoon," he said.

"My task force is meeting at six tomorrow morning," said Rychman tentatively. "I don't suppose . . ."

"Police Plaza One? I'll be there. Give you what I've got."

"That's very generous of you," said Jessica.

"With a madman like this, we all must do what we can."

Fifteen

~

When he was alone, Dr. Ames immediately started to analyze the poem. It was literate, which told him something
about the killer. It was forced, however, and not what one
might call good poetry by any standard, including that
strange, bizarre and measured poetry he had seen written
under the classification of *horror*. And yet, knowing of its
discovery, hidden in the corpse of the victim as it was, and
going on the assumption that the Claw himself had penned
the work, gave it all of the horrific overtones required to
make the thing chilling in its every aspect.

Still, he knew he must remain objective to look at the
words in the context of psychiatry.

He knew it would take some time. He buzzed his secretary
and asked that she send in some sandwiches, a cola and a
large Snickers bar. He'd need sustenance, he told himself, and
a little sugar kick to get finished by 6 A.M. tomorrow.

He then turned back to the words before him. One phrase
seemed to leap out at him, as if it were underlined, and yet it
wasn't. "Your sins will be eaten away." He read it aloud, and
then he scanned down to find its sister line: "By eating away
your sin . . ."

Instantly Ames realized the author of the piece was the
worst kind of sociopath, the sort that was truly deranged, following the urgings of a voice or voices in his head, not unlike
the Son of Sam, David Berkowitz. Berkowitz had claimed
that Satan had come to him using the name of Sam and had
convinced Berkowitz that he was in fact his true father, having used his mother in some unholy fashion to conceive him.
Satan's instructions were to go about the city with a
.44-caliber handgun and blow away couples parked in cars.

137

It seemed obvious to Ames as he considered the latent meaning in the phrase "eating away your sin" that the Claw felt he had been selected or chosen by a higher power to do so.

Following the instructions of Satan or some other such evil father figure, he was doing his victims a favor, sending them on to a new and better life without the excess baggage of their inherent sins. If the poetry could be believed, these sins were being taken on by the killer, ingested with each swallowed bite of the victim. By extension, the more sins ingested by the Claw, the more evil and powerful he became.

One sick sonofabitch, Ames moaned inwardly. He had kept up with the Claw in the news and had even read many of the police reports on the victims. He had asked for and gotten placement on the task force as a special consultant. He knew it was an important case, but more important to him than the political clout breaking such a case would give him within the community, he honestly wished to put an end to the madman's reign of terror. No one looking at the photos of the victims could want anything else.

It was now almost 3 A.M.; he had only a few hours to dictate his notes and prepare some graphics that might assist him in explaining to Rychman precisely what he had. Priscilla, asleep on the couch beside him, would have to be awakened shortly.

He rushed on through the poem again, reading it once more in its entirety.

He realized there was something that didn't ring true with the rest of the poem. It was the fifth line, ending with *him* instead of *me*. The entire poem was cast in the first person, as though the author was speaking of himself and his own inhuman accomplishments. But suddenly, in the middle, he called himself *him*.

He read it aloud. "The Claw is no name for *him*."

He considered it the other way with the personal pronoun. "The Claw is no name for *me*."

He thought and stared at the line for some time. "Is it *him* or is it *me*?" he asked the empty room. "He just needed the *him* to sorta rhyme with sin?" he asked himself.

He stared longer. It was *my* teeth, *my* rabid, hungry sin-feast, and all so as to give *you* eternal peace without *your* sins following you to the grave, if *I* hadn't come along and saved you from *yourself*. At the bottom the "I" was proclaimed in the signature as Ovid, Divine Protector. In the reference to divine protector, it was all too evident that this guy had honed a helpful rationalization for his cannibalism, that he felt it was a *benevolent cannibalism*. The third person encroached almost like a Freudian slip. The Claw is no name for *him* . . . who gives *you* eternal life . . . by eating away your sin.

Who was *him*? Ames wondered. What psychosis-fed creature came to this poor devil, Ovid, to send uncontrollable urges of murder and cannibalism coursing through his mind? Was it the same brain monster that spoke to John Wayne Gacy, Richard Speck, Jeffrey Dahmer and Morgan Sayer, Chicago's infamous Handyman? Was it the same demon of the mind that spoke to the Son of Sam killer, the Boston Strangler, the Hillside Strangler and a host of other sociopaths who were unable to empathize in the slightest with the suffering they caused in their victims? Was the Claw totally at the mercy of the demonic urges that moved him to commit the most heinous of crimes? He was obviously capable of rationalizing away his own part in the proceedings, as if he weren't really responsible. That's where Ames parted with the soft approach of other psychiatrists, for he firmly believed that such men as this, men who were dominated by an inner "spirit" that drove them ever onward to commit vicious acts against humanity, were by definition insane.

Those other sociopaths who were driven purely by lust and libido were fodder for the electric chair, but men like Morgan Sayer, driven by the demons of their childhoods, controlled by the demons of past horrors and abuses unimaginable, were legally and medically insane. To destroy them in an electric chair or gas chamber was tantamount to destroying a wolf by the same means. An animal instinct for "survival," not one of evil, seemed at work here. Such men were to be restricted for life, certainly, but such men were also valuable to scientific laboratories. Given the current state of brain research and neurosurgery, it was evident to Ames that one day such men could be medically cured of their insane behaviors . . . one day . . .

Richard Ames had read, heard or seen every kind of human

rationalization associated with cannibals, but this "divine protector" thing was something new in the annals of cannibalistic behavior. Ames was now convinced that the killer was working in tandem with an *inner demon*.

He wasn't sure how Rychman and Coran would react to his educated guesses, but given the time frame, it was the best he could do.

His secretary rolled to her side, the blanket covering her falling away to reveal her nudity. He went to her and tenderly began to caress her inviting skin. She'd uprooted from home and family in Chicago to remain with him. He momentarily wondered why she put up with him, and when he would commit himself wholly to her.

"That'll do just fine, Priscilla . . . just fine," he said in an escape of breath when her hand went instinctively to his inner thigh.

Others might see New York City as an earth mother in repose, or even a lovely, sensual goddess, but Jessica had no such illusions toward this cruel city. Like Chicago, its character was molded from the butcher's block of commerce and profit, and those without were damned to poverty, homelessness, infirmity—to become easy prey to wolves like the Claw who flourished in shadow and darkness.

Jessica wondered where her personal joy in life had gone; another more youthful and innocent Jessica might have felt that joy encircling her, even here in New York, as a kind of lifeforce or energy shield. There'd once been a time when the teeming life of a New York would've easily excited her imagination and sense of play, no matter how dire her reasons for being there, but now she saw all life through a darker lens.

Staring through the rain beading up on Alan's car window and paying no heed to the constant buzz on his police-band radio, she mentally toyed with life as it was lived in the towering buildings that made up the city's famous skyline. Alan had tried to improve her mood by giving her a quick tour, pointing out landmarks, museums, art galleries, the Met. He obviously loved his city, despite, or perhaps because of, its many flaws. His professional life, like Jessica's, hinged on

he sins of those he policed. The uneasy relationship between
hunter and hunted made Rychman as much a part of the equa-
ion as the Claw.

"Look, whataya think about my suppositions in light of the
Claw's stepped-up agenda, and what we found at the Phillips
apartment?" Rychman asked, breaking the silence between
hem.

"I'm glad you've opened your mind to the possibility of a
second perpetrator, but still we need more to go on."

"It's not something we can ignore."

"I dunno, maybe I just don't want to face another Gerald
Ray Sims," she replied, "I dunno . . ."

Her voice gave her away. She was tired and didn't want to
pursue it, but this gave Rychman the opening he'd been waiting for. "Look, I've got two show tickets and—"

"The theater?"

"You needn't sound so surprised. I've even been known to
stay awake, especially for a Neil Simon."

"I don't know, Alan. There's just so much to—"

"You've got to get in some R&R sometime, Jess, or else
you'll fall apart on me, and then you'll be of no use to anyone, including yourself."

She seethed a moment before she got hold of herself, realizing he hadn't meant it the way it sounded. He couldn't
possibly know of her therapy with Dr. Lemonte, or her very
real fear at times that she would come unglued. She calmly
replied, "I'm that transparent, am I?"

"Come on, it'll be good for you. This case's enough to make
O'Toole give up drink, and Mannion to give up women."

She laughed at this and dropped her guard. "All right. I
know I push myself hard. Guess I could use some stress-free
time . . . but I'm not convinced it ought to be with you!"

"Hey, I'm not so bad, and I promise to keep a hands-off
posture all evening long."

"A cop's promise, hmmmmmm."

"Is that a yes or no?" he demanded, wheeling the car into
the underground garage at Police Plaza One.

"Maybe yes . . . maybe no . . . maybe maybe. Call me at
the end of the day, and we'll see."

It took all Rychman's strength to resist saying another word, and to content himself with the *maybes* and the *we'll sees* which he wasn't particularly fond of or used to.

They were now in Rychman's ready room, awaiting others for the six A.M. meeting. Jessica sat near a window, staring out.

This morning New York shared a collective fear that permeated the air like a coarse, uneven blanket. Lying over the skyline, smothering the streets, the nightmare was heralded in bold black headlines at every corner. News of the double murder filled everyone's conversation, and with the morning's coffee, every New Yorker had something far more bitter to swallow: *the fact that the Claw had gone inside this time,* finding his prey in their homes, no longer content with the occasional streetwalker or those foolish enough to be wandering after dark. Now there was no place safe from the cannibal. The monster might choose any woman in the city, no matter her neighborhood or habits. Jessica could almost reach out and touch the palpable fear that was all around her.

Lingering clouds played a tumbling game of seesaw above the city, capturing industrial smoke and exhaust fumes. By 5:30 A.M. a fog of hazy heat was accumulating, causing the tops of the spiraling temples of Manhattan to wink and disappear.

Her thoughts were cut short by Alan's angry words. "That SOB Eldritch had the nerve to call this morning to ask what we were doing to calm the public mind, and how we're going to play the press. Ever see such a jag-off?"

"I've run into more than my share," she confided, reaching into her purse for a mint, offering him one.

Declining her offer, he snatched out a pack of Rolaids instead. "I just hope I can keep my mind from exploding along with my stomach."

"Don't let the stress get to you, Alan." She reached across and laid her hand over his, squeezing momentarily, a gesture that made him look across at her. He visibly relaxed, the creases in his face smoothing.

Stress came with the strain of having to face death in it

myriad forms, and while a cop had to harden himself against it so as to appear in control, he still internalized such brutality—such as that meted out on the victims of the Claw—as would incapacitate a lesser man. He had to console those left behind, had to relive the events via the mountain of paperwork each case spawned; even then he must contend with his own feelings, not to mention the system and those higher-ups in it, who, like Eldritch, only poured salt on the wounds. The scars left on a homicide investigator often became visible only when a man smoked himself with his own gun.

"You okay, Alan?" she asked.

"Yeah, sure . . . fine . . ." he managed in his best tough-guy brogue. "God, I hope we can keep the friggin' press from learning about his taking the brain matter out."

"I agree."

"We're batting zero with controlling leaks."

She nodded and took her hand away. "As it is, when an arrest is made, it's going to be difficult to prove it's not just another lunatic who reads."

"The real Claw will have secrets to share with us that no one else could know . . . things we don't even know. Things we can't even imagine. Or worse, things we have imagined. What is it they say in Disneyland? If you can imagine it, you can do it? Tell it to the Claw."

She didn't answer, allowing him to vent.

"Still," he continued, "if ever I find out where the leaks are coming from . . . well, God help the fool."

"These press guys like Drake are real smart about getting people to slip or cooperate. They've got more tricks than divorce lawyers."

He blanched a little at the mention of divorce lawyers. "Once again, you're not telling me anything I don't already know."

"Sorry . . ."

Rychman changed the subject. "We're searching like hell through the backgrounds of the victims, sticking with old-fashioned police work."

"So what's it gotten you?" she asked.

"A lot of upset relatives who think we've got no business

asking questions. They don't want us to know their loved one frequented a neighborhood bar, mixed it up with some character in a one-night stand ... you know, the usual."

"Still no common threads?"

"Does he like them lean and mean? Does he like them young or old? Hell, what happened in Scarsdale tells us emphatically, he isn't a choosy bastard. He'll take his tall or short, brunette or blonde, in her teens or in her eighties."

"Frustrating."

"We have sniffed out one item of interest, though. It took us long enough to see it, but I got a little curious; something you said about the killer's knowing something about medicine, anatomy maybe."

"Yeah, and ... ?"

"So it appears all the vics were relatively poor, on food stamps, on small incomes, Medicare."

She brightened and sat up. "That could be very important."

"At least some of them were having some sort of medical problem. We're checking into each of their medical histories and running down doctors they've been seeing, trying to cross-check, but so far nothing."

"Has it occurred to you that one of the killers likes them young, while the other likes them old?"

"Then you've definitely found forensic support for your theory that there're two of them at work here?"

"No, not yet, but we're working on it, and if that poem is interpreted as I believe it will be ... well, it lends credence to the idea."

"Because if you and Darius are sure, I could get my task force going in that direction. Some of them have already been thinking along those lines. Anyway, it's coming clear to me that the killer or killers knew at least one of the victims, and perhaps others."

Mulling it over, she said, "If he knew them, then perhaps he knew them from where they received their medical assistance. Someone working in the medical community, or a closely related field, say insurance, would be in a position to get information on Medicare patients."

"We're already working on it. We're comparing all the victims' preferences regarding medical clinics, hospitals and private doctors. Of course, the guy could be anybody working in the health or health-related professions. We're talking medics, nurses, pharmaceutical supply companies, clinics, hospitals, the goddamned housing authority, the health authority, HUD, for God's sake."

"It's still a trail worth pursuing, Alan."

"So we start with the victims' medical records, which I've already got my detectives searching through. Maybe we'll get lucky."

"Then you did have something to tell Eldritch. Why didn't you get him off your back with this news?"

"I'm done with letting Eldritch make a fool of me. I know what he'd do with the information."

"You're not saying he's the leak!"

"No, but I am saying he takes all the kudos when everything goes well, but he's the invisible man when things fall apart."

"This could prove the most important lead we have, Alan." She brightened. "It gives me hope. And we're overdue to be due, as Casey Stengel would say."

This made Rychman laugh. "I didn't know you were a baseball fan."

"Baseball, football, sure. My dad did not neglect his duty to me."

"So what do you think of the Giants' chances this year for the Super Bowl?"

"Do you really want me to answer that? But," she added, again looking out at the passing traffic of the city, seeing a glimmer of the sun that had been shut out for the past few days, "I just might feel up to the theater, after all."

"Great, great." Rychman felt a sudden surge of excitement himself.

Rychman called the meeting of the task force to order a little past six, delaying as long as he could for Dr. Ames' arrival. Everyone was still buzzing about the double homicide and the equally puzzling double crime scenes. None of the detectives knew about the bizarre poetry sent to them by Ovid.

"Gentlemen, ladies," began Rychman, "we have a great deal to cover this morning, so let's get to it. First, suffice it to say that last night's double murder was most certainly the work of the man known to us as the Claw, no question. But the killer left us with a little more to go on this time than he—or they—have in the past."

"They? Whataya saying, Captain? That the Claw is two men instead of one?" asked O'Toole's partner, a burly detective named Mannion.

"That possibility is being discussed in light of new evidence that has come to our . . . well, that was placed under our noses. Dr. Darius and Dr. Coran fished a note from the body of the Phillips woman from a man signing himself Ovid. He claimed knowledge of the killer."

"A note?"

"What kind of note?"

Rychman held up his hands. "You'll see the note in due time. At the moment, I'd like you to rethink your quarry; this bird may be two birds. Meanwhile, Forensics is trying to pursue the case from the same angle."

O'Toole, sitting near the front, said in his baritone voice, "So the creep had to reach out and touch somebody . . ."

"More like Western Union," said Rychman. "He sent a *message*, which I'll let Dr. Coran tell you about."

Jessica came to the front and leaned her cane against the podium. "Our killer, or one of our killers, is into poetry. At 1100 hours yesterday, when we were about to close Amelia Phillips up after autopsy, Dr. Darius found a wadded-up piece of paper below the rib cage with a message from this man calling himself Ovid. I'll read it to you in its entirety." Jessica read the bizarre poem to her audience as the mutilated faces of the Claw's victims looked on from the photos along the walls in the ready room.

A collective sense of curious bewilderment filled the room. The silence was broken by O'Toole, who asked, "Is it literate; I mean, how's the spelling, punctuation, all that?"

"Not a problem."

"Holy shit," said Mannion. "It does sound like there're two guys. This guy signs as Ovid and he talks about the Claw like he's another guy."

"Why'd he leave the poem inside her?" asked Detective Emmons. "How'd he know you'd find it?" she added.

"He likely knows that on autopsy we'd be pretty thorough," she replied. "So far, no other messages had been found in this manner, and a recheck has turned up nothing further, according to Dr. Darius."

"What Emmons means, Dr. Coran," said Mannion, "is why'd the creep jam it inside the dead woman? Why not write it on the goddamned wall in blood like a Manson might do?"

She considered this and looked to Alan for a reply. Rychman stepped closer to the mic and said, "People, this is one indication we may be dealing with two separate personalities here: one being fearful and timid, the other dominant and daring. The fearful Ovid is in awe of his more potent accomplice."

Jessica jumped back in. "Maybe Ovid doesn't want the other killer to know that he took this step."

"And he's counting on us not to leak this information, maybe, and maybe he's as good as dead if the other one finds out," added Rychman. "Least, that's the way Dr. Coran and I see it at this point. Call it educated conjecture, if you wish."

This seemed to satisfy most in the room. Emmons' thin hand went up as she raised another question. "What does he have to gain by this act? Does he want to be caught? Is he trying to end the killing spree?"

"We don't have all the answers, not by a long shot," replied Rychman. "The poem shows a lot of misguided, insane notions are swimming around in the guy's head, like the business of the Claw's doing the world a good turn, servicing us, you might say, by getting rid of the wretched among us."

"This ties in with a related theory that Captain Rychman is working on, about the killer or killers knowing that some and perhaps all of his victims were having medical problems," Jessica added.

This brought a rumble from the assembled detectives. Only a handful were working on the probe of the medical histories.

Rychman asked these few to report any new findings, but they'd just begun to scratch the surface and each begged for more time.

O'Toole asked the question that seemed now on everyone's mind. "Then this bastard, or these bastards, *knew* their victims?"

"We can't say that's a for-sure at this point," countered Rychman. "But we're betting that he had prior knowledge of their weaknesses through their medical histories or records. Believe me, people, it has been a leap of faith to take our speculations this far, but that's why we're lucky to have Dr. Coran on our side."

The group acknowledged this with positive grunts and nods. Emmons asked in her quiet voice, "You got all this from that poem? Maybe I'd better go back to school, because I don't see it."

"The medical history trail came independently through Captain Rychman's investigation," Jessica answered. "All we truly got from the poem is the belief that Ovid is a weak and subordinated personality at the mercy of the one he calls the Claw. It was Ovid who contacted the radio station after the initial attacks way back in November of last year. Ovid has remained silent until now—out of fear, we believe. But just as with his radio appearance, he is championing the work of the Claw with his poem."

"Sorry," said Emmons. "I just don't get that much out of this loon's poem, Doctor, and if you're wrong we could be looking in all the wrong places."

"The poem doesn't really say all that much," agreed another detective.

"But it *does*," Jessica disagreed. "It's a sick rationalization for the Claw's cannibalistic nature, and it places the Claw in a godlike role, doing the work of an archangel of death. It tells us a great deal about the killer, and about his accomplice, this Ovid who is in fear for his own life and quite surely in awe of the other man, who has convinced him somehow to be a part of some glorious master plan."

"Obviously delusionary," said Dr. Richard Ames, who had stepped through the door, his secretary beside him with a handful of slides. "However, I'm not convinced that you have two men with murderous intent and cannibalistic urges, and not one man with a dual personality disorder."

Dr. Ames' contradiction took both Rychman and Jessica by surprise. Jessica tried to minimize the damage already done. "No, this is not a case of one man with two identities, Doctor, but two men with a *shared* psychosis, acting out a *shared* fantasy."

"If you will bear with me, please," Ames pleaded with an upraised palm, displaying his huge hand. He then gave a nod to his secretary, who looked disgruntled to be working so early. Priscilla obviously knew the routine, going for the slide projector at the rear of the room. Rychman pulled down a screen from overhead.

Meanwhile, Ames was saying, "I will provide you with my opinion regarding the Claw as he has revealed himself through his writing. Beginning with his handwriting, it is clear that he has a great reservoir of self-hatred and is lacking in self-esteem. As to how many killers you have? I believe this a case of encroaching possession of one personality over the other—that is to say, what the press has dubbed the Claw is another Gerald Ray Sims, i.e., Sims equals Ovid, Stainlype equals the Claw."

"No, no," Jessica started to object, unable to hide her disappointment, her eyes meeting Rychman's. He, too, was upset, realizing that Ames' conclusions toppled all that they had so carefully built up in the minds of his detectives. They had been suddenly clipped at the knees.

Ames had taken the podium, and seeing the dismay in their eyes, he said to Jessica and Rychman, "Aren't you even curious as to how I arrived at my conclusions? Shall I go on, Captain?"

Rychman bit his lip and nodded. "Please ... please do."

Jessica sat down alongside Alan, the two of them waiting for Ames, who was waiting for Priscilla, to continue. Rychman began tapping with a pencil, his confused people looking on.

Sixteen

❧

The room was darkened, and overhead, larger than life, was the handwriting of the Claw. The childish script of huge swirls and loops looked almost as if it had been intentionally used to throw police off. Dr. Ames, a huge, dark shadow beside the screen, pointed at each line as he discussed it.

"His rage and anger have been sublimated by this fantastic idea that he has somehow done the right thing; his words here and here, about tearing out his victims' eyes, feeding on the soft flesh, are balanced by his holier-than-thou attitude that he is somehow the agent of a spirit beyond this world, an angel or archangel. He feels that the power controlling him is in fact superhuman, and so if it tells him to kill, if it tells him to feed on those he kills, he does so. Not that he is without fear of the spirit that has overtaken him, but it is this fear that motivates him. He would rather eat out the sins of his victims, swallow them down and accumulate them, than face this being from another world that has taken control of him."

"Then there are two killers and not one," said someone in the group.

"No," Ames disagreed. "There is only one killer, but he is a psychopath who receives visits from a second, more powerful *personality*, the dire, black side of his own soul, perhaps. Voices he takes to be that of God or God-directed."

"Then he's one guy with two personalities?"

"Two personalities, yes, but one is at the beck and call of the other, the weaker will subjugated by the more demonic."

Jessica was unnerved by Ames' profile of the killer. He was describing Gerald Ray Sims and a host of others either behind bars or executed long ago.

Rychman said in her ear, "We should've postponed this,

gotten together with Ames ourselves and hashed it out before we presented it in front of my people. This is going to send them out with a lot of mixed signals."

Jessica interrupted Ames. "Dr. Ames, isn't it at all possible that the two personalities you're referring to are, in fact, two physically separate men? One dominated by the other?"

"This is my interpretation of the poem the man has written. It fits the classic pattern of a dangerous psychopath."

"But isn't it possible that he could just as well be writing about himself and his dominant partner, the one he protects?"

Ames was decisive. "No ... not in my estimation."

Damn, she thought. "I really need those reports from J.T. now," she told Rychman.

The lights came up on the confusion of sixty creased faces, each person and each team trying to weigh the theories and decide whether the Claw was a single individual with a dual personality, or a killing couple.

Rychman was as upset with the way things had gone as Jessica, and it appeared, finally, that Dr. Ames realized just how upset they were with him. "I'm sorry if my diagnosis of the situation does not fit neatly into your plans, but I must be honest," he told them as he began to pack up his notes and files. Priscilla had already abandoned the overhead and was now waiting for him at the door.

Rychman shook Ames' hand and thanked him for coming, as did Jessica. When Ames disappeared, hands went up all over the room. Rychman said in his firmest voice, "I believe Dr. Ames is half-right, and Dr. Coran is half-right. At any rate, quite soon, we will have forensics evidence to prove one theory or the other. In the meantime, you have your assignments. Dig into the medical records of each victim, and think about—think about—the possibility of the Claw being the *Claws*. Dismissed."

The room cleared quickly, leaving Rychman and Jessica alone. She said, "Sorry it went so badly."

"Oh, I don't think it went too badly," he politely lied.

"You're a terrible liar."

"When I wanna be, yeah."

She shook her head, and her knuckles went white when she

gripped her cane. "We completely confused your entire task force. It was a fiasco, admit it."

"They needed shaking up. Come on, you don't have to take this all on your shoulders, Jess."

They had moved toward the door, and he turned off the light, leaving them in the dark, at close quarters. She could feel the strength and the heat coming off him as he nudged still closer, dipped his head downward and pressed his lips tenderly against hers. When he pulled away, he said, "I hope this is better than the elevator."

"You can't blame it on the wine this time," she replied, reaching around his neck and kissing him in return.

Her cane slipped away and slapped against the floor with a crack that made her start.

Rychman felt her tremble under his touch, realizing she was teetering; he sensed that part of her wanted to give in to him, while another part wanted no romantic entanglements. He wisely let her go, lifted her cane and returned it to her, saying, "I hope we're still on for tonight."

"Tonight?"

"The play? Dinner?"

"Oh, I don't know, Alan."

"Come on, we both need to get some relief from this case, and what better way than an evening at the theater?"

She didn't readily answer. "Alan, there're a million things to do around here right now, and Dr. Darius and Archer can't do it alone, and—"

"You've got a bad case of the *ands*, Doctor, *and* what is it they say? Physician, heal thyself?"

She smiled back at him. "Is that your prescription?"

"Stop thinking in *ands* and show a little concern for your blood pressure, that's right."

She knew it would be easy to become stressed-out if she chose to work at the lab tonight. And staying alone with her thoughts in her hotel room, uneasy about sleep for fear she'd return to the nightmares that featured Teach Matisak would be just as bad. With an expectant look into Alan's eyes, she finally replied, "What do you propose? Take an evening off and call you in the morning?"

"Things'll look a whole lot better in the morning," he assured her, taking her hands in his. "Trust me."

"I want to, Alan, but—"

"But what?"

"I've . . . we've got important work to do here and to get involved in any but a professional relationship . . . well, it could jeopardize the investigation in ways neither of us can predict, and, and—"

"There's those *ands* again. I told you it was a sickness. You're worrying about things that haven't happened and may not!"

"And besides, there's just no future in our becoming romantically—"

He kissed her firmly yet gently, his passion once more getting the better of him. She felt her breath taken away and she returned his kiss. When they parted, he said simply, "We'll just see the play, have dinner. Anything else will be up to you."

She laughed lightly. "I guess I do have a bad case of the *ands*. Maybe you're right. Maybe I do need a little time to call my own. Although I don't believe my boss at Quantico would understand."

"Is that an acceptance?"

She put her hands to her temples and said, "Yes *and* yes."

It was getting very late, but Dr. Luther Darius was driven, refusing all overtures from his associate, Dr. Simon Archer, to vacate the lab and relent. First there was the double autopsy of the day before, and then a re-examination of the Hamner cadaver, and now personally overseeing every aspect of the laboratory follow-up work on Olin and Phillips. It was too much for any man, but when Simon Archer asked him if he didn't need rest, the old man told Archer that he planned to push himself further by re-examining all earlier evidence-taking that'd accompanied the various Claw-case autopsies.

"Searching for what?"

"Any iota of evidence that may've been missed either by Perkins, you, Dr. Coran or myself."

By now everyone in the lab understood that Darius was obsessing, and that although Archer'd been of great help, assisting in the re-examinations of the Olin and Hamner cadavers, they'd found nothing further. During their close work on the now wooden and grisly Hamner corpse, Darius confided much in Archer, and told him, "Somewhere along the way we've all missed some vital clue. This macabre poem we found wadded up inside the Phillips woman is just the tip of the iceberg, Simon." Coran had since explained the nature of the communication to Darius. "Dr. Coran believes the killer to be not one but two people, and coincidentally, I have held the same suspicion for some time myself."

"I find it all rather doubtful, given the facts," Archer said.

Still, Darius insisted they comb back through every shred and fiber of evidence with the exactitude he was famous for before his recent illness and bouts with depression and alcohol.

"You forget, sir, that in your absence during your illness, I've been in charge, and ... well ... I've found nothing to point to two perpetrators. In fact, all the evidence points to a single individual."

Darius bit at the inside of his cheek, deep in thought. "Yes ... yes, well ... of course, Simon ... you may well be proven correct."

"I'm sure, sir, that I will be, and I am anxious for Dr. Coran's people at the FBI to fully corroborate my findings."

"We shall see, Dr. Archer. As for now ... would you please close her up and see to final dispensation of Miss Olin here?"

Archer, ever the faithful associate, said, "Of course, sir. I think you may have overtaxed yourself, Dr. Darius. You'd best get a car home."

"I can remember a time I could have done four or five autopsies in a twenty-four-hour period; God, when your stamina goes, Simon, it's a horrible thing. Your mind is as fully functional and alive as when you were twenty, but your body begins to resist what your mind tells it to do."

"I'm sorry for your ... difficulties, Dr. Darius. I take it your doctor's advice hasn't—"

"Isn't worth a damn, Simon."

Archer smiled and waved him off, Darius hobbling from the area, his body racked with pain.

Alone, Dr. Darius now sat on a bench in the changing room before the locker he had used for so many years, trying to regain enough strength to get himself home. Finally he stood and opened his locker. He began to pull off his green surgeon's shirt, and in doing so, felt as if he were being watched. He saw the eyeless head of Mrs. Hamner staring down from the top tray of his locker.

Darius, shocked, backed into the bench, fell over it and knocked his head against a locker, sending him into unconsciousness.

Darius was found this way by a passing attendant. Medics were called and he was rushed to the hospital, his forehead bleeding.

He woke up in a hospital bed with an IV unit strung over his head, trying to recall what had happened. Then he remembered the black holes staring at him from the head that had been placed in his locker. Or had it materialized out of delirium tremens? He had gone for several days without a drop of liquor and his nerves had been shot as a result of the double autopsy and the way he'd been pushing himself on the Claw case. Maybe he had just imagined Mrs. Hamner's eyeless, severed head there in his locker. Maybe he was going crazy with all the stress that had been placed on him. They couldn't leave him to die in peace? No, the mayor and the C.P. had to push him into this hideous case, likely the final hideous case of his career.

When the doctors had told him about the cancer atop his heart condition, and how short the remainder of his life would be, he had taken to drinking heavily and secretly. So far, only a few need-to-knows had been informed and even these people only knew that half of it. But now all his secrets might surface.

He lay gasping, wondering how he could get a drink. His every nerve felt like brittle paper about to snap. He didn't care about the Claw any longer; he just wanted to find a corner to crawl into with a bottle of J&B.

His head pounded from where it had come into contact

with the locker. He wanted the pounding to stop. He wanted life, his fevered brain with its obsessions, to end.

He once again began to contemplate suicide. It would be a clean break, and perhaps that way, no one would ever have to know about his weakness and his transgressions. No one would have to know about his cowardly fears, his mental blackouts, his awful visions like the head in his locker.

He swore to himself that no one would ever know the depths to which he had fallen.

Her time with Alan off duty was precisely what she needed, Jessica decided. The kindly Dr. Darius had urged her to follow all passions, as he put it. Now Alan managed to take her mind off the demanding burdens she had been subjected to since arriving in New York, not only those of the baffling, frustrating Claw case but all of the painful memories she had brought with her. She was transported out of herself and her narrow self-interest, and now the stress she'd felt over the past few days had melted away.

Dinner was a sumptuous meal at a wonderful harborfront restaurant high above the city. They'd gotten a window looking out over the glassy expanse of New York Harbor, the boat lights reflecting up at them. She could not recall a time when she'd been more relaxed, more herself, and she genuinely liked Alan, who apparently felt the same way about her.

After dinner he took her for a ride to a place called Belmont Harbor on the Hudson River where they got out and walked along a wharf and past the boats. The rigging beat out a chorus of soft metal clinks, a lilting sound created by the same wind that swept through her hair. In a few moments they stood before a beautiful sailboat with the name *MVP* painted boldly at the stern. Rychman stepped aboard and said, "Coming?"

"Is this yours?"

"Still making payments, but I like to think it's mine, yes."

"*Wow*, do you ever get her out of her slip?"

"Not often enough." He held out his hand to her and she accepted it, stepping aboard with her cane, fearful of slipping. He held her firmly and she managed well.

"You've got to come out with me sometime. You'd love it. We could take a whole day, make our way to Nantucket Island."

She had a fearful, flitting premonition of a time when, having allowed herself to love Boutine, she suddenly and explosively lost him. Any relationship with a cop could end this way, she knew. She also knew she was projecting her feelings for Otto Boutine onto Alan, and these feelings felt right and sure, but they brought with them a great price. Finally she said, "I'd like that; it's a beautiful sailboat, Alan, just lovely."

"One of my larger and more expensive vices. Can't afford anything larger, or I'd have a Cobra XS-2100, believe me."

"Why didn't you tell me about it before?"

"Showin's better'n tellin' in circumstances such as these, I've learned. Want to see the rest of her?" He unlocked the cabin door and held it open to her. "Careful of that first step."

She lay the cane aside and used the handrails, going down into the cabin after he clicked on the lights. It was a beautiful interior, almost entirely of teak, shining and warm. It felt like the coziest, safest place on the planet, she thought.

"I love it."

"I hoped you would."

He went for the little refrigerator and an icy bottle of zinfandel materialized in his hands. "I've got some nice glasses somewhere," he continued as he searched. "Here they are." He removed the cork as she glanced out through the portholes at the dark expanse of the big river, which looked as calm as peace itself.

"I've got my scuba gear stowed below the bed," he said as he poured the wine.

"So how's the diving here?"

"Not terrific, but it keeps me in shape. I mean it's not like Mexico or Florida. But we've got a few man-made reefs. Keeps me in practice."

She took the wine he offered and sipped at it. They then talked about diving and seriously planning a dive trip together once all this was over. He assured her that he would meet her anywhere, anytime. They talked about other concerns, and she told him about her father and how he had

taught her to be independent and self-sufficient and strong.
Alan spoke of his childhood, which was in no way so harmo-
nious as hers, citing frequent battles with his father, who simply never understood him or his brother. He said he envied
her relationship with her father.

They talked so easily and so long that they'd both lost
track of time and suddenly she realized it was past midnight.
"Perhaps I should go now," she suggested, putting aside the
wine she held, getting to her feet and looking about for her
cane.

"You left it on deck," he said. Then he approached her
there in the cramped cabin and put his arms around her. She
allowed him to hold her. In her ear, he said, "I can't remember a time when I was so comfortable with a woman, Jess. I
want you to know that."

She looked into his eyes and read the depth of sincerity
there. She lifted her mouth to his in an open invitation to him
and he did not fail her. Their passionate kiss lingered and became a long, breathtaking one. When they parted, their eyes
were fixed on one another. He wanted to say something but
was afraid that words would fail him, and she sensed this.

"Don't say anything," she instructed him. "You've heard
me go on and on about all the places I've been, all the things
I've done."

"And I've enjoyed every word."

"I've never been *here* before, and I've never made love on
a sailboat before."

He lowered her to the bed. "Neither have I."

Their lovemaking had them both believing that it would be
endless as they fulfilled their desires. Each time they parted,
exhausted and panting, a new wave of passion swept over
them, erupting like a powerful tide neither wished to stem.

Alan's body was powerful, his muscles like stone. He was
strong, pinning her against the bed, driving into her with sure
yet gentle strokes, surging and retreating and surging again.

Alan somehow made her feel weightless and without care.
She had become Jessica Coran again, someone she had long
missed. With him, she realized, she did not have to put up

any fronts. She was accepted as his equal yet he managed also to make her feel like a woman again. She hadn't been touched by a man this way since Otto.

Sometime in the night they left the boat and returned to her hotel, where they showered and made love under the spray. When they finally shut off the water, they heard her phone ringing. It was like a death knell to their night. It was almost four in the morning.

Lou Pierce was on the other end of the line, asking for Alan, saying he'd tried him everywhere else he could think of, and that she was his last hope.

"He's right here, Lou. Hold on," she told the sergeant, unhappy that she and Rychman had been "found out."

Rychman came across the room in a towel and took the phone from her, barking into it, "What's the problem, Lou?"

"It's bad news, Captain, having to do with Dr. Darius, sir."

"What is it, Lou? Spit it out." To Jessica, he said, "Something's up with Luther Darius."

"I'm afraid, sir, he's . . . well, it looks like he's committed suicide, sir."

"Suicide?"

Jessica's face went white as she repeated the horrible word. "Suicide?"

"How did it happen, Lou?" Rychman asked.

"Jumped from his hospital window, Captain."

"Hospital? What hospital? When I last saw him—"

"He suffered some sort of seizure at the lab, was carried out sometime around seven last evening, after you'd gone. I tried to locate you, but—"

"Who's handling it, Lou?"

"O'Toole and Mannion were in the area, checking on some lead, something to do with a clinic in the medical complex; you know that strip of medical buildings along there, several city blocks long. We got Archer in on the cleanup and the E.T. work, sir."

"I'm on my way, Lou."

"He was a good man, Captain."

"Right . . . right you are, Lou."

Jessica hung on Alan's every word, trying to piece things

together, tears welling up. Rychman got the name of the hospital, which he knew well, and after he hung up he tried to put the pathetic scenario into focus for her as best he could, finishing with, "That old man was working cases when I was a rookie. Got to know him very well. He was a friend, Jess, a close friend, I thought. But I guess you never really know what's going on inside another person's head. Guess the difficulties he'd been having, and now this latest bout, put him over the top . . ."

"He didn't strike me as suicidal," she countered. "I didn't know him long, but I got the impression that giving up wasn't in his nature. He loved his work and life."

"I've got to get down there."

"So do I."

"It's not necessary you go down, Jess. Archer's got it, Lou tells me."

"I'm going with you," she said, turning from his touch and starting to dress.

"Fine, you're coming." He began to dress quickly as well, and when they'd finished and were halfway out the door, the phone rang again. They looked at each other.

"Probably someone else calling with the dire news," she said, going back for the phone. But when she answered, she heard J.T.'s voice from Quantico, apologizing about the hour.

"You okay, Jess? You sound a little down," said J.T., who surely expected a happier note since they hadn't spoken in a while.

"Got some bad news this morning, J.T."

"Oh, sorry to hear that. Anything I can do?"

She briefly explained about Darius.

"God, sad loss to everyone there and the profession," he said.

"So, J.T., what is it?"

"What is it? I've finally got results for you, that's what. I tried reaching you all evening but obviously you were indisposed? Anyway, I left messages with the desk. Didn't you check your messages, Jess?"

" 'Fraid I failed to."

"Christ, Jess, O'Rourke's been trying to get you, too.

Wants to know what's cooking with the case; wants an update. You'd better call her as soon as it's a decent hour."

"Thanks for the tip, J.T. Now, what'd you learn about our Claw?"

"Well, it's not what you think, Jess. Sorry, but I've looked at the samples you sent six ways to Sunday and it all adds up to the same guy in every case, same bite impressions."

She let out a soft groan of disappointment but composed herself the moment she realized that Alan was staring. "No doubt in your mind?"

"None whatever, Jess. If it *is* two guys, one of them's not a meat-eater."

She thanked J.T. for his troubles, disappointed by this news, but it was the weight of Darius' death that she felt most strongly as she said goodbye and hung up.

"Jess," said Alan, "you really don't have to go down to the scene."

"I'm going," she insisted, grabbing her cane and pushing past him for the door. He stopped her, taking her in his arms and feeling her fight for her freedom until finally she gave in to her sobs.

Seventeen

❧

Suicides were treated as homicides until murder was completely ruled out, and that was how the NYPD was working the death of Dr. Luther Darius. The story of one of the foremost authorities in forensic science who, facing cancer and despair, took his own life would be splashed across newspapers all over America.

And yet it didn't fit him, didn't stand to reason. The man Jessica had breakfasted with the previous morning hadn't appeared in the least suicidal. But appearances were often a masquerade.

Stories about Dr. Darius began to circulate, about his problem with drink, about his growing morbidity. People who worked in close association with him had known for some time now of his despair over his inability to perform at peak performance.

Dr. Simon Archer was on hand at the hospital to tell Rychman word for word the dire and prophetic last conversation he had had with Dr. Darius only hours before in the autopsy room.

"Then you have it on tape?" asked Jessica.

"Matter of fact," Archer replied thoughtfully, "I do believe the tape was still on at that time. I'll . . . I'll fetch it for your investigation, Captain."

"Good, good . . . If it's as bleak as you say, then I guess we can assume the worst here."

Darius' body had been scooped from the pavement, eleven stories down. Blood still pooled about the spot where the police chalk outlined the man's small form.

"I'd like to know if there was anything in his system to indicate—" began Rychman.

"I'd like to assist in the autopsy, Dr. Archer," Jessica interrupted.

"You sure that's wise, Jess ... ah, Dr. Coran?" asked Rychman.

"Dr. Archer?"

Archer nodded like a grieving pallbearer. "Certainly, certainly."

Rychman took her aside. "Don't you think you'd be better served by concentrating on the case you were sent here to work on?"

"Dr. Darius was a friend of my father's, Alan. I owe him this much."

"To what end? And at what emotional cost to yourself? Do you think Darius or your father—"

"I've got a room upstairs to investigate," she said, storming away from him.

He shook his head and watched her as she went, the cane lightly tapping out her anthem.

Archer said to him, "She's quite a strong-willed woman."

"You could say so."

"An exceptional woman, I think."

Rychman stared at Archer. "So I've noticed." Archer, too, was watching her disappear into the hospital as the siren blared its warning, the ambulance pulling off with Darius' body, taking him to what had been his morgue for the last forty-two years.

"What sent him here, to the hospital?" Jessica asked Archer, who had followed her to the room Darius had leapt from.

"He apparently had some sort of fall. He was working himself extremely hard ... going back over the Hamner cadaver and all our earlier findings ... all for you, Dr. Coran." Archer supplied her with what few details he knew, ending with, "And he suffered a concussion where his head had struck the locker."

"All that about his drinking and his despair ... all true?"

Archer frowned. "Life gets the best of the best of us. I'm sorry."

She went to the IV bottle, the loose tubing dangling, the contents spilled across the floor. Other tubing, connected to a heart regulator, lay on the soiled bedclothes. The window had been smashed, presumably with the chair that had lain along-side the body downstairs.

"It must've happened all in a matter of seconds after he pulled the plug on his heart regulator," she said. "The nurse told me that the buzz was loud enough to wake the dead when he snatched the electrodes off his chest."

"That's how I pictured it," agreed Archer.

"Then you've already examined the room?"

"I have, yes."

"Everything points to suicide, but I just didn't figure Darius for the kind of man who—"

"The kind of man . . . There is no suicide type, Dr. Coran. Suicide comes when there is a breakdown in brain stimulants and proper judgment is impaired when connections and cause and effect cannot be put together by the struggling, desperate mind. No, I'm afraid our dear friend simply felt he must end his despair."

She swallowed hard, watching the dark shadow cast against the wall. It was part her shadow, part Dr. Archer's. "I suppose he gave in to his *shadow*," she mumbled.

"Pardon?"

She took a deep, long breath and said, "Nothing . . . nothing." With this she rushed from the room where Darius had spent his last hours in desperation and loneliness while she was making love to Alan Rychman and had, for the first time since Boutine's death, felt whole again.

Jessica Coran had to get away. She needed time alone to mull over the situation and the emotions the death of Dr. Darius had sent surging up to the surface. She was angry with Darius for committing suicide, especially after all that he had said to her about wishing to end his career with a solution to the grandest and most gruesome case he had ever witnessed firsthand, the case of the Claw.

She had returned to the place on the harbor where she and

Darius had breakfasted together, where they'd watched the ships in the channel. Alone now, she watched the sea gulls overhead. She recalled Darius' inner strength, his vibrant and tenacious will—which could not be overcome, she had thought, and yet he had given in.

Why? Why had he jumped from that window?

Was it the grueling hours he had put in both at the scene of the Olin murder in Scarsdale and later at the laboratory performing autopsies on two victims? Even with her and Archer's assistance, the amount of work might simply have been too much of a strain.

He'd come back to the M.E.'s office against doctor's orders, at the behest of Mayor Halle and Commissioner Eldritch, or so Alan had confided, saying, "Perhaps we were all expecting too damned much of Darius."

In a sense, the deadly Claw had claimed yet another victim, but the sun rose over New York Harbor just the same, setting the Statue of Liberty ablaze in a red-orange hue, while all around her city sounds from tugboats to fire trucks signaled that New York was clamoring for this new day like none before. The sun-dappled water reflected back the tall skyscrapers, turning their shapes into living, moving images. Nothing in this city was as it seemed, and everyone held secrets, her included. The only truth to be found was below a microscope, and even then the truth mocked her, proving her wrong, showing in no uncertain terms that the killer was one man and not two. On several of the victims she had taken her own findings and had personally overseen to their dispensation—she had thought: the samples sent to the FBI labs at Quantico to be examined by the best in the business. There seemed no way that the evidence could have been tampered with unless . . . She ruminated further, allowing herself the ugly thought. Only a man of Luther Darius' caliber could send a lab technician away from his duties of processing and properly packaging such evidentiary items for shipment. Might he have dared to open her samples to replace them with others? *Nothing . . . no one is completely as he seems,* she told herself again.

It was a terrifying, fluttering, wild bird of a thought, trapped in the building of her head, screeching, flapping, not wanting to be there. It was the kind of thought Jessica wished she might banish the moment it entered her consciousness, because it felt evil even in its instinctive conception. Could it be that Darius, unhappy at her coming in on the case, had used his charm and flattery to beguile her in an elaborate ruse to gain her confidence? Perhaps he had wanted to retire in a blaze of glory, reason number one for coming back onto the case after his serious bout with illness. Perhaps he didn't in fact want her arriving at the same Sherlockian presumptions about the Claw as he had won through his hard work and determination? By now she couldn't recall which of them had arrived at the two-killer theory first, but even if Matisak had arrived at this same conclusion from his asylum, it hardly seemed improbable for Luther Darius to do the same from a hospital bed where he may've spawned a plan to "unveil" the true nature of the Claw in the grand style for which he had, over the years, become famous.

The sun shined now like a giant fiery fingernail over the horizon beyond the great harbor where the Statue of Liberty stood. Jessica gazed at the sun as it rose in increments, turning from a fingertip to a crescent and soon to a huge, blood-red orb in the sky, the eye of God, she thought. Nothing was as it seemed, and yet how could she refute the microscopic evidence that proved her wrong, the teeth marks sent to J.T. She had taken the samples herself. They had been in no one else's hands save Dr. Darius' when he had sent them to Quantico.

The terrifying unwanted thought fluttered back into her brain.

It was the kind of thought Jessica Coran wished on no one: Darius perhaps had not actually been happy with her coming on to the case his flattery about her father was all a ruse; he had not wanted her to come to the exact same theory he had of two killers instead of one, because it was a notion he had had long before her, one that he had been carefully nurturing along; he was secretly upset with her.

Darker thought still: Darius was in a position to do something about how he secretly felt.

He always stood in a position to *subvert* her forensics work on the case, especially after lulling her into thinking him a worthy associate. But worthy associates didn't commit suicide . . .

Darius was also in a unique position to divert or sabotage the work of his other colleagues, Simon Archer and Perkins before her. Even from a hospital bed, a man of his reputation could see to it that the wrong files were sent to the wrong locations. In an M.E.'s office such mix-ups were common enough without someone deliberately destroying or withholding evidence.

She recalled the doctor's reluctance when she had wanted to take the additional bite mark cuttings from the throat, and how he had kept the head covered, and how she had placed the materials to go out to J.T. into his hands.

But why? she asked herself several times. Why would the old man sabotage her work? In an attempt to regain his former stature within the medicolegal community as something of an amazing guru? It seemed almost too farfetched, but recently *farfetched* was the rule of the day.

No! no! she told herself, not wishing to hear it. Then she wondered if Darius had been pursued to come back on the case initially, or if he had put the idea into Eldritch's mind. According to Dr. Darius' own statements, they were actively seeking a replacement for him. Was he hoping to so dazzle them with the Claw case that they'd ask him to stay on permanently?

There were not too many men who, after so long a service, could gracefully walk away from such an all-encompassing career as that of Dr. Luther Darius.

But then why kill himself? If he thought to make a comeback of a spectacular nature, to crack the biggest case in New York City . . . why? Archer had said that the old man had fallen in the locker room outside the autopsy theater, and when he awoke, he must have found himself alone in that hospital room, his body connected to an IV, machines registering his heartbeat, blood pressure and breathing. It was perhaps too much for him to bear, this enormous setback.

Thinking he could no longer cut it . . .

Alan Rychman had called the lab and everywhere else he could think of in his attempt to locate Jessica, but no one seemed to know where she was, and she wasn't answering her phone at the Marriott. Then he recalled how she and Darius had disappeared the previous day. He went searching for her himself and found her strolling a harbor sidewalk, stopping to stare off into the bay, occasionally reaching up to gulls that hovered nearby. From a distance she looked to be in conversation with the birds, who were simply fooled into believing she had something for them in her hand.

Rychman beat a path over the aged, discolored wharf, straight for her.

"Talking to the birds?" he shouted as he approached.

"To myself, actually."

"Come up with any solutions?" He slipped an arm over her shoulder and she leaned into him.

"Why is it always that beauty . . . integrity . . . honor . . . all fine things in this city of yours come wrapped in such ugly packages?"

"What's that supposed to mean?"

"I mean that Darius was all those things, at least outwardly . . . beautiful in his soul, and yet he was also deceptive and dangerous at the same time . . . cloaking his own personal mystery and pain so well, working in the lab at the same time."

"A man's got a right to a few secrets, Jess. Hell, without them, we're all . . . well, naked and at the mercy of others who aren't often kind."

She said no more. It seemed strange how the city had come to life around her, but in her state of mind she hadn't before noticed the melee of activity and bustle from cars and buses to pedestrians.

He looked into her shimmering eyes. "I tried reaching you at your hotel ... then thought of here. Listen, Jess, I'm ... I couldn't be sorrier about Luther. He was a hell of a doctor and a fine man."

"I only knew him for a short time." She sniffled and dabbed her eye with a handkerchief. "Foolish, I guess, standing out here crying over him. Fearful for his memory."

"Nothing foolish in it at all," he countered. "Might do us all some good. As to fearful ... well, no one can hurt him now. Hell, no one would want to, Jess."

"Yeah, I guess Archer and the rest of the people in the lab have to be feeling pretty low over it. I should get back, do what I can to ... to straighten out a few things."

He was confused and curious at once. "Straighten out what?"

"I think maybe Dr. Darius had more reason than alcoholism or depression to take that jump. He ... he had to, and perhaps ..."

"You're getting me confused, Jess. Perhaps what?"

"You had a high opinion of Dr. Darius."

"Of course."

"Everyone did, right?"

"Right. So?" Rychman held her to a dead stop.

"He was above reproach, above question. His reputation alone—"

"What's this all about, Jess?"

"The first coroner worked for the king as a watchdog, overseeing suspicious deaths in the kingdom, Alan. Mostly the king wanted someone to represent his interests, so that he got his due on the death of a subject—taxes, lands, whatever. Nowadays things have changed, sure, but just like the king, you and others in government have to rely on the coroner to tell you the truth. In other words, the king may have a man watching out for his own interests, but who's going to question the king's man?"

Rychman didn't understand what she was driving at. He looked deep and questioningly into her eyes. "Jess, I don't do riddles. What're you saying?"

"You up for some coffee? Let's get some."

Over coffee she confided her dark suspicions of Dr. Luther Darius. Rychman listened with quiet reserve the entire time, flinching only once, at the idea that Darius would sabotage his own investigation.

"To heighten the payoff," she suggested. "At the end he would pull the rabbit out of the hat. He'd thought he could do that when he discovered some small clue that the Claw was two men instead of one."

"So he withheld information on the bite marks?"

"I think so."

"And he diverted some of the tissue samples you sent to Quantico?"

"I know it sounds crazy, but—"

"It sounds crazy, all right."

"—but, Alan, it also makes crazy sense. He was the first besides me to suggest that the Claw was two men."

"It's so unbelievable. Darius?"

She was quickly angered by his coolness to the idea. "I know I'm right."

"Now you sound like Luther."

She relented. "You knew him a lot better than I did. But all the time you knew him, Alan, he was in good health and mentally capable. Perhaps, with his failing health—"

"He was a fighter, Jess."

"So, dammit, what made him go through that window?"

"You tell me. I'm going to make a phone call." Alan was upset with what he saw as her wild suspicions.

Alan returned and sat down heavily, his brow creased.

"What is it?" she asked.

"I've just talked with Archer ... Blood tests show no drugs, nothing foreign in Luther's system, and nothing to indicate anything other than a jump from the window."

She breathed in a deep gulp of air, filling her lungs and releasing it in exasperation.

"I think our next step is to talk with Archer, find out if he thinks Dr. Darius was acting strangely, and if he thinks anything strange was going on with respect to the forensics evidence in the case."

"A careful accounting will show you're wrong, Jess," he said. "You've got to be."

She nodded. "I've been wrong before, and this time I also hope I am . . ."

Eighteen

❦

Alan escorted her back to the NYPD forensics laboratories, where they parted company. Jessica feared making any further commitment in their runaway relationship. She feared anything more with a man like Rychman. Like Otto, he lived too close to danger. As far as she was concerned, their lovemaking was an offshoot of the war they were engaged in, two people thrown together due to circumstances, their attraction the only thing bonding them. And yet, she cared deeply for Alan.

In the laboratory she returned to a project she'd begun the day before. Using computer graphics, she matched the ugliest wounds inflicted on the victims, trying to determine the exact nature of the weapon used against these women. She had programmed-in the depth of the wounds and the abrasive nature of the instrument used to turn flesh into jagged scars. She fed every detail to the computer. The computer's job was to find a weapon to fit the wound as closely as possible.

It was determined quickly that in the case of each victim all three rents to the torso had been done simultaneously, and not—as earlier suspected—one at a time. This explained the exacting parallelism of the wounds. The image that was slowly surfacing on the computer screen was that of a three-pronged garden hoe, the prongs sharply bent, the ends like ice picks with razorlike serrated edges.

The Claw lived up to his name.

She stayed with it into the evening, soon realizing that the computer's insistence on the perfection of the three simultaneous jagged lines signaled something else significant. For each of the long tears to be so similar, the pressure had to be extremely even. With a hand-held tool this seemed unlikely. But if not hand-held, what else was there?

Dr. Archer, fascinated with her tack, had become increasingly interested, asking questions. "You don't think the guy's got talons, do you?"

"That's what the computer's saying; that it's the work of a bird of prey with talons created for ripping flesh."

"But that's impossible." Archer suddenly realized that he had lost track of the time and said he must rush off.

Word was circulating in the building that Archer was up for Darius' vacant position, and she guessed that he had an important meeting regarding this possibility. "Good luck," Archer said as he was leaving.

"Good luck to you," she countered, making him stop for a moment and stare.

She qualified her statement, "I mean ... well, I've heard that you may be stepping in to ... to fill ... into the coroner's seat. Good luck."

He bit his lip and dropped his gaze. "I ... I ... wouldn't take it if they offered ... not under the circumstances. I'm not in Dr. Darius' league, anyway ..."

Archer was so self-effacing, perhaps too much so. This was very likely the character trait that had kept him here for so long, working in Darius' shadow.

"Actually, I think you'd do a fine job," she told him.

He laughed boyishly at this. "Coming from you, Dr. Coran, that ... that's quite a compliment."

"Go for it, Simon. God knows you've worked hard enough over the years."

"That's true enough, but it takes more than years of work and dedication ... I mean, running this place? Me?"

"Who they gonna call?" she quipped.

"Hell, any number of good M.E.s across the country. Perhaps they'll even offer the job to you, Doctor."

"No," she said with a laugh, "it's definitely not for me."

"Oh? And why not?"

"I tried a big-city coroner's job once, in Washington."

"And once was enough?"

"Too much politicking; had my hands tied at every turn. Guess I just didn't have the right . . . mind-set."

"Is it so different with the FBI?"

"There're some problems with the Bureau, too, don't misunderstand, but in my present situation I'm given more latitude, more freedom, more . . ." She searched for the word.

"Respect?"

"Yeah, at least by most of the people I work with."

He nodded. "A valuable asset such as yourself? They best respect you, Doctor."

She blushed and looked away but kept talking. "As for you, Dr. Archer, you seem to function so well here. You know how to beat them at their own game."

"Beat them at their own game?" He was momentarily confused.

"Politics inherent in the umbilical tie between the medical and the legal worlds. You've managed the office for Dr. Darius in his absence; you took care of everything and remained above the pressure. That's all rather commendable and they must see that."

"Yes, all true. Well, I appreciate the fact that at least *you* have noticed my contribution," he said with a warm smile. "Must run now. Please, excuse me."

Even as he spoke his last words to her, she managed to keep her expression convivial, although her thoughts were running toward darkness like a mouse down a drain pipe. She had begun to listen to herself as she complimented Archer on how well he had managed things during Darius' convalescence. Even as she spoke she had begun to wonder about Archer's part in Darius' cover-up; then she began to wonder if it wasn't *Archer's* cover-up, and if so, was he covering for Darius or for himself? After all, Archer had been in charge of several of the Claw cases himself. He was in a unique position to alter or obstruct the flow of the investigation.

The thought was like a wild horse galloping through her brain. She tried to catch a complete glimpse of it, but it was too fast. She needed time to mull it over, view it from all angles.

Was she being foolish? Alan's reaction to her suspicions

about Darius now tempered her new suspicions about Archer. Had she targeted the wrong man? Would Alan understand if she went to him with her latest dark deduction?

Had Archer heard the innuendo in her voice? Had he seen any moment's hesitation or shift in expression that gave her away? His having to leave left her little chance to study any reaction, and finally she wondered if Luther Darius had ever entertained like suspicions, and if so was Archer aware of such suspicions? Was it possible that Archer was far more ambitious a man than he let on? And if so, to what lengths would he go to have Darius' position? If he began with lies and cover-ups which escalated with each Claw case in a blind attempt to gain prominence in the lab, and Darius learned of this and threatened him with revelation of the fact, what would the tightly bound Dr. Simon Archer do?

Was he capable of striking out at Darius? Had Darius' locker-room fall more to do with a blow than previously suspected? Worse thought yet, had Darius' jump from his hospital window been helped along by Archer?

The skittering, nebulous suspicions had taken on the complexity and color of a solidified and dreadful idea. While everyone else was busting their humps to bring in a maniacal killer, Dr. Archer was playing a sinister little game of his own right under their noses, so bent was he on being Luther Darius' heir.

"Son of a bitch," she muttered to herself.

But doubts lingered. Could Archer have killed Darius for the top rung on the ladder here?

Her mind was now racing faster than the computer, which was still refining the graphic display on the possible weapon used by the Claw.

Darius found out. He somehow stumbled onto the fact there were two sets of teeth marks, after all, and therefore someone within his organization was, or had been, tampering with physical evidence. It all made sense.

He suspected a number of people before getting around to Archer, but he finally had. Bringing this to light would ruin Archer's career forever. He'd never again see the inside of a forensics lab. Tampering with the medicolegal materials of the crime was against every precept of the medical examiner's office.

Could it be? she asked herself. If so, how could she best prove it? No doubt, Archer had by now covered his tracks thoroughly.

She could review the original autopsy tapes on every victim, cull through them for nuggets of information that might or might not lead to an obvious wrong done, but such an error could be seen as a mistake, a fumble or a bad judgment call. Even if she found out that Archer had ordered slivers of flesh taken before from each and every bite mark on the victims, the lab had such a jumble of tissue samples taken from so many bodies that she couldn't prove a thing, one way or the other. At best she might prove the NYPD coroner's office was guilty of being overburdened.

The obvious goal to Dr. Archer's scheme was the moment when he, and he alone, would unveil telling evidence that would lead directly to the Claw. It had been Archer who was in control of all the chips. All this hidden beneath a veneer of the reticent, self-effacing, loyal and trusted assistant. It almost ranked with the nightmare of the Claw himself.

Bastard, she thought. Or was it *bitch*? Had she been turned into a suspicious bitch by the years, by the terrible convolutions of the plots she had unraveled? By virtue of having seen so much mendacity, was she overly suspicious?

Still, even if he hadn't actually physically pushed Luther Darius through that window, Archer may well have driven his superior to jump.

This made her wonder anew about Darius' fall in the dressing area. Might they have had an argument? Might Archer have shoved Dr. Darius?

It was all too perfect and all too mad. Darius' return marked a move back down the ladder for Simon Archer, just when Archer felt secure in the position he had yearned for, for so many years.

The computer had become insistent, flashing a single graphic on and off at her, as if the machine were daring her to turn and look at it.

She did so and came face-to-face with the actual claw used

by the killer. It was a deadly, three-pronged prostheticlike attachment or glove that fit over the human hand. The killer had fashioned his own cougarlike claw, his own killing machine. Rychman had to see this.

But Jessica was almost afraid to tell him her theory about Archer. He might think she was mad, especially since she'd already accused Darius of tampering with his own "sacrosanct" evidence for personal and professional gain. It had been Archer all along, but she'd been blind, or rather he had been *invisible*. Either way, she had no proof, only the gut-wrenching certainty of her intuition, and that wouldn't cut any ice with Rychman any longer.

She got on the phone to Quantico and caught J.T. in the lab there. She asked twenty questions about how he had received the forensic materials from the NYPD, what kind of postal service was used, how it was boxed, how it was labeled and how many actual samples were forwarded to him.

It all checked out. Archer had covered himself well. She began to feel like a drowning victim gasping for air. She started to hang up but stopped to make another request. "Oh, J.T., see what you can find out for me about a Dr. Simon Archer. You know, what schools he attended, where he worked before here, that sort of thing."

"Sure, Jess." He knew her well enough not to ask why. When she wanted to tell him she would, but not before.

"Call me when you've got it."

He hung up, and she was sure that she had thoroughly confused him.

She dialed Rychman, who was out. She left a message for him to see her at the lab the moment he returned. Alone, she turned to stare at the computer replica of the deadly weapon used on the eight victims of the Claw.

Somehow, she sensed that the body count was going to escalate, largely because police were being stymied by their own forensics people. As before, despite the so-called evidence, despite Dr. Ames' assessment of the killer's mind, she continued to believe there were two monsters at work in all this, and she felt it strangely scary that only she and, of course, the killers knew the truth about the Claw.

One of the lab assistants was coming, a cup of coffee in one hand, the daily paper in another. Jessica shut off the monitor with the graphic detail of the claw as she watched Laurie Marks approaching.

"Dr. Coran, have you seen this?" asked Laurie, her eyes wide.

"What is it?"

Splashed across the front page was Ovid's poem.

"Christ, how'd the papers get hold of it? Damn!"

She began scanning for the informant, but beneath Jim Drake's byline and all through the rutting piece, she saw only references to "sources" close to the investigation.

"All hell's going to break loose," said Laurie. "I hear Captain Rychman didn't tell the mayor's office or the C.P. about the poem, and they just got it by the papers, and Rychman's on the warpath for whoever leaked it to the press."

Jessica's mind flashed on the image of Rychman choking Dr. Ames to death in his office. "I've got to find Rychman," she said. But she first went back to her computer and pressed for the file menu, storing her information under a code known only to her. Impatiently waiting for the computer to run through its final program, she asked Laurie a few questions about Dr. Archer, about how he seemed around the office and the labs, especially lately.

"Nervous, kinda touchy if you ask me, but who wouldn't be? I mean with this kind of an investigation going on, with Dr. Darius killing himself, and with the possibility of his having to take on—"

"Has he ever asked you to do anything . . . *questionable* or anything that you've wondered about?"

She hesitated. "Once . . ."

The computer whine turned into a click, telling her that storage was complete and that she could now pop the disk and take it to Rychman. But now Laurie had her undivided attention.

"Please, Laurie, it could be important."

"Well, once . . . maybe it was an accident . . . we were working late—"

"Yes?"

"And he ... his hand just kinda grazed my ... my breast ... I ... I don't think he meant anything by it, but maybe he did, but he ... he just isn't my type."

Jessica's disappointment was painted in broad strokes across her face. "I'm off to locate Rychman."

"You ... you won't tell him I said anything about ... will you?"

She shook her head, grabbed the computer disk, the autopsy tape and her cane before she rushed out. Laurie Marks frowned as she watched Dr. Coran march away, wondering to herself if the sometimes clumsy, sometimes callous Dr. Archer had hit on the FBI woman. Then she thought of some of the strange stories she'd heard about Archer, stories she'd never repeat to anyone—the kind of sick tales told about a lot of people in their profession.

Nineteen

e

Leon Helfer was hungry and tired; his head ached, his sinuses were clogged and he feared that soon the Claw would know what he had done. If his poem was discovered, and surely it would be, and if the news leaked out, the Claw would know. Even if the news didn't leak out, the Claw would know. Somehow he'd pluck it from Ovid's brain.

Leon had just finished work for the day. His job was a boring one, filled as it was, from hour to hour, with the same mechanical process. And him like a robot for the duration of time he was in the factory. But it was a living, and it kept his mind off the Claw and off killing, off what he had become.

It was his job to inspect pipe. The company made every kind of pipe known, from plumbing pipe to irrigation and city lines, some of the pipe large enough to walk through. The Claw might need to lower his head, but the average man could stand fully upright inside the largest concrete pipe the company made.

Once the pipe was inspected for safety and quality-control purposes, it was loaded onto trucks and sent out into the world. Sometimes Leon felt that his work here was important, but the Claw made it clear that there was only one important task in Leon's life . . .

Machine noises at the factory were deafening, so much so that Leon could talk at the top of his lungs to himself about the Claw and no one could hear. Sometimes he caught his coworkers staring, but he'd gotten used to that, and they'd gotten used to his talking to himself. Or so it seemed.

Then suddenly today Mr. Malthuesen called him into his office and told him that he needn't come back; he said the company was facing hard economic times, and that layoffs were necessary. He said that he was sorry, and that he'd write him a letter to help him find another job, but that he could do no more.

Leon thought it strange that only he was being laid off, especially since there were any number of men who had come to work for the company after he had, people he had seniority over. He guessed it was due to his behavior since his mother's death . . . since the Claw had come.

Maybe the Claw had arranged for him to be fired.

The Claw wanted all of his time . . . wanted him all to himself, wanted Leon to become Ovid twenty-four hours a day.

That seemed quite possible. He would not put it past the Claw to visit Malthuesen in the night to convince him to fire Leon, so that Leon could devote himself completely to being Ovid.

It made sense . . . made perfect sense . . .

Now, home alone except for the dead remains surrounding him in every cupboard and cabinet, Leon awaited with mounting apprehension the Claw's certain arrival. He waited hour on hour for him to come, knowing that in having killed *two* victims the night before last, the Claw would be craving even more, and tonight he'd want to attack and take apart three, and maybe four victims next. This certainly seemed logical to him.

The Claw would come when Leon least expected it.

He'd better be prepared . . . better be a good Ovid.

Better pray that the Claw was in a merciful mood.

God help him if he had angered the Claw too greatly by planting the poem.

The light-emitting diode of a digital clock began to get on Leon's nerves. He wondered what he'd do now without a job. He knew that if the Claw could get him fired from one job, it'd be a simple matter to keep him from getting another.

The Claw most likely wanted Leon to use his days to increase the number of victims they could take. The Claw wanted the city to run with blood . . . wanted the skies to rain blood.

And if Leon was not a good provider . . . a good Ovid, he'd become a good victim.

As the night stretched on, Leon Helfer waited in dread anticipation of his master, his fears colliding with one another to form a knot of anxiety he thought would burst his brain, until late evening turned into morning, and he came to realize that the Claw wasn't coming.

Going with only haphazard sleep where he sat with his knees to his chin in a corner of his living room, thinking about poor Mrs. Phillips, the only victim he had known. Leon realized just how cruel the Claw could be. He had taken old Mrs. Phillips for only one reason, knowing Leon would be devastated by his having to eat from her entrails, to take on the old woman's sins, as the Claw had taught him. Mrs. Phillips had always had a kind word for Leon, always with a smile on her lips. She had seemed innocent of any sins, and yet the Claw had, by virtue of having dispatched her, claimed that her body was riddled with the maggots of sin upon which they must feed.

And so the Claw had fed like a voracious animal over her.

Then the Claw, as if it were just an afterthought, had begun to replace one victim's organs with another's, taking some from the jars he had brought with them, refilling these with the younger organs of the Olin woman.

It was then that Ovid, taking a moment when the Claw was not looking, impetuously shoved the wadded-up poem into Mrs. Phillips' body.

He had felt compelled to communicate with someone outside himself, as compelled as he had been the night Leon had telephoned the all-night radio talk show. He had had to blame it on Leon because this action had made the Claw grow large with anger and strike Ovid with the deadly claw, a razor-sharp series of talons fastened to the Claw's right arm. It was in sharp contrast to the human hand that dangled at the end of his left forearm. The claw itself was made up of three fingerlike extensions, ice-pick sharp, tapered, with cold-steel edges, extending from beneath the black coat at the wrist. It was far deadlier than a hook, each of the three talons having a jagged edge, like those of a fish scaler.

Ovid was the only one alive who had seen the Claw's weapon . . . and he had seen it in action.

It was so fast his eyes could not possibly follow.

Swwwwissssh, swwwwissssh, swwwwissssh. He heard the

horrible sound of it as if it were in the room now with him. It made him get up, stumble around in the dark and cry and shout, but he found himself alone, after all, alone except for the odor of what was in his kitchen cabinets.

It was the first night in so long that the Claw had failed to materialize.

What did it mean? he wondered.

He couldn't hazard a guess, but an overwhelming fear gripped his heart, a double-edged fear. He was afraid that the Claw would come again, but he was equally afraid that the Claw would never come again . . .

At almost nine the next day Leon was awakened by an insistent knock at the outer door. He owned the building. It was paid off finally with his mother's inheritance, and he had evicted the tenants from upstairs so that now only he and the Claw kept house here. Who could be at the door?

He never had visitors.

He was still in the same clothes as when he had left work the day before. He hadn't brushed his hair or his teeth in all this time. He stared out between the curtains at two people, a man and a woman, both dressed relatively well for the neighborhood. The woman banged on the door again, staring, trying to make out the movement inside from behind the faded curtains, when she decided to hold up a badge. She shouted, "Police, please open up!"

Her partner muttered something about forgetting about it, but she swore she saw some movement from inside, and so she banged again.

Leon wondered if it was a test; if the Claw was testing his loyalty.

Suddenly the glass shattered where the female cop hit it with the butt of her gun. She was shouting an apology to the occupant or occupants inside.

Leon, shocked into action by the shattered glass, fearful of their coming in, rushed to the door, shouting, "What the hell're you doing, breaking my glass? You're going to pay for that."

"Mr. Helfer?" she asked.

He was shaken that she should know his name.

"We stopped by last night and yesterday to speak with you, but you're always out, it seems."

"Speak with me? About what?"

"You must be aware that a neighbor of yours was killed a few doors down," she replied. "Look, I'm Sergeant Detective Louise Emmons, and this is my partner, Sergeant Turner. We've been assigned to question everybody in the building about—"

"I'm the only one in the building."

"So we've been told."

"Don't like boarders . . . don't trust them . . . can't."

Turner, who had come closer, eyeballing Helfer, said, "I know what you mean. I rent a space over my garage . . . real nightmare."

Both Emmons and Turner were staring at the way Helfer was dressed. He looked as if he had been ejected from a boxcar with the train going forty. His bloodshot eyes were wide and wild. An odor exuded from his body that spoke of more than mere perspiration and bad breath. Emmons tried to place the odor but it was elusive.

"Can we come in and ask you a few questions about Mrs. Phillips down the street?"

"No, no! I mean, I've got to get to work, and . . . and the place is a mess, and besides . . . I don't *know* anything."

Emmons took in a great breath, her breasts rising in exasperation, but she was also trying desperately to place the odor that seemed to be wafting out to her from the building. "Smells like you've been using cleaning fluids," she said. "Place can't be any worse than mine."

He blocked her way. "No, I'm sorry, but I got no time. I'll be fired if I'm late. I got a nasty boss, real nasty."

"Mr. Helfer," said Turner, sounding stern, "am I to understand that you're refusing us entrance to your domicile?"

Leon stared at him, weighing his options, it appeared. "You . . . you got a warrant? If not, you ask your questions right here and now, and let me get on with my life. I'm sorry about Mrs. Phillips, but I don't know anything and there's nothing I can tell you that will change the fact she's dead."

She and Leon stared back at one another. Leon finally said, "Go ahead. Ask your questions. I don't have all day."

Emmons asked the questions while Turner reached for a cigarette and asked Leon if he wanted one.

"How well did you know Mrs. Phillips?"

"Cigarette?" repeated Turner, holding the packet up to him.

"No, no thanks ... Not well. Just seen her around."

"Like at the park?"

"Sure."

"And the supermarket?"

"Yeah, places like that."

Emmons noted something in her little book that made Leon nervous. Turner was puffing heatedly on his Marlboro.

Emmons looked Leon directly in the eye for a second time and said, "Your neighbors said you once or twice visited her in her home."

"What?" he asked. "Me? That's ... that's a lie."

"Said when your mother died, she had you over for dinner once."

"No, no ... not me. I mean, yeah, my mother died ... left me ... but no, I never had a meal at Mrs. Phillips' place. Talked with her in the park. We ... she'd feed the pigeons, and I'd feed the pigeons and—"

Turner piped in. "What'd you talk about?"

"Weather, the Mets, stuff like that ... nothing big."

"You know anyone that would want to hurt Mrs. Phillips, Mr. Helfer?"

"No, no one."

Emmons asked him his whereabouts the night of her death.

"I was out ... to a movie ... with a cousin. Spent the night."

She asked him where he worked.

He hesitated. "What's where I work got to do with it?"

"Please, Mr. Helfer," she said, "it's just for the record." She pointed to her notebook.

"Oleander Pipes."

"Pipes?" asked Turner. "Smokin' pipes? You think maybe I could get a sample of one of them?"

"No, it's not smoking pipes, it's industrial pipe."

"All right," said Emmons. "Thanks for your time, Mr. Helfer."

"Yeah, thanks, Leon," added Turner.

Helfer closed the door quickly on them. Emmons recognized the signs of a man who had *something* to hide, and she continued to wonder about the odor she sniffed at the door. As they walked away from the premises, they could feel Leon's eyes on them.

"Let's make him sweat," said Turner.

"You're on."

They stood outside for some time, staring up at the building, talking in guarded remarks, using frequent hand gestures, Emmons jotting down items in her notebook. Leon couldn't hear them.

"Whataya call that kind of brick? Stucco?"

"Stucco Royale, I think," she replied. "Think that's bad; look at the weedy yard and that shack out back."

"What a junk pile."

"Breeding ground for a killer?"

"This guy can't be the Claw. He's a wuss. I figure the Claw's got to be something more than Leon."

"You heard the captain and that lady FBI agent," she challenged him.

"What, that there's *two* Claws?"

"Or that there's one guy with two heads like Ames says."

He nodded, considering this. "Still, Leon would be a pretty sorry catch when the TV cameras hit him, but then so was Richard Speck and Jeffrey Dahmer."

"Damn sure would like to get inside."

"No legal way. And breaking his window was dumb, Louise."

"We got probable cause. He refused us entrance. The broken glass was purely accidental."

"There's no probable cause for a warrant. No way."

"What if we examine him a little closer; catch him in a lie or two?"

"Like whether he ate with the old girl or not?"

"Let's talk to some more of his neighbors and maybe his boss at this pipe place."

"You're on," agreed Turner, tossing away a butt, "only first we find some coffee and a can. I gotta go."

Twenty

❧

Unable for the time being to locate Rychman, Jessica slowed long enough to retrieve a copy of the tape made while Darius and Archer were reopening the bodies of Olin and Hamner. She located a tape player and some privacy, listening to the report for any sign of friction between the two M.E.s. To her consternation, she could make out no such difficulties whatever, and this made her doubt her own earlier misgivings about Simon Archer. A straight arrow, Rychman had called him, and suppose he was? And suppose she raised questions about him only to learn that she had sullied his reputation for nothing? Suppose her imagination had run amok? It could cause enough of a stink that her superiors in Quantico might smell it. Yeah, just what O'Rourke would like most of all to come out of her investigation of the Claw. Hadn't O'Rourke gone behind her back to put Matisak in her way?

Her convictions regarding Archer hadn't yet solidified and she was already second-guessing herself: What would Rychman do? How would others react? Would everyone think her mad?

She was unsure what to do with her suspicion, but she knew that she wanted to pay a great deal more attention to Archer than she had. At the moment, she assumed he was meeting with the C.P. and the mayor, his interim status as manager of the coroner's office being made permanent, naming him as the new M.E. in charge. Was it a dream he would sabotage for . . . possibly kill for? Men killed for far, far less.

She went searching for Alan, expecting to find a very upset man who'd no doubt respond badly to the irresponsible publication of Ovid's poem. Rychman, she learned, was in conference with Mayor Halle and C.P. Eldritch. No doubt he was being informed of Archer's new appointment and all of them were hashing out a public relations ploy to combat remarks in Drake's *Times* story, which alleged that the police had knowingly arrested the wrong man in the Claw case, and that he was not the author of the horrid poem. Telephones were shrilly crying out the message that the newspaper account had had a great ripple effect throughout the city, and that Jim Drake's career with the paper was solidified.

"I'm afraid he can't be disturbed now," Rychman's matronly secretary said to her, pursuing Jessica as she pushed by, anyway.

The men in the room fell silent the moment she pressed through the door, except for Rychman, who told his secretary that it was all right.

"You may as well know, Dr. Coran, that the C.P. here wants someone else to head the Claw task force, that I'm being held responsible for the leaks getting out to the press, and that maybe I'm the Deep Throat here . . . for Christ's sake."

"That's crazy," she said, going toward the mayor. "Alan's done everything in his power to contain such information leaks—*everything*." She realized now that Dr. Archer wasn't in the room.

"We've traced this thing. Ames didn't do it," said Eldritch, his thin frame almost quaking with his anger. "His secretary was grilled for hours, and nothing there."

"But Lathrope's people knew," she countered.

"All screened and let go."

"The secretary . . . she made copies that day," replied Jessica.

"She's the most likely, but she swears otherwise," Alan replied. "I'm not a hundred percent convinced of her innocence but—"

"Darius was the only other person to have any knowledge of it, and he's dead," said the mayor.

"No," she countered. "There was also Simon Archer."

They all stared at her. Rychman asked, "Archer? What could Simon possibly have to gain?"

"You're considering him for Darius' position, aren't you?"

"Yes, but it's not an appointment. He must go through various boards, committees, and compete with other applicants," said the mayor. "Of course, he . . . he has solicited my backing and I . . . I gave it, of course. But why do you suspect . . . What possible reason would he have to . . . to sabotage Rychman's investigation in such a way?"

"I'm not completely sure. Call it free association, but I believe he has some plan to . . . to dazzle you, sir, to ensure he gets the position as chief M.E. of the city, and the more sensationalized the case, well . . ."

"That's . . . that is a very serious accusation, Dr. Coran. I hope you have some evidence to support it."

"At the moment, I have very little . . . only circumstantial." She held up the tape she'd just listened to. "Proof that he knew something had been found is in here." She then showed them the computer disk. "And in here is a computer representation of the weapon used by the Claw, a representation that I believe Dr. Archer himself could have created given the evidentiary materials in his possession, and yet he failed to do so."

"What the weapon looks like?" Rychman was instantly curious. "Let's see it."

The C.P. and the mayor were equally curious. Rychman led them to a secluded room with a computer terminal, and in moments Jessica had them staring at what she believed the Claw used on his victims. Rychman was amazed, as were the others. Before their eyes a graphic representation done in geometric red lines afforded them their first glance into the nature of the weapon, and with it the nature of the beast.

"It looks like some kind of meat-cleaving glove," said Halle.

"It is that," said Jessica.

"Look at that," said Eldritch. "You ever see anything like it before?"

"Closest thing to it is a prosthetic hook," said Rychman. "Kind you see on some longshoremen working the docks."

"Maybe the bastard's a sailor, then, a merchant marine."

"I think he's more into gardening tools," countered Jessica.

"Notice how similar the three prongs are to a hand-held garden hoe."

"Yeah ... yeah," agreed Alan, nodding. "You're right."

"You have absolutely no doubt that this is the weapon used on his victims?"

"None whatever."

"How did you possibly come to—"

"A special forensics program designed by my mentor, Dr. Holecraft, Washington's chief M.E. for over thirty years. He had for years dreamed of and worked on a program that would collect all information on the wounds inflicted, compute this to the last degree and reassemble it to mirror back the exact nature of the device used in an attack, from blunt objects to blades and even to caliber of a handgun via the bullet's entrance and exit wounds."

"But if you brought the program with you from Quantico, there's no reason to assume that Dr. Archer would have been proficient in its use, or had had the time—" countered Eldritch, who seemed anxious to defend Archer.

"But he was proficient in its use, and he did have the time." She stopped him with upraised hands.

"You're sure of this, Dr. Coran?" asked Alan.

"The program was sent to the NYPD M.E.'s office two months ago, and Darius didn't seem to know that it was on hand when I asked him about it. Of course, then he became excited about its use, and he asked me—since I'd had practical experience with it—to do the honors. I've been working on this image ever since. But prior to this, for whatever strange reason, the program wasn't being used."

"Perhaps Archer was incapable of using it." Eldritch's hands went skyward. "I, personally, have a phobia when it comes to computers."

"Archer and every medical examiner in the country wants this program. It's being tested now in a number of cities. One of them, from the beginning, had to be New York."

"So the question arises, why wasn't it being used?"

The mayor's question resounded about the room.

"Are you certain of your suspicions of Archer?" Alan pointedly asked.

"I'd stake my reputation on it."

"And are you equally sure that Dr. Archer dragged his feet on providing this information?"

"I don't know that with hundred percent certainty. As I said, my ... my instincts are based on circumstantial findings. But I do know that he knew something had been found in the Phillips cadaver. Dr. Darius confided in him."

"I see."

"That still doesn't prove he told the press about it," said Eldritch.

"No, no, it doesn't, but he's the only one you haven't talked to."

"But we did talk to him," said the mayor.

"About this very subject?"

"He denied having known anything about it. Said he had been left out of the loop since your arrival, Doctor."

"Then I suggest you speak with him again." She popped the tape into a player beside her. She had earlier cued it to the spot she wished Rychman to hear. Darius' distinctive voice was followed by Archer's, a clear exchange of the information Archer claimed now to have no knowledge of. It wasn't the worst of his lies, she guessed.

She hazarded a tentative word. "If he'll lie about this ... what else is he capable of lying about?"

"What do you mean, Doctor?" asked Halle, dumbfounded.

"I fear that he only forwarded selective information out to Quantico, that which would back up *his* theory of the crime, that the Claw is a single individual."

"My God," said the mayor. "If this is true ... think of it ... It could ruin us all if a bastard like that Drake fellow got hold of it."

"Drake doesn't have to get hold of it," said Rychman, "all he has to do is imagine it. Half what he writes is pure conjecture."

"And the other half?" said Eldritch. "Half-truths have been destroying us in the press—you included, Dr. Coran."

"I've learned it's best to ignore my critics," she countered. She knew that Rychman was taking most of the heat that had been flamed by Drake's biting, irresponsible series.

"Lathrope's secretary has ties with Drake," Alan said. "She's just as likely a candidate as Archer, more so even."

"But you saw the woman, you heard her," countered Eldritch.

The mayor added, "I believe she was telling the truth, else she would not have told of her former involvement with the man and his phone call pleading for the very information we were grilling her about."

Rychman conceded that he felt Marilyn Khoen was being honest with them, and he was trained to know a liar when he spoke to one. He considered his senses more reliable than a polygraph, which Marilyn had agreed to take.

"When I think of how I charged into Ames' place," said Rychman, falling into a chair, "accusing everybody in sight . . . damn . . . damn . . ."

"So what're we going to do?" asked Eldritch. "About Archer? How're we going to trip him up, if he is indeed behind all this?"

"The man appears unflappable," said the mayor.

"I'll be working a great deal closer now," Jessica said, "and I'll keep my eyes wide open, you can be assured of that. But we need something to shake him up. I suggest a wholesale investigation of Dr. Darius' department, from mislaid toe tags to broken beakers. I suggest a call for an exhumation of the first victim or victims. I suggest a second autopsy of some of the victims, perhaps Dr. Darius' autopsy as well. Chalk it up to a departmental investigation of what appears shoddy practices since Dr. Darius first fell ill. Give it to the papers, if you like."

"Not at all bad," said Eldritch, thinking like the politician he was. "Hey, Rychman? It'd certainly take some of the heat off of our asses, move it downstage, so to speak."

"No, we give the papers nothing," countered Rychman. "We investigate our own in-house, and the M.E.'s office is part of the network of government offices serving the people. We leak this to the papers and we're no better than Archer, if he's guilty. Who knows, he may have just been following orders." This made Eldritch blanch and fidget.

Jessica thought of her initial suspicions focusing on Darius instead of Archer, and she felt ashamed of herself but proud of Alan for standing so firm on his friend's memory.

"Don't be a damned fool, Rychman," said Eldritch, standing in Alan's face now. "You can't possibly think I had anything to do with some alleged wrongdoing in the M.E.'s office."

"Screw it, Eldritch. I'm not handling any allegation aimed at the coroner's office in the damned press. I'll do it, but I'll do it by the book, using IAD."

"Internal Affairs is fine," said Mayor Halle, "and should Dr. Coran's fears be borne out, *then* we go to the press." The mayor didn't appear anxious to deal with differences between Rychman and Eldritch here and now.

Eldritch backed off and Alan struggled to hide his pleasure.

"You will keep us posted every step of the way," Eldritch told Rychman before barging out.

The mayor stopped at the door, turned and looked back at Coran and Rychman. "Keep up the good work, people. Little wonder we've had difficulty catching the Claw if what you say about Archer is true. Imagine it . . . If he's guilty of subverting information vital to the case, he's . . . well, he may be an accessory to murder."

Twenty-One

~

Sgt. Louise Emmons and her partner, Dave Turner, had continued all day long in Leon's neighborhood, asking questions. More and more their questions led them back to the strange character named Helfer at the center of the block down from Mrs. Phillips. It seemed everyone thought Leon Helfer a little queer in the head, especially since his mother had died and he was on his own. They heard how he had gotten rid of all of the former tenants in the building when their leases were up, isolating himself inside. They heard about his late night drives and how he talked to himself all the time. But they heard nothing that could be in any way construed as evidence.

Emmons, tiring of the door-to-door, went back to her idea regarding the man's boss at the pipe factory. After arranging to see him late that afternoon, she and Turner went to the factory, where Leon's immediate supervisor promptly said, "He don't work here no more."

"Whoa, Mr. Malthuesen. He told us he was in your employ."

"*Was*, yes, but not no more."

"When was he fired?"

"We like to say *let go*."

"All right, then. When was he—"

"Yesterday, just yesterday. Why? Is the little weasel in some kind of trouble?"

"We're only interested in what you know about him, sir."

Malthuesen revealed things they had already heard about Helfer: that he had changed dramatically after his mother's death, that it seemed to have had a profound effect on him. Malthuesen also explained why he had let Leon go.

Emmons sensed intuitively that there was something the man was either lying about or omitting. She dug at him, with Turner's help, but he wouldn't come out with it all. They threatened with legal jargon, and still the man would not tell them anything else.

When they left the plant, Emmons shared her feelings about Leon's boss with Turner, and Turner agreed that the man seemed to be sincere about his reasons for firing Leon, but that he was nervous and fidgety and closemouthed, all tell-tale signs that he was uneasy with the police.

"But that could mean a million things unrelated to the case," he cautioned her. "Who knows, maybe he's got outstanding tickets."

"Who doesn't in New York?"

"Or that he's had a brush with the law in the past himself. Doesn't necessarily mean what he's hiding is relevant to our case, Louise."

She scratched behind her ear and said, "Maybe."

"It's almost quitting time and I'm hungry," said Turner.

"You're always hungry, but you're going to have to postpone eating, pal."

"Whataya mean?"

"Leon lied to us. That's a little more heavy-duty than denying us entry to his place."

"Probably not enough for a judge to issue a search warrant, and if I go down there now, I won't see my kids tonight."

"You bailing out on me? Hell, Turner, this creep could be the Claw. I'm dropping you off at the courthouse and I want you to get us some paper on this."

"That could take hours. Why don't we do it tomorrow?"

"Because if he is the Claw, we've scared hell out of him and he could run, if he hasn't already."

As they drove for the courthouse, he asked, "What're you going to be doing while I'm busting my chops with some judge?"

"I'm going to get back to his place, keep him under surveillance. You'll have to get another car and join me."

"Whoa, I don't like the sound of that," he argued. "You're not going anywhere near that creep without me."

"For Christ's sake, Turner, I'm just going to keep an eye on him. I won't go inside until you get back with the paper, got it?"

"We can't add on another false arrest. We do and it's our butts, Louise. You know that, don't you?"

"I got a feeling about this guy."

"Like your feeling about Conrad Shaw? Look, maybe we'd better not communicate this to the other task force guys just yet, you know?"

They were both smarting about the Conrad Shaw arrest, which had looked so good but had been so wrong. They had been working Shaw for two months. It seemed unlikely that they might have simply stumbled onto the real Claw so easily. It felt like winning the lottery on a found ticket.

"Agreed," Emmons said. "Let's first see what a search uncovers."

"Be careful out there," Turner cautioned.

"Don't worry," she said. "I was born careful."

Once again, it was growing late and still no further word from the Claw. Inside his apartment building, Leon was panic-stricken. The cops were on his doorstep, for God's sake, and where was the Claw? Had the Claw abandoned him? He had killed old Mrs. Phillips, he'd said, because she was a useless person, just taking up space on the planet, without value to anyone or anything beyond the pigeons she fed in the park. Decrepit, her body riddled with pain and injury and disease, the Claw said that he had done the old woman a service, ending her suffering. But now Leon wondered if the Claw hadn't had a more deceptive purpose in mind for Mrs. Phillips all along, an ulterior motive for killing someone so close to Leon.

It led the police into *his* neighborhood, up to *his* front step, to point a finger at *him*.

Had the Claw turned against him?

He had long feared it, yet he had thought that when it came, it would come in a murderous rage with the Claw skewering him as it had all the victims before now. He had not expected this kind of chicanery and deceit and yet it couldn't have been any other way.

He had lied to the police. They need only run a few checks, ask about him where he used to work. Then they would be back.

He realized as if coming from out of a deep cave and into the light that all around him was the smell of death and the evidence to convict him. It had been the Claw's plan all along . . . not to destroy others, but to destroy Leon "Ovid" Helfer.

And the plan had begun when Ovid telephoned the radio talk show; the plan had been solidified when he wrote his poem. Finally the Claw's plan for Ovid and Leon was acted on after Leon had planted his poem inside that corpse. The Claw knew. He knew, and his anger could not be quenched until Ovid and Leon were destroyed.

For a time, Leon had begun to believe that the Claw was one with him; that by virtue of what they shared, the flesh and the sins of their victims, they were in some cosmic way united, that in fact the Claw was Ovid and Ovid was Leon and, by extension, Leon was the Claw. But no more. He knew he could not knowingly destroy himself this way, that it was out of the question, that the Claw was a second person, a second entity, and not a second personality somehow projected by Leon's brain like some goddamned unholy hologram he interacted with.

He must do something about the evidence, the jars filled with human organs in formaldehyde which lined his kitchen cabinets. He must transport everything to someplace where it could never be traced back to him. He must air out the place, remove all signs of Ovid and the Claw. He must think clearly and not overlook a single item that might be a clue to his part in the mutilation and cannibalism of those women. And he must begin *now*.

He shook with the fear now pervading his mind. The Claw *wanted* him to be caught, wanted to see him suffer for the deaths of all those women, be shot down by police like a sniveling dog. Having digested so many sins of the victims, Leon would go to Hell, where the Claw could control him further.

Was that it? Was that what this was all about?

Leon thought of how the monster had come to him in his lowest moment of weakness, when he was most vulnerable, at the side of his mother's coffin; how *it* had materialized out of nowhere to make promises to him, to befriend and console him. There had been no one else.

But it had all been a lie . . . a lie leading to this . . . And the reason was simple. The Claw was no angel; the Claw was an agent of Satan that'd been lurking about the funeral parlor for years, no doubt, just waiting for someone like him—the perfect victim—to come along.

And now this devil had led him to his own end.

"I won't let him get away with it! No!" shouted Leon, rushing to the kitchen, tearing open cabinets, locating every horrible, disgusting object that he and the Claw had ever collected. In the basement, he searched for and found several crates and boxes, and in a black corner of the room he thought he saw the specter of the Claw staring at him.

Snatching on the light, he saw that it was just an old coatrack that'd been here for years, and yet, moments before, he would have sworn it was the Claw come for him.

Shaken, he dragged the crates upstairs, where, in the brightly lit kitchen, he began to pack them with the awful remains, each jar sloshing with his excited hands. There weren't enough crates. He'd have to return to the basement for a box. He did so cautiously, this time taking a flash with him and turning on the light before he dared look again at the coatrack. It was still a coatrack.

He snatched up the sturdiest-looking box, flicking away at a cockroach that scurried along its flap. He then returned quickly to the work remaining in the kitchen.

Finally it was all packed, and he stood wondering how he could get each crate and box outside without drawing attention to himself. Then he flushed red with heat, wondering if the cops were having the place watched. If he stepped outside with a single crate, they'd snatch him up, the evidence on his person. All they'd have to say is that he was acting in a suspicious manner.

He went from window to window, his paranoia rising. Every car on the street looked like an unmarked squad car or surveillance vehicle. He had to calm himself, maybe wait until nightfall. But by nightfall, they could be back with a search warrant. He must dispose of the bloody evidence and he hadn't the time or stomach to ingest it all at once.

He had been such a fool . . .

He froze where he stood because the deathly silence of his house was whispering to him in the voice of the Claw, asking, "Where're you going, Ovid? *Whhhherrrrrr're yooooou goooo-ing? O-vid . . . O-vid?*"

A strange wind was sweeping up from the open basement door that looked now like the throat of Hell, ready to swallow him whole.

The telephone rang shrilly and the *whirr* and whisper within the *whirr* was suddenly gone, the house raging with silence again, save for the intermittent, insistent ring of the phone.

He went to the phone hesitantly but once there he grabbed it up, saying, "Hel-hello?"

"*We're* going, Ovid." It was him, the Claw, on the line. He'd never telephoned him before.

"Going?" He tried to swallow but his mouth was dry and cottony. In the background, he could hear the sounds of rushing traffic, suggesting a phone booth or perhaps a car phone. "Where?"

"We'll disappear . . . go elsewhere . . . where they can't find us. Just wait for me there."

He was momentarily confused. Could he trust the Claw? "For how long?"

"For as long as it takes."

"I thought when you didn't come last night . . . and the cops came this morning . . ."

"Cops?"

"Police were here, asking questions."

"Yes, I see they've fixed on locating Leon. That's why we must disappear."

"Another country, another city, where?"

"You will know in time."

"I don't have any time. They're bound to come back."

"Leave them to me."

"All right . . . all right, I will."

The Claw hung up. Ovid knew now that the Claw was not an imagined creature of the dark or some other facet of Leon's own personality. The phone call had been *real*. This, along with the fact that the Claw hadn't abandoned him, after all, went a long way to quell Leon's frazzled nerves. As much as he feared the Claw, he realized, he needed him; that, in a sense, *the Claw was him*.

Still, he must dispense with the incriminating evidence he had so foolishly allowed to accumulate all around him. He must give some thought to the boxes. While he sat there, staring at them, his eyes wandered into the living room, where an old carpet reminded him of the blood-soaked Oriental rug still in the trunk of his car. He remembered, too, that his tools had been used in every killing.

There was so much to think of, so much to do. He returned to the windows, going about the house, staring out. He saw no strange cars now. Every car on the block could be accounted for; he had stared down this length of asphalt for years, so he was sure. He saw a few people milling about, but he saw no one that looked out of place.

He went to the rear of his house and gazed for a long time before he decided that the alleyway was at peace with itself, and that there weren't a thousand cops hiding behind trash cans, garage doors, telephone poles and bushes. He had to traverse his backyard to the garage, where his little car was kept. He had a good notion of what he wanted to do with all the evidence, although he wasn't sure he could get away with it.

For now, relatively sure of his safety, he began to make trips to the car and back, carrying one crate at a time, carefully placing them into the trunk atop the soiled, bloodied rug that had been Mrs. Phillips' shroud only two nights before. Leon was cautious with each crate, but when he lifted one of the less sturdy boxes, the bottom gave way and he went to his knees in an attempt to keep the jars from hitting the kitchen floor. But one containing a victim's heart shattered, sending a slick of formaldehyde out from his knees. Through this the organ slid across the floor, slapped against the first rung of the basement steps and then flip-flopped down and down, leaving a thin liquid trail of gruel in its wake.

"Damn, damn," Leon cursed at the delay. It meant more cleanup, more wasted time. He went down into the basement, fetched the now soiled heart and brought it back up to the kitchen. He found tape, reinforced the box that had come loose and jammed the dirty heart down into the box between the other jars.

He then looked down at the broken jar and the mess created by the formaldehyde. He had always detested the odor, but it had never bothered the Claw. It was, however, sure to go rank if he did not clean it up quickly. He grabbed a kitchen towel, but knew this would not be enough. He needed newspapers, lots of them.

He found a stack in the corner in the living room and threw them about the kitchen floor, stomping over them in a wild dance. He saw the headlines about the Claw and knew he must destroy the papers, too.

"That'll do it," he promised himself.

In five minutes he had the problem soaked up, and with a damp mop and Cheer he cleaned the linoleum, much pleased with his progress. But he knew that the heat outside was not doing the other organs much good in the trunk of his car.

He now crushed all the newspapers into a Hefty bag and tied it off. This he took outside to the trash cans and shoved it all into a can belonging to him. This done, he retrieved the now well-taped box, returned to the garage and grabbed his toolbox. He put the last box and his tools on the backseat of the car and in a moment was cautiously making his way out of the area.

Jim Drake's star was rising at the *Times* and he owed it entirely to the Claw, not that he had ever dreamed that such evil could be a meal ticket. It just happened, he kept telling himself; it didn't mean he was a bad person. If he didn't write the stories, someone else would, and someone else would get the prestige, money and power coming to him nowadays. He also knew that he owed much of his success to Archer. If Dr.

Archer weren't as concerned a citizen as he was, Drake's information trail might've shriveled away long before, but Archer was what he was, a real concerned citizen who for reasons of his own—ambitious ones—leaked useful information to Drake.

Now there was heat being put on the good doctor, or so Archer thought; maybe the man was just feeling paranoid, and little wonder with that FBI lady watching his every move, not to mention Rychman, who was enough to frighten a sumo wrestler.

A dampness made the dark air all around feel like a shroud, and once again Drake cursed Archer for picking such a deserted area to meet. An occasional car fired by the open alleyway, and earlier someone had parked a car in the dark recesses of the shadows here. Now that his eyes were accustomed to the dark, Drake thought the car in the alley might be Dr. Archer's BMW. He went nearer, scanning for any sign of anyone at the wheel or nearby, but he saw no one. The alley was a complicated one with a Y-fork, one branch dead-ending at the back of a factory.

A step closer and he thought he saw a shrouded form at the wheel, but it was so still, it didn't look human. Suddenly the engine kicked into life and the car came at Drake, tires smoking. Drake ran for the Y-fork, pretending at first to go toward the dead end, but at the last moment he dove the other way. The car shot by uncontrollably, and Drake got to his feet, racing for the exit and the street for his own car, his mind trying to fathom the reason for the attack, but for now he must think of one thing and one thing alone: *survival.*

He was out in the open, running toward his car, which was parked halfway down the street, when the BMW tore into view behind him. It was coming down on him at sixty, seventy, eighty. Drake prepared to swerve at the last moment, but the killing machine anticipated him, driving his body into a parked car, driving the blood from within him to all the orifices. He was literally squashed between the metal of the two vehicles.

As he drove off, Archer glanced into his rearview mirror.

Drake wouldn't be talking to Coran or Rychman. One less worry in Archer's life.

Detective Emmons pulled her unmarked car into view of the building where Helfer resided alone. There were several lights on, but she saw no movement or shadow. She feared he had already fled. She would like nothing better than to get inside the little prick's place for a look. She cautiously slipped out and walked through a gangway to the rear alley that would lead her to Helfer's backyard.

She could still smell the strange odor that earlier emanated from the house; it was a stench she would not soon forget. As she rounded the garage at the back she found it standing open, the black interior a gaping maw, and to her surprise the little weasel had a silvery BMW nosed squarely at the front of the open garage. The fool was asking for it to be ripped off or stolen. She wondered how he could possibly afford it, but she gave more thought to how pleased she was to find him in. A cursory search of the car with her flashlight turned up the fact it had recently been in an accident that had damaged the front grillework and fender. She started for the license when a sudden noise startled her, making her whip around and draw down on a black cat that spit at her and showed two venomous shining eyes. She breathed deeper and took down the license plate, noting that it could not be Helfer's, as it was a medical plate, signifying the owner was a doctor.

Maybe she had the wrong garage, she thought. It made no sense.

She dared not open a door or the trunk, not without the warrant. Where was Turner! Had he stopped for a burger? Her light then found the creep's trash cans against the fence in the alleyway.

"Public domain," she whispered to herself, and smiled. She didn't need a warrant to go through the trash and there was no telling what she might unearth there.

She dragged out a Hefty bag and carried it behind the garage, where she dumped it. She was immediately assailed by the bizarre odor that had hit her full force when she was standing at Leon's front door earlier that day.

"Christ, what's this guy been eating?" she muttered, and then thought of the cannibal called the Claw. With the only light a streetlamp some distance from her, her flash seemed the only warm thing in the alley. She wished that Turner were with her. She squeezed her gun back into its holster, glad for the feel of its protection. She silently told herself the same words that were the last she'd said to Turner. "I was born careful."

Soon Emmons' hands were filthy with tomatoes, with little somethings that looked like raisins buried in wet coffee grounds, with oatmeal and she didn't want to know what else. Had she gotten into the wrong trash can, as she had the wrong garage? Not a chance. That unholy odor that rose above the rank decay of vegetable matter was the same as in the strange house. She had flung aside several balled-up newspapers, one with headlines about the Claw staring her in the face. Maybe she was way off base, she told herself after a time.

What had she expected to find, she asked herself now, an ugly pair of collapsed Ping-Pong balls that turned out to be decaying eyeballs? Maybe it was time for a reality check, maybe a shot of Jim Beam. But if she could find something—*anything*—to implicate this creep in the death of the Phillips woman, she would thereby implicate him in the Olin woman's death, too, and if he wasn't the freaking Claw, he damned well knew who was.

Turner was right about Helfer's puny appearance. She had imagined the Claw would be a masterful man with hypnotic eyes like those of Bela Lugosi in *Dracula*. It was hard to believe that any woman worth her salt could be overpowered by such a loser as this shrimpy Lee Harvey Oswald look-alike. Then again, most of the serial killers on the books were small in stature, from Manson to the skinny Richard Speck, most with acne problems like they were stuck in puberty, and all of them with serious sexual dysfunctions of one sort or another. And if Leon was one of two men involved in this killing rampage, as Dr. Coran believed, Leon certainly could fill the bill for the dominated half of the duo.

Still, his trash, although malodorous, wasn't filled with human organs or tissues.

She thought of what she knew of the victims, how they had died: first with a hammerblow to the head, rendering them unconscious. Totally in keeping with a little creep like Helfer. She wished only that she could get one chance at him. If anyone like him came at her with a hammer, she wouldn't hesitate to blow his fucking face away.

Then she thought of the awful damage that the killer's blades had done to the women, and this, with the lingering odors around her, conspired to make her want to puke. She'd deliberately stayed away from the morgue after seeing the first set of pictures on the first victim, well aware that to see them in real time would be too much for her. Turner had been more than sympathetic and helpful in keeping her secret. Turner hadn't razzed her about it, either. In fact, he stood in every time for her, making sure there was nothing in the reports that indicated she hadn't been involved one hundred percent.

Maybe that's why she felt compelled to work harder on the case than all the others combined, she told herself now. Maybe that's why she was getting so good at sniffing these low-life *sonsofbitches* out, like Shaw and now Leon Helfer. Regardless of what anyone else said, Shaw, even if he wasn't the Claw, shouldn't be on the streets. Leon was cut of the same cloth; she just knew it.

Continuing to sift through his garbage, she imagined a scenario in which Leon, learning of Shaw's arrest, had deliberately gone out and committed the horrid double murder in order to make Shaw appear innocent and thus gain his freedom back, because maybe Leon felt like only half a man without Shaw. But nothing she could uncover showed any connection between Shaw and Leon. Although the idea was in keeping, the shoe didn't quite fit.

A curious man going by the alley entranceway glanced toward her, no doubt thinking her mad. Another man came around a corner, shocking her, and she fully expected it to be Helfer coming for her, but it was a tall man in a black overcoat and he asked, "You're Emmons, aren't you?"

"Yes, that's me. Who're you?"

"Perkins, M.E.'s office," the stranger flashed his M.E.'s badge. "Got a call to be here from . . . from, ahh . . . HQ, that there was going to be a search and seizure?"

"Paperwork's rolling on it, yeah."

"Oh, good . . . then I'm not too late. How long you think it'll be? I got kids at home and one of 'em's in recital to-night."

She smiled at this and relaxed, taking her hands out of the garbage, grabbing up some of the newspapers and wiping with them when she noticed the gruesome stains on the paper and again that odd, disturbing odor. Suddenly she realized that it was the kind of preservative they used on cadavers at the morgue. Then she remembered the medical plate on the car in Helfer's garage. But it was too late.

The man lifted his black valise in one surgically gloved hand and for a moment dangled it before her eyes, when a sudden swipe of icy steel and wind tore across her eyes, shredding them. He was laughing as if it were all a magic trick. She blindly stumbled away, trying to pull her gun while he said, "Meet the real Claw."

As she reached for the gun in her shoulder holster, the claw crashed into her with light reflecting from somewhere, and the flash of light lobbed off her right hand, the severed limb thudding against her shoe, making her shriek and pull away, backing deeper into the garage, blood spurting from her wrist, pumping like a geyser and making her light-headed. Blood streamed down her face from her wounded eyes. She reached wildly at her gun with her one good hand, fumbling and finally getting the weapon into her grasp when she felt the powerful claw clap around her neck, severing arteries and cutting off her choked, gurgling scream, pinning her against the car. Unable to turn, she clung tightly to the gun held now at her midriff, waiting for him to turn her over and drive the damnable claw into her breasts and drag it jaggedly to her navel, as she had seen in countless horrible photographs.

She was the ninth victim.

She tried to feel the gun in her hand but everything had gone numb. She could feel consciousness evaporating, knowing that if she could not remain conscious, she was certainly dead, and yet, to remain conscious meant excruciating pain if he got at her again with the claw. Already she had lost a limb, already her neck was showered in her own blood.

He turned her around and saw the gun clenched in her fist and he fully expected to be shot to death on seeing it gripped so, but then he realized that she was too weak to lift it, too weak to pull the trigger, and this brought a smile to his lips as he raised the claw over his head and brought it down in one powerful dig, feeling it take root in her where the ice-pick ends jaggedly made their way through her, making her twist and squeal again.

He had gotten lucky seeing Emmons from the house going through Leon's trash. She must also have seen his car. He tore from her the little notepad she carried. He'd destroy it later.

He had never expected to enjoy the killing as an explosive orgiastic experience, but that's precisely what it had become, and in the sheer pleasure of brutally taking life, he had found that brute part of himself he called *Casadessus* who had been locked away just below the surface his entire life; that part of him that had hated all the constraints, all the nagging, needling commandments, all the pressure to conform, all the voices telling him his entire life what to do; that part of him that secretly murdered his father and mother once a night every night during his years under their roof; that part of him that had been restrained from hanging his sister; that part of him that *had* hung her dog instead; that part of him that fought his entire life to be unleashed and unfettered. Now he had given over to that side, and yet he was well adjusted enough to do so in careful increments, and to do so with a master plan in mind.

While at the same time that he could watch women squirm beneath the impaling claw before he completely gutted them, he could also be comforted in the thought that he could never be caught—*ever*. He had Leon to assure this, and he had Dr. Simon Archer to assure it as well. Leon, his Ovid, was the perfect dupe, a perfect victim in his own right. Dr. Simon Archer had learned all about poor Leon from his dying mother at the hospital where Archer did his *pro bono* work. Archer knew precisely the state of mind her death would leave the weak-minded Leon in, and that he would be helpful to Casadessus, the real Claw. Leon was so impressionable, like a child, so easily molded.

But apparently Leon had some ideas of his own. The poem had come as a shock, but a bigger shock was when Dr. Darius told him of its discovery *inside* the body. Darius had gotten a copy from Lathrope and had shared its content with Archer. Little bastard had disobeyed him, and now Archer's cleverly laid plans were unraveling at the seams, unless he could quickly put everything right.

The first step to putting things right was to rip the flesh of Detective Emmons from top to bottom with the tool that had come from the mind of Casadessus, an idea polished and improved on by Archer. He covered himself in a smock taken from his valise, lifted her sagging form and carried her dying body into Helfer's house.

Twenty-Two

꒚

Once inside Leon's house with Emmons, who was still alive, Archer took further hideous delight over her. Here he disemboweled her, tearing her intestines from her stomach cavity, curling them in a heap beside her, as was the Claw's custom. Rychman, Coran and the others would find her eviscerated, gutted open like a fish on a slab. And Leon was the perfect suspect. Archer had seen to that.

Archer's clothing was bloodstained, but he had a change of clothing in his trunk. He had been careful once more to wear a hair net and surgical gloves, even under the glove of the claw so as to leave no prints *inside* the claw itself. Coran would think to investigate the interior of it, he was sure. Now, ready to feed on the dead Emmons, he covered even his teeth with an acrylic coverlet that duplicated the impressions made by Leon Helfer. His plan was one of genius, thanks to the ruminations of his alter ego, Casadessus, whom he kept secret from even Leon.

The teeth impressions were compliments of Leon's dentist, a Dr. Parke, who had been most pliable when presented with the sight of $25,000. The good dentist had a number of outstanding gambling debts he was anxious to be shed of. The transaction had gone smoothly, and when Casadessus had visited Dr. Parke again, the dentist had no fear or suspicion of him. He just wanted to know if there was anything else he could do for him, for payment. "There is one thing," Casadessus told him just before pushing him down an open elevator shaft. "You can die for me."

Archer had agreed that Parke, like Jim Drake, had to be eliminated. It just tidied things up and he was cautious to a fault.

209

He fed over Emmons' organs now, feeling the warm blood and tissue traveling down his throat. Her soul would add power to his, become one with him as the prey and predator met in the ultimate union. She would go a long way to empower him with the strength needed for what lay ahead. But he hadn't much time before Leon might return and before Emmons' partner or other police might show up.

Sergeant Emmons had been a pleasant surprise, coming on his heels as she had. Archer had entered Leon's stinking place with a key he'd fashioned long before. Expecting Leon to be there, he became incensed to learn that Leon had not only disobeyed him by leaving but had removed all the organ jars.

He had gone to the window and peered out, recalling how he had once watched from this same window to see Leon with Mrs. Phillips in the park, feeding pigeons. He had known then that Casadessus, his other self—known to all others as the Claw—would kill Mrs. Phillips in order to implicate Leon further in the Claw killings. After Leon was taken into custody, Simon would prove beyond any doubt that Helfer was the one and *only* Claw. It was the type of attention-grabbing case that would catapult him into the kind of prominence demanded of his profession. If he were ever to be given the serious consideration granted people like Luther Darius, he must carry through with Casadessus' diabolical plan. Once accomplished, Simon Archer would be whole, Casadessus had promised.

He'd then seen Emmons out the rear window going through Leon's trash. He went down the street, fearful at first, and when he saw her unmarked police car, and no one near, he got in and called dispatch, who asked, "Unit 234, what is your position?"

When he did not answer, the dispatcher said, "Turner? Are you there? Emmons? Louise, are you there?" Louise Emmons was the lady cop at the trash, but there was no sign of her partner. She must be moonlighting on her own. She had undoubtedly seen his BMW and possibly the smashed fender. He decided he could use her in his scheme to implicate Leon and extricate himself from any possible suspicion. He'd fortunately carried his black valise into Leon's with him, intending to plant the murder weapon in Leon's bedroom closet. Now he'd leave Emmons' body as well as the damning murder weapon to ensure Leon's absolute guilt. It could not have worked out better. Not even his sinister other self had planned such a climactic end to the Claw.

Now, his lips red with her blood, he swallowed another piece of Emmons, knowing the protein was good for him.

Having fed to his liking, he reached with his bloodied and gloved right hand into his mouth and snatched off the hard, acrylic tooth coverlets that Leon's dentist had fashioned for him at a dear price. These he carefully wrapped in cellophane and placed in his pocket.

He stood over the body where it lay in the kitchen. Emmons had been a lovely woman in life, and she had sustained him in death. His strong, inner self, Casadessus, grew in strength and energy each time he fed, and Simon Archer, too, was strengthened. With each kill, Simon became more and more adept at getting what he wanted.

Now he had only to let things fall as they may. He stepped away from the last feeding he would have in some time. The masquerade must be finished, the Claw captured and his reign of terror ended, all for Simon.

Archer sat in the middle of Leon Helfer's living room, his knees pulled up to his chest, rocking and biding his time, determined to keep calm and to cover his own tracks as carefully as he had throughout the year of the Claw. He'd soon take his final step as the Claw, and all would end with Leon's capture or—preferably—his death.

It was odd, he thought, how he had become a murderer, and why. He hadn't planned it, not really . . . at least not the first time, yet it had grown out of who he was and what he did. He'd begun in the lab where he stripped the bodies of the women; knowing he could not mutilate them, knowing that if he did, it would surely end in his dismissal, if not his arrest, he took what delights he could. He knew he must refrain from any cutting other than the coroner's Y-cut, unless there was some overriding and urgent need to cut elsewhere. But he had such urges; sometimes he wanted to tear the corpse from head to toe. It had just started creeping over his mind like a growth, a snaking vine. He *could* mutilate the insides, that which did not show. And so he began ... He ripped apart the organs in the privacy of his lab, and finding this not satisfying enough, he had begun to cannibalize the internal flesh.

He did not know exactly why.

He was not sure he wanted to know why.

Why had his appetite for flesh suddenly blossomed? Was it hereditary? An ancient lust, genetically coded? Or had it a cerebral origin coming out of a nasty childhood in which his mother often bit him repeatedly as punishment for wrongdoing? Either way, why did he now feel the need for a *fresh kill* when before, the quiet, silent feeding over corpses entering the morgue had been enough?

Ambition, he guessed. He might have gone on feeding his prurient, unusual tastes just as he had for years in the depths of the city morgue but for his other self, that self who was ambitious enough to want Dr. Darius' position.

Archer kept his secrets well from everyone; however, he kept no secrets well from himself. He knew that there were two Simon Archers, and the Mr. Hyde was aware of Dr. Archer, and vice versa.

He must get up, make the call and get out.

He gathered up his black valise and other things, leaving only the poorly hidden tell-tale claw and the gutted, motionless body of Detective Emmons, her eyes gone from their sockets, delicacies that Archer had taken for himself.

He dialed 911 and clicked on the spliced-together tape recording he had forced from Leon several months before, knowing the day would come when he'd have to use it. Leon's taped voice said, "Someone's been killed ... send help ... quickly." Leon then gave his address and Archer hung up over the protests of the operator.

Archer then quickly disappeared from the premises.

When Dave Turner pulled within sight of Leon Helfer's squat little apartment complex, his heart felt as if it were in ice, his nerves completely dulled, and his vision blurring like that of a drunk's. It was true ... It was true, what they were

saying on the radio: another victim of the Claw had been discovered, and it was a cop. He knew it was Emmons.

"Dammit, Louise, damn you! Why didn't you wait?" He
was holding the search warrant in his hand, waving it at the
unfeeling night sky.

Capt. Alan Rychman stood on the very steps where Turner
and Emmons had questioned Leon Helfer. He seemed to be
directing an orchestra of cops. Sergeant Pierce was beside
Rychman and now he pointed out Turner, who was fighting
his way through the crowd toward them. Rychman looked as
if he'd swallowed hemlock, and he started straight for Turner,
grabbing him and holding on, saying, "Where the hell were
you, Turner?"

"I . . . I . . . went for a search warrant, Captain. She . . . she
wasn't supposed to go in until I got back."

Rychman snatched the warrant from him and looked at it.

Turner's face was stricken with grief. "Did she . . . did she
die badly?"

Pierce said simply, "You don't want to go in there,
Turner."

Turner tried to push past him, but Rychman held on, ordering him to stand down.

"Bastard! Bastard! Little weasel, Captain. The guy's a
weasel. Why didn't she wait? Why'd she go in alone?
Doesn't make sense. She promised; she knew the danger;
knew I was on my way. So, why? *Why?*"

Turner leaned across the top of a vehicle, his body shaking
with pent-up rage and tears.

Pierce just stared at the back of Turner's head, saying,
"She'll be taken care of, Turner. She's in no pain now."

Rychman frowned and nervously nodded, adding, "She
cornered the Claw, Turner . . . Now we know who the creep
is. With an APB out on Helfer, he's as good as dead."

Inside Leon Helfer's apartment house, Jessica Coran first
took a cursory look at the condition and situation of the body,
finding the fact that Emmons' eyes were missing far more
disturbing for some reason than the fact that every organ in
her body had been turned out, some resting near the body

while others, like most of the brain, had been heaved across the room. Some of the organs had large chunks missing, presumably eaten by the cannibal.

Just to get away from the body and to draw her breath, Jessica toured each room, examining for any clues that might tell her where Emmons was when she was first attacked. It appeared from the trajectory of blood against the walls in the kitchen that the killing had occurred there, as if she had been surprised and attacked on entry at the back door. A trail of her blood led Jessica deeper into the kitchen, where the body had been splayed open, her organs squandered about the room in what appeared to be a more violent rage than the Claw had heretofore exhibited.

Emmons was hardly recognizable.

The sight gave Jessica pause, which the police photographer and the evidence team seemed to take as a sign of weakness. She brought herself up quickly when she heard someone say that Dr. Archer had been located and was on his way.

She wanted to get as much accomplished as possible before Archer arrived. She gave orders for the E.T. people to concentrate elsewhere, and in particular to search for tools and deadly instruments. One of the men went straight for the open door of the basement, stepping directly into a smear of fluid. Jessica's shout—that he watch his step—came too late.

She placed her black valise within reach and knelt over Louise Emmons' disfigured corpse, trying to control her nerves, which threatened to erupt at any moment. Her immediate reaction was that the body had been here less than an hour. Even so, the flies had found it.

As she cut away patches of stained clothing, bagging these in paper, as was necessary in properly drying and preserving bloodstains, she thought once again about the letter of the law with regard to the chain of custody of medicolegal evidence of this nature.

She knew that the practicalities of proof did not require the State of New York to exclude every possibility of substitution or tampering; that it need only establish a reasonable assumption that there was *no* substitution, alteration or tampering of the sacrosanct evidence. All that was required was to establish a "chain of custody," a reasonable assurance that the exhibits of trial were the same as those taken from the scene, and that they remained in the same condition.

A lot of assumptions and assurances were made and taken for granted along the way between scene of event and the medical examiner's office. She had learned from Dr. Aaron Holecraft that it was not sufficient merely to show the authenticity of the item on which analysis was based, but also to prove that the custody of the materials analyzed was absolutely reliable.

There was always danger of adulteration, even confusion, of materials in a busy lab, but worse, there was always the possibility, however remote, of tampering. She could recall word for word what Holecraft had said on the subject.

"It is unnecessary that all possibility of tampering be negated, but where the forensic substance is passed through several hands, the evidence must not leave it to conjecture as to *who* had it and what was done with it!"

The bottom line, even for a bad M.E. who was faking it, was merely to establish a chain that afforded reasonable assurance. Archer knew this. Every M.E. knew this.

Could he have used it to his advantage, to further his career? It would be a simple matter for the acting head of the medical examiner's office, like a Mafia accountant doctoring and falsifying books.

As her mind played over the importance of the chain of custody in the Claw case, she took nail scrapings from below Emmons' already paper-white, stiff fingers.

She tried desperately to tell herself that perhaps she was being too critical of Archer's performance; that given the circumstances of his situation—a shortage of people, the sudden loss of strong leadership in the department, her own threatening presence—that maybe she herself had simply become overly suspicious of everyone's motives. She wasn't happy with the idea, for she was beginning to suspect even her friends of plotting against her, like J.T. He had put off her request for other, pressing work at Quantico, and there had been something in his voice the last time he had spoken with her, a kind of backscatter that was saying between the lines how sorry he was for something unspoken. As for the background check on Archer, he'd given her only a long series of generalizations, nothing concrete.

Maybe her growing paranoia was getting out of hand, affecting how she viewed people. Maybe . . .

"Oh, God . . . God damn!" shouted the policeman in the basement.

She went to the door and peered down to where the flash lit up a lump of flesh. "What is it?"

"Looks like her spleen or a kidney . . . I don't know," he replied.

"Leave it exactly as you've found it. Don't touch anything. Any tools down there?"

"Nothing other than brooms and rakes. It's weird."

"What's weird?"

"Got a workbench but no tool chest, no tools."

"They travel with this creep," she said. "They're probably in his car. See if you can find a light switch down there, and I'll get that photographer back."

It was a fundamental precept of jurisprudence that a jury, upon seeing the items presented in evidence relevant to a case, was powerfully affected. She knew from the Matisak case, in which she and J.T. has amassed a small mountain of forensic evidence, that such items as those from the basement of Leon Helfer's house would most certainly put him away for life. All she had to do was make sure that the genuineness of the article from here to trial was carefully authenticated by tracing its every movement and repository, and into whose hands it had passed from place to place. Only in this manner could a judge rule that the chain of custody was appropriate and thus the evidence permissible in a court of law.

A close reading of the records with respect to each of the Claw's victims had revealed—to her way of thinking—that Dr. Simon Archer had not always been careful about the integrity of the chain of custody. She thought surely that this must have been a very abrasive thorn in Luther Darius' side; no doubt they had arguments over it. On the surface, and especially to anyone who was not an M.E., it might look like simple relaxing of rules, carelessness, errors, but to Jessica

Coran, a perfectionist, it looked far more like tampering, or at the very least negligence.

She'd earlier gone to the *New York Times* and had found Jim Drake at his desk, looking smug and pleased with himself. She asked him point-blank about who it was that had supplied him with the information about the poem written by the killer. He had refused to tell her.

"You knew this would compromise our case, and yet you went ahead with the story without even giving us the benefit of knowing you had it or that you were publishing it, Drake. Don't you see that every time you do something like this, you erode any trust, confidence or cooperation built up between the press and the police?"

He rocked forward in his squeaky chair and stood up all in one fluid motion, speaking as he did so. "It was my editor's decision to run it, and I respect him for showing good sense and guts."

"That's a cop-out and you know it."

"Look, Dr. Coran," he said, raising his voice, looking around at those who'd begun to stare, "I'm thirty-three years old, a veteran investigative reporter, and my first loyalty is to the story!"

"The *story*?" she said snidely.

"The story, the newspaper, the public—"

She snorted in disdain. "You don't give a rat's ass about the public's right to know. We both know that."

"All right, maybe I'm not so sure what the public wants or thinks, but—"

"Public interest too big an abstraction for you?"

He stared a moment, realizing she was making him sound like a fool. "When I get any information that makes a good story, and it doesn't break the law, then I'm going to use it. If it upsets you or Rychman, the D.A. or the friggin' mayor, then that's no concern of mine."

"It just might be more concern of yours than you think, Mr. Drake. I happen to know that you obtained your information from Simon Archer, and that it was *off* the record."

"There was nothing off the—" He had stopped himself, his guilty eyes giving the rest away.

She'd then turned and rushed away, leaving the reporter to stare after the cane-wielding FBI agent.

She learned tonight that Drake was dead, the victim of a hit-and-run while out on what was described as a dangerous assignment having to do with street gangs and drugs. An assistant of Simon Archer's had done the crime scene, collecting paint chips and drug paraphernalia found near the scene. Archer was curiously unavailable.

An awful lot of people were dying around Simon Archer. First there was Darius and now Drake. Coincidence? She had seen coincidence at work on her side in the case involving Matisak, but this coincidence bordered on the impossible.

Could she possibly *not* harbor doubts about Dr. Archer? She had already besmirched his reputation, telling the mayor, the C.P. and Rychman that she believed he had leaked the information about Ovid to Drake. Suppose that was his worst crime? Suppose the rest was all due to her history around such criminal minds as Sims and Matisak, that she found it near impossible to believe anyone was without some hidden motive or secret or ambitious drive?

Just then Archer entered the scene, the look of shock and horror on his face convincing her how much the work of the Claw turned his stomach, and that he wanted to get this bastard as much as anyone. The killer, particularly vicious with Emmons, was their goal. All else must be shunted aside now.

"One of her kidneys was thrown down the stairs and is in the basement," she told Archer.

Archer's face worked the grimace away, turning to the granite surface required of the M.E., and she understood clearly the need to throw up a protective barrier of hard professionalism.

"Dr. Coran, you look as if you could stand some air," he said. "If you'd like to step out for a breath, I'll be here."

It made her recall how solicitous he had been at the scene of Darius' death.

"No, I'm quite all right. Over the initial blow, you might say."

He shook his head and pursed his lips. "It's hideous . . . just awful what this madman has done."

"What I can't understand is why he did it here. In his own place. When before he was so careful."

He shrugged. "She obviously surprised him, and perhaps . . . Well, panic doesn't take time for calculation."

"But he's been so careful in the past, so organized and calculated."

"As I said, Doctor, it must've been the shock of her coming in on him."

"I don't understand that, either. Why she came in alone, against all regulation, without backup, no warrant, nothing."

"I understand that you once did the same thing, Doctor."

She could find no words of reply.

Archer kept talking. "Has the man been apprehended?"

"No . . . not to my knowledge."

He nodded. "With a citywide APB, it's just a matter of time."

"More likely he'll be shot dead after this, if I know cops."

"Yes, well . . . either way, it's . . . it's at an end; just too bad for Emmons that her last official act, while it pointed straight to him, cost her her life."

His tone was sincere, and she believed he must feel some guilt, if he had indeed slowed an investigation that cost more lives as a result, merely to feed his ambition. Part of her pitied him. Part of her hated him.

He seemed to see either the pity part or the hatred, and so he quickly drew back his eyes, going for the body to begin his own scrapings and specimen-gatherings. She, too, returned to Emmons' body to finish her own findings.

"Looks like a lot of duplication of effort here, Dr. Coran," he said after a time. "I hope you will be willing to share? Save a lot of time and effort, and frankly, the less time with this . . . Afraid my heart and stomach aren't as strong as they should be. Not at all like Dr. Darius in that regard. Now, there was a man who could look at any deformity or disfigurement . . . So clinical . . . so . . ."

"So like me?"

He was taken by surprise, obviously not thinking this at all. "I . . . I didn't mean to imply . . ."

"The samples I've taken are not going to be shared, Dr. Archer," she said flatly.

"What? But why not if—?"

"I understand your department will soon be under investigation for chain of custody lapses; I'm afraid the FBI cannot align itself any closer to your department than absolutely necessary for the duration of this case, and I've been ordered," she lied, "to . . . well, create my own chain, as it were."

He stared coldly at her now, all his former solicitousness having vanished. "No secret, is it? Well, they'll find nothing. They'll look, sure. And they may find clerical errors, missteps, but nothing your own laboratory is not guilty of at times. They'll see we have worked for years under extreme handicaps and . . . and . . . Well, why am I boring you with this? I guess I understand your situation, and if you're under orders . . . FBI'll change its tune when I break this case."

"Sorry, but that's how it must be, Doctor," she said.

He nodded and went back to his work. He had put on a surgical mask, surgical gloves and a hair net. As she went back to her own work, her own surgical precautions seemed limited by comparison. She merely wore gloves. However, she had taken every precaution with the samples she'd now fixed to slides, packeted, bottled and bagged, down to the precise time that she placed each label onto the gathered evidence. She had also brought along a separate officer, Sergeant Pierce, Rychman's aide, to take custody of the materials. In his safekeeping, the materials would go to the medical lockup, where each was catalogued, and only then could she regain them for laboratory examination. In some instances, Archer had been remiss with such materials for fifteen, twenty and sometimes forty minutes, easily enough time to subvert or tamper with the material for reasons only he fully understood.

"One way or another," she told him across Emmons' body, "I'm going to prove there is a second killer."

"You're still clinging to that impossible notion? Doctor, one would think you obsessive."

Meanwhile, the entire apartment building was still being scoured, turned inside out for any sign of a murder weapon, or anything else that might further incriminate Leon Helfer, the owner and resident of the premises.

As she worked she felt eyes on her. Archer was watching askance from where he worked. Some of the men in the room were watching them both. It was difficult working a corpse whose face was familiar, the woman having been a walking, talking, laughing associate not a few hours before. For Jessica, it brought back lurid memories of the terror of being rendered helpless by a maniac bent on slowly taking her life from her, bleeding her like a stock animal. At least Emmons' suffering appeared to have been short-lived, far shorter than the suffering Jessica had tolerated at the hands of Mad Matisak. But she was alive.

She reached up to her throat where all the scar tissue had been surgically repaired.

Twenty-Three

❧

Leon Helfer had cut his lights as he pulled off the overpass and down into the dirty little construction road that led into the depths of Holland Construction Company. The place had been recently shut down over debts owed to creditors, one of them the place Leon had worked for, Oleander Pipes. Leon had been out to the site on more than one occasion to inspect the use of the pipes in the field, because Holland had been claiming there were a number of costly problems attributable to faulty pipe.

He had long had it in his head that this area, with its direct open pipe to the raw sewage of the city, would be the ideal dumping ground for the organs if and when he had to go against the Claw. He searched in the darkness for a night watchman but saw no one, nothing but signs warning people off. He drove up to the fence, and letting the motor idle, got out his bolt cutters. It was a simple matter to get inside now.

He snapped the giant lock and yanked back both sides of the gate. In moments he was cruising over the stone path. He knew exactly where he wanted to go and was quickly parked and unloading the cargo that could implicate him in the killings.

He worked steadily, dumping the contents of each jar down an enormous drain pipe, the bottom of which could barely be made out. The organs slipped like dead fish into the mire below, never to be seen again.

He would bury the jars in a dump heap on the other side of the delapidated buildings. He unscrewed another cap, dumped the contents, screwed the cap back on and placed the empty jar back into its box.

The work was going well when he noticed a police cruiser

with its lights out on the overpass that he'd come off of. His heart felt like an enormous stone inside his chest, weighing him down. His hands froze on the jar he held, and he held himself statue-still, his eyes scanning for any movement, his ears pricked, listening. He saw nothing, heard nothing. But what was the meaning of the silent cruiser overhead? Were they laying in wait for him? Had he been spotted coming in? Was a SWAT team on its way to the sight?

He had to rush. He unscrewed all the lids. He began tossing the full jars clattering down the pipe. He knew that closed jars would float on the surface, and he meant to have them sink.

Suddenly flashlight beams hit him from two separate directions and then a third, and men were shouting at him. "Freeze!"

"Police! Drop what you're doing and lie facedown on the dirt! Now! Now!"

The lights blinded him, but in a panic, he lifted the last of the boxes and began dumping its contents into the pipe. The lights were racing for him, closing the distance, when suddenly Leon felt the powerful boot of one of the men slam into his jaw. The force sent him reeling backward, and he dropped the empty box in his hand. One of the jars had spilled over the side and lay in the sand at his feet. He lurched for it, trying desperately to knock it out of sight just before a nightstick caught him in the temple, bloodying his face, sending him down again, the pain shooting through him as he took another kick, this time to the stomach.

Demons, he thought. They surrounded him, continuing to kick and beat him. They were sent, no doubt, by the Claw himself. He tried to get up and was sent flying into a mound of brick and debris. He felt the nightsticks rain down until he was senseless with the beating.

"Kill the bastard here and now!" one of them was shouting.

"We can make our own death penalty for cop killers!" agreed a second.

Leon blubbered and sputtered from a near broken jaw, trying to speak with a mouth full of blood. "I . . . I'm not the Claw! I didn't do it! *He* did it!"

He was hit again, so hard he saw only blackness over him. Still he cried out, "*He* made me do it! The Claw made me do it! I didn't wanna! Didn't wanna!"

Another boot came up, striking Leon in the right eye, breaking off his words and his consciousness.

At the same instant a squad car careened into the yard, kicking up rock and gravel and a fog of sand. The watch sergeant for the area leapt out, tore into the men and pulled them off Helfer. "Get an ambulance for this bastard! This ain't a goddamn kick-fest, and this ain't L.A."

"He tried running."

"We had to stop him."

"Picked up a lead pipe."

"Came at Connors."

Helfer was beaten near to death.

"Confiscate all this crap of his," ordered the sergeant.

"He was dumping jars like this down that hole over there, Sergeant," said the cop named Connors, holding the single confiscated jar up.

"Looks like we got the fuckin' Claw, all right."

Alan Rychman was not blind to the fact that the two M.E.s weren't working well together when he reentered the scene of the mutilation murder. But his men were circling him with the bagged items they'd discovered during their room-to-room search.

"This freak's collected women's underwear, some still with bloodstains on them, Captain," said one man.

"We got lipstick tubes, hair nets, brushes with hair in them."

"And a shit load of women's bags, Captain, but none of the missing organs or parts."

Rychman held up a hand to his excited men and said clearly, "Turn it all over to Lou, and it'll be logged in along with Dr. Archer's and Dr. Coran's findings."

Rychman neared Emmons' body for the second time, the eyeless face, the blood, and the shredded carcass profoundly disturbing him. It was different when you knew the deceased, when the corpse was more than just a stranger. Emmons' familiar face wasn't so familiar anymore, but her body proportions and her clothing were.

"I want absolutely nothing left to chance, Doctors," he told them.

Jessica looked over her shoulder at Rychman, hearing the pain in his voice. He must have known Detective Emmons for several years.

"Can you verify it as the same work as that of the Claw?" asked Rychman.

"If you're interested in unsubstantiated guesswork—" she began, but was cut off by Archer's reply.

"There's no doubt in my mind. It's the work of the same maniac."

"That's good," replied Rychman, "because I've just learned that Helfer's been picked up."

"Alive?" asked Jessica.

"A bit roughed-up, but yeah, very much alive."

"Alive and talking, I hope," she said. "We need him alive. We can learn from him, fill in the information blanks."

Archer was nodding and saying, "Yes, good. Once he has been questioned, the details can be sorted out."

Someone was shouting from an upstairs bedroom. It sounded like a major discovery. Rychman raced upstairs, followed by the others. On the second floor, in a back bedroom, lying in a shoe box in the closet, was the claw itself.

A young detective was almost hyperventilating over it. "Captain, it's . . . it's the damned murder weapon. Has to be! Has to be!"

"Don't touch it!" shouted Jessica over the men crowding in to see the murderer's weapon of choice.

"I've got it, Jess," said Rychman.

"This is going to nail the bastard six ways to Sunday," said the young detective who had made the discovery.

"Can't hurt your career, either, Marty," said Sergeant Pierce.

Rychman carefully lifted the box out and then placed it on a bureau top. Jessica looked over his shoulder at the awful tool of terror, a thick, three-pronged metal rake with ice-pick ends and razored serrated edges set into a glove that had a thick thong of Velcro.

Rychman used the barrel end of his .38 Police Special to lift the awful claw from its resting place in the shoe box. The metal, kept meticulously clean by the killer, sparkled and shined in the light, yet microscopic analysis would reveal Emmons' blood and minute particles of flesh clinging like electrified particles to the surface.

Rychman said, "The thing has heft. It's a hand-attachment weapon and it looks extremely close to the computer depiction you created, Jessica."

Standing just beside and behind Rychman, looking at the chilling thing, she involuntarily shivered. It looked like something a gardener would use for tearing into the soil.

"How extremely awful," said Archer.

"Yeah," said one of the cops in the room, " 'magine that going through your gut."

"Archer, take this into custody, and I don't want anything—anything—happening to this piece of evidence. It's vital to our nailing this bastard."

"Understand, Captain," replied Archer, who allowed the brawny detective holding the ugly instrument of death to drop it into a large polyethelene bag, which Archer produced like a magician.

"It looks as though we've finally caught the sicko bastard, men," said Rychman to the group. "And we're going to see him carefully every step of the way to a lifetime behind bars."

Someone screamed, a hair-curling, ear-splitting screech from the kitchen. Rychman got to Turner first, ushering him away from the sight of Emmons' body.

Helfer was under twenty-four-hour watch, no chances being taken with his safety; nor was any stone being left unturned in providing every shred of evidence against the man. No missteps or mishaps must be made. The D.A. was personally overseeing the conviction of the Claw, and so he asked Dr. Simon Archer to draw up an airtight medicolegal presentation that would bury Helfer and at the same time be easily understood by a jury. The entire, enormous machinery of City Hall was put into motion against the frail, little man named Leon who had become the city's most notorious serial killer.

Meanwhile, Jessica received a fax at the crime lab from her headquarters ordering her return. She faxed O'Rourke back that she needed to stay longer, to help build the case against Helfer. When this was granted her, and Archer learned of it, he seemed nervous, ostensibly concerned for her, that she'd been away from her own duties at Quantico far longer than she ought to have been, and that he could manage. Alan Rychman, by comparison, was delighted that she had postponed her leaving.

Jessica took the first opportunity granted her to speak with Helfer; she didn't approach it as an interrogation, knowing that Helfer had been interrogated by everyone else. She wished to put him at ease and had asked beforehand if she could tape their conversation. He had consented.

When Leon entered the interrogation room, he was so manacled she thought the chains must weigh more than the man. He had the bloodshot eyes and emaciated look of a prisoner of war, and his nervous movements, jerking head and distrustful eyes reminded her of a disturbed, caged animal. The small man's eyes were brown, beady, ratlike. Every nerve ending appeared delicate, frayed and ready to sputter like a loose wire. Looking at him was like seeing a ghost. It was Gerald Ray Sims all over again, she thought.

He searched the corners and the shadows of the interrogation room before his eyes fell on her. A nervous tick plucked intermittently at his left temple and eye; his lower jaw quivered, indicating the onset of tears was not far off.

Rather than the horror story antagonist, some creature out of a Geoffrey Caine novel, this man was a mewing, simpering mole. She tried to imagine him overpowering his victims, some of whom were heavier and taller than he.

She offered him a cigarette, which he accepted with the caution of a stray cat, his hand reaching out only to be snatched away, afraid that she meant to trick him. She then tossed the pack of cigarettes across to him and loudly intro-

duced herself, trying to break through the altered state of in-
sensitivity he had built up around himself.

"You do remember agreeing to speak with me?"

"Yeeeah," he muttered just above a whisper.

"Leon, do you hear or see things that no one else hears or
sees?"

He looked confused. He took a long time to curry her favor
with a meaningful reply. "Whataya talking about?"

"Oh, I don't know. Your mother's voice, for instance, in
your head."

Once more he took his time in replying, weighing the
sound and sense of his words. "Sure . . . sure, I hear . . .
sometimes . . . something she said all the time, sure, but it's
just my memory is all."

"What does she say?"

"Do right. Do the right thing. Listen and obey, that kind of
thing."

"Anything else?"

"Nah, she just kept me in line. I never killed nobody when
my mother was alive. It started when the Claw came, with
him lying to me, saying it was *her* talking through him. He
got me all twisted around and confused."

"What about the Claw? His voice like your mom's, in your
head? Like maybe a ghost?"

She didn't want to put words in his mouth, but at the rate
it was going, she had to coax him along. The tape was running, and he seemed keenly aware of it.

He failed to answer, biting his lip instead.

"Do you, on occasion, hear voices, Leon?" she persisted.

"Voices?"

"Telling you what to do . . . telling you to murder people?"

"You mean like voices in my head?"

"Yes."

"No, no voices in my head."

"I see."

He went on. "And I never saw ghosts, not like, you know,
my mother's or anything; no, but I saw the Claw all the time,
and nobody else has seen him."

"Leon, do you think there are people out there who are out to get you?"

"Damned straight there are."

"I mean before you were arrested, Leon, *before*, were there people out to get you?"

"My boss, yeah . . . and my dentist never liked me. Think he thought I was a carrier or something, like I had AIDS maybe, I don't know."

"Are you aware that your dentist is dead?"

"What? No . . . when?"

"Seems he fell down an elevator shaft that was being repaired there in his building."

"I didn't have nothing to do with that."

"And your boss, at the pipe factory, had an unfortunate accident recently."

Leon looked amazed.

"Some large pipe fell on him, crushing him."

Leon shook his head. "I didn't know."

"Same day Detective Emmons was killed. Malthuesen's death looked like an accident, but that's rather coincidental, isn't it? I mean you on trial for murder and two people close to you die accidental deaths?"

"It's the Claw's doing . . . *got to be*," he replied, and fell silent.

She sighed and took in a deep breath, about to go on when he volunteered, "I was nowhere near the pipe factory, and I ain't been back to the dentist in over six months."

She began asking him some general questions to determine his fund of knowledge. "How much is seven times eight, Leon?"

"What? Oh, ahh . . . fifty-six."

"Who's the mayor of New York?"

"Halle, the big guy."

She nodded. "Who's out in right field for the L.A. Dodgers?"

"Daryl Strawberry . . . funny name."

"You follow sports?"

"Not much no more," he said. "Not lately, not since . . . since Momma died and the Claw came."

She had already heard the general outline of the story of
how he had met the Claw for the first time and that it was at
his mother's funeral.

She asked him to repeat the story for her. She found it in-
triguing.

"Your mother was ill, then, for some time?"

"Yes."

"What kind of medication was she on?"

"Painkillers mostly. She died of inoperable cancer—the
brain. That's what they told me."

"Who told you?"

"Her doctors."

"And where was she getting medical assistance, Leon?"

He hesitated. "Why's that so important?"

She shrugged. "It could be very important. Why're you reluctant to talk about it?"

"Momma never liked to accept charity, but our money was
running out, and we were down to the apartment building,
and she didn't want to lose that, so she went to the free clinic
in the end. Her Medicare wasn't enough. I drove her to the
free clinic when she needed more painkillers, until she
couldn't even get out of bed."

"What's the name of this clinic, Leon, and where's it located?"

"You can give blood there for money. It's called the Street
Hospital on Fourth and Union, near Byrne Park, South Bronx.
Good way's from home, but cheap."

"I'm sorry, Leon, for your loss."

He looked blankly up at her.

"Your mother, I mean."

"Oh . . . oh, yeah . . . It was bad."

"Now, I want you to be honest with me on the next question." •

"All right."

"Leon, Leon, listen to me. Is there any other proof that you
can present to us that will verify what you're saying, that
you didn't act alone?"

He grinned and said, "Well, ma'am, I didn't take no pictures, but when I wrote my poem and called the radio show—

and nearly got myself killed for it—*I was trying to tell you about him.*"

"Leon, we've got proof that *you* fashioned the weapon where you used to work. Isn't that true?"

"He tol' me what he wanted; gave me the exact details. He knew I could make them. Knew all about me the moment he showed up at Momma's funeral. He knew."

"Evidence, Leon, evidence. Do you have any proof?"

"The *other* claw."

"What other claw?"

"He had me make two claws, two right-handed ones."

"Two? Why two?"

"Only the Claw knows that, but sometimes he'd make me wear one, so I could be more like him. Wanted me to eat on the women, too. Always at me to eat up."

Jessica, fatigued and more confused than ever about what kind of basket case she sat across from, wanted to conclude the interview, but something in Leon's eye held her a moment longer. "What is it, Leon?"

"You got to promise to keep *him* away from me, please."

Gerald Ray Sims had made the same plea regarding Stainlype.

"By all means, Mr. Helfer, we will do so, by all means," she replied with clenched hands, knowing they'd been unable to do so in Sims' case.

At the door, she turned and asked him, "Leon, why did you let this other man do this to you? Why did you allow him to bully you and turn you into a killer and a cannibal?"

"I ain't no cannibal, not really. *He* is . . . He's crazy for the organs. I . . . me, I mostly just bit and chewed a little . . . not much. It was him that did the real damage."

"Where did you bite the women, what parts of the body, Leon?"

"Just the . . . the behinds . . ."

"Come on. Where else?"

"Throat sometimes when the Claw told me, but mostly the sex parts. I only swallowed flesh maybe twice and that was just so the Claw wouldn't get angry with me."

"But why . . . why'd you let him lead you to this?"

"I was so . . ." He began to shiver and rattle in his chains. "I still am afraid. He could get me even here. He even came to me last night, appeared right outside my cell. He . . . he terrifies me."

Unable to take any more of this little man, Jessica left with many, many questions still unresolved.

She returned to the NYPD headquarters to continue the search for the elusive Claw, because she still refused to believe that Leon Helfer, by himself, was capable of carrying out the various atrocities inflicted on the Claw's victims. She made her position clear to Alan, whom she forced to sit to listen to her.

"I've heard all this," Alan complained, "and Ames has interpreted his remarks as just the opposite—"

She pointed out Helfer's responses on the deaths of his dentist and his boss, and that Helfer's mother had been under medical care at a Bronx clinic known as Street Hospital.

He slapped down several files before her.

"What're these?"

"Didn't take much digging, once we hit on this angle, to learn that all the women were ill, some terminally so."

"That means you've discovered the first true link between the victims," she said. "That's great."

"With the exception of Mrs. Phillips, they were all traveling far from their homes to that same clinic Helfer mentioned. Storefront operation, low overhead, cheap medicine, *pro bono* stuff, lots of starry-eyed interns doing their bit for the homeless and indigent."

"So who's on staff there regularly?"

"No one who looks suspicious, but the average stay for a doctor is brief, and there's one, a Dr. Casadessus, who interests me."

"Have you talked to him?"

"No, unable to locate. All information on him at the clinic was falsified."

"It's him. I know it. I can feel it. They must have some record of who's practicing—"

"Hey, from the look of the place, they're just happy to have someone who can hold a scalpel right-end up."

She breathed deeply. "But you're not letting go?"

"No, not at all. I don't like blatant coincidence in a murder investigation."

"Then it is a continuing investigation?"

"Only so far as you and I know. The C.P. ordered it a closed case yesterday."

"Alan, it can't be mere coincidence alone that all these victims were getting their health care at the same place."

"Agreed," he replied. "Now what about Simon Archer? How does he feel about your staying on, I mean?"

"He isn't completely thrilled with the idea."

"Sounds good." Alan's sarcasm made her frown.

They then kissed and parted, telling one another to be careful, Alan taking Lou Pierce with him to make additional discreet inquiries at the free clinic.

Jessica returned to the laboratories where she had worked alongside Darius. From time to time she saw Archer look up from his own work, his eyes penetrating the glass partitions between them, his reflection caught by a myriad of glass panes, making it appear as if he were on all sides of her. She continued to work through the forensic materials that had been placed at her disposal by the acknowledged new chief coroner of the city, Simon Archer.

While she worked over the leather glove claw, Jessica was haunted by the image of another deadly weapon. All during the chase for Matthew Matisak they'd had so much difficulty determining the exact nature of the weapon used by the killer. It had finally come down to a bastardized form of the tracheotomy tube through which the vampiristic Matisak drained the blood of his victims into canning jars which he put up for his leisure-time activities.

The Claw's terrible weapon, which Jessica now held in her hands, was weighty, the prongs trying to pull themselves from her grasp, until she pulled it over her gloved hand and tied off the thong that held it cinched to her, making her think of a falconer's harness for an osprey, a coverlet to protect the trainer's flesh from the bird's talons.

There was blood on the casing and thongs, Emmons' blood. But when they picked up the weaselly little man who had supposedly overpowered Emmons, his clothes were free of blood, as were his hands. In fact, not so much as a fiber of Emmons' hair had been found on the man's clothing. Furthermore, Emmons had not suffered a hammerblow to the skull.

Jessica had now to slit open the coverlet of the weapon in order to run the MAGNA brush over the interior for any telltale prints the killer might have left *inside* the glove. The sable-hair brush was used to lift the grease stain for a print, but there was nothing here. Could Leon Helfer have been so methodical as to *wear a glove* beneath the gloved weapon?

Not the Leon Helfer she had met and spoken with. To be so precise and careful and organized in his thinking while he hacked away at the life of his victims . . . not Helfer. There had to be another Claw. Leon simply could not have been so methodical.

Proving it would be quite another matter, however, and she knew she'd get no help from Archer, who kept his own secrets now.

She certainly hadn't time for Archer's well-hidden pettiness, not now; not if she wanted to lash out at Leon's still-unknown accomplice. The real Claw was still at large. She wanted to shake this creature to his core, to make him feel fear, fear that his carefully constructed walls would come crumbling down like brittle parchment.

He surely must believe, as did the papers and everyone else in the city, that the police were satisfied with Leon Helfer's life. Leon was fattened and ready to die for his master. She believed that the dominant half of the killing duo had set up the weaker half to take the fall, so that the Claw someday might again take up where he left off, perhaps in another city in another state, perhaps next month, perhaps next year, perhaps ten years hence.

Twenty-Four

ᕮ

At his pretrial hearing a week later, Leon Helfer presented
a pitiful sight, a man that had sunk so low as to become a
cannibal, a true human monster whom the press painted in as
lurid a color as possible and then some. He argued at the beginning that he had not killed alone, that there was an accomplice, and that the *other* was the real Claw; he argued that he
had just been the Claw's dupe, his procurer, his Igor.

The few inclined to believe Helfer's side of things, anyone
with doubts about the Claw's being in custody, quickly lost
that position when Leon began calling himself Ovid in open
court. Then *Ovid* was questioned on the stand by Dr. Richard
Ames, who had been appointed by the court to determine if
Leon Helfer was criminally insane.

Ames found himself in a quandary. He believed Helfer was
not criminally insane by the strict letter of the law, but that
he was clinically insane. Ames drew out the second personality even further. Ovid did not do as expected on the stand;
rather than accuse Leon of the murder spree, he accused a
third party, someone Ovid knew only as the Claw, someone
Leon had met in some mystical interlude at a darkened funeral home where his mother's body lay in waiting.

"The Claw," said Ovid in a near whisper as his eyes
moved about the room as if searching for this *other*, "the
Claw is powerful and strong. He has eyes that glow red in the
dark ... like a mad dog ... like Satan. He keeps coming
back to me, in my cell at night."

"In your dreams, Mr. Helfer?" asked the prosecutor.

"No, not in my dreams. He's just there, standing right
there."

"In your cell?"

"No, just outside, just staring in."

"What did he say to you?"

"Nothing. He won't talk to me anymore. He won't help me. He's . . . he's abandoned me."

Leon slumped in the witness stand. "He comes and goes right through the concrete walls."

It was generally agreed in that moment by almost everyone in the courtroom that Leon Helfer was quite mad, and that he was the maniac with the unquenchable hunger for flesh and blood; that the ugly instrument entered as people's exhibit A was fashioned by Leon after hours at the pipe factory where he worked, coworkers testifying to seeing him fashioning what they had thought to be a garden tool. "In fact," said one woman who had worked in the same department as Leon, "I think he made more than one of them things."

Alongside the jars and several organs that were near unrecognizable as such, hammers, axes, and tire irons, all with flecks of blood from a variety of victims, were entered into evidence. Dr. Elliot Andersen, a thin, handsome serologist under Archer's guidance, laid out the various damning evidence, convincing everyone that Leon Helfer was none other than the Claw.

Ames capped off the thinking when he told the court that when Leon became Ovid, Ovid was in fact the Claw. There was very little to add after that.

All the ends were neatly joined together, the package tightly bound.

Throughout the swift trial, which had been held quickly to appease public demand, Jessica had labored over the findings she had brought back from the last of the Claw's victims. She had put in late hours, upsetting Alan Rychman among others, Alan now as certain of Helfer's guilt as the rest, as nothing he or his men could do could turn up a mysterious doctor at the Street Hospital who had disappeared, a man named Casadessus. According to the hospital, the papers the doctor had filed were accepted without question, and they had felt glad to have him. From their description, the man sported a mustache, was well-proportioned and tall, with dark hair and blue eyes.

He disappeared a few days before Emmons' death and was not seen again.

Jessica had stopped going to the courtroom to watch the pitiful Helfer and the mounting case against him, utilizing whatever time remained to scrutinize the slides and scrapings she had taken from Emmons, knowing that O'Rourke had pulled the plug and ordered her back to Quantico. To offset this, she had already taken preliminary steps to see that Emmons' body and all the materials she had taken at the scene would travel back with her to Quantico for further investigation. Thus far, she had told no one about her plans, but everyone would know soon enough, and she expected a fight.

She knew that Emmons' family was already upset that the body had been kept this long. But she expected an even greater fight from Archer.

And maybe another from Alan, not to mention her chief, Theresa O'Rourke.

As she was giving thought to the hurdles she faced and while she worked over several fibers and hairs she had tweezered off the dead Emmons and placed in a plastic bag and labeled, she realized with almost a photographic sense of déjà vu that what was staring back at her from the bottom of the microscope, she had seen somewhere before. The hair with its unmistakable patterns was that of Dr. Simon Archer, once again. His hair, like Luther Darius', Perkins', and her own, had had to be ruled out from the outset of the investigation, as the various hairs of the investigators, working in such close quarters with the corpses, usually showed up somewhere under a microscope. But there was a significant difference about *this* particular specimen.

Her hand began to shake. She had circumstantial evidence in her possession that Dr. Simon Archer had been in the vicinity of the deceased *before* she had died, *before* Jessica had shown up at the death scene. She looked again at the tiny packet, labeled in her handwriting, the time clearly marked. It was tagged seven minutes *before* Archer's arrival. How had his hair adhered to the body? How did it get there *before* him?

She shivered over the discovery, wondering who would believe it. If she raced to Alan with it, he'd dismiss it. A single hair, a labeled packet. She could have been wrong about the time, he would say. The D.A. would say the same thing. So would O'Rourke; so would anyone.

Perhaps she *had* made a mistake; she could hardly believe it herself. It could easily be refuted and no one suspected Archer of murder, of being the Claw . . . no one now but her.

And she was scheduled on a flight to D.C. tomorrow. Since there had been no Claw attacks since Leon Helfer's incarceration, everyone connected with the case was at blissful peace with the notion of *case closed*, and that was nowhere more true than in the mayor's mansion and in C. P. Eldritch's office. Rychman, too, was basking in new celebrity as the head of the task force that had brought down the Claw.

She still must tell Alan her new and terrible suspicion brought on by the errant hair strand. At the same time, she feared letting it out of her hands, unsure if she could trust that it would be in the medical lockup when she again looked for it. She decided to take a high-intensity photograph of the strand of hair and she pulled the one on file with Archer's name on it. If nothing else, she could show this to Alan, perhaps convince him that she wasn't completely crazy.

She next logged her findings and put these under lock and key in her office and, following chain of custody procedure, returned the tiny packet and the hair to its place, signing the register for it and everything else she had removed from the lockup, realizing how simple it would have been for her, the attending M.E., to substitute another strand of hair for Archer's.

Was that how he had altered the evidence to make the Claw one man instead of two? To hide his own ugly tracks?

She was seeing Alan tonight to bid him farewell. In fact, time was running late and she must go to her hotel, freshen up and prepare for their parting. She was halfway out the door when Laurie Marks shouted that there was an important phone call for her.

"From Quantico?"

"Some guy in Philadelphia. Says he's a shrink."

Arnold at the loony bin. She hesitated, wanting to run from

the call, but thought better of it and said she'd take it in her office.

"This better be important, Arnold," she said impatiently.

"Matisak wants to speak to you."

"Come on, Arnold! Case closed, or don't you have any newspapers in Philly?"

"Matisak's read every paper, every account ... following this case as if his life depended upon it, and ... and he says he's got something more to report to you."

"Who's in control there, Arnold? Dammit, you or your fucked inmates?"

"Why ... I ... Dr. Coran, I am just doing my part! At the request, I might add, of *your* superiors!"

"O'Rourke," she said. The woman could do nothing right. No way could she step in for Otto Boutine. She wasn't even in his league. "All right, put the creep on," she finally told Arnold.

Matisak was insanely polite. She endured him for as long as she could before she said, "To the point, Matisak."

"This Leon Helfer is not the Claw."

"And just how do you know that?"

"You don't believe it yourself, Dr. Coran. Do you? Well, do you?"

There had been remarks made in the papers. Matisak was picking up cues from the news items. He must have put it together, must have decided that her staying on this long on a case that was supposedly closed signaled that there was more. Ironically he had more confidence in her intuition than her superiors did. How fitting, she thought, that the only one who had any faith in her at the moment was a madman and serial killer.

"You're right, you know," he said. "I was wrong before. Helfer is crazy, and he has been a bad boy, but he doesn't really turn into the Claw any more than he's this Ovid character. He's just a weak kitchen mop, a dishrag, used by the Claw, set up by him. That's what you believe and that's what I've come to believe."

"What have you based your belief on, Matisak?"

"You, Dr. Coran. I'm basing it on you."

"A vote of confidence from you isn't going to do me much good."

"But it has."

"What're you talking about?"

"Why do you suppose O'Rourke allowed you to stay on?"

"Sonofabitch," she muttered into the phone.

"That may be, but all the same—"

"Why are you even interested, Matisak?"

"You know the answer to that. Besides which this guy is as cunning and dangerous as I am, and I wouldn't want to read of your death, Jessica. I still fervently believe you're mine, and one day when you least expect it, Doctor, you and I will return to that interrupted dance. I still taste the blood I drew from your throat as fresh and as wonderful as if it were only—"

"Shut up!" she shouted.

"Look for a nurse who knew this guy Archer when he was a punk intern."

She hung up on the madman in Philadelphia. She was shaken by both his threat and the revelation that O'Rourke was more willing to accept the recommendation of a convicted serial killer than her own. But she was even more shaken by his suggestion to investigate Archer's past. Her reports were being funneled to Matisak. She resolved to have it out with Chief O'Rourke on her return.

Matisak was playing his own game of averages. Since he knew that Simon Archer had interned *somewhere*, the doctor would have had to work with many other doctors and nurses during his residency. Doctors kept secrets while nurses didn't. Matisak also knew that the grueling "boot camp" of a residency could make or break a would-be doctor. With all his time to think about the case from his safe and objective distance, Matisak was telling her what she already knew.

Jessica had embarked on her own search into Archer's background, and it had quickly led to rumors of the sort that cling to anyone in the profession—her included—that the doctor who sliced and diced the dead perhaps enjoyed himself just a little too much for the comfort of others. So came the usual stigma. Archer was called names behind his back. Just as Jessica was called "the Scavenger," Dr. Archer'd come to be known as both "Arrowhead" and "Dr. Ghoul" for his penchant of getting his "head" deep into his work, and for the undeniably long hours he spent in the company of the female bodies in particular. Morgue humor was something that followed every M.E. she had ever known, but usually such remarks were made by cops and lab assistants in gallows jest with some redeeming quality of black humor about them. In Archer's case, for some unaccountable reason, the remarks seemed devoid of humor, black, white, yellow or otherwise.

She continued to dig into his past, and the trail led to a retired nurse named Felona Hankersen. Lou Pierce had been persuaded to drive Jessica into the ghetto where Mrs. Hankersen lived. The thin, once pretty Mrs. Hankersen didn't want to talk to her, had nothing to say and pleaded with her to leave, but Jessica kept hammering at her with a barrage of questions about Dr. Simon Archer. As soon as Felona Hankersen heard the name, she blanched, weakened and crumpled, retreating to the safety that the interior of her apartment afforded.

Inside, several grandchildren scampered and played with toy pistols.

"I took early retirement. Left that part of me behind. Don't know nothing about Dr. Archer anymore."

"I just want to ask you a few questions," Jessica insisted, baring her teeth.

"I've been out of that so long. I can't help you."

"From your record, from what I saw, you were an excellent nurse, and then something happened. A lawsuit settled out of court—a wrongful-death claim—and suddenly you were taking early retirement. Is that right?"

Her eyes had filled with thick tears.

"I'm sorry, Mrs. Hankersen, but it's *very* important."

"I . . . I took the fall," she muttered.

"You were blamed for the boy's death, Mrs. Hankersen? Is that right?"

"That was a lie!" Her tears left milky gray streaks along her black face.

"Who lied, Mrs. Hankersen?"

"What difference it make now? I just don't want no more of it. Said my piece at the time and there wasn't one of them wanted to hear the truth, not one!"

"I do, Mrs. Hankersen . . . I do."

"It's been too long."

"Please."

"They believed the intern and I was quietly let go, and the parents were paid to keep shut. Officially the boy died of pneumonia with complications, but it all come about because of a mistake."

"Whose mistake?"

"Mistaken dosage."

"Who ordered the dosage?"

"Dr. Archer, but then you already know that. Whatchu need me for?"

"You told the hospital authorities? There's no record of any such thing."

Her eyes flared in anger. "You expect there to be? I saw and I told, and it got me *gone*. I questioned Dr. Archer's motives but nobody was listening. Now, I don't care to talk 'bout it no more. Now, if you will, please, just go."

"I can't do that," Jessica fired back. "Please, what you say to me could save another's life."

The elderly woman's eyes had been held by Jessica's gaze, but now they went to her trembling hands. Jessica reached across and covered her hands with her own. "I know it's difficult."

"He . . . the little boy . . ." she began tentatively, her lip quivering, "was gettin' better when he . . . he got into some mischief. Climbed out of bed night before . . . got to wanderin' the halls, you know. God . . . good God . . ." She sniffled and fought back more tears. "I . . . I wasn't believing a word the boy said. He looked like one of my own when they was little, sweet thing, and I just thought he was having a nightmare, you know, or maybe he was full of a devilish imagination . . . I don't know."

"What did the boy tell you?"

"Told me"—she gasped for air—"told me he saw one of

the doctors, and the man was cuttin' out a woman's heart and
. . . and that he was *eating* the heart."

Jessica drew in her own breath now, surprised by this, having expected something else. "Did he say where he had seen
this?"

"Somewhere in the basement. He was running when I
caught him. Ran frightened into my arms."

"Basement in a hospital," she muttered. It added up to the
morgue in her mind.

"Boy said, this doctor had blood all over his face, like a
hungry dog. Said he saw the boy scramblin' outta there."

"And the boy was hysterical?"

"Screamin' this mad tale? Yeah, he was hysterical."

"And you gave him sedatives? Valium?"

"I didn't put nothing into that boy," she said firmly.

"The reports say otherwise."

"The reports are full of lies."

"What steps did you take, then?"

She looked off as if to do so helped her think. "I called for
help. Called the boy's doctor, who, over the phone, prescribed
sedatives."

"Then you administered the sedative?"

"I did, on doctor's orders."

"A Dr. Grisham?"

"Yeah, Grisham . . . later threw me to the wolves to protect
one of his own."

"Then what? Did Grisham come down?"

She shook her head in slow, thoughtful motion, saying,
"No. Said to get the resident intern to look in on the boy."

"Archer?"

"I protested but didn't do no good."

"Archer was the intern on duty that night?"

"Yes'm."

"Where did you locate him?"

"Rang the intern quarters. He was sleeping in there."

"And he came in and another drug was prescribed over and
above the Valium?"

"Pentobarbital over Valium in an eleven-year-old child,
yes'm." Her head was held high now, giving her a haughty

and angry appearance. "It was wrong and I told Dr. Archer it was wrong and he told me to shut up."

Jessica knew that pentobarbital was routinely used about hospitals everywhere for a litany of ailments. Primarily given before a patient's surgery to stave off nervous insomnia, it was also used to control seizures, and little Rodney Bishop was in the hospital for an epileptic seizure and resulting injuries.

"Did you try to physically stop Dr. Archer?"

"We argued and I telephoned Dr. Grisham, who ordered Dr. Archer to the phone, but by then the damned fool had killed Rodney."

The use of the boy's name brought a new welt of tears to assail the woman.

"And the boy never regained consciousness?"

"Went into coma and there was no bringing him back after his heart seized up."

"Did you ever tell anyone about the boy's story of the doctor in the basement?"

"I tried . . . I truly did. But it was dismissed 'long with me. What does an ol' woman like me know 'bout anything? That was the attitude of them doctors. Felt so awful for that boy's people. Terrible thing . . . just terrible . . ."

"And then you were set up?"

"Like Alice in Wonderland in the Queen's court. Hospital was fearful of a major lawsuit. I was coerced, threatened, cajoled, pleaded with and begged, and finally they just plain scared hell out of me. They were going to take my pension, everything I worked for all my life. They left me no choice but to resign. I put it from my mind so long ago, and now here you are."

"I'm investigating some irregularities regarding Dr. Archer."

"Irregularities?"

"Of a more recent vintage."

Mrs. Hankersen took a deep breath, eyes blinking and said, "Think of it, the FBI, coming to me for information on that man. Saw a picture of him in the papers just the other day.

Wanted to burn the thing and stomp on it, but I just put it out with the rest of the trash."

"Do you think that what occurred back in 1965 at St. Stephen's Hospital was an accident, Mrs. Hankersen?"

"I got two ways to go with that."

"Oh?"

"If the boy's story of a ghoul in the morgue was true, and I have never seen a more frightened child in my life, then it was no accident. If the boy was just fibbing or nightmaring, then the overdose was likely an accident in judgment."

"You've given it a lot of thought over the years, haven't you?"

"When I rang the interns' quarters where they're on call twenty-four hours, I got no answer for four, maybe five rings. That place was like a closet with a few bunk beds and nobody could sleep through a ringing phone, and when Dr. Archer did come on, he was breathing real heavy, like he'd been running. I didn't think anything of it at the time, but yeah, I've had lots of time to think about it since."

She left Mrs. Hankersen soon after, but not before asking her to be prepared to one day repeat her story in a court of law. Mrs. Hankersen said she would not dare do so.

Then she wanted to know what Archer had done that had the FBI after him. Jessica had to decline giving her any information on a "pending" case, but she assured her that one day Dr. Archer would pay for his sins.

"That much I already know," Mrs. Hankersen had finished in the doorway.

Outside and all the way back downtown she remained silent, Lou Pierce obviously curious, staring over from time to time and asking if she was okay.

She assured him with little clichés of custom.

She was fighting a war within her the whole time, however, and Lou was not fooled. How could she bring to light any of the Hankersen story? It was hardly the kind of compelling evidence that men were indicted on. All she had were a handful of questionable hospital statements and the word of a lone nurse to contradict the records. No D.A.'s office in the land would touch such circumstantial evidence in an attempt to topple a man of Archer's growing reputation and position.

As for going to Alan Rychman with this, she feared that he was coming to imagine her a suspicious bitch by nature, and spiteful where Archer was concerned. But suppose Archer was in the morgue taking a bizarre necrophiliac's desire out over the body of a woman he'd helped autopsy that day? Suppose the now dead Rodney Bishop *had* seen his vile performance? Suppose Archer *had* murdered the boy in retaliation, out of fear and panic?

What did that make Archer? Besides a cannibalistic ghoul, like the Claw, a murderer of the innocent. And if he was capable of killing a helpless Rodney Bishop, why not an equally helpless Luther Darius? And if he was capable of necrophilia and cannibalism and of killing such innocents, why not, by extension and with the help of an accomplice, infirm, aged and weak women he found on the street?

Had Alan's words of the night before been meant simply to appease her? She had told him in no uncertain terms that she distrusted Archer, but to now go to him with these allegations? He'd likely think her mad.

Still, she had to present what she instinctively felt about Archer. At any rate, he was guilty of conspiracy to subvert the medicolegal evidence being compiled against the killer known as the Claw. Alan must at the very least accept this, and he must know that Archer's reasons for doing so may've gone far deeper than earlier thought. Like an onion, one layer peeled away only revealed a denser layer beneath.

Lou's radio crackled with the dispatcher's signals, 10-11s and 10-12s mostly, vandalism, minor disturbing the public, domestic violence. Lou's unit signal was 10-55 and he immediately picked up his transmitter and called into it, saying, "10-55 here. Go ahead."

It was late, almost 7 P.M. Alan Rychman's voice came over, asking Lou if he knew of Dr. Coran's whereabouts. Lou looked to his right where she sat alongside him in the patrol car, and when she nodded, he said, "She's right here with me, Captain."

"And where's right here?"

"Let me talk to him, Lou," she said, taking the transmitter into her left hand.

"Captain Rychman, if you'll meet me at the Marriott, I have some things to discuss with you before I leave for Quantico."

"Fine, but where've you been?"

"We'll discuss it over that dinner you promised me, remember?"

"Very well. See you then."

Lou returned the transmitter to its cradle and sped through the tunnel for Manhattan. "You and the captain seem to have hit it off, Dr. Coran."

"We have a great deal of respect for one another, Lou, a good basis for a relationship, wouldn't you say?"

"I would indeed, ma'am. He's a good man and you, well, you've put a spring in his step, I can tell you."

She smiled across at Lou, who had earlier confirmed the nature of the rumors that went around about Archer, but Lou, like most, shrugged it off as "normal morgue bull" as he colorfully put it. She wondered what Rychman would call it; wondered how far she dare go in revealing her ugly suspicions of Simon Archer.

Perhaps it *was* too farfetched to say that Archer not only covered up evidence of the Claw but *was* the Claw. Perhaps Alan would choke on the notion. She knew she must temper what she said, so that Alan would take her seriously.

She leaned back into the cushioned seat, the weight of the day coming down on her, fatigue threatening to overtake her. She closed her eyes and recalled the tearful features of Mrs. Felona Hankersen, and she once again imagined a wide-eyed little black boy named Rodney who may have been the first person to have had an idea of the true nature of one Dr. Simon Archer.

Rychman met her in the lobby and they walked to a restaurant nearby, a place called the Social Contract. The ambience was surprisingly one of flora and fauna and jungle sounds, everything bringing up the image of Africa, and some of the dishes were most exotic. After a drink and after laughing over some of the items on the menu, she ordered chicken and he opted for the "rhino steak" after learning that "rhino" referred to the size of the thing.

After a moment's silence, a toast; Alan promised that he would soon break away and visit, for the first time in his life, the nation's Capital, "Now that I've got my own personal guide," he'd finished.

"If you make a promise to me, mister, I expect it to be fulfilled. I hope you know that."

"Count on it."

"I'll count the days."

"Soon as we put this Claw thing to rest for good."

She looked off into the distance, chewed a bit on her "tiger-striped" grilled chicken and then dropped her head.

Rychman, reading her body language, asked, "What's troubling you, Jess?"

"Nothing."

"Nothing or everything?"

"All right, Alan, I still think Leon's only half the equation, and I think . . . I think . . ."

"And you think everybody else is rushing this thing over the falls? Is that it?"

"Damn straight that's it."

"Everybody's got their teeth into this, Jess."

"And that means the bite's on you? I know how important being commissioner is to you, Alan, but this isn't the way to do it."

He stared coldly at her, his anger rising. "I haven't cut any deals on that score with anybody, kid, and you can take that to the bank."

"Have I said that?" She backed off a bit, sorry for getting into this the night before she planned to leave.

"No, but it's what you're thinking. You give me something other than a lot of suppositions and questionable circumstantial evidence, and I'll move on it, Jess. You know that as well as I do."

Frustrated, Jessica sipped at her wine, shaking her head, saying, "I know that, Alan . . . I know."

"You're some kind of holdout, Jess. You're the only one who still thinks that Leon had an accomplice."

"I'm not the only one who thinks so."

His eyebrows rose. "Who else thinks so?"

"Forget it."

"Who?" he demanded.

"A nurse," she said. "A nurse who knew Archer when he was interning at St. Stephen's Hospital in '65."

"All right, tell me the whole story."

She took Alan carefully through the paper trail that led to Felona Hankersen. She told him how impressed she'd been with the woman's sincerity and how unimpressed she was with the hospital's paperwork, citing odd discrepancies. Finally she told him about Rodney's story, of his fear of a doctor he'd seen in the morgue, feeding on a human heart wrenched from a cadaver.

"Okay, Jess, is that it?" he said in a tone that spoke of fatigue and disappointment. "The secondhand story of a dead boy from a sad old woman fired from her job? You know what you can do with that kind of evidence. And what're you saying here? How've you gone from Archer's being a petty and jealous assistant to Darius, trying to make himself look good, to a . . . to a cannibal . . . to Leon Helfer's accomplice . . . to being the *Claw*? It's just too outrageous, Jess. No one would believe it."

"Least of all you," she said coldly.

"Look, if you had anything corroborative, any hard evidence—"

"Felona Hankersen isn't the only one who thinks he's a ghoul. You've heard the hallway gossip about Archer."

He shook his head, saying, "Don't you think I've heard the same about you, especially since word's out we're seeing each other?"

This took her aback and she shook her head repeatedly. "Word's out *how*?" she wanted to know.

"Damned if I know, but it is, and so every jerk in the department wants to know what it's like, seeing . . . someone like you . . . after hours. Point is I've heard the same nasty crap about you as I've heard about Archer: about how you like cutting thin slices of organ meat for a quick sandwich over the autopsy table. All crap, Jess, and you know it."

"Just the same, Felona Hankersen's not the only one who thinks Simon Archer is a *fiend*."

"And just who else is there, Jess? The night janitor at the lab?"

"Never mind. Guess I've said too much already," she whispered in her whiskey voice, leaning back into the cushion of the booth.

"Who else?" he insisted.

"Never you fucking mind. It's no one you'd approve of, anyway."

He stared in dismay and she muttered, "Not sure I do myself, it's just ... Well, the more I learn about Archer, the more twists and turns I—"

His eyes lit with an unexpected fire she could not at first fathom. He looked about to explode, about to smash the table with his fists.

"Christ, it's Matisak again, isn't it? I thought you wrote that bastard off? What can a madman in a cell hundreds of miles away possibly know that we don't, Jess?"

She took in a great breath of air and shivered as if a draft passed over her. "I don't know how he does it, Alan, but Matisak has shadowed my every move, my every hunch on this case."

"He's just got you spooked."

"He's creepy, all right, uncanny."

"Bastard's just got you confused, Jess. You must see that."

"Confused? Hysterical is what you mean, isn't it?" She looked sternly up at him, her eyes fiery. "That's so convenient for you, Alan: chalk my suspicions up to those of a hysterical woman. Damn you."

"I'm just saying that this creep's gotten into your head, maybe."

"That's bullshit, Alan, pure—"

"All right, all right," he said, trying to calm her. "So you harbor doubts. Tell me about them. Talk to me, Jess."

She calmed, dabbed with her napkin at a spot of wine she'd spilled and said evenly, "I still think there's something to this Dr. Casadessus at the Street Hospital you got a line on. Where has that led you?"

He scratched his head and said apologetically, "Nowhere, I'm afraid. The guy disappeared like smoke, without a trace."

"So you've given up?"

"I still have men working on it."

"Have you ever considered the not so remote possibility that this Dr. Casadessus might be someone close to the case?"

"You're back to Simon Archer."

"I am. Alan, you realize it was rather a convenient coincidence for Archer that Jim Drake was killed by a hit-and-run?"

"Drake's death is still under investigation."

"Have you checked Archer's car for recent repairs?"

"We have, and it led nowhere."

"Then maybe he's got two cars?"

"You're reaching, Jess."

"And what about Dr. Darius?"

"What about him?"

"His so-called suicide. Also overseen by Simon Archer."

"Jess, you sound like . . . like—"

"Don't say it, Alan."

"—like you've got some sort of vendetta against Archer."

"My vendetta is against the Claw, Alan, and in my book a Leon Helfer isn't capable on his own of the damage done by the Claw. He's told us that he fashioned the murder weapon while under the spell of this other man, and that it was designed by the other. He was very specific. He told us that the killer had two claws made but used only one, normally, reserving the kill for himself."

"Nobody, Jess, believes what Helfer has had to say." He put his hand over hers and added, "I know how hard you took Darius' death, but to think that Archer actually helped him out that hospital window, Jess . . . Well, there's not one speck of evidence to support that contention. I know you got close to Darius. Maybe it's clouded your judgment—"

"Clouded, confused woman, huh? So we're back to that."

"You do admit to being human, to being emotionally involved?"

She did not answer this, stubbornly persisting in her own questions instead. "So what're you saying? Helfer killed his boss and his dentist as well?"

"It seems much more likely that Helfer did these men than Simon Archer, Jess. Look, I'm . . . we are continuing investigations into both Parke's and Malthuesen's deaths. We have good reason to believe both were murdered, but that leaves Leon as prime suspect in these deaths, and this morning, Leon confessed to both murders."

No one had bothered to tell her, and she was caught off guard. "Leon'll confess to anything anyone puts to him now, so long as you promise to keep him safe from the Claw; but tell me this, Alan."

"Yes?"

"Has he confessed to *being* the Claw?" Before he could answer, she added, "Look at this," and took from her purse a manila envelope, spreading its contents before him: two electronic photos of Archer's hair which she had taken from the lab.

"What is it I'm looking at, Jess?"

"This was taken a few hours ago, and this was on file. It's a strand of Archer's hair."

"Does this mean something?"

She explained how she had gotten the first strand, her belief that it was lifted from the body a good seven minutes before Archer arrived on scene.

He looked over the two photos for some time, his features not giving anything away, but his eyes showing a dubious and steady blink, the big hands folding about the photos. "You sure that you labeled it correctly?"

"Yes! Dammit, I knew you'd say that."

"Even if *I* believe you, Jess, it's slim evidence at best. Do you have anything else on the man?"

She couldn't hide the look of disappointment on her face.

"D.A. wouldn't touch this. It'd be your word against Archer's, and Archer could make a case for your having a long-standing poisoned relationship that—"

"Forget it," she said abruptly.

"Wait a minute, Jess."

"Just forget it, Alan."

The waiter arrived to clear their dishes, and they fell silent.

After he left, Alan began, "Jess, it's not that I don't believe that you believe—"

"I won't bore you with any more of my doubts, Alan."

"Come on, Jess. That's not fair."

"I wouldn't want to bring you down from that high you've been riding since Helfer was cuffed."

He tossed down his napkin and leaned in across the table. "That's bull, Jessica. I'm not railroading this creep. He's as guilty as guilty gets and—"

"And so is someone else, someone who drove him, controlled Helfer, gave him a new name, a new identity, and gave him *orders*."

"There's not a shred of forensics evidence to support you, nothing other than Leon Helfer's word, which is less than nothing, Jess."

"All true, thanks in large part to Archer, who, by the way, still has not been so much as reprimanded for his part in slowing this investigation."

"Internal Affairs is looking into your allegations."

"Allegations?"

"Yes."

"And what does Internal Affairs know about hiding evidence in a test tube or beneath a microscope?"

"Christ, it's not as if Archer conspired with the killer. If he let some things go, if he became a little careless, it was for mundane, perhaps petty reasons."

"Well, I'm not so sure."

She got up to leave, but he stood also and grabbed her by the wrist. "What's that supposed to mean?"

"I'm still unconvinced he had nothing to do with Dr. Darius' fall prior to his going into the hospital, if not his so-called suicide."

"Christ, you really dislike this guy, don't you?"

"Don't you see? Archer did all he could to slow the progress of the investigation until he was firmly in place as

Darius' logical successor. And I don't understand why you and the others choose to look the other way."

She hurled away, and he threw money on the table and rushed after her. Neither of them had noticed the darkly clad, heavily made-up man at the booth beside them who now stood and quietly left in their wake.

Twenty-Five

❧

"I want Emmons' body shipped to Quantico." Jessica stood over Simon Archer's desk, her tone lean and spiced with a tinge of officiousness. "I'd like your cooperation."

"What can you possibly expect will come of carting the poor woman's body to and from Virginia, Dr. Coran?"

"Well, I won't know that until—"

"Then you can speak with the family members. I'll not be a party to unnecessary pain and injury to the bereaved."

"I'll deal with her family."

She started away from his office when he got to his feet and said, "Do you really think Quantico can do any better than we've managed here?"

"We have the most sophisticated equipment on earth, Doctor, some of which you've only read about, the experimental laser photography, for instance, and our electron microscopy is of the most recent vintage. If any minute differences . . . *ahh* . . . Doctor, at this point, I'm asking your cooperation, but if you try to stand in my way, I'll steamroll this right over your head."

"You have no jurisdiction here. It ended with that retch's arrest."

"Oh, but I do. So long as the FBI holds open the case, and since the NYPD asked us in . . . Well, just check with the commissioner and the mayor, if you like."

Archer stared a hole in her but said nothing. She smiled, saying, "Being at the top's a bitch, Simon, especially when the top isn't the top."

"Just what is it you think you will find?" he persisted.

"Look, Dr. Archer, we're not in this to prove your team in error, or—"

"What, then?"

Others about the lab heard the raised voices and began to stare.

"We're interested in looking more deeply into the physical evidence, and the best way to do that is to transport, whole, one of the victims, perhaps two."

"Two? But the others are all in the ground."

"That didn't stop us during the Chicago Vampire man-hunt." They had unearthed two bodies for exhumation then, and she knew that Archer was aware of the case history.

"Look," she said solicitously, "I've got a military plane on standby and we'll take the body to Quantico with or without your consent."

He put up a palm to her. "No, no, you know you have my full support, Dr. Coran. It's just . . . well, I'd hoped we had put this horror behind us."

"I can certainly understand that."

"With Helfer in custody—"

"That's not enough. We have to be absolutely certain, and I'm afraid the forensics evidence provided to prove him guilty beyond a reasonable doubt—"

Archer's shoulders hunched with his raised arms as he pro-tested, "I oversaw that evidence myself, and it is enough to bury Helfer several times over. What can you possibly mean, reasonable doubt?"

"Reasonable doubt that he acted alone."

"But all the evidence points to that single fact."

"I know . . . I know, and it's all so pat."

He was again staring at her before he caught himself. He cast his dark gaze elsewhere, but not before she registered the pent-up rage seething below, held in check. The unflappable Dr. Archer had been *flapped*.

"Well," he muttered, "it sounds as if you need nothing from me."

"No, I don't. I'll take the heat from the family and any other interested parties."

"I guess you've been made aware that they've ordered some sort of internal investigation of the department."

"No, really? I had no idea," she lied.

"Routine, they say."

"Oh, yes, I suppose so when such a position is held for so many years by someone such as Dr. Darius."

"Yes, well, they do seem to be concentrating on efficiency levels, that sort of thing. Who knows, perhaps we'll get some additional influx of funds. God knows we need it."

"I'll keep my fingers crossed for you."

She turned on her heels and disappeared down the hall, tapping out a light Morse code with her heels and cane as she did so. Dr. Archer flicked a switch on his intercom and spoke to Laurie Marks, telling her to prepare the Emmons body for transportation.

He clicked off the intercom and said to the empty room, "Fine, Dr. Coran, you will have your cadaver, but you will never get the eyes back."

Later that day, Jessica stopped by Rychman's incident room, where everything had been dismantled. Desks and secretaries were being rerouted, but Alan was still working out of the central office here, and he was concentrating deeply on what Dr. Simon Archer was telling him.

Jessica could only guess at what Archer was saying. Both men stood up when she entered.

"Well, I'm on my way, gentlemen, and not likely to return soon."

"You'll be missed," Rychman said, their eyes meeting.

Archer, who had seen them make up in the parking lot outside the restaurant and who had followed them to where she was staying, knew that Rychman had spent the night with her.

"Got to catch up with Emmons' body," she told them.

"Can't give up on that two-man theory, can you?" asked Rychman. "Suit yourself, but I think you're wasting your time, Jess . . . ahh, Dr. Coran."

"If we could just find some corroborating evidence like a second set of hairs—other than yours, Dr. Archer!" she said. "Of course, everyone expects to find some of the coroner's hair on the body." She watched him for a reaction but there was none.

"Par for the course," said Archer.

"Well, look, I've got to get down to interrogation. Seems Leon's wanting to talk some more," said Rychman.

"Is he still claiming his innocence?" asked Archer.

"He never claimed to be innocent," countered Rychman. "But he does claim that he was *used* by the Claw."

"But Ames says—"

"I know what Ames says, and I agree. It's Dr. Coran here who disputes Ames' findings, not me. But I listen to Leon because the more he talks, well, the more we get on him. He's described most of the murder scenes down to the dots on the *i*'s."

"Lot of pent-up rage, anger toward his mother, I've heard," said Archer.

"You've heard right, and it got directed at women in general."

"I'll offer you a final word of advice, Captain," Archer said.

"Yes?"

"With Helfer's type you want to threaten and intimidate every chance you get. Wear the bastard down; don't let up; intimate that you have his DNA, his hair, his fingerprints, his teeth marks on the body. In time, he'll crack like a dried eggshell."

Rychman's smile was wide. "Say, Dr. Archer, you sure you won't come along, take a shot at Leon? Sounds like you'd make a great interrogator."

"I'll leave it to the professionals. Besides, I have to get back to my lab. A lot of people want a lot of information from me right now, so as much as I'd like to . . ."

"Understood," replied Rychman, walking him to the door and a little way down the hall.

"I hope you're not still buying into Dr. Coran's notion that Leon Helfer did not act alone. Not one shred of forensics evidence we have supports her claim, you know."

"No, Dr. Archer, you needn't worry on that score, and with her going back to Quantico, so goes her theories. Can't prosecute on a theory."

"No, no, you can't, and we should do nothing to jeopardize

the case against Helfer. The man deserves the full extent of the law. There's no way he can escape justice now."

"Depends."

Archer looked closely at Rychman's eyes. "What do you mean, depends?"

"You know how the game is played, Doc. Defense'll try for an NGI—"

"But Ames says he's not insane in the legal sense."

"Defense shrinks will say he is and it'll be bargained down to a manslaughter with intent, diminished capacity, all that crap. Our boy'll spend the rest of his natural life in an asylum 'longside guys like Jeffrey Dahmer, John Wayne Gacy and Matisak. Long as we've got no death penalty in New York . . ."

"No justice anymore, is there, Captain."

"You got that right, Doc." Rychman took Archer's hand and shook it, saying, "You did a hell of a job amassing information against this creep, Archer. Don't worry, news like that travels through the ranks fast, and when the D.A. puts Leon away, one way or another, IAD'll get word to back off."

"Being a division chief really puts the spotlight on you," replied Archer. "Have to say, I'm tired of those guys snooping around my records and my lab."

"You'll learn that being in charge means priority one is to cover your ass and keep fault away from your sector. Divert attention to someone else, if you must."

"I may have to come to you for advice from time to time," he said.

"Sorry, but at the moment, if I stepped in, said anything on your behalf like you ask, it'd just backfire on both of us. Let the snoops snoop, so long as you've got nothing to hide. So far, what've they turned up? A few clerical errors? A broken chain or two. Come on, when Darius ran the department, errors were made, right?"

"Guess you're right. I'll stop worrying."

"You really ought to at least come down and watch Helfer sweat. You can stay behind the mirror. He's really coming unglued now, waiving off his attorney's advice to shut up, breaking out into cold sweats. Part of the fun of the chase, once it's over, is to toy with your prey."

"Maybe . . . I'll drop by, then, if I can. Later," said Archer.

Jessica joined Alan in the hallway where he stood watching Archer disappear. "What was that all about?"

"Seems he wants my advice about how to deal with IAD. Guess they're making him antsy."

"Where there's paranoia there's fire?"

"IAD spooks everybody, Jess."

"I doubt that they could spook you."

"I'm keeping an eye on Archer, Jess. Right now, that's all I can do."

She bit her lower lip and nodded. "Fair enough. Well, I've got to go . . . got a plane to catch."

"And you won't reconsider the foolishness about taking Emmons with you?"

She shook her head. "No, it's a must-do."

"You know that if Archer were guilty of any . . . *entanglement* with Helfer . . . if he were a schizoid killer, your taking that body out of here . . . well, it's got to be viewed as a direct threat to him. Everybody knows your reputation in the lab is—"

"Why, Alan, I almost believe you have some suspicions regarding the unimpeachable Dr. Archer!"

"I guess I may."

"To be so worried about a hypothetical danger?"

"I worry for you, that's all."

"Don't. I'm a big girl, and I'll be safe in Quantico."

She punched him in his meaty arm. "Now, walk me to the elevator and say goodbye for now."

He did so and kissed her at the elevator as personnel in the building moved by them, some staring. "I will be seeing you sooner than you think. I am going to visit, and—"

The doors had opened and she had stepped through but she held it open for him to finish.

"Yes?"

"I think I love you, Jess."

She smiled in reply, her eyes misting up. "I'll miss you." She wasn't prepared to tell him that she loved him. She wasn't sure she could love anyone again. Certainly it would

take more time, a change of setting, more privacy with Rychman, if it were ever to happen.

"Bye, Rychman."

As the doors closed between them he shouted, "Going to
miss you around here, FBI lady."

"Me, too, Alan," she said back, unsure if he had heard.

Dr. Simon Archer wondered if his having gone to Captain
Alan Rychman ostensibly for advice, but actually to "read"
the man's reactions to him after whatever revelations Coran
had made the night before, had been wise. He was satisfied
that Rychman, while interested in the woman sexually, was
not about to make a fool of himself otherwise.

Archer had no intention of seeing Leon Helfer in the presence of others. He had visited Leon's cell when he was in
lockup the first night to throw a scare into the little creep.
Still, Rychman's suggestion that he come down to interrogation and see how it was going was a provocative one. While
it could be a trap that Rychman and Coran had set for him,
somehow manipulating Leon and him into the same room to
see what the reaction would be, he didn't think so.

Coran had left the building, of this he was quite certain. So
had Emmons' body. Both were bound for Quantico, and perhaps now everything in New York might return to a sem-
blance of normalcy. With Leon's coffin being nailed shut by
Archer's own forensics team, with precious little added by
the FBI woman, it would be Dr. Simon Archer who would be
credited with putting an end to the Claw, and he would realize the goal that at first he had felt was far beyond his reach
and ability. With Dr. Darius gone, at long last, it was *his* department, and now his reputation would flourish.

As for the Claw, he must forever remain dead along with
Leon. To satisfy his taste for flesh, Archer told himself that
he could go back to his old methods, forget about the mutilation deaths he had engineered, forget about the fresh smell
of a kill, the mouth-watering urges that welled up at the smell
of blood. He could do it, he told himself, and if he could not,
he'd have to fashion a new weapon, something that could not
be linked to the Claw or to him.

Finding everything calm in the lab, he excused himself, saying he would be at the interrogation center with Rychman. Within ten minutes, he was sitting behind a one-way mirror listening to Rychman grill Leon. Helfer had apparently agreed to fully cooperate in return for leniency and mercy. He was desperately trying to answer any and all questions put to him. He continued to declare that the Claw was a physical second person and not a second personality manifestation. Dr. Ames, sitting in a corner of the interrogation room, slipped in questions between Rychman's. Ames had his own tape recorder going and he jotted down notes as well, his eyes seldom leaving Helfer, reading the man's body language. Several times Ames looked puzzled, Archer thought.

Helfer was pleading now. "I told you . . . I told you, I . . . I don't know where he lives or who he was."

"You say you let this guy lead you around by the nose and you never once learned his name?"

"That's right, that's right . . ." Leon was blubbering.

"So he always initiated the contact?"

"Yes."

"And he always told you where to drive to? What street corner to stand on?"

"Yes, yes . . . I've told you that."

"And as if by magic, here comes the exact victim he wanted?"

"That's how it happened. I hit them over the head and dragged 'em down where he told me earlier to bring them, but he cut them open, and he . . . he ate from their insides. I . . . I just faked that part. It made me sick." A lie as the forensics evidence had shown.

"How did he contact you? By phone?"

"No. He'd just show up."

"And you sat around waiting for him?" asked Dr. Ames.

"But you told Dr. Coran that he telephoned you."

"No, no! Only the once, the time he set me up . . . just before he killed the policewoman."

Rychman pounded his hand on the table, causing a gunshot sound that made Ames jump along with Leon. "How do you expect anyone to believe such shit, Leon? Leon, nobody just shows up out of nowhere, out of the curtains at your mother's funeral home, out of the dark in your house, out of the fuckin' thin air!"

Lou Pierce stepped into the room. He'd been behind the mirror with Dr. Archer. And now he asked a few questions, spelling Captain Rychman. "You know, Leon, we've got the ball peen hammer you used on the women, the axe, the other tools, all with blood on them."

"We've got DNA counts on your blood and all the victims' blood, Leon," added Rychman, turning and facing the little man again, towering over him. We've got your hair, your coat fibers, your rug fibers, your fingerprints and your teeth marks, and not a single piece of microscopic evidence otherwise to point to a second killer, Leon. No, Leon, you did all these killings all on your own, and you're going to tell us the truth, Leon, here and now! The goddamned truth!"

"No, I told the truth! Dr. Coran believed me! Talk to her. Talk to Dr. Coran!"

Archer could feel the muscles in his face tighten and twitch and his brain replayed Leon's words in refrain: "Dr. Coran believes me! Talk to Dr. Coran!"

"We found all that stuff you stole from the women, too, Leon, from their purses," Lou continued. "Mascara, rouge, lipstick, earrings, hairpins, brushes with the dead women's hair and odor still on 'em. We know you acted alone, Leon."

"You saved a lot of their underthings, Leon," said Rychman, "and Mrs. Phillips' Oriental rug splattered with her blood was in the trunk of your car, Leon."

Archer had heard enough. He was convinced of two things. Rychman and the others believed what he wanted them to believe all along, that Leon had worked out his lurid fantasies alone, and secondly, Dr. Coran believed otherwise. She remained his only threat.

When Rychman stepped out of the interrogation room, all he saw of Archer was his back as the M.E. disappeared along a corridor. He cursed his luck. Had he known Archer was outside, he would have found a way for Helfer to meet Dr. Archer face-to-face.

Twenty-Six

❧

Simon Archer lay restless in his large four-poster mahogany bed, unable to sleep, his peace disturbed by a woman who was over two hundred miles away. He knew that Coran was no typical medical examiner, that she was known among her close associates as thorough. Very little to nothing got past her. Her intimations of impropriety on his part had led to an investigation of his newly acquired department. He wasn't worried that the investigation would turn up anything as incriminating as murder and cannibalism, but he was worried about Jessica Coran. Even Darius had called her brilliant, an adjective he had never used to describe Archer. And now she had Emmons' body under her full scrutiny.

Perhaps he was foolish to worry: the stronger voice within him tried to soothe his fears, calling them irrational.

"After all," he told himself, "you took every precaution with Emmons, every possible precaution: gloves, hair net, the specially designed tooth sheath that simulated Leon Helfer's bite, now a somewhat useless item."

Giving it further thought, he told himself, "I really should destroy and discard the sheath." He held up the two rows of hard, acrylic tooth coverings with Helfer's signature on every edge and molar. They were self-incriminating, after all.

He cupped them in his hand and placed them beside his bed and felt the old urges welling up. His need for living flesh had come full circle.

He tried to close his eyes, get some rest. But each time he did a mad cinema of images flashed before him: first the writhing body, the half-conscious victim simpering, and he bending over, a shadow-man looking on in stark horror and curiosity. Closer and closer he brought his face down to the

264

victim's throat, his animal's claw poised for the final tear, but his mouth wanting to tear first into the still-flexing arteries of the throat, when suddenly he saw her face. It was Coran's face and her eyes opened, staring straight through him, daring him to continue to kill her.

His dream self lashed madly and monstrously at her with the claw again and again, but her flesh withstood each blow. She began to laugh, and he was unable to make her stop, and the claw was breaking apart under his repeated attempt to rend her iron flesh from her.

His eyes came open with a start. She knew. He did not know how she knew, but she *knew*.

"Forget about her," he told himself in a chastising voice. "Even if she knows, she can't prove a thing."

"Not yet, she can't," he answered himself. "But one day she might."

Responding to a nervous Malthuesen who had telephoned in a panic, he had gone after hours to Leon's place of work. Malthuesen had immediately contacted him after two police detectives, one named Emmons, had grilled him about Leon. Malthuesen was surprised when Archer had shown up after the place had cleared out. Malthuesen didn't know he was about to die of a tragic accident, the trap already set before Dr. Archer led him to the snare. Malthuesen didn't understand Archer's interest in Leon and had thought it all to do with a gay liaison between them, and Archer hadn't dissuaded the notion until the end. But as a result of the police snooping, Malthuesen had become greatly curious, and he was asking too many questions.

"Come with me," Archer had told him. "I'll clear everything up for you."

"What if the cops come back? They seemed to want to get more out of me," said Malthuesen.

"I'd appreciate your not saying anything about my . . . association with Leon."

"But what if they ask?"

"You do as I say, and there's more money in it for you, much more."

Malthuesen was interested. "How much?"

"Three times what I've given you already."

Malthuesen whistled. "When do I get it?"

"It's in my car. Come with me."

He maneuvered Malthuesen into a long corridor where piping had been stored to the ceiling. He rushed ahead of the other man, getting to the safety of the other side of the room, and in the dark he threw a switch that released a row of the pipe at the bottom. This sent an avalanche of heavy metal over Malthuesen, whose cries were quickly drowned out.

Archer exited quietly the way he had come as a night watchman raced to the scene of the noise and clatter.

Now Archer smiled anew at the memory. He was an efficient man, smart to have had Leon actually design the claw. He had been efficient with Leon's dentist as well, the man who had designed for him a set of tooth coverlets. He lifted the set of acrylic teeth to his eyes once more and stared at them in the darkened bedroom.

Its contours were so beautiful, and holding it in his hand made him want to put the instrument to good use. But he couldn't . . . not for a long time, and when he did, he'd have to use a completely different approach, different cuts, and a new dupe. It would take some time to find another Leon, someone as pliable as he, someone with a helpful dentist.

Leon's dentist had put up a struggle. He had grabbed onto Archer's coat and shirt, worrying Archer that fibers below the man's nails would show signs of the struggle. When he pushed the thin, bespectacled Dr. Parke over the edge, the man had grabbed onto the cables, his briefcase and his glasses preceding him down the sixteen stories of black hole. For a few minutes, as the man's hands were rubbed raw against the thick metal cable, their eyes met, and in that moment the fool knew he was about to die, and then he slipped, grabbed again, grunted, cried out and was gone like a pebble down a well.

Archer had slipped from the area only to return in his official capacity to see to it that the dead man told no tales. The death was ruled accidental, as had Malthuesen's, but in Malthuesen's case, an associate M.E. handled the cleanup.

So far as he knew, no one other than that suspicious bitch,

Coran, had thought the death of Leon's dentist anything but a freak accident, the sort that happened all too often in high rises lately. Rychman didn't need the dentist to convict Helfer; all he needed were the dental records and the testimony of another qualified dental expert, in fact, one in forensics, Dr. Donald Altman, who worked under Archer now as his paleontologist and dental forensics man. Altman had done a superb job on the witness stand, so much so that Archer had turned over all the evidence to him and had sent him and serologist Elliot Andersen back to court to oversee the presentation of the case against Leon Helfer. Both Altman and Andersen were pleased with the confidence Archer had placed in them, and Archer hadn't had to face Helfer, fearing the little weasel would recognize either his face or his voice and cry out in open court that he was the Claw.

Of course it would only make Leon look even more crazy than he already did, and it would be interpreted as ludicrous, but Archer had already taken enough chances and there was no point in tempting fate. Nor did he want to fuel Coran and Rychman's combined distrust of him any more than he already had.

"They've got nothing on you ... nothing," he told himself. "Get your rest. Forget about that bitch. She can't prove a thing ... not a single thing."

But the rest of the night, his sleep remained disturbed by the image of the woman and the incessant tapping of her cane. Matisak had only maimed her. If he had one chance at her, he would do far more than maim her.

"Let ... it ... go ..."

But how sweet her flesh must taste, he thought. How lovely to roll her eyes around in his mouth ...

Jessica's apartment never looked so good. She loved being surrounded with her familiar trappings, the photos on the walls, many blow-ups of her underwater shots taken when she had gone on various diving excursions in Jamaica, the Keys, Martinique and elsewhere. She also had photos of her parents, herself as a child and her best friends and closest working associates adorning another wall.

The beige to white furnishings with glass tops and glass cases throughout the apartment had also collected knick-knacks from her many travels and hunting and diving trips, from first-prize awards for the biggest or the most game in a season to miniature deer, bear and fowl, many of which were hand-carved by American and Canadian Indians.

Here, more than anywhere on earth, she felt secure and comforted, and she received a transfusion of sorts, a transfusion of identity and soul that was often much needed. She already missed Alan Rychman, however, and it would be some time, as she had told her girlfriend, Amanda Cairn, over the phone, before Alan could break away to take her on that diving trip they had planned before she had left New York City.

When she had arrived at the airport at Quantico there was faithful J.T. to take full charge of the Emmons body, seeing to its final transportation to the morgue. And as ever, J.T. was full of questions, starting with, "I don't get it, Jess. Why're we examining a body the New York people have already designated as the work of this nut case Helfer? You want to fill me in?"

"Just treat Emmons as a murder victim, J.T., and run every test we have on her. I mean every damned test, and no short-cuts."

"All right, but you'd better know up front—"

"What?"

"O'Rourke doesn't like it."

"What doesn't she like?"

"Carting the body here like this, pulling it from this guy Archer's jurisdiction. Says . . . thinks it's not good form, that sort of thing. Says we've got to respect and cooperate with the local officials for times when we really need them, all that crap."

She could not hide her exasperation with O'Rourke. "I suppose she wants to see me on the double?"

"You must be psychic."

She frowned. "First she gives Matisak carte blanche with the information on my case, has that filthy creep telling me long-distance how to investigate it, and now she's questioning decisions of mine of a forensics nature? You know what she wants, don't you, J.T.?"

"If I didn't know better, I'd say she wants your ass in a can, Doctor."

"Great being home, J.T., and it's great to talk to someone who's going to be straight with me."

"It's great having you home, Jess."

Their relationship had grown over the years of their association and had solidified with the Matisak vampire-stalker case. Her cane was a constant reminder to both her and J.T. of how close she had come to being killed by Matisak, but there was something else she remembered when around J.T., and that was her old confidence in her deft abilities. J.T. fanned the flame of her positive self-image. He was a good friend.

"O'Rourke thinks she'll cut me loose and that she can more easily *control* you, John," she told him. "You know that, don't you?"

They stared at one another there on the tarmac, the sound of aircraft near deafening.

"I'll see to the body now," he said without another word, and as she watched him go toward the open cargo bay and the box within, she wondered if J.T. had changed. It shouldn't come as any surprise, not with O'Rourke's keen manipulations. O'Rourke was very happy playing queen to Chief Bill Leamy's king on the FBI chessboard. She'd been made chief of the psychological profiling unit which had been built from the ground floor by Otto Boutine, and to which Jessica and J.T. belonged.

She went straight from the airport to O'Rourke's office. O'Rourke was a strong woman, firm and sure of herself, always dressed to kill, and she had worked her way up through the ranks to get where she was, but her affair with Bill Leamy hadn't hurt, either. Otto had had great respect for O'Rourke's ability at crime detection and, in particular, psychological profiling—her avenue up the rungs of the FBI ladder.

Their meeting was brief and predictable. O'Rourke was sorely upset. She'd gotten a call from the chief medical examiner of New York City, a Dr. Archer, who felt his entire staff had been maligned by Agent Coran, and that the unnecessary removal of Louise Emmons' body was the final straw. "Archer feels you're out to ruin his reputation in the forensics community, that you bear him some personal animosity, something to do with Dr. Darius' being made some kind of god in your eyes to which no one could possibly measure up; said the entire time you two worked together, you were second-guessing his every finding."

"Somebody had to."

"Is that all you've got to say?"

"Why're you so concerned about Archer's feelings?"

"It's quite simple, Dr. Coran. We will need New York someday in the future, and cooperation between our agencies has to be optimal. You, of all people, should know that."

Jessica realized that the conversation was being taped, that everything she said was on the record and that her boss was now amassing her own evidence to prove Jessica incompetent and unable to continue in her present position, that her psychological problems were overtaking her.

Something must have shown in her eyes, because O'Rourke, staring coldly at her, said, "You know, Jessica, we're all concerned about you. The FBI family wants only what's best for you, and I, personally, care only to see that we do what's best for you."

"Yes, I realized that when you sent me to Philadelphia that first time, to see Matisak . . . to see the bastard alive and well fed and biding his time. Yes, Theresa . . . Chief . . . I've always known that you took my . . . my problems . . . as seriously as I."

"Are you still seeing Dr. Lemonte?"

"No . . . not professionally, but thank you for asking," she lied.

"Then you are feeling . . . emotionally stronger? Good."

"I'm so glad that you can see that."

"And your . . . physical impairment? How is that doing?"

She held up the cane. "It's not going to go away, if that's what you mean, but it hasn't kept me from doing my job."

"Of course not."

"And another thing, Theresa." Her voice like acid, Jessica was emphasizing her words with a tongue that flicked across her upper lip and disappeared. "You won't win against me; you won't take my job here. I'm too good at what I do."

O'Rourke pointedly pressed the recorder attachment to her desk to off. Then she came around the desk and stood toe-to-toe with Jessica. "Dr. Archer telephoned Leamy when he finished with me, and—"

"At your urging, no doubt."

"Archer didn't need any urging. Regardless of Archer, it's just this simple, Dr. Coran: you didn't get the collar in New York; you weren't involved in the manhunt to the extent you should have been. Very likely because you were too busy sleeping with Captain Rychman."

Jessica's jaw stiffened but she refrained from saying another word or raising the hand that so wanted to slap O'Rourke.

"You're not being credited with the end of the Claw case, Jessica, and you got Otto killed in Chicago. Facts like that have a way of haunting a person's career. Careers here rise and fall on the basis of one's most recent case, not yesterday's laurels. Fact of life here . . . what have you done for me lately, Dr. Coran? Then there's Matisak . . ."

"Matisak?" Jessica's right hand quivered now with a power of its own. Had O'Rourke set her up from the beginning, anxious from the start to see her crumble under the physical and psychological strain of dealing with men like Sims and Matisak? O'Rourke had known from the beginning that Jessica believed O'Rourke's leadership was far inferior to Otto Boutine's as head of the division. It seemed a particularly nasty way to clean house, but then O'Rourke had proven nasty in the past, especially to other women whom she felt threatened by.

"Yes, he claims you've failed to listen to him—"

"I don't believe I'm hearing this."

"—that you've been uncooperative and extremely rude, and—"

"For Christ's sake, O'Rourke!"

"—and the fact you entered his cell with a gun hidden on

your person, Dr. Coran. Very bad . . . very bad form. That alone—"

"I deny it all! All the fucking crap that Gabriel Arnold, your penitentiary pimp, has told you. And his word will not hold up against mine! Now, I'm leaving before I actually do commit a punishable act."

Jessica made it to the door but hadn't cleared it before hearing O'Rourke say, "Well, you have regained some of your old strength, dear, haven't you?"

Jessica had kept going, afraid if she did not clear the building, she'd return and knock O'Rourke on her ass.

Time was crawling by. To keep everything completely objective and unimpeachable, she had turned the Emmons examination over to J.T. and a team that was unlikely to miss the smallest hair or fiber on the slate-white tissues of the body.

And so she had gone home.

How she now missed Alan.

Would she soon be missing J.T.?

She felt alone in her comforting little world, snuggled deeply into the cushions of her soft, beige couch, staring up at the walls, the silence, taunting time and memory, beating out a rhythm not unlike that of her saddened heart. It was not just her loneliness that was poisoning her homecoming, but her fear. She realized now that all this time, since she had recovered from the attack on her by Matisak, O'Rourke had played on her weaknesses and Jessica had become *afraid* not only of her own decisions but those of others, and of O'Rourke's in particular. O'Rourke held sway over her and had been trying to use her like a dangling marionette first here and then there. It had been O'Rourke who pushed her into taking the Claw case, and she had manipulated her to the interviews with Matisak long before this, and urged her into Gerald Ray Sims' cell, all the time knowing what it must be doing to her, eroding away her mental stability, washing away her strength.

And like a weak and bullied kitten, Jessica had allowed this to continue. No wonder J.T. seemed so estranged. J.T.

didn't know her anymore, didn't recognize her, because she had changed long before J.T. had. The tragic effect was that their relationship had also been eroding away. She wondered if it could yet be saved.

In the past, J.T. would never have doubted her actions; in fact, he had always been her chief advocate and champion. The memories flooded in. Cheering her, J.T. was always there to dig in and learn from her actions, to become a principal player in her sometimes dubious attacks and feints, never quite fully apprised of her motivations, and yet trusting her on faith alone, the way Alan Rychman had come to trust her, she thought. John Thorpe had never questioned her ability as a super-sleuth M.E. who worked hard to please the memory of her father.

But she had let J.T. down somewhere along the way. She had let herself down, and the wolves were waiting on the periphery of her waning strength, prepared to tear her apart. And J.T.? Was he among them?

Theresa O'Rourke was her division head now, and Jessica must answer to her, must work with her instead of around her as she had in the past, but she must first face her down, show the woman what she was made of. Until now O'Rourke had only known the wounded Jessica Coran. It might take some doing, and the confrontation might end in her dismissal, but on her way out, she would see that J.T. got her position. No one was more qualified.

Another full day at the lab had netted her nothing, and now Jessica had returned home where her thoughts wandered back to New York City, to Alan Rychman. Alan had calmed down later that night of their last evening together and had allowed her to speculate on the possibilities, had held her and had comforted and counseled her. In light of there being no evidence, he had likely been humoring her when he said he would continue to investigate, to locate the shadowy Casadessus, and to try to link him with Archer, as they were both medical men. Had it just been Alan's way of soothing her, his way of leading her back into bed?

She covered her eyes now with both hands and recalled every sumptuous moment of their lovemaking; they were good together, good for each other, too.

Alan was gentle with her, his touch so light, at odds with his size and the hardness of his body and muscles. But she knew she could not depend on him—or any man, for that matter. In the end, she knew that her full recovery from the fear and suffering the Matisaks of the world had caused her would come only through her own hard-fought, inner battle with the demons residing deep within.

Unable to sleep, she wondered if she ought not to return to the lab, if it hadn't been a mistake to leave Emmons' body in J.T.'s hands; if she shouldn't be there overseeing his every move. In her absence from Quantico, it seemed that J.T. and O'Rourke had found a little too much common ground for her liking.

She sat up and checked the blinking, light-emitting diode signal coming from her alarm clock. The patterns went on and off at 11:07.51, 11:07.52, 11:07.53. Time was in slow motion, she thought.

Unable to stand things as they were a moment longer, she got up, stumbled in the dark and found a pair of jeans in the closet and pulled a sweatshirt on, forgoing a bra. She found her shoulder holster, thinking that since the range was open all night, she might go there instead of the lab. Over the gun she placed a light jacket with the insignia of the Washington Redskins on it. Uncertain of her destination at the moment, she nonetheless rang for a cab. She then grabbed up her cane and her keys and was out the door.

On the street outside the lobby doors to her condo complex, she beat out a rhythm on the sidewalk with her cane, a little angry at herself for slipping backward again, allowing sleeplessness its way with her. At least, she told herself, she wasn't on any pills anymore, and she wasn't drinking heavily as in the early days of her battle with the shadows that came in on all sides, turning even her spacious haven upstairs into a claustrophobic vise.

If shadows were without substance, then how did they crawl up from out of her psyche to do a lurid dance along the walls? How could they take shape and stand and stare back at her? Dr. Lemont said she had to stare her fears down. When Alan was near, the phantoms had let her be, afraid to show themselves to another human being—or maybe just afraid of Alan! Now that he was no longer near, they'd slinked back on stealth feet: all her self-doubt, her remorse over Otto's death, her guilt and shame.

She was relieved to see the taxi's lights when it pulled into view. When she got into the cab she knew where she wanted to be, a well-lit place with others around her.

"Quantico gates, please," she told the cabbie, who grunted in response.

After a moment, he said, "Whataya do out there?"

"I'm a doctor," she told him.

"Oh, yeah? That must be in-ner-resting work."

She said no more, thinking of J.T. instead. She wondered why he hadn't telephoned with something. The old J.T. would have.

As the cab pulled from the curb, the cabbie caught a rear-view glimpse of someone who'd stepped from the shadows.

He said in a smoker's rasp, "You was alone, wasn't you?"

"What?"

"A single fare?"

"You see anyone with me?"

"No, no . . . Sorry, Doctor."

Twenty-Seven

❧

Simon Archer had arrived in Quantico, Virginia, very early that morning.

Casadessus wouldn't leave Archer alone about Jessica Coran; he would not let Archer sleep. Days had gone by in which he had fought the influential force within him that kept saying over and over that he must have her, must see Jessica Coran's insides turned out, must feed on her. Casadessus' appetite for the more youthful and powerful was not surprising. Casadessus believed that by feeding on the physical energies of others, by feeding on organs such as the heart, that Archer simultaneously fed on the psychic energy of his victims, thereby making him stronger. Of all the hundreds involved on the case of the Claw only she had an inkling of what had actually occurred, and it stood to reason that only she, now with Emmons' body under her full control, might someday show others that she was right: that Simon Archer was the Claw.

He had carefully arranged to leave New York without anyone's knowing, booking his flight under the name of Ernest Casadessus, the name belonging to his grandfather, a man who took delight in beating, torturing and biting his own children, if his mother's rendition of her upbringing could be believed.

His work in Quantico, Virginia, must be swift and sure, he knew, and he must be back in New York on Monday, at the office, as if nothing had happened. So far, he had had no trouble either at the airport or at Quantico, where he had successfully taken the tour of the grounds and had learned the whereabouts of Dr. Coran's office and labs. He followed this with phone calls asking about her whereabouts and how he could get in touch with her, careful never to leave a message, but always making it sound urgent.

He had learned that the Emmons autopsy by the FBI was going on tonight, but he had been stymied when he learned that Dr. Coran wasn't among the doctors doing the final autopsy. She could be the only one capable of interpreting errant fibers or other clues of minutia he may have inadvertently left on the body, so he resumed stalking the FBI woman.

Before the rather superficial tour of Quantico ended, he had located a safe place into which he stepped and disappeared. He had waited for hours, very patiently, for the right moment, when a security guard came toward the door where he stood on the opposite side, inside a stairwell.

He grabbed the man quickly and surely, driving the needle into the man's chest like a spoke in a hurricane. The man's body went instantly limp, his eyes alone moving, searching for some reasoning in Archer's eyes, but only Casadessus' bottomless eyes were looking back.

Casadessus wanted very much to take the man's eyes and feed on them, but Archer argued with him, saying that it would undermine the larger goal. He had such a finely tuned plan in mind for Coran that nothing, not even his own appetites, must get in the way. It would be exquisite, poetic even; even the poet, Leon/Ovid, would appreciate it when he read about it in the papers.

Archer quickly stripped the security guard and replaced his own clothes with those of the guard. He acquired the guard's gun, badge and identification. Carefully he scooped up his other clothes and placed everything, including the guard's brown-bag lunch, in a cloth handbag he had earlier folded and stuffed under his shirt. He dragged the dead man's naked carcass to the concrete cave just below the steps, dumped it there and strolled out of the stairwell.

He was careful to keep to this floor of the building, staring out a full-length window at the security vehicles below. He then took his time, learning as much as he could about the security in the building, the alarm systems and where the keys to the vehicles were kept. After he finished with Dr. Coran, he must get quickly to the airport.

And so he haunted the halls with great care and caution. At the central switchboard was another security man. For a moment they stared at one another, the black security guard asking him what section he was from.

"Subbing, just temporary assignment," he muttered as he lifted his bag in one hand, the needle in the other, and jabbed the guard with the paralyzing, killing snake serum. He quickly dragged the body through a stairwell door and deposited it in a utility closet. He returned to the panel and looked everywhere for a list of telephone numbers. Finally he found one with Jessica Coran's name on it.

He quickly dialed and it rang without answer until an answering machine beeped on and her recorded voice began giving him instructions. He didn't know what to do. If he left a message, they'd have his voiceprint; if he didn't leave a message, she might not come within his grasp, and time was of the essence.

He hung up, trying to think. Could she have already entered the building?

He dug through the signatures of people coming and going through this area, his eyes scanning for her name. There it was. While he was upstairs, she had entered the building. The time she signed in read 11:47 P.M. His heart raced. She was here, very close, within his grasp.

She must be in her lab, must be poring over the autopsy results on Emmons, must be digging for the single thread of evidence that would lead back to him. But it wasn't about to happen that way. Dr. Coran was in for a great shock.

Archer carried with him another hypodermic. Meant to incapacitate rather than kill, the drug would effectively paralyze her. She'd stiffen and her eyes would be frozen open long enough to watch him torture her body, to take what he wanted. But not here. It would be done far from here, and the trademark of the killer that now would be stalking D.C. would be very different from the Claw who terrorized New York. The weapon he'd devised was every bit as deadly as the claw, and of far more precision. It utilized a scalpel that fit over the hand, razor-sharp and deadly, but it would leave an entirely different marking than the claw's three-pronged ruptures.

The body would be discovered on the street, perhaps pinned to a chain-link fence just outside the darkened interior he had found earlier in the day. He had done it all this time without any help from the bungling Ovid. He didn't need Ovid. All he needed was Casadessus.

He went for the elevator, which opened on a number of tired faces, none of whom seemed to pay him any attention as they made for the register and signed out of the building. They were talking about finding a night spot for drinks, but one moaned he was far too tired after the grueling day they'd had. The others tried to get this one, called J.T., to join them, but he remained steadfast, saying, "Dr. Coran'll be expecting me at the crack of dawn."

"You let her run your life, too?" asked another.

"Hey, why not?" asked another.

"Imagine her with that cane beating your—"

"Knock it off!" shouted the one called J.T., who looked up at the guard who'd remained near the elevators, saying, "Where's Tuttle tonight?"

"Wasn't feeling well," said Archer flatly.

"Hmmmmm. Well, g'night."

Archer stood in the hallway on the floor where Dr. Coran's lab was located when he saw a door opening ahead of him. He dropped back into a parallel hallway. All around him were glass partitions through which he saw laboratories. Given the fact it was so late and that it was Labor Day weekend, the place was nearly deserted. Still, the lights over various lab tables confirmed that there were some people yet in the building.

But where was Jessica Coran?

Then he heard her, or rather he heard her cane as it tapped out a singular chorus to him. She was approaching from the door that'd burst open, sending him hiding. She was coming straight toward him: *tap, tap, tap* . . . coming for the elevators, no doubt.

He readied his hypodermic and listened as she approached. Closer and closer, *tap, tap, tap* . . .

He was acutely aware that the hallway corridor formed a complete square at the center of which were elevators on both sides.

When she was within inches, he lurched from around the corner and stabbed her full in the chest with the hypodermic, *but it wasn't her.* It was an elderly man in a white lab coat who now stood clutching at his heart, certain he had been killed by a madman, going to his knees, his cane skittering away, clattering against the floor.

"Damn, damn, damn," Archer moaned where he stood over the fallen old man, whose eyes had rolled back in his head, the whites staring up at Archer without seeing him. But somewhere he felt eyes upon him and when he turned back he saw her. Dr. Coran was several offices away from the incident in the hallway, but through the panes of glass through which she had watched, she saw a poorly disguised Dr. Simon Archer attack her serologist, Dr. Robertson. Her eyes told him that she knew that he had come for her.

For a moment they simply stared at one another, hunter and hunted. Then she revealed to him that she had a gun. Pointing it, aiming it at Archer and firing, she burst the three panes of glass between them, but Archer had disappeared. She could not tell if she had hit him or not, but drawing up her nerve, she rushed toward Steve Robertson's prone and still form. Archer had somehow escaped. She wheeled about with the gun extended, her white lab coat flapping about her legs, her cane tucked below her arm. She fought to keep balance, knowing her full weight on her ankles was not good, but she must be prepared to fire again if need be.

She saw that the elevator was taking someone down, possibly Simon Archer being true to form—a coward when faced with a victim who fought back. Every victim of the Claw before now had been defenseless and taken by surprise.

She knelt over Robertson, seeing blood on the floor beside him. She took his pulse and found it weak and erratic, searched frantically for a wound, fearing that flying glass had hit him. But there were no wounds. Robertson was unable to speak and quite possibly unable to hear. Paralyzed somehow by Archer, she knew that but for the grace of God it might well be her lying here paralyzed, in the complete and utter control of the Claw.

"I hope you can hear me, Robertson ... Robertson!" she called out to the injured man. "I'm calling 911. You're going to be all right. Just hang on!"

She realized now that the blood beside Robertson was Archer's blood, that she had wounded him. She saw a trail of it leading in the direction of the elevators. She now pushed upward against her cane to regain her feet, but the cane slipped from beneath her when it found blood. She lay on her back when she saw a shadow dart across the hall down from her, going toward her office and lab. She held firmly to the gun, and hearing something metallic skitter away from her, she found an odd glove with a scalpel firmly attached to it: Archer's new weapon of choice. She placed it safely away— evidence for later.

She wanted to hunt Archer down. Turn the tables on the sonofabitch, see him in the position of his victims, avenge Dr. Darius and all those other victims of the man's madness. One thing she did not want was to see this freak Archer incarcerated in Gabe Arnold's Philadelphia madhouse alongside Matisak. She wanted some modicum of justice this time around.

Regaining her feet, she saw that the elevator she had thought to be going down was coming up. Was he aboard it, or had he taken refuge in the labs, hiding in wait there? She could not be certain. She waited for the elevator to arrive and for the doors to open, her gun extended, at the ready.

The door opened on a stranger to her, his hands going up on seeing her gun pointed at his eyes. "Don't shoot," he said.

"Who the hell are you?"

"Frakley, FBI, like you, Dr. Coran." He flashed an ID and said, "I got a call from a Captain Alan Rychman, NYPD, about you. The captain was real worried, pressed us for a twenty-four-hour surveillance of your place."

"Why the hell wasn't I told?"

"There's been no time. Something to do with your Claw

case and that you might be a target for some guy named Archer you've been trying to nail. Rychman made it sound real urgent."

"Jesus, it takes Archer's coming to assassinate me for everyone to believe me. How long've you been watching me?"

"Just since seven this evening." Frakley saw Robertson beside her on the floor. He rushed to have a look. "I heard the shot, came straight up."

"Get to a phone, Frakley; get help."

"Where're you going?"

"Back to my lab."

"But where's this guy Archer?"

"I don't know, but he's wounded."

"I can't leave you like this."

"If Robertson doesn't get medical attention now, he'll die. You see to that and I'll secure the floor."

Frakley reluctantly went in search of a telephone.

In the movies, Rychman would have come racing to her side, instead of sending a Frakley, she thought, moving cautiously through the glass maze of the laboratories here, in search of any sign of the madman. Archer had perhaps found the stairwell and was holed up there somewhere. She only thought that she had seen him duck in here. She relaxed a bit; the place was empty. She had to get the building sealed off, and where the hell was security? She went into her office and dialed. As she did so, she stared out at the lab table where J.T. had been studying a replica that had been made of the claw, something to be used, he said, as a teaching tool for next semester's newcomers. It was in the vise when she had gone out, but now it was gone.

Out of the shadows, as if materializing from air, the claw came crashing down at her, swiping out at her throat and latching onto the telephone receiver instead as she leapt away. Her gun flew off the desk where she had laid it down. The phone went through a glass partition, making enough noise to wake the dead, and certainly to cause Frakley to race in from wherever he was, she thought. But he did not come and she was knocked down and now, standing over her was the Claw,

Archer's eyes like those of a raging, mad stallion as he raised the deadly instrument above his head and was about to strike.

"God damn you, Archer, you've screwed up everything," said Frakley as he entered, his weapon holstered.

Archer's voice had taken on the croaking sounds of a man in pain. "The bitch shot me. My blood is all over the place."

"We can't do her here."

Archer moved closer to Frakley, the claw dangling at his side like that of a giant crab, his form hideous in the darkened room where the lamp had been overturned. Somewhere on the floor lay her gun. If she could only find it. Her mind raced to piece things together. Somehow Archer had found another weak, easily dominated dupe for him. Somehow the man had hypnotic power over others of a certain personality type.

"After all, Frakley, *you* killed her here, not me. I tried to stop you and was wounded in the ensuing struggle," Archer was saying as he turned Frakley's gun on him and twisted and fired. Frakley fell in a heap on the floor, dead.

Jessica took the opportunity to grab up her cane and she brought it around just at the precise moment that Archer's jaw turned into it, knocking him, claw and all, across her desk, sending what remained there onto the floor with his weight. She scrambled about for a few moments for the gun she had lost. On hand and knee, she wildly pursued the missing gun but could not find it before Archer began clawing his way back up, holding onto the desk, stunned but far from incapacitated.

Jessica tore from the office through a door that led deeper into the labyrinth of the labs. She made her way to another door that opened onto an autopsy room, where she left a spinning stainless-steel table in her wake. She went from room B to C and to D before she remembered the service elevator on the other side of the hall. She struggled on without using her cane, acutely aware that Archer and his deadly claw were right behind her.

When she stepped into the hallway, she saw him at the other end, his dark form like an alien from another planet, the deadly claw clacking as if in anticipation of her blood. He'd kill her and set up the bodies, hers and Frakley's, to make it look as if they'd killed one another, to both prove her right about the dual nature of the Claw and to end any further speculation about him.

There was little telling what the maniac had in mind other than her death. After she was splayed open like a tarpon, he'd feed on her, stuff portions of her into Frakley's mouth for good measure.

She streaked for the service elevator, praying the car was on this floor. It was used for bringing bodies to and from the morgue in the basement. She had a fifty-fifty chance that it would be there. She fairly fell against the big red button that opened the sluggish doors, and the moment they opened, she hurled herself against the far wall. Turning, she saw that Archer was racing at top speed toward her, the claw extended at eye level, and as he came crashing into the closing doors, the claw dove through, as if it had a life of its own, snatching at her.

She was too afraid to scream and instead seized the moment to tear out at the coverlet about the claw, trying desperately to rip it from his hand. He fought back, jabbing her, causing a bloody tear in her cheek, another to her forehead. Her hands were bloodied, but she continued to fight for control of the weapon when he finally snatched it back, allowing the elevator doors to close. She jammed at the controls to take it down as quickly as possible, but there was no hurrying the machinery.

She tried desperately to catch her breath. She had to get to a phone. There was one in the morgue. But he knew she'd be there, and he'd be taking the stairs two and three at a time; he'd be there waiting for her when the doors opened.

She jammed the emergency stop button and found herself between two floors. From the floor level below, the awful claw was scratching to get at her, tearing at her ankles, causing her to feel weak and terrified with the memory of how Matisak had immobilized her by cutting both her Achilles tendons. She jumped for the upper floor, pulling herself up. Archer climbed halfway into the cab after her. She quickly pulled herself to the floor above, reached up and slammed home the control button, sending the car down, but the mechanism was too slow for any chance of cutting Archer in two. However, the action did send him to the floor below.

She raced for the stairwell but she heard him coming toward her. Glancing around, she saw a storage closet, and praying it was not locked, raced for this hiding place. She pulled the door wide and gasped at what it revealed. There in the dark, amid the clutter of broken glass from a smashed light, mops, brooms and fallen debris, lay the body of a security guard, a large black man she knew as Amos Croombs. The dead man's uniform matched the one Archer was wearing. Behind her she heard Archer's approach. She hadn't any choice. She pulled the door closed behind her and sought refuge here with the dead man.

She could hear Archer nearing; she could feel him on the other side of the door. She'd been a fool to come into this dead end, she now told herself. He'd whip the door open any moment and kill her here. She didn't stand a chance.

If she could see, she might arm herself with something, a bottle of bleach to throw into his eyes—anything—the moment he opened the door.

But it was too late to dare make a sound. He was turning the doorknob.

When Archer looked into the dark interior of the closet where he had dragged Croombs' body, he saw only what he had left there before, the dead security guard. He scanned the deep shadows for any sign of Jessica Coran, but found none. In a moment, he quietly closed the door and moved on in pursuit of his prey.

Below the deadweight of the security guard, Jessica could hardly breathe and she felt the steady drip of blood as it oozed from the corpse's mouth, soiling her. She must wait patiently until Archer was out of earshot before she dared free herself of the position she was in. Once she was sure, she toppled the body, making more noise than she had wished to, and in the bargain feeling something heavy and metallic, like a hefty tool, cold and icy against her thigh. She reached down and found Amos Croombs' firearm. It was like a godsend.

Archer had no doubt killed both security men on duty, but he'd foolishly left Croombs' .38 behind.

She checked the cylinder and learned by touch that every chamber had a round. She now held the weapon to her breast, hoping Archer had heard the noise she'd made, hoping he *would* return, throw open the door again. She'd blow his brains out.

She waited, kicked out at some metal shelving to make more noise, and shouted for him by name, but he didn't return. He was on another floor, gone in search of her, hunting her as if she were an animal. But now it was time for her to hunt, to make *him* sweat.

Cautiously she made her way from the closet. She knew she was close to the lobby, that it was just down the corridor. Was he lying in wait for her there? Expecting her to try to escape the building through the obvious route? She rounded a corner and saw the big glass doors and the darkness beyond. Was he outside, waiting for her? She had her chance now at escape, but should she take it?

Where was the bastard? *She didn't want to escape him now.* Now she wanted to hunt him down and place a bullet in his brain.

She surmised that he had done one of two things. He had panicked and run with the claw in hand, or he had remained calm and had returned to Frakley's body to plant the claw on him. It would still be his word against hers in a court of law, no matter what. There were no witnesses to his attack and he had Frakley to explain away everything. The bastard was shrewd, and even if his plan had gone awry, he would remain calm. She knew where he could be found, if she moved quickly. She rushed to the elevators, seeing that another car had come to a standstill on the floor where Frakley's body lay dead in her office.

She got into the other car and went hunting. If she killed him, there would be justice. She could prove forensically that he had attacked both Frakley and her, that he had been shot by her when he attacked Dr. Robertson with the hypodermic needle; that he had killed the security guards. She had proven the guilt of Matthew Matisak ten times over, but what justice had come of it? She wanted to blow this bastard away as she had so often dreamed of blowing Matisak away.

This was her chance.

He would see now how it felt to be hunted.

How it felt to be helpless.

To plead for life, to beg, to know you're going to die.

To be like his many victims in their last moments on earth.

She stopped at the floor below and located an office, into which she stepped and turned on the building intercom. She said carefully into the mic, "Archer ... Dr. Simon Archer, now I'm coming for you; I intend to kill you for all that you've done. I'm coming for you, Doctor ... coming ..."

Archer got the message loud and clear where he stood over Frakley's body, securing the claw to the dead man's hand. He looked up and around, fearful that *she* was watching him this moment. She had somehow armed herself, or otherwise she would have fled into the night. Her voice sounded full of venom and fury.

Knowing the danger to himself now, he made his way back toward the service elevator she had introduced him to. He rushed past some of the same objects he'd seen the first time around, coming to a standstill suddenly in a refrigeration room, where one of the vaults was standing open. Sitting up, its eyeless face staring back at him, was the Emmons cadaver. The ghoulish sight did not frighten him. It was the idea that Coran was watching him so closely. He dove for the floor at the instant a shot rang out, a shot that would have taken off his head.

He crawled along the floor on his belly, making his way toward the service elevator. Where was she? How could he get free? Questions came in a tumult as he crawled animal-like to get away. At the elevator a bullet ripped past his ear and into the metal door. He was still bleeding from his earlier shoulder wound.

He ran for the stairwell and disappeared ahead of the gunwoman, who seemed to be toying with him. In the stairwell he hesitated a moment, unsure which way he should run, up or down. He felt like a rat in a maze, and she was making him run in the direction she wanted. She'd like to get him on the roof, force him over the side, watch him catapult to the concrete below. By the same token, she could be waiting for him if he rushed to the bottom. Which way? he asked himself. Then he heard her coming. Heard her cane going *tap, tap, tap* behind him.

Twenty-Eight

Jessica thought of how many people had been on this floor only a half hour before, how she had sent J.T. and the others away for much deserved rest while she reviewed each expert finding. Most every area of the lab had shut down and was now in darkness. She stretched out along the floor, dragging herself military fashion along by her elbows, certain that the madman was somewhere nearby, hiding like a frightened animal now, feeling the fear she had long wanted to instill in him.

Leon Helfer would not die in a gas chamber or at the end of a rope, but now she had Archer in Virginia, where the death penalty was in full effect for capital crimes. He had murdered Frakley before her eyes. He had murdered the guard she had found and Robertson could well die. He was still alive, still breathing. She could see his chest swell with his gasps.

She wanted to do what she could for Robertson, but she dare not allow one moment's concentration to be taken off her prey. Archer could turn and strike at any moment.

She kept going, cornering from one cubicle to the next in the labyrinth, wondering from moment to moment when he would strike again, and how.

She tried to calm her own breathing, thinking it so loud that he could monitor her movements by her breaths. When she made it to the next cubicle, she came face-to-face with another pair of eyes in the dark, and books and files suddenly were raining down over her. She lifted the gun, prepared to fire, when she realized the screaming person staring wide-eyed at her was Audrey Robel, a lab assistant she had thought had gone with the others.

"Audrey!"

"Dr. Coran, it's you!"

"Thank God, you're here. Did you see anyone pass this way?"

"Heard, but I didn't see. I kept myself out of sight. What's happening, Dr. Coran? Who-who-who's trying to kill us?"

"You mean, you've been here the whole time and you haven't phoned for help?"

"I was frozen stiff. When I heard the struggle, saw what was happening."

She grabbed the younger woman roughly by the arm and pushed her out into the hallway, forcing her to look down at Dr. Robertson. "He may die, Audrey. Get to a phone. Now! Call 911. Get medical help and backup."

She started away. "Where are you going, Doctor?"

She said nothing, disappearing down the blackened corridor, pursuing Archer. She stopped before the stairwell door where she believed he had gone, taking a deep breath, maintaining her composure as best she could. The hefty weapon in her hand had gone a long way to restore her courage.

She no longer felt helpless. In fact, with her training and expertise, she knew that it was correct for Archer to be afraid now. Somehow she knew that he was aware of just how dangerous she had become. Then she heard the clatter of metal steps inside the stairwell. He was desperate to put as much distance between them as possible.

Still, she must control her hands, stop the trembling. But her every nerve had been struck as if by flint, her entire nervous system hot-wired.

She straightened and arched her backbone, took a deep breath and drew on her FBI training.

She pushed the door wide, sending it thundering against the wall, echoing up and down the stairwell. Archer, wherever he was, went silent. She searched the upward spiral of the stairs and then the down, her cane tapping a metallic warning to him. She could see no sign of him.

"I hope, you bastard . . . I hope you went in the direction I wanted you to go," she shouted, taking the stairs up.

From below, Archer dared stick his head over the rail to

look upward; seeing her shadow along one wall, he was mildly struck by the fact that she had regained her cane and seemed perfectly capable of quick forward movement. Acting on adrenaline, he thought. He hesitated in making a decision to follow the shadow or go ahead as planned. He knew time was running from him like a river now, and that he must save himself, survive to catch her another day when her defenses were lowered.

Quietly, quickly, he continued with his original plan.

Alan Rychman shouted at the Quantico authorities in the front of the six-passenger helicopter. "Can't you radio ahead? Can't you get us there any faster?"

"No one's responding at security in the building where she works, and she's not responding to calls at her home," replied Agent Stan Corvella, who had picked Rychman up at the airport.

A second agent then turned and said, "Don't want to alarm you any more than you already are, Captain Rychman, but there's been an emergency 911 call out of the same location as Dr. Coran's laboratory."

"Jesus, oh, God," he moaned. "We're too late."

"Hold on," said the pilot through their headphones. "I'm bringing this bird in."

Below, on the runway at the military base at Quantico, strobe lights were flashing in a myriad of colors, indicating state, local and federal authorities had been alerted to the danger. Thanks to Alan Rychman's repeated attempts to get help, everyone was aware by now that Dr. Jessica Coran's life was in danger.

He hadn't time to call from New York, as he had raced out to the airport in an attempt to catch Archer before he got off the ground, but he learned at La Guardia that there were no flight lists with Archer's name on it; however, he did come across a Dr. Casadessus on a flight far earlier in the day going to D.C. Rychman then got on the first available flight, which was held for his boarding. Flashing his badge and credentials, he was allowed to retain his .38 for the flight.

It was en route and from the plane that he telephoned the

FBI in Quantico. With a bad connection, he finally got someone to understand that Jessica was in imminent danger. He
gave a full description of Simon Archer and was assured that
Dr. Coran would be safe. He then sat down and waited for
what seemed an endless flight—actually only fifty minutes—at the end of which he located the FBI chopper waiting
for him on the tarmac.

They had bad news, one agent said, as he shook hands with
the two men. The phrase almost knocked Rychman down until the second agent qualified it. "Dr. Coran was not at her
place, and at the moment no one's quite certain where she is,
but we assume she may be in her lab and that's where we're
going."

"Why haven't you sent someone to the lab?"

"We've sent word ahead for security to be beefed up and
we asked the guard if Dr. Coran was in the building. At that
time, we were told that she was not on the premises."

"Other areas are being checked," said the second agent.

"We've got to find her," muttered Rychman, drained and
fearful.

Rychman had spent the previous several days going over
every shred of legitimate information about Simon Archer,
with Lou Pierce's help the entire time. He had done what he
could to reconstruct Simon Archer's past, but large gaps remained, especially those related to his childhood, young man-
hood and schooling years. So Rychman had put his best
detectives on it, sending a pair to visit Mrs. Felona
Hankersen, the woman who'd been fired from St. Stephen's
when Archer—allegedly—made a mistake.

Meanwhile, IAD detectives had apprised Rychman of a
shopping list of grievances, all relatively minor when viewed
alone: incidental procedural errors, some a first-year med stu-
dent might make. The accumulation of errors, however,
pointed toward an unusual picture, just as Jessica had tried to
tell him. There were wide gaps in the chain of custody of
evidence—a breach of ethics and conduct—not only with the
Claw victims but with the evidence that had indicted and con-
demned Leon Helfer to his cell. Had Leon had a better de-

fense attorney, he might have gotten off on chain of custody violations large enough to drive a truck through.

Altogether, the shadow of wrongdoing in the laboratory had only grown larger during the short time since Jessica had left. Archer's motives must be questioned. Was it blind ambition, an attempt to best Dr. Darius' record? Was there, buried below Archer's machinations, evidence of far more sinister motives and crimes? Jessica had suspected Archer of intentionally poisoning an eleven-year-old boy who may or may not have witnessed a ghastly perversion, and if he was capable of that, was he also capable of helping Dr. Darius out that hospital window?

His careful plan to outwit Dr. Darius had unraveled when Jessica came on the scene and Dr. Darius returned. From that point on, there was never a right time to expose the "truth" about the Claw as Dr. Archer had created it.

Things began to really smell bad as Rychman examined closely how Archer had mishandled the Claw case. Archer had been M.E. of record on the second, third, fifth and ninth killings. Perkins had been on the scene for the sixth case, but Archer had done the autopsy. The first, fourth, seventh and eighth autopsies had fallen to Darius. The seventh, eighth and ninth victims had also seen input from Jessica Coran. In all cases where Archer had not participated, the integrity of the chain of custody of evidence was maintained assiduously. Even Perkins concerned himself with this. But with Archer there were serious time lapses between crime scene and lab, between tagged information and missing tags and lost evidence. He had placed clothing into plastic rather than paper bags, knowing that plastic hampered the natural air-drying process, which greatly enhanced microscopic opportunities for blood and seminal stains. He also had failed to chalk-mark notable stains on occasion. Through various "misunderstandings" evidence had been accidentally destroyed or lost or had gotten out of his hands. A trail of responsibility for such indiscretions led to lab assistants and sometimes Perkins, but in all cases, it ought to have been Archer's responsibility.

He added to the equation the deaths of Leon Helfer's boss

and dentist, and the fact that both men's bank accounts had swelled with thousands of dollars only weeks before. Leon Helfer couldn't have laid out the kind of money that was going to Dr. Parke and Malthuesen, so who did? And if these men were paid for services rendered, what were those services? Obviously, a dentist's services had to do with teeth, and a large part of the case against Leon rested on his tooth impressions.

Rychman had gone to Parke's office personally to have a look around, and when he found any number of casts for teeth lying about, it got him to thinking further. Jessica had somehow guessed right about the bite marks; they were identical, yes, but suppose that some—or even all—of them had been made by a cast? He had then gone down the hall to other dentists in the building and inquired about the possibilities, and he came away with a set of teeth that fit over his own, teeth that slipped over his gums and remained fixed tightly against the skin with a little coat of adhesive.

And if Archer liked chewing on human organs and eyeballs, he well could be up to his own eyeballs in guilt as Leon Helfer's accomplice, the dominant half of the duo, as Jessica had believed.

Rychman had next gone to Archer's office to confront him, but he found the doctor had taken the day off, leaving early for the long holiday weekend. He then pursued him to his condominium complex, where he got no response from his apartment. Picking about the lobby, asking questions, he learned that Dr. Archer simply was not findable. The doorman had said that Archer could not be away long, that he was carrying no bags, that he hailed no cab, that he must be in the vicinity of the condo. But no amount of searching had turned up any sign of Archer.

By 7 P.M. Rychman's unofficial APB on the coroner had gotten him nowhere. The man was not even answering his page beeper, which Rychman was told was unlike Dr. Archer. No one seemed to know where he'd gone.

Then Rychman's imagination went into overdrive, sending him into a panic. Suppose he's not answering his beeper because he's out of range? he asked himself. Suppose he was on a plane for D.C.? Suppose he was afraid of Jessica, knowing she wouldn't let it rest? Suppose he'd decided to get rid of her?

Rychman tore for the airport, radioing ahead that he was on police business and that he must have a seat on the next flight to the Virginia/D.C. area.

That had been several hours before. Now he was in Quantico, in the company of Quantico police and FBI men, all of whom had their orders. Rychman wanted Jessica safe at all costs; he also wanted Simon Archer alive, if possible, but he would be the first to blow his head away if he had harmed Jess.

The chopper now put down with a jarring thud, its rotor blades sending a cascade of debris in all directions around the bubble. The men jumped from their seats, and even as he raced for the waiting car, Rychman kept damning himself for not having trusted Jessica's instincts earlier. He prayed she was safe and unharmed, but Archer had had a long head start on him.

Why hadn't I been listening sooner? he silently berated himself as he and the others now sped for the nearby Quantico labs. Like everyone else in New York at the time, he had wanted to wrap up the case of the Claw as quickly as possible, get a conviction, smile for the damned press, one of whose members had also mysteriously died.

Little smoke clouds, one upon another, rose off the wet pavement that had earlier been heated by a baking sun and was now being doused with a weak, intermittent drizzle. The car, leading a motorcade of others, fishtailed along the slick street and out of the compound.

It was only a matter of minutes before they came to a gate and a guardpost. Here they found the phone off the hook and the guard's throat cut. "The bastard's here!" Rychman shouted, and behind them they heard the sirens of an ambulance.

They raced forward, circling one of the taller structures on the FBI Academy grounds, shattering the usual calm of the campuslike setting, lights going on at the academy dorms nearby. Rychman held his breath, his heart beating a mad chant against his chest, afraid for Jessica with every fiber of his being.

Jessica debated her options before leaving the relative safety of the hallway for the roof, almost certain that the perverted Dr. Archer had gone in the direction she had hoped he would take. He must surely now feel safe, she thought, safe and out of range of her deadly gunfire. It was exactly what she wanted him to believe.

The roof was black with night and wind that whipped around her, tearing at the bloodied lab coat where Frakley's and the security guard's blood had soaked her. She went to the north ledge of the building, cautious of the blacker shadows that crossed and fed upon one another here, fearing that Archer could leap out at her at any moment. But the silence and the darkness were total. There was no human soul here save hers. The weasel had scurried exactly as she had believed he would, possibly thinking that if he escaped now he would have another chance at her another time.

She shivered at the thought of his invading her home, of defiling it. It was the one place she had always felt safe.

She looked out over the edge feeling a bit dizzy, seeing the stable of security vehicles at the rear of the building, sensing that Archer would go for one of these. She also saw the distance from here, twenty-nine stories up; the distance between herself and her target would be great. Suppose she missed? Had she made a foolish choice in coming up here, rather than giving close pursuit? Fearing she might miss, she tried desperately to adjust her eyes on the aim required. She had to take into consideration the wind factor as well as the distance and the trajectory of the bullet as it would wend its way down. Her largest target would be his skull from this angle. She had four shots left. She must make each count.

Where the hell was he? Had he decided to double back? Had he remained in the building? Where was he?

"Show yourself, dammit," she muttered, her eyes never veering from the area below where she expected to see him streak for the security vehicles.

Then she saw the lights and faint scream of sirens. An ambulance was approaching. Audrey had gotten help for Robertson, thank God. The noise and lights distracted her for a moment, and as if waiting for the confusion to begin, Archer chose this same moment to dash for the safety of the security vehicle he had selected.

He was running at top speed. She aimed, drew a bead and fired, anticipating his step. The bullet blew up smoke at his ankles. She drew another bead, sent the second shot just ahead of him, and it struck him in the shoulder, sending him reeling into the truck he latched onto. She fired a third shot that hit the cab, sending paint shards into his eyes, but he threw himself into the truck before she could get off a last shot.

Police below were suddenly firing up at her, their bullets going far wide, but making her leap back. "Dammit, I'm FBI! He's getting away!" she shouted, but only the wind up here could hear her.

She leaned out over the ledge and saw the truck moving off, veering down a loping lane that would take Archer to the gate. In a few minutes, he would be out of range.

She was suddenly hit by flying debris from a bullet that impacted the ledge in front of her. She screamed with pain, tore away from the north wall to the west wall, where she leaned out over the edge, aimed and drew a bead on the cab of the truck. She couldn't make the shot at anything resembling a horizontal through the window, as the truck was almost straight below her. If she waited for a horizontal shot, he'd be out of range.

The police and FBI below, understandably thinking her a sniper, were gauging her new position and readying to open fire on her again at any moment. In the distance, she could hear a helicopter and knew that sharpshooters would be aboard. Soon its searchlight and airborne guns would be trained on her.

She had but one shot left if she was to stop Archer. She concentrated with every fiber in her being, remembering all the years of practice since childhood, everything her father had taught her, all that she had learned at the academy and on the firing range.

She guessed at what point below the square of the cab Archer's head would be if he were sitting in an upright, driving position. She drew a bead on the imaginary cranium below the metal rooftop. Her finger was steady, her reasoning good, her eyesight perfect when she pulled hard on the trigger and the clap of the bullet's response came seconds later.

She'd fired through the roof of the moving truck but it remained on the road, moving easily off. She'd missed.

More bullets rained around her, and the helicopter was now within range. Her own people were about to kill her. She stood up, holding the weapon high above her head, her white coat flapping about her like a flag of truce.

For one horrible moment, she feared the men in the flying machine were going to open fire, fillet her with their automatics, but they held as the helicopter put down on the roof and she tossed away the .38.

She then relaxed and leaned back against the ledge, turning to stare down at the brown and beige security truck. Suddenly it toppled like a dying elephant off the roadbed and into a ditch.

"Christ," she said to herself, "I did it . . . I got him."

The euphoria she felt wasn't dampened even by the rough handling she was suddenly receiving and the handcuffs that locked her arms behind her. As she was being searched for other weapons, Alan Rychman rushed out onto the rooftop and pushed people from her, shouting, "It's Dr. Coran, you fools! Step aside! Let her go!"

He took her in his arms, holding on firmly, her hands still cuffed behind her back. She thought he would crush her. "Jess, oh, Jess! I thought . . . I thought that he . . . that he got to you."

"He almost did. But he underestimated me."

"Where is he?"

"You'll find him on the road out there, in that truck that's turned over." She pointed it out to him with a flick of her head and her eyes. He followed the gestures down to the truck.

"You made a hit like that from here?"

"I had to stop him, to place him at this scene. You'll find

a security guard dead along with a stand-in for the Claw named Frakley and my serologist, Dr. Robertson."

"Robertson's all right," said J.T., who had followed Rychman up.

"We found two dead security guards below," added an agent, who ordered that Dr. Coran be released from the cuffs.

"He must've been crazy to try a stunt like this here," said J.T.

"He was a lunatic," replied Rychman.

"I don't think he planned to kill me here. He and Frakley meant the paralyzing agent for me, not for Robertson. I think they meant to overpower me, take me somewhere else to torture and kill me."

"It's over now," said Alan. "That bastard can never again hurt you or anyone else."

Alan strengthened his hold on her and helped her toward the stairs. J.T. and the other men watched until J.T. shouted, "All right, secure this area. M.E.'s going to want to go over this area just the same as down in the lab and the lobby. Get a photo man up here. I'll call in our people for evidence-gathering. We don't want anything screwed up here. We've got to protect our own."

Simon Archer was in desperate, horrid pain, his eyes having gone blind with the last impact to his cranium, his body slumped so tightly below the wheel and on the floor of the cab that he had to be pried out by the hands that reached him. He was bleeding from three wounds, the head wound the most severe. It would likely kill him within hours if not minutes. The ambulance attendants nonetheless began their regimen, placing him on fluids and IV-drip, stabilizing him as much as possible as the ambulance driver got the signal to transport. This was all happening as Jessica and Rychman got to the ground floor and came out to the waiting car that would take her home.

"Dammit," she said, "he's not dead. He's not dead!"

Her eyes were bulging with a murderous rage.

"He's in the hands of God now, Jess. Leave it . . . come away," said Rychman, pulling at her.

She tugged back and came away with the gun from his shoulder holster, pointing it at the ambulance just as the attendant closed the door, the man's eyes going wide at seeing her. Rychman grabbed the gun and sent the muzzle skyward, but she didn't pull the trigger.

"Are you crazy? You might've hit one of the attendants."

"That's the only reason I hesitated."

He took the full measure of her hatred in all at once, and he found it immeasurable.

She lifted her cane. "You got any scars to match this, Rychman?"

"If you want to match scars, let's do it somewhere more private, shall we? Come on, Jess. Enough for one night. You've got to let it go now."

"In God's hands? Do you think God will put that bastard in a cell next to Matisak?"

He had no answer for her. Instead, he held her once more in his arms. She wrapped her own arms around him and sobbed.

Twenty-Nine

❧

"The bullet entered here." The doctor pointed to the occipital lobe of the brain represented by the plaster-cast model he was using. "It completely fractured the occipital bone, here; and this in turn destroyed much of the occipital artery, which is why the man is on a heart-lung, because that artery supplies the head and scalp with blood from the carotid."

"Is he in any pain?" Jessica wanted to know.

"When he's conscious, which isn't often, yes, considerable pain."

She nodded. It was all she wanted to know. But the doctor continued with his explanation just the same.

"We've done successive brain scans to determine the sites of blood clotting and the extent of damage. Radioisotopes indicate far more damage than can be repaired in any one operation, and in his condition any single operation could kill him."

Alan Rychman pointed to a computer chart beside the brain model. "What's this, Doctor?"

"Oh, the BEAM."

"Beam?"

"Brain map, brain electric activity map," he replied, lifting the chart and pointing out the evidence of brain activity going on inside the head of the dying man not fifteen feet from them. "The computer map of the brain responds to the brain's electrical signals, monitoring them and creating a map for us every hour. Abnormal patterns, blocked and distorted signals, like those you see here and here indicate extensive damage. Of course, you realize the violent jarring of a bullet into the brain is, well, tantamount to a Hiroshima bomb exploded in that contained miniature world. Little wonder his body reaction is one of paralysis and long periods of unconsciousness. I'm surprised the man has not lapsed into irreversible coma and brain death."

"But he will, eventually, won't he?" asked Jessica.

"'It's very difficult to say."

She took the BEAM chart from him, staring at it and asking aloud, "What do you suppose he's thinking in there? What kind of thoughts are going through his mind?"

"Mostly just pain and suffering, I should think."

"Who deserves it more?"

There was a silence among them which was only accentuated by the blips and electronic hum of the life-support system that Simon Archer was attached to.

"As I said, there is extensive damage throughout the brain. Even if he should, by some strange force, manage to live, he would be a simpering idiot."

"A jury would be hard-pressed to give a simpering idiot the death penalty," she said coldly. "Despite the fact he engineered the deaths of so many others."

"It's out of our hands, Jess," said Alan, trying to lead her away.

She pulled from Alan's hold and went to the glass partition that separated her from Simon Archer's helpless form, wishing only a few minutes alone with him. As she stared at the evil encased in the glass room, his orifices jammed with tubes, his head covered in a turban of white linen, she wondered if the evil within him would not somehow beat death, would not somehow transcend it. She thought of Gerald Ray Sims' insistence that his deadly other self, Stainlype, would infect someone else upon his death. He had warned her that it could be her, and at this moment, standing over another human being, wishing it only suffering, pain and death, she began to think that maybe Gerald Ray Sims, Matthew Matisak and Simon Archer had, after all, infected her with their madness and rage.

She could almost see the floating parasite rising above Archer, the evil of his Casadessus, lying in wait for a host to come near enough and stay long enough to be infected and corrupted by it. And perhaps the process had already occurred.

Dr. Phillip C. Graf, chief of brain surgery and neurological disorders at Walter Reed Hospital in Washington, D.C., exchanged a long glance with Alan Rychman. Taking him aside, he said, "You may want to get your friend a little psychiatric assistance on this. Now, if you'll excuse me, I have a department to run."

Graf was gone, and now Alan took her in his arms and held her. Her holding onto him was like grabbing onto the side of a boat in the midst of drowning. She said in his ear, "Thanks for staying on, Alan."

Over his shoulder she stared at the pathetic form of the man she had so maimed.

That was the last she had seen of Simon Archer, and now she was in the Cayman Islands, some 150 feet below the surface, as far from the horrors of her profession as she could bodily get. Alongside her, in the vivid blue-white of the deep, outlined against the stark beauty of the coral reef, was Alan Rychman. They had together run away, and being here, in the ocean, there was no chance either one would be disturbed for some time.

Alan held her each night on the boat as it cradled her to sleep in the soft foam. They made love beneath the brilliant sun on deck, not a soul within sight, and they dove together, marveling at the beauty that life could, in its proper course, create.

But she was not blind to the predatory nature of the creatures that sometimes surrounded the area, sharks of every size and stripe, mean-looking barracudas and other aggressives, given to taking what they required of life, feeding on life as Simon Archer had, as Matisak had, as other killers in her future would.

Alan signaled that his air tank was low, and when she checked her watch and the gauge that dangled from her octopus, she realized that down here where the human spirit soared, time was different, that it went by in a flash. In the

deep her soul was unfettered, without constraints, that it enjoyed a kind of flying.

Kelp and minute creatures were carried by her mask in the
current that swirled in eddies, dovetailed and returned, fan-
ning the coral in its wake. She reluctantly followed Alan to
the surface, perhaps for the last time, as they were down to
a single tank of air, and zero days.

Their time here had been beautiful and she didn't want it
to end. In the water she needed no cane, and she felt whole
and complete again. In the water even her memories were
washed away, but on the surface the memories came creeping
into the back of her mind, even as she lay in Alan's arms.

She'd think about how her own dark side had been ap-
peased by just seeing Simon Archer's struggling body, suffering in his coma. It filled her with a sense of retribution she
could never feel when looking through the bars at Matisak's
smug countenance.

Matisak had sent a letter to her while she had still been in
Virginia, immediately after Simon Archer had been apprehended. He had said that they had made a good team. He reminded her that when no one else had accepted her theory of
the crime, he had remained the only faithful voice among a
pack of jackals that wanted to see her proven wrong. His final words had made her physically ill at the time she had read
them: "You and I are more alike than we are different, Dr.
Coran. And now you see it, don't you? I preyed on my victims, and you prey on yours. If you were not on the side of
righteousness, if your dark side gripped you as mine does me,
then perhaps you, too, would be locked away. Congratulations . . ."

She had felt in the grip of her darkest self, that black
shadow self that Donna Lemonte had told her she must give
vent to at times, when she had shot Simon Archer. She had
been elated that she had had the strength and the ability to
make that final shot, but she was also displeased at having
been under the control of the dark, evil instinct that welled up
from within, even for that moment—to end Archer's life.
Still, she had mastered the evil, had countered the rumbling
beast within. Unlike Matisak and men of his ilk, she had not

been overtaken by her sinister self; she instead had forced that part of her to give her the strength and determination to allow Jessica Coran to act as she must.

She would be stronger still in the future, a thing that O'Rourke had taken note of on their last encounter, a fact that J.T. applauded and a fact that Alan Rychman perhaps feared as he might an approaching storm. They both knew that their relationship faced many obstacles, that once they returned to the real world, she would continue at her FBI laboratory, and he as C.P. of New York.

Aboard ship, Alan said to her, "We'd better get in." He pointed to a dark patch of sky moving toward them in the distance.

She nodded and went about the business of dressing down, helping him get his tanks off, he reciprocating. They'd have to hurry if they wished to stay out of rough waters. Below, both had noticed the marked change in the underwater currents, like a harbinger of what awaited them above. Lightning strikes streaked the sky in the distance where darkness seemed to be reaching toward them, eclipsing the horizon.

Soon Alan had the sailboat moving toward the islands. Thunder rolled across the distances of the sea like the angry spirits of men. Alan gave her the tiller as the motor pushed them shoreward. She watched Alan tie off lines and secure others. All the sails were bound by thick ropes, like the ropes that held her in check, she thought, like the ropes that held all men and women in check, until one snapped.

The little ship was streamlined and the motor was powerful. They skittered across the top of green waters toward the white sand, the darkness at their backs, the wind and waves lifting, sending them rolling from side to side.

The peace of the ocean floor had, she realized, been a façade, as false as the peace of civilization. The calm of the ocean, too, had been false, lulling them into a sense of its having a warm and caring identity when in reality it was an unforgiving, often cruel god, this ocean that had the night before cradled them like children. Now it wanted to kill them.

• • •

As soon as they got to the hotel, messages were pushed at them by hotel people who had been saving them up for days. Rychman had more than she, but both of them were being pressed hard to return to their duties. They looked into one another's eyes. Rychman just threw his arm over her shoulder, saying, "The New York natives're getting restless again."

"Pressing problems, I know," she said, her cane tapping across the floor where their wet bodies left a trail of water that seeped from beneath the wraps they wore over their suits. Outside, the gale was beating ferociously at the building's windows. It was the only ill weather they'd seen since arriving several weeks before.

Her cane's *rap, tap, tap* came to an abrupt end when she stopped, frozen in place. It was a cryptic message from J.T. that read: "Archer finally dead." It was dated two days before.

Alan, holding onto her, asking after her, took the note from her clenched fingers. He read the note, saying, "Amen."

"Yes, amen," she agreed.

"Guess we'll never know what drove him to it."

"Demons," she said. "That much we know."

"Get changed. We'll have dinner and then . . ."

He let his words hang in the air, teasing. "And then we'll book a flight back?" she asked.

"Yeah, that . . . but we'll also make love."

She kissed him. "I do love you, Alan."

He was taken aback. "That's . . . that's news to me."

"Me, too."

"What're we going to do about it?"

"Do we have to do anything about it?"

He breathed deeply. "I want to be with you as many hours in the day as possible," he confessed. He sounded like a schoolboy, she thought, and she loved him for his enthusiasm.

"If it's really love, Alan, it can survive time and distance. We'll find a way."

"Chief coroner spot's still open in New York. You could—"

"No, no sudden changes. Not right now. I've got to have time and it's got to be right."

He nodded. "Sure, sure . . . I understand."

Someone called her name, a man coming toward them through the spacious lobby of the hotel, a black man in an island police uniform. "You are Dr. Coran? Captain Rychman?"

"NYPD," said Rychman.

"Yes, I am Dr. Coran."

"FBI?" he asked.

"Apparently, you know more about me than I know about you, Officer ahhh—"

"Okinleye, Ja Okinleye, Lieutenant Investigatory, Cayman. There's . . . there's been a murder. Someone knew of your being here. Could you look at the body, Dr. Coran? We hear of your work in the United States. The deceased is . . . *was* an important man in the islands, a grower and an owner in this hotel you are staying in."

"You have no coroner?"

"He comes from Martinique, but it will be a day, maybe two."

"Give me time to change," she said.

Alan stopped her. "You sure you want to get involved in this?"

"Got to get my feet wet again sometime. May as well take the leap."

"Wait up. I'll go with you."

"You'd best answer your calls and book our flight."

"Yeah, maybe you're right."

Lieutenant Investigator Okinleye could not help but see that the two Americans were very much in love. He said abruptly, "Of course, I hate to intrude on your holiday, and I would not have, except that . . . well, this is the third such murder on the island, and the man died in so . . . such . . . an unusual manner."

"Really?" she asked. "Tell me about it."

About the Author

ROBERT W. WALKER is the author of *Killer Instinct*, which was recommended for the coveted Bram Stoker Award for 1993, and many other novels of psychological terror. Walker has made forensic sleuthing his hallmark. Born in Corinth, Mississippi, and raised in Chicago, Illinois, he is a graduate of Northwestern University. He has lived in Upstate New York and currently resides with his wife, Cheryl, and son, Stephen, in Daytona Beach, Florida, where he teaches writing at Bethune-Cookman College and Daytona Beach Community College.